FINISH WHAT YOU STARTED

FINISH WHAT YOU STARTED

THE KURTHERIAN ENDGAME™ BOOK FIVE

MICHAEL ANDERLE

DISRUPTIVE IMAGINATION

Copyright © 2010 Michael Anderle
Cover by Andrew Dobell, www.creativeedgestudios.co.uk
Cover copyright © LMBPN Publishing
Interior Images by Eric Quigley
Interior Images © LMBPN Publishing
This book is a Michael Anderle Production

LMBPN Publishing
PMB 196, 2540 South Maryland Pkwy
Las Vegas, NV 89109

First US edition, May 2019
Version 1.03, Oct 2020
Print ISBN: 978-1-64202-285-8

FINISH WHAT YOU STARTED TEAM

Thanks to our Beta Readers:

Tim Cox, Tom Dickerson, Dorene Johnson, and Diane Velasquez

Thanks to the JIT Readers

Kelly O'Donnell
Crystal Wren
Diane L. Smith
Jeff Eaton
Dave Hicks
James Caplan
Jeff Goode
Shari Regan
Angel LaVey
Daniel Weigert
John Ashmore
Jackey Hankard-Brodie
Nicole Emens
Dorothy Lloyd
Micky Cocker
Peter Manis
Larry Omans

If I've missed anyone, please let me know!

Editor
Lynne Stiegler

To Family, Friends and
Those Who Love
to Read.
May We All Enjoy Grace
to Live the Life We Are
Called.

GLOSSARY OF CHARACTERS, LOCATIONS, AND SHIPS

Characters

- **Bethany Anne Nacht (BA)**

Super-enhanced human, part of a triumvirate consisting of her, TOM, and ADAM. Can walk the Etheric (see locations). Has the ability to manipulate Etheric energy to her will. Will stamp out injustice without mercy wherever she finds it.

Ex-Empress of the Etheric Empire, BA took voluntary exile to bring in the Federation and now fights to protect it from the Kurtherians. As her alter ego she controls a growing buffer around the Federation border.

Currently based out of the QBS *Izanami* on Devon, fighting a war against the Ooken—who are connected to the Kurtherians.

Wife to Michael, mother to Alexis and Gabriel.

- **Baba Yaga**

Bethany Anne's alter ego. Aka "The Witch."

Originally formed during a time of difficulty, Baba Yaga has become the face BA uses in public to sidestep her little exile issue. This way, BA has been able to extend a level of protection to the Federation without them knowing.

- **TOM – "Thales of Miletus"**

Kurtherian, hosted within Bethany Anne's body. Enhanced Michael in an attempt to warn humanity of the coming invasion and got it wrong, inadvertently creating the vampire myth on Earth. A thousand years later he got a second chance and got it SO right.

- **ADAM**

AI, hosted within Bethany Anne's body (see AI's and EI's)

- **Michael Nacht**

Ancient, super-enhanced human.

Formerly known as the Patriarch, Michael was the first "vampire." He has ever-increasing skill with the Etheric and a short temper. Ruled the UnknownWorld on Earth for over a thousand years before choosing Bethany Anne to replace him.

Currently based out of the QBS *Izanami* on Devon.

Husband to Bethany Anne, father to Alexis and Gabriel.

- **Alexis Nacht**

Super-enhanced human, Bethany Anne and Michael's daughter. Twin of Gabriel. Highly trained from a young age in martial arts and close combat, weapons.

Has an affinity for technology, and a habit of hacking to get answers. Has shown telepathic ability, and has growing control of the Etheric. Outgoing, loves fashion.

• Gabriel Nacht

Super-enhanced human, Bethany Anne and Michael's son. Twin of Alexis. Highly trained from a young age in martial arts and close combat, weapons.

Has specialized in "spy skills," as well as engineering, history, and languages. Appears introverted, collects blades.

• John Grimes

Enhanced human. Queen's Bitch—Bethany Anne's Wherever Bethany Anne goes, so does John.

Currently based on the QBBS *Guardian* (see ships and stations).

Husband to Jean, father to Lillian, grandfather to Nickie.

• Scott English

Enhanced human. Queen's Bitch—Bethany Anne's personal bodyguard, and close friend.

Currently based on the QBBS *Guardian* (see ships and stations).

Husband to Cheryl-Lynn (cousin of John Grimes).

- **Darryl Jackson**

Enhanced human. Queen's Bitch—Bethany Anne's personal bodyguard, and close friend.

Currently based on the QBBS *Guardian* (see ships and stations).

- **Eric Escobar**

Enhanced human. Queen's Bitch—Bethany Anne's personal bodyguard, and close friend.

Currently based on Devon with Gabrielle.

Husband to Gabrielle.

- **Gabrielle Escobar**

Super-enhanced human, daughter of Stephen. Head of the Queen's Bitches—one of Bethany Anne's closest friends.

Currently based on Devon with Eric.

Wife to Eric.

- **Tabitha Nacht**

Super-enhanced human, hacker extraordinaire. A sister of the heart to BA. Held the rank of Ranger 2 during the Age of Empire, she chose exile with Bethany Anne when the Federation was formed.

Currently located on Devon with her partner, Peter, and their son, Todd Michael.

- **Peter Silvers**

Super-enhanced human, has Were form called 'Pricolici.'

The first Guardian. Held the rank of Guardian Commander during the Age of Empire, he had reason to remain in the Federation but chose to leave and settle down with Tabitha after the death of his best friend.

Currently located on Devon with Tabitha, holds an advisory position in the Guardians while on paternity leave.

- **Todd Michael Nacht Silvers**

Super-enhanced human, abilities unknown as yet. Son of Tabitha and Peter. Tiny terror.

- **Akio**

Super enhanced human. Head of the former Elite guard. Queen's Bitch. Remained behind to protect Earth, returned to BA after the Second Dark Age.

Michael's closest friend, mentor/father figure to Sabine.

Currently located on High Tortuga.

- **Hirotoshi**

Super enhanced human, former Elite guard, Queen's Bitch.

Friend, mentor and guard to Tabitha.

Currently located on Devon.

- **Ryu**

Super enhanced human. Former Elite guard.

Friend and guard to Tabitha.

Currently located on Devon.

- **Jean Grimes (née Dukes)**

Super-enhanced human. Inventor of the infamous Jean Dukes Special. Weapons R&D genius, legendary across galaxies for her weaponry.

Currently located at QT2, working to expand the fleet.

Wife of John, mother of Lillian, grandmother of Nickie.

- **Bartholomew Thomas**

Admiral of Bethany Anne's fleet. Based at QT2, travels aboard the QBS *ArchAngel II*. Permanently mildly annoyed.

Husband of Giselle, father of three infants.

- **Barnabas Nacht**

Super-enhanced human. One of seven firstborn "children" of Michael, former monk.

Currently located on High Tortuga, where BA has made him Steward of the planet in her absence.

- **Lance Reynolds**

Enhanced human, aka "the General." Bethany Anne's father.

Remained to chair the Federation when Bethany Anne went into exile.

Currently located on the QBBS *Meredith Reynolds*, stationed at Yoll.

Husband to Patricia, father also to Kevin.

- **Kael-ven**

Enhanced Yollin, captain of the QBS *G'laxix Sphaea*. Potentate of Yoll during the Age of Empire, he divorced his awful wife and rejoined Bethany Anne when she took exile.

Currently stationed at Location Three (see locations)

- **Kiel**

Enhanced Yollin.

Former mercenary, Marine during the Age of Empire. Weapons officer aboard the QBS *G'laxix Sphaea*.

Currently located at Location Three.

- **K'aia**

Enhanced Yollin, four-legged. Former mine slave on Devon, rescued herself and met Bethany Anne and Michael who helped her free the other slaves. Followed BA to High

Tortuga, was given the role of Alexis and Gabriel's personal guard.

Current location, Devon.

- **Eve**

(see AIs and EIs)

- **Addix**

Enhanced Ixtali, Bethany Anne's Spymistress. Sometime guardian and governess to Alexis and Gabriel, has returned to spying now the twins are teenagers.

Currently located around Devon.

- **Nickie Grimes**

Naturally enhanced human. Birth name, Meredith Nicole, aka Merry. Daughter of Lillian, granddaughter of John and Jean. Sent on a sabbatical by BA in her late teens as a consequence of her poor choices—which can be read about in the Deuces Wild series. Is returning a (mostly) changed woman.

Currently working out of High Tortuga, where she and her crew are acting as vigilantes under the guidance of Barnabas.

- **Sabine**

Enhanced human, rescued on Earth by Michael,

Jacqueline, and Akio during the Second Dark Age. Crack shot, excellent fighter. "Adopted daughter" of Akio.

Currently located on Devon, co-owner of The Hexagon (see locations).

In a relationship with Tim Kinley.

• Jacqueline

Enhanced human, Were with Pricolici form. Daughter of North American pack leader, Gerry. Rescued by Michael during the Second Dark Ages.

Currently located on Devon, co-owner of The Hexagon. Excellent fighter, skills with managing the media.

In a long-term relationship with Mark.

• Mark

Enhanced human. Rescued by Michael and Jacqueline in NYC during the Second Dark Ages.

Currently located on Devon, co-owner of The Hexagon. Skills in technology and invention.

In a long-term relationship with Jacqueline.

• Ricole

Enhanced Noel-ni, originally from High Tortuga. Would choose knowledge over profit, and a fight over all else.

Currently located on Devon, co-owner of The Hexagon. Excellent fighter, even better at business. Runs a team of young adult apprentices who work around The Hexagon.

• Demon

Enhanced mountain lion. Rescued from an animal testing facility on Earth by Michael & co. during the Second Dark Age. Was treated in a Pod-doc to fix faulty nanocytes and have her claws regrown.

Currently located on Devon, co-owner of The Hexagon. Especially attached to Sabine.

• Tim Kinley

Enhanced human, Were. Aka "Rocky," aka "Mr. Meaty."

One of the original Guardians, Tim joined BA as a young man looking for a better path. Spent time as a bouncer at All Guns Blazing (bar) during the Age of Empire.

Currently located at Devon, where he is the Commander of the QBBS *Guardian*.

In a relationship with Sabine.

• Giselle Foxton-Thomas

Human. Civilian resources manager at QT2 (see locations).

Originally from the colonies, daughter of Helena. Has a sunny disposition, is relentlessly efficient.

Wife to Admiral Thomas, mother to their three children.

Good friends with Jean and Qui'nan.

- **Lady Helena Foxton**

Human, indeterminate age. Mother of Giselle, grand-mother to Giselle and the Admiral's children, generally harmless pain in the ass.

- **Qui'nan**

Yollin, four-legged. Architect, engineer, grumbler.
Currently based at QT2, responsible for ship design as part of Jean's R&D team.
Good friends with Jean and Giselle.

- **Mahi'Takar**

Baka. Nominal leader of the Bakas on Devon.

- **Takar'Tu'Reigd**

Baka. Son of Mahi'Takar.

- **Da'Mahin**

Baka, one of several younger brothers of Mahi'Takar.

- **Ch'Irzt, Em'Eir, Em'Ain, Kn'Ille**

Bakas, niece and nephews of Mahi'Takar.

- **Meon**

Moen leader.

Other Species

- **The Collective**

Co-dependent, water-dwelling species enslaved by the Ooken. Peaceful, enormous telepathic ability. They get their name from their group consciousness, their true name is as yet unknown.

Bethany Anne came across one of the Collective, known as "the Prisoner" in an Ooken outpost.

Bethany Anne granted the being's dying wish, but not before learning where the Ooken were hiding via the Collective's shared memories.

- **The Ooken**

Invasive species with connections to the Kurtherians.

Attacked at QT2, then Devon.

Not much is known about where they come from, or their connection to the Kurtherians. They share the same type of group telepathy as the Collective.

Behave like mindless killers, have committed genocide on a nameless number of planets and stolen the technology.

Have been pushing to get closer to the Federation, only Bethany Anne and her people stand in the way.

- **Kurtherians**

Powerful alien species divided. Seven clans are bent on dominating others, five clans are peaceful and chose to eradicate the capability for violence from their genome. Both sides strive to reach a higher consciousness—known as Ascension.

Bethany Anne has sworn to eradicate the Seven in order to protect Earth, and has been either hunting or fighting their puppets for over two centuries. Seven is no longer an accurate name, since BA wiped out all but a couple of the Phraim-'Eh clan.

AIs and EIs

- **ADAM**

AI, resides in an organic computer within Bethany Anne's body.

Bethany Anne's close friend and advisor. All BA's AIs and EIs come from ADAM.

- **ArchAngel, AI**

This is the second iteration of ArchAngel as an AI. She serves aboard the QBS *ArchAngel II* and travels with the Admiral between locations.

- **Eve**

AI, date of ascension unknown. Resides in a short android body. Remained to protect Earth with Akio and Yuko when Bethany Anne left for space, and rejoined BA at the end of the Second Dark Age.

Currently located at High Tortuga.

- **ArchAngel, EI**

This is an EI copy of the original ArchAngel. She serves aboard the QBS *G'laxix Sphaea*.
Currently located at Location Three.

- **CEREBRO**

EI group/s, consisting of digital entities left without a purpose after the Empire became the Federation. Began as the EIs for the base at High Tortuga and have expanded into the battlestations at Devon, QT2, and Location Three.

- **Winstanley**

Building EI for The Hexagon.

Locations

- **The Etheric**

Unknown location, possibly outside of our universe. Source of limitless energy for those who can access it.

The Kurtherians developed technology that enabled them to access the energy—known as nanocytes. The Seven used nanocytes to dominate every species they came across for millennia, while some among the Five used them to "prepare" other species for the fight.

TOM changed everything when he came to prepare Earth and gave humanity the technology.

- Devon

Originally a mercenary hideout until Baba Yaga took over and renamed the planet Devon as part of the plan to divert attention from High Tortuga.

The planet is protected by its end of the Interdiction—a three-layer security system comprised of a long-range early-warning system, the BYPS network around the planet, and the QBBS *Guardian*.

The planet below consists of two major cities, and one smaller city around the lake system.

First City is the location of The Hexagon, the bazaar, and various communities of settlers.

Current location of Bethany Anne in response to the Ooken attack in the previous book.

- **High Tortuga**

The planet Bethany Anne prepared for her exile. A safe haven, highly defended and hidden from knowledge.

BA has a base on the northern continent, where the planet is populated. The southern continent is wild land.

Bethany Anne has now left High Tortuga in Barnabas' hands while she fights from Devon.

- **QT2 System**

Site of the original Ooken incursion. Bethany Anne built wide-ranging defenses similar to those at High Tortuga and Devon. In addition to the battlestation QBBS

Helena is the shipyard, where the fleet expansion is being managed from.

- **The Federation**

Coalition of planetary governments born after the Empress of the Etheric Empire stepped down. Governed by the leaders of the people from both the former empire and other peoples (such as the Leath), it is headed by General Lance Reynolds.

It was facilitated by Bethany Anne before she left and went into exile.

The Federation is still young, and the leaders fear BA's return as she is a powerful person who would upset the balance of power between the members of the Federation. The revelation that BA is right on their doorstep would end with the various governments withdrawing from their agreement to work together for the good of all.

- **Moen**

Planet occupied by the Ooken. Bethany Anne has been attempting to free the planet.

Ships
Transport class:

- QTS *Lucky Run*
- QTS *Shanks' Express*
- QTS *Polaris*

Shinigami-class:

- QBS *Izanami*
- QBS *Sayomi*
- QBS *Defiant*
- QBS *Cambridge*
- QBS *Revolution*
- QBS *Shufur*

Sphaea-class:

- QBS *G'laxix Sphaea*
- QBS *Widow's Tears*

Battlestations:

- QBBS *Guardian*
- QBBS *Helena*
- QBBS *L3*

Superdreadnoughts:

- QBS *ArchAngel II*
- SD *Ballista*
- SD *Astraea*
- SD *Adrastea*

PROLOGUE

THE ETHERIC

Bethany Anne held the mercurial storm energy tightly in her mental grip, her hands clenched into tight fists. The thrashing mists around her blazed red, lit by the fire bleeding from her eyes.

SUBMIT.

The force in Bethany Anne's command manifested physically in an outward wave that left her body and rippled through the mists, solidifying each molecule as it was overlaid by her will.

ADAM and TOM regarded Bethany Anne in their private space with something approaching awe.

>>**Should we say something?**<< ADAM fretted. >>**She's been pushing this hard since she and Tabitha found the Ooken staging post. She has to take a break** *sometime,* **right? I'm concerned that her focus on following the Prisoner's mental map is taking her attention away from everything else that's been going on.**<<

You're not the only one concerned. TOM felt relief at

1

getting the subject aired between them. **Perhaps we can nudge her into taking a short break.**

>>**Good luck getting Bethany Anne to do anything she hasn't already got a mind to do,**<< ADAM scoffed. >>**She's not going to step back until she gets the result she's looking for. We'll be doing this until we locate the Ooken homeworld.**<<

She shouldn't be able to do "this" in the first place, TOM contended, most of his attention on maintaining Bethany Anne's body. **The most adept Kurtherian wouldn't so much as approach an Etheric storm, much less grab hold of one and use it to open a window looking out on wherever the hell they wanted. Why you shared your research on the storms with her I'll never understand.**

>>**Um, because she asked nicely? And by asked nicely I mean threatened to tear my chip out of her brain and crush it under her heel if I didn't. It could be worse,**<< ADAM muttered as the energy around Bethany Anne began to shift. >>**She could have figured out how to tear an actual path through the storm. Then we'd both be monumentally screwed.**<<

True. TOM snickered as a thought occurred to him. **We should thank whoever will accept it for small mercies.**

ADAM chuckled dryly. >>**You can pray for us both since you're the religious one.**<< ADAM tuned TOM out, preparing himself for whatever alien operating systems the Ooken had on the other side of the storm.

The energy quieted a touch as Bethany Anne exerted her complete control one droplet of vapor at a time. She felt the strain bending so much Etheric energy to her purpose was taking on her body, but a nosebleed or two had never stopped her before. She increased her grip until the energy was leashed at her command into total obedience.

The energy almost frozen, she felt along the paths she'd learned from the Prisoner, searching for the mental signature of the Ooken hive mind. *I've got one.* She flexed her will and opened a window onto the location. *ADAM,* she ground out with effort, *are you in?*

>>**Almost,**<< ADAM grumbled, feeling a little bit of the strain himself. >> **You know, you could say "wow," or something, BA. I'm hacking reality itself, and you're not even impressed.**<<

Bethany Anne wiped the twin rivulets of blood from her nose. *Sure, it's a challenge. Do you want a gold star? I wouldn't allow you to even try if I didn't have faith in your ability. You wanted to play with the Etheric? Well, suck it up. This is how the grown-ups play. Now, readings, before I start having brain hemorrhages from holding this much volatile energy.*

TOM cleared a throat he didn't possess. **Actually, Bethany Anne, you have already had several minor bleeds. I'm directing everything I can toward keeping your brain intact.**

Bethany Anne raised an eyebrow. *I should hope so, since all three of us kind of need it to be functioning if we want to survive this. How long before it gets dangerous?*

TOM paused for a moment while he did the calculations. **I estimate another thirty seconds, twenty to be on the safe side. That's a marked improvement on your last effort.**

>>**Close the window,**<< ADAM announced. The strain in his voice had dropped off considerably. >>**I have the readings.**<<

Bethany Anne gradually released her hold and the Etheric energy dissipated, spent. *Well? Was it what we wanted to find?*

>>**Give me... Dammit. I'm going to say we missed again. It's definitely an Ooken location, but it's not a planet. It's closest to Admiral Thomas' location.**<<

Bethany Anne's jaw twitched. *Fucksticks. I need to refine this. Stabbing in the dark is too fucking inefficient.*

ADAM stayed silent.

It's still a sizeable colony, TOM demurred, feeling the need to divert Bethany Anne before their fears became a reality. **And it's not so close. It's out of immediate reach, so that's progress again. You'll find it.**

I don't give a shiny shit. It's not the homeworld. Bethany Anne released a breath slowly, forcing the frustration down. *Never mind. We can still send them a nice-to-meet-you gift.*

She received confirmation from Michael that Bart's section of the fleet was underway to the coordinates. She breathed slowly again to center herself, gathering her strength once more before moving on. *Next storm. Next target.*

>>**Really?**<<

Yes, ADAM. Really. I want this done. We have the capability to hit another target, and I sense my next storm. Bethany Anne grasped the temperamental energy. *Get ready.*

The storm bucked and twisted to escape her hold, but

she was stronger than some upstart energy ball with delusions of sentience. Bethany Anne raised her hands as the energy whipped her hair around her body.

It was more about intent than anything else, and she intended to *own* it.

Submit or be crushed.

The Etheric fought capture like an unbroken colt—if a young horse were capable of reducing the person breaking it down to their constituent atoms, then scattering those atoms to every corner of time and space if they lost control for the merest fraction of a second.

Bethany Anne had heard all the old vampire myths back on Earth. Shit, she'd been the one to debunk most of them. Somehow, she thought, being scattered that far and wide might be beyond even *her* ability to heal from.

Best not to risk it.

She clamped down hard with her will, exerting her absolute assurance over the storm that its power was hers to use as she saw fit.

It belonged to her.

It *wanted* to serve her purpose.

Bethany Anne opened her window as the vortex calmed at her touch, unable to resist. *That's more like it. Good storm. ADAM, you're up.*

>>**Already in,**<< he told her smugly. >>**We have a colony. Mid-level tech, nothing unexpected. The architecture is less than a century old.**<<

Time to send in the Bitches, Bethany Anne decided. She reached out to Michael to pass on the instruction, finding the connection weak. *TOM, do something about my link to Michael. I can barely hear him.*

Oh? There was a pause. **I'm doing what I can to make up for you two being on different planes. Try now.**

She did, finding her mental connection to her beloved restored. Michael's voice caressed her mind, calming her as it always did, even in such extenuating circumstances.

Do we have Gate coordinates for our next target?

We do, she replied, sending them over. **How many is that now? I've lost count.**

Today? Seven. Over the last few months? One hundred twenty-nine. Michael's voice was low and laced with anger. *The bastards keep popping up as quickly as we can exterminate them.*

Bethany Anne's lip curled. *I know. They're like fucking roaches. Worse, since every nest we find leads to a fucktuple more. If it wasn't for the help we got from the Prisoner...well, shit. I don't even want to think about how this war would be going.*

We owe that poor soul a great debt, Michael agreed. *Without the mental map it gave you, the Ooken would have all the resources we have deprived them of to bring against us. We might have been left with more than hurt feelings.*

Feelings? We're way beyond emotions. This is duty, plain and simple. The Kurtherians have unleashed a plague, and I am the scourge that makes them fear in the night. Bethany Anne touched her fingers to her nose, feeling the blood well again. **I have to go. I'll be home soon, so keep safe.**

You too, my love.

Devon, First City, The Hexagon, Network Command Center

Tabitha's shoulders lost some of the tension she was carrying as she exited the elevator into the dim, screen-lit room. There was something about the familiarity of the setup that spoke to her deep inside her little hacker's heart.

It felt homey to her.

She pushed Mark's wheeled chair out of the way with her foot, dragging the next one over to sit down and commandeer the keyboard as his chair kept moving. "What is so important that you had to call me down here? Don't you know us moms have to sleep when we can?"

Mark raised his hands in apology as his chair came to a stop in the middle of the floor. "I'm really sorry. I wouldn't have called if I didn't think you needed to be here." He scooted his chair back over with his feet and reclaimed his keyboard. "I don't know what to do about this."

Tabitha glanced at the screens, her eyes flicking over the silent crowd gathered outside in Hexagon Plaza. Her half-asleep brain refused point-blank to provide a reasonable explanation as to why the people were there at this unholy hour. "What the hell do they want?"

Mark dropped his hands. "Fuck if I know. Winstanley alerted me an hour ago. They just turned up, and they keep coming. They're not doing anything, just hanging around like they're waiting for something."

Tabitha narrowed her eyes at the screens. "Yeah, well, I don't like it." She got to her feet and headed for the door. "I'm gonna go down and see what they want." She caught sight of her reflection as she left the command center and sighed, running a hand through her hair to smooth some of the sleep from it. "Ugh. Six AM is *so* not my best time of day."

Tabitha made her way to the side entrance—the one the public didn't know about—and listened to the murmurs of the gathered citizens. There was no malice coming from the crowd, just a determined resolution to find a way they could contribute to the defense of their homeworld.

She slipped back in through the door and walked around to the main entrance. "Winstanley, let them in."

One of Ricole's students was operating the front desk. She dropped her handset at Tabitha's command and stared openmouthed as the building's EI opened the great glass doors to admit the crowd. "Where did they come from?"

Tabitha waved her off as she crossed the foyer. "It's okay, Trixa."

They entered, slowly at first, but then with more confidence when Tabitha called them in. The girl behind the desk sat back in her chair, eyes wide and mouth open as she witnessed the goings on.

Tabitha stepped forward to meet the people. "Hey, what can we do for you all?"

The people turned at the sound of a voice. A few began to speak, followed by the rest.

Tabitha raised her arms and waved for quiet. "Just one of you." She pointed at the crowd. "What's going on?"

A group of four Bakas stepped forward. The shortest, a slightly less shaggy individual dressed in an odd combination of orange monk's robes and crisscrossed leather utility belts spoke up. "We want to fight. We were told by the human Hirotoshi that we would be welcome here. That you would train us."

Tabitha was too distracted by the enormous toenails on the hairy feet protruding from the bottom of the Baka's robe to be angry. Still... *Damn you, Hirotoshi. If I've got to be awake, so do you. You're not getting away with this.*

Hirotoshi's chuckle echoed darkly through her mind. *But, my Lady Kemosabe, you were just recently saying how bored you were. Are you going to turn these potential allies away?*

Tabitha growled over their link. *That was before this war broke out. I won't turn them away, but I hope you're ready to reprise your mentor role. If I'm teaching, so are you and Ryu.*

As you wish, came the reply from her other loyal Tonto.

Tabitha flashed Ryu the mental image of her giving him the finger. *Screw you, Ryu. Screw you.*

Hirotoshi chuckled. *Tread carefully, my friend. If our lady is reduced to words that rhyme, you may be digging yourself in deeper than you planned.*

Listen to Hirotoshi, Ryu. Quit while I'm telling you that you can't get ahead—and don't think you've gotten away with it, either, Tabitha told Hirotoshi. She promised herself that she would pay them both back, right before she erased every copy of that damned movie from the record. She gave the gathered citizens her brightest smile and opened her mouth to speak.

Unfortunately, she didn't have a word to say.

For once.

Her hesitation caused a ripple of unease in the crowd.

The Baka spoke again. "We don't want any trouble," he told her quietly, glancing at his three companions. "We'll leave if we're not welcome here."

Tabitha tried to speak. *How did Bethany Anne do this on the fly all the time?* "Of *course* you're welcome here," she finally pushed out.

The people looked at each other, murmuring among themselves. Tabitha felt a wave of pride that they'd all turned out in support, but she needed the crowd to disperse for now. What would Bethany Anne do?

Although… Bethany Anne wasn't the owner of *this* planet.

Tabitha's mouth twitched as inspiration came to her. "It makes me feel very good to see the people of Devon come together when we're threatened. This city has become a safer place to live thanks to good people like you. People I'm proud to call neighbors. I'm glad this is the place I'm raising my son." She swept her arms out over the crowd. "I just don't know what to do with, well, all of you. I have to speak to Baba Yaga."

There were a few gasps. "You know Baba Yaga?" one of the young Bakas asked.

Tabitha flashed a crooked grin. "Oh, yeah. Me and Baba

Yaga, we go *way* back." That did the job. She waved a hand at the front desk, satisfied with the results. "Everyone who is really serious about training can leave their contact details with Trixa, and I'll get back to you once Baba Yaga gives me her orders."

The crowd moved over to the desk, making Trixa's morning a lot more interesting than the young Noel-ni had been expecting.

Tabitha headed back inside the main building with revenge on her mind. She took the private elevator up to the penthouse apartment, where the offending Tontos were hanging out with Peter in the kitchen, waiting for the coffee maker to deliver the liquid gold.

Ryu held his hands up, looking at the others for help as Tabitha stalked toward them.

"I'll deal with you later," she told Ryu. She lifted an accusatory finger in Hirotoshi's direction. "*You*, on the other hand, are dead meat, Mister."

Hirotoshi turned an accusatory finger on Peter. "You told me she wanted to get into teaching."

His accusation only changed the course of Hurricane Tabitha by a few degrees.

"Oh, really?" She darted around the counter, grabbing a dish towel as she passed. "So *you're* the ass-face responsible for my sleep getting disturbed." She wound up the towel, her mouth twisting into a wicked grin. "You'd better run!"

Peter hopped the counter to escape the sting of the towel. "If I'm an ass-face, doesn't that mean you like kissing ass?" He ducked the towel and made a break for the sitting area.

Tabitha blocked him with a flick of the towel. "I've

never killed anybody with a towel before, but I'm sure I can figure it out easily enough. Todd and I will just have to get by without you."

Peter slid around Tabitha and vaulted the couch, grabbing an armful of cushions as he went. "Wait until his nanocytes kick in and see if you feel the same. You need me, but I don't need these." He raised one of the cushions.

"Don't you dare!" Tabitha squealed, and scrambled for the corridor with Peter on her heels.

Hirotoshi exchanged amused glances with Ryu. "They're going to wake the baby."

Ryu chuckled. "It is good to see her happy."

Hirotoshi nodded, smiling. "That it is, my friend. It has been a long time coming." He looked out the window at the dissipating crowd far below. "There are rather a lot of people down there."

"You don't say," Tabitha cut in as she and Peter returned to the living area.

Hirotoshi turned from the window to look at Peter. "Surely a percentage of them would be more suited to the military?"

Peter nodded. "I'll have Tim filter those out. This isn't the first group of angry citizens who have turned up in the last month wanting to defend their planet from the Ooken." He grinned. "I'll say this: for a planet that's mostly nonhuman, they sure had a human reaction to that invasion."

Tabitha smiled. "I know, right? I *love* this place. If you don't count the weird flora and fauna, it's pretty much just like Earth used to be, only without the politics spoiling things for everyone."

"Bethany Anne had it right," Peter agreed. "Some people just do better outside of a regimented society." There was a giggle from the baby monitor.

Tabitha's eyes lit up at the sound of her son's laughter. "Looks like we woke Todd up with all the shenanigans."

"I'll get him," Peter offered. "I have the day off. I'm going to take Trouble up to the *Guardian* to see his Uncle Tim. You have the space to work this out."

Tabitha headed for the nursery. "No way, my turn. Besides, I'm coming with you guys. Tim is just the person I need to see before I leave for High Tortuga."

High Tortuga, Space Fleet Base, Requisitions and Stores

Jean met her daughter's old school friend and the base's sometime quartermaster, Sofia Gutierrez, in front of the massive warehouse area.

Sofia's cheerful face was split by an even wider grin than usual. "Nice to have you back, Jean." Her eyes narrowed, although the grin stayed. "But something tells me I'm going to have a lot less inventory to keep track of once you leave."

Jean returned her grin as the two women walked into the first building, each grabbing a large antigrav cart from the rows by the door. "Yes…and no. I brought a few things to leave here with you."

Curiosity added an extra glint to Sofia's smile. "Oh?"

Jean nodded. "It's a gift. For my granddaughter."

Sofia's eyes sparkled with hope. "Merry's coming home?"

Jean wiped away the shine in her own eyes, closing

them tightly. "I don't know, but I fucking hope so, Sofia. I want my baby girl back." She snorted softly. "Nickie hasn't been my baby for a long time, but the reports are looking better."

Sofia laced her hands over her chest. "Really? I hadn't lost hope, but when her exile ended and she didn't come back..."

Jean patted her old friend's arm in sympathy. "I know. You did a lot for her when she was younger. Her exile hit us all hard. But she's not alone."

Sofia's eyebrows went up, and concern replaced her hopeful smile. "She's fallen in with another gang?"

Jean saw Sofia's face and remembered the heartache the woman had gone through back when Nickie had first succumbed to the temptation of not giving a shit. She shook her head, flushing with pride—and the relief of being able to give her some good news. "No. She's gotten herself a crew, and she's been taking care of a colony that was hit by the Skaines. She's doing well."

Sofia hid her emotion with a joke. "The Skaines are still a problem?" Her mouth twitched. "Don't tell Tabitha."

Jean snickered. "Tabitha has her hands full with that gorgeous boy of hers. My Nickie has taken up the mantle. She'll be home, Sofia, and when she gets here, she's going to know *exactly* how proud I am of her." She indicated the seemingly endless rows of multi-tiered racks filled with crates and boxes of all sizes and shapes. "I'll get the crates for Nickie sent over before I leave. For now, Bethany Anne wants ships, and she's in one of her oh-so-rare impatient moods. I'm about to get *very* creative."

. . .

Devon, The Hexagon, Underground Hangar, QBS *Izanami*

Michael sat on the couch in the remodeled cargo bay, his arms spread along the back and his feet up on a box he'd repurposed. His gaze was firmly on the screen, where Bethany Anne laughed and joked with Alexis and Gabriel while she guided them through the exercises they had carefully constructed to test the twins' capabilities.

Michael could have made his observations from inside the scenario, but sometimes the beauty of his wife in competition was an art form best enjoyed from a distance.

With popcorn.

Bethany Anne called instructions while the children sparred as a team against her. She deflected everything Alexis and Gabriel threw at her, encouraging them to dare while giving them no quarter whatsoever.

Michael snickered as her lips moved and he read her favorite training mantra. "There are no prizes for trying and no commiseration for missing. In this situation, there is only surviving to fight another day. If you land a single finger on me—and make no mistake, one day you will—it's going to happen because you damn well *earned* it. Until then, well, failure is still an attempt, and I'm proud of you both."

All the while, Bethany Anne fought Gabriel and Alexis off without once causing them pain, in contrast to her traditional training methods. Every move she made was an improvement on a technique the twins had believed they'd mastered before she showed them differently.

There was a detachment to her, a determination to extract the best from Alexis and Gabriel that made even his admittedly epic relentless streak appear reasonable. Nevertheless, both children responded to her teaching methods with the same enthusiasm as always.

He popped a piece of popcorn into his mouth absentmindedly, forgetting about the rest when the twins attempted a risky maneuver.

Gabriel blinked out of reality as Alexis tossed one of the two energy balls she was holding at Bethany Anne. The other she threw underarm to Gabriel, who had appeared high above Bethany Anne's head to catch it and send it hurtling ahead of him toward his mother.

Bethany Anne deflected the energy balls, halting Gabriel's freefall with a wave.

Michael was on the edge of his seat when Eve appeared at the side door leading to her lab—or lair—distracting him from the outcome.

"How is it going in there?" she asked, making her way over.

An almost pensive look flickered across Michael's face for a second before his usual imperturbable mask came down. "It's all good. Alexis and Gabriel are doing well."

As if Eve couldn't read micro-expressions. Michael's outwardly relaxed demeanor wasn't fooling her for a second. She crossed the floor and took a seat on the couch. "You're worried about Bethany Anne. Why don't you just ask her how she is?"

He regarded his wife and children, who were still playing onscreen. "I did, and she wouldn't tell me," he admitted. "In fact, the query as to her wellbeing was met with what I can only describe as a distinct feeling of 'oh shit, what bomb did I just set off?'"

Eve nodded in sympathy. "She is extremely focused at the moment."

"Focused, obsessed; it's a matter of how you look at it." His tone was quiet. "Touching the prisoner's mind affected her. You know how she feels about the innocent being made to suffer. Add to that her insistence she avoid repeating her supposed mistakes with the Leath."

Eve tilted her head. "Still?"

Michael nodded. "I've looked over the records. To my mind, she did everything she could. The time it took to overcome the Phraim-'Eh was unavoidable."

"And yet she still feels responsible for the toll it took on both sides," Eve whispered, her head bowed. "That is why she is our Queen, whether she wants to be or not. She cannot do anything but fight for whoever needs her. Her heart is too pure for the evil she has to face, but I have faith that she's equal to the challenge."

The corner of Michael's mouth turned up at her choice of phrase. "That isn't in question."

Eve scrutinized him for a moment. "You're wondering how much of your wife will be left once the dust settles."

Michael looked long and hard at her.

Eve lifted her hands. "What, the android can't understand emotion?"

He shrugged and returned to watching the screen. "I didn't say that. You surprised me is all."

Eve nodded, her eyes wide and innocent. "The only obstacle to growth is the decision to stop learning." She lifted a finger. "Or snooping on Bethany Anne. That's for people who wish for a short life expectancy, and I plan on living a *long* time yet."

Michael swept a hand in Eve's direction without looking away. "And there's the almost-but-not-quite Zen adage which tells me absolutely nothing. Will you help me or not?"

"Not." Eve got to her feet and sailed out of the room, waving a hand as she went. "Talk to your wife."

Michael contained the urge to fling a bolt of lightning through the open door after Eve. It wouldn't be the most honorable thing to do, given that she was right. Instead, he resumed his careful observation, watching his wife even as he kept track of Alexis' and Gabriel's efforts.

He'd noticed the recent difference in Bethany Anne during lighter moments like this, when the weight of galaxies dropped away and she existed solely in the memories the four of them were creating together.

However hard the face he presented to the world, his heart softened at the sight of his wife. The woman he would die without.

She was his strength and weakness in one, his equal and his better. The mother of his children. How he had lived for a thousand years without knowing what light she would bring to his life, he couldn't contemplate.

Michael didn't care one bit about galactic politics. He didn't care if the Estarians and the Oggs ever managed to get along. Let the Bakas hold themselves separately, and the Noel-nis cheat the Leath to score points. The Torcellans could go fuck themselves with their systematic oppression of the males, and the Shrillexians—well, he felt a little for them. They didn't ask to be compelled to fight.

What he cared about was the woman in that machine. The one who fought for them, one and all.

He would never forget the blur of nothing his life had become before Bethany Anne swept into his existence demanding her Justice. She had walked her high heels into his life and brought him back—*twice*.

To see Bethany Anne in any kind of turmoil was a constant burning. She had given him her heart to keep him grounded, and he would offer himself up like Prometheus upon the rock to keep it safe.

He was restricted in his course of action by his personal war; the internal pull to action which also demanded he be the parent his children needed. His duty to Gabriel and Alexis prevented him from bringing down unholy hell on the Ooken until they were laid waste to a one, as his instinct demanded.

However, it did not prevent him from unleashing the Patriarch given the necessity. Quite the opposite. He would tear this entire universe to atoms and rebuild it from scratch if that was what his love required to be at peace.

Bethany Anne and the children vanished from the screen as the scenario ended. Michael collected their water bottles and waited for the Vid-docs to cycle open before handing them out. "Very well done," he told Alexis and Gabriel. "I'm impressed with your improvement in your control of the Etheric, and even more so in your tactical thinking."

Bethany Anne kissed Michael as she took her water from him. "Honey, we have to find somewhere planetside for the children to train. Somewhere it won't matter if we make a mess."

Gabriel pumped the air with a fist. "Yes! I want to try that flip thing in reality." He looked up at Michael, the distance not so large these days. "D'you think I can make the midair turn and land it, Dad?"

Michael grinned. "I think you would do better to make the fall in the Etheric. You will both wear armor during practice. I don't want you missing the catch and getting blown up again."

Alexis squirted Michael with her water. "Let it go, Dad. I blew him up one time." She huffed a stray strand of hair out of her face. "No wonder Aunt Tabbie gets so annoyed with you."

Bethany Anne chuckled. "One time was more than enough, thank you, Alexis. Now, you two have what going on for the rest of the day while your father and I are in meetings?"

Gabriel reeled off their afternoon schedule on his fingers. "Math with ADAM and TOM, socioeconomics with Sabine, galactic history with Phyrro, then Uncle William promised we could blow some stuff up because that counts as chemistry and it's a lesson."

Alexis let out a little squeak. "Gabriel! You weren't supposed to say!"

Bethany Anne chuckled and shooed Gabriel and Alexis toward the door. "It's okay, William already cleared it with us. We'll walk out together."

A smile for the loves of his life graced Michael's lips as he slipped his arm around Bethany Anne's waist, savoring the chaos of a life he'd always believed would be denied him.

Alexis' and Gabriel's nonstop chatter filled him with the same deep urge to protect them that burned in his wife. It gave him strength and reinforced his determination.

Bethany Anne settled into the hollow of Michael's shoulder as Alexis and Gabriel headed down the ramp first. "We have to do something about a permanent place to live," she murmured against his cheek. "They're starting to settle, and we are *not* raising our children on a ship."

2

Location Three, QBS *Glaxix Sphaea*, Bridge

Kael-ven looked over from the viewscreen when the door to his ready room opened and the Admiral rejoined him and Kiel on the bridge. "What's the word from our Queen?"

Admiral Thomas glanced at the screen as he made his way over to his station. "The word is that she's on her way here to deal with the Moen personally."

Kael-ven considered that for a moment. "No change in how we deal with the Ooken in the meantime? She still wants us to stand back?"

The Admiral arched an eyebrow at his old friend. "What do you think? Bethany Anne is not the most patient, but neither does she change her mind once it's made up." He thought for a moment. "If she happens to change her mind, remember that was in the plan as well and don't comment on it."

Kael-ven chuckled as he discarded the orders he'd been

about to send to the ground teams, his hands hovering over the comm. "You're leaving?"

Admiral Thomas shook his head. "As much as I wish I could spare the time to see my wife and children, no."

Kael-ven turned in his seat, his face sympathetic to the Admiral's plight. "That's how it goes in this life. You sacrifice your time with your family, knowing it's the right thing to do to keep them safe. They understand eventually if they don't get it at the start."

The Admiral sighed. "That sounds like experience talking."

Kael-ven nodded. "My children are grown now, don't forget."

"And your wife is a distant nightmare," Kiel chipped in.

All three shuddered at the memory of Kael-ven's ex-wife.

Kael-ven shook it off. "What is Bethany Anne's plan for the Moen?"

Admiral Thomas lifted his hands. "I couldn't tell you, since she didn't bother to divulge it."

"We all know how she deals with things 'personally,'" Kiel conjectured. "It would take the patience of a saint to keep coming up against a wall and still not give up."

Kael-ven snorted. "The only saint we'll see will be Saint Payback when Bethany Anne gets here. This is possibly the oddest standoff I've ever encountered."

Admiral Thomas pointed at him. "Got it in one. None of it sits well with any of us, but there's no way of getting rid of the Ooken when the Moen willingly sacrifice themselves to protect them every time we move in."

Kael-ven saw a flaw in the reasoning. "We haven't taken

a single Moen life, so they must understand we value their lives more than their masters do."

Admiral Thomas grimaced. "You would think so. It's a wonder they haven't gone extinct already."

ArchAngel spoke up from the screen. "There are several species on record who are submissive in this way."

"Yes." Admiral Thomas nodded at the avatar. "But not to this extreme. The species' whole reason for existing seems to be nothing more than to obey. How have they survived?"

ArchAngel looked off to the side for a moment. "My conclusion, based on the data we have, is that the Moen have evolved to be indispensable to a stronger group who are able to protect them. In this way, they are able to survive, and given the right circumstances, thrive. It could be something as simple as them sticking with the oppressors they are familiar with as the more certain choice."

Kiel grunted in annoyance. "Then why are we still here? There's a bigger war going on out there, and we're missing it."

Kael-ven shrugged. "We know they're smart. The tech they produce is proof of that, so why not make some provisions for defense? I agree with Kiel; we would be of more use to the fleet right now. If not for the people suffering down there, I would take the argument to Bethany Anne."

"It is common among many of the species we have contact with to have a split within their societal structures," ArchAngel informed them. "The strong defend, and the intellectuals innovate—at least in the successful examples, although war is the other single largest driving factor for technological innovation across the galaxies. The curiosity here is that the Moen lack such a component in their society, which in turn leaves them vulnerable to predation from species like the Ooken."

"It's not so much a curiosity as a damn crying shame," the Admiral stated flatly. "No sentient being should live at the mercy of another."

"Unless that mercy is Bethany Anne's," Kael-ven amended.

Admiral Thomas nodded. "Amen to that."

"Would it be beyond the bounds of reason to assume that the Moen began as one of these 'split' societies?" Kiel inquired. "ArchAngel, I wonder if your data can provide an answer as to whether this is the Moen's planet of origin. Perhaps their homeworld suffered some cataclysmic disaster and those we know are the descendants of the survivors?"

They turned to the screen as one for the answer.

ArchAngel lifted a shoulder. "I couldn't possibly confirm either way," the EI told them. "However, I *can* tell you that the actions of the on-ground troops have not gone unnoticed. I have been listening in to the Moen's communications in an attempt to discern the hiding places of the Ooken leadership, and there is much confusion as to why our Marines did not fire upon them when the Ooken used them as living shields."

Admiral Thomas growled, "Because we are not monsters! Those Ooken bastards deserve to die painfully for this." He began to pace in an attempt to burn off the anger radiating from him. "So the Moen know that we mean them no harm. The question is, how do we capitalize on that to get them out from under the thumb of the Ooken?"

Kiel held up a hand. "We could put our resources into finding out what passes for leadership among the Moen. Make contact on behalf of Bethany Anne before she gets here?"

"Baba Yaga," Admiral Thomas corrected. "Our Queen does not wish to be caught on video."

Kael-ven shrugged. "It's not that simple. Is it?"

Admiral Thomas wasn't hearing him. "I like the idea. Find the Moen leaders, reach out to them with kindness. Which is their due, anyway. Bethany Anne's aim has always been to reach hearts and minds, and she's right." His pacing slowed some, his hands linking at the small of his back as he worked through his thoughts. "The Moen don't want to be free since they have no idea what freedom is. Bethany Anne wants the Ooken out, so I wouldn't waste money betting they'll be on Moen for much longer. Then...I don't know. She'll probably want them edged slowly toward independence, right?"

The two Yollins looked at each other, then nodded at the Admiral.

"Sounds about right," Kael-ven agreed. "So we institute the same systems for education, healthcare, and employment we have on High Tortuga and Devon?"

Kiel looked skeptical. "Isn't that basically tricking them? What if the system doesn't work? This isn't the same situation as High Tortuga or Devon."

Admiral Thomas shrugged. "The system is designed to be adaptable to whatever needs the people living within it have. We'll work out what the Moen need."

Kiel shook his head. "I'm not asking if it's possible. I mean, how does this come out ethically?"

The Admiral raised an eyebrow. "This isn't *Star Trek*, Kiel. If interfering with the constitution of a planet is what we need to do to protect the people, then that's exactly what we're going to do."

ArchAngel reappeared on the main screen. "I have just received an alert from the early warning system. Multiple Gate signatures just lit the network in all directions."

Admiral Thomas cracked his knuckles. "Time to get busy, boys. Looks like we have company on the way."

"How long until they get here?" Kael-ven asked, turning back to his console to get the information out to the defense line.

"I cannot say until they trip another layer of the system," ArchAngel replied.

Admiral Thomas cursed softly. "You will inform me the second we have new data."

Archangel narrowed her eyes. "Of course. Should I inform the Queen that the Ooken are on their way?"

Admiral Thomas considered the options. "No need to alarm Bethany Anne," he replied. "We have the BYPS keeping the planet out of the equation, and the Ooken don't know we have control of all of their defense platforms as well as our own. Send a brief report to Devon, and tell the captains to prepare for a brawl."

QT2, QBBS *Helena*, Shipyard, R&D Lab

Jean and Qui'nan stood separated by the hard light hologram of Qui'nan's proposed design, as well as the gulf between Jean's expectations and the Yollin architect's interpretation of them.

Jean double-checked to make sure she hadn't misread the scale. "Qui'nan, this isn't a battleship. It's a fucking floating continent."

Qui'nan lifted her shoulders in the Yollin equivalent of a shrug. "What do you expect me to do? The Queen wants her superdreadnoughts to be able to Gate farther. We either upgrade our technology or we—"

"Supersize them," Jean finished. She sighed, brushing her hair off her forehead. "I know. I'd hoped for more progress with the nanocytes Bethany Anne brought back."

Qui'nan hissed. "Do not speak to me of that ginormous waste of time and effort. Weeks, and all we have to show for it is a whole lot of illegible code we can't decipher because it's too degraded to tell what's useful and what's junk put there to throw us off the trail."

Jean frowned in consideration. "You think it's in there on purpose?"

Qui'nan turned from the hologram. "You don't?"

"I hadn't considered it," Jean admitted. "My priority is to reverse-engineer whatever tech we get our hands on and get it working for us."

Qui'nan's anger ebbed. "There is always the possibility that Bethany Anne will find the Ooken homeworld at any moment," she commiserated. "We need to take a break from this."

Jean chuckled and followed Qui'nan out into the corridor. "You mean you're hungry."

The Yollin did not pause in her stride. "You have that right. There is entirely too much blood in my sugar system for proper consideration of the issues we've had working this *drek* out."

"Don't sweat it. We'll solve it soon enough." Jean bumped her with a shoulder as they walked into the cantina. "Trust me, I've catered to Bethany Anne's demands for more years than a lady would admit to having lived, and I've never failed to find a solution yet."

Qui'nan looked somewhat doubtful as they split up to get their food.

A few moments later, they met back up at an empty table with their trays. Jean snickered at Qui'nan's choices. "What will you do when you outgrow your carapace?"

Qui'nan looked up from her cheesecake, her fork hovering halfway to her mouth. "What are you talking about? This is perfect Yollin fuel. Better than…what's that you have?"

Jean waved her fork over her plate. "An actual meal."

Qui'nan snorted. "Enjoy your veggies. I'm good with dessert." She made a show of enjoying the bite on her fork, drawing another chuckle from Jean.

They ate in silence for a few minutes, both their minds on the issue blocking their progress.

Jean pushed her tray away, her plate clear. "We need to talk about the elephant in the room."

Qui'nan looked at her in confusion for a moment. "Idiom, right? There are no pachyderms here. I can only assume you mean that the unavoidable is coming, and we are almost at the bottleneck I predicted some time ago?"

Jean massaged around her eyes with a thumb and fore-finger. "Uh-huh. My teams are doing good work removing everything of value from the territory we've gained, including strip-mining the systems to make sure there's no value in the Ooken returning."

Qui'nan made a face. "Giselle is working to find more suppliers of raw materials."

Jean grimaced. "It's not enough. This shit was so much easier when we didn't have to organize it all in the dark. Sneaking so as to not get caught with our asses out by the Federation isn't exactly conducive to building a state-of-the-art fleet."

Qui'nan raised her Coke bottle. "I'll drink to that. I can't pretend to understand the Queen's motivation in declining to form a new empire, but we can only work with what she gives us."

Jean chuckled inwardly at Qui'nan's philosophical mindset. Personally, she didn't see Bethany Anne taking the Empress route again, since she had never chosen it for herself in the first place.

Oh, she had accepted the role. Begrudgingly. In the beginning, but it had been a necessary step toward fulfilling her vow to wipe out the Kurtherian threat. However, as time passed and the years rolled into decades, that duty had become a burden that prevented Bethany Anne from reaching her goal. Jean had witnessed her friend's relief at being "forced" to step down as Empress.

Jean knew that if it came down to it, Bethany Anne would make the same self-sacrifice again. She also knew that if it wasn't on Bethany Anne's agenda, it wasn't likely to occur. Her friend was no dewy-eyed ingénue this turn of the carousel. "We need to get with a solution. We need processed metals, plastics, and a shit-ton of other resources, and we have the grace of a few more months before our concerns mutate into a shutdown."

Qui'nan was not unaware of the dire situation they were headed for. "We cannot allow that to happen. Ongoing fleet growth is key to our continued advantage. The maintenance on the superdreadnoughts alone is putting pressure on us."

Jean nodded. "Yeah, and that's just considering the superdreadnoughts we already have. We haven't even started on the bitch of a job building the next class of superdreadnoughts is going to be without a stable source of uncommon elements. Not to mention an ancillary fleet that doesn't require bodies to run it without specialist plastics."

"We need a solution," Qui'nan stated.

Jean snorted and met Qui'nan's eyes with a hard look. "Fuck if I know where we're gonna get *that* from. That's the problem with living in the shadows; you have to stay hidden."

Devon, First City, The Hexagon, Indoor Arena Two

Michael walked through the Hexagon, heading for Arena Two on Winstanley's directions.

He expected to find Tabitha teaching since Alexis' and Gabriel's schedule had them with her for the afternoon. However, instead of the clash of weapons he'd thought to hear coming from the training area, Michael heard music.

Further investigation did not clear up his confusion. For some unknown reason, Tabitha appeared to be throwing a party for her students.

Michael glanced around, noting that while most of the students were happy to mix with each other, the adolescent Bakas sat off to the side while the others socialized around them.

He was pleased to see his children making the effort to include them. Alexis and Gabriel acknowledged Michael's presence without breaking from their conversation with the group they were trying to persuade to join in.

Tabitha grinned when she saw Michael. She waved a hand, and the music faded out. "Guys, we have a visitor! Everyone say hi to Michael."

Michael froze as every child in the room turned their curious stares on him. What was he supposed to say to children whose alienness to him had nothing whatsoever to do with their species?

Tabitha cracked up. "Don't look so scared. They don't bite."

"Speak for yourself," one of the Bakas called. "If he comes at me, I'm definitely gonna bite."

Michael snorted, amused by the youth's spirit. "You will find that my teeth are a little sharper than yours, young one."

Tabitha sighed, her hands on her hips. "Boys, play nice, now. Trey, come over here and introduce yourself to our guest."

Tu'Reigd, aka "Trey"

The Baka looked a little less certain of himself on being singled out. Nevertheless, he walked over and offered his hairy hand to Michael. "I am Takar'Tu'Reigd, only surviving son of Mahi'Takar. You can call me 'Trey.'"

Michael allowed Trey to engulf his hand and pump it vigorously, amused by the young male's earnest enthusiasm. "Nice to meet you, Trey."

Tabitha clapped her hands and the music started up again. "Great, that was just like we practiced."

Michael raised an eyebrow at Tabitha. "What exactly is the purpose of this class?"

Tabitha grinned. "I'm teaching social skills. You wanna stay and learn some?"

Michael narrowed his eyes. "You do enjoy pushing me. Maybe a bit too much." He grinned at Tabitha's momentary uncertainty. "I'm here to get acquainted with the Bakas. Baba Yaga wishes to know what kind of people they are."

Trey's head whipped between Michael and Tabitha during the exchange, a small, surprised growl sneaking out at the mention of Baba Yaga. "You... You're Her consort!"

The young Baka hopped from one foot to another in his excitement. "You have to... *I* have to... Ohhhhh!"

Michael frowned at the teen's inability to form a complete sentence. "Are you well, Trey?"

Tabitha chuckled. "He'll slow down in a second. Trey's mom is the one who authorized the youths to train here."

Michael inclined his head and patted Trey's shoulder. "Good woman. You'll learn a lot from training with Tabitha."

Trey was still bubbling over. "I have to take you to meet Mahi'. The Mistress, too, if she will come."

Tabitha sucked in a breath. "I'm not sure that's a good idea, Trey."

Michael noted her sideways glance at him. "Why not?"

Tabitha grimaced. "Let's just say that you're not likely to visit the Enclave without getting into a fight. We need to be on good terms with the Bakas, so ixnay on the unchingpay, and no visiting the Enclave until we're on solid ground with them."

"How are we to build relations if we cannot meet?" Michael demanded. "Does your mother agree that we have to work together to defeat the Ooken?"

Trey snorted. "Yeah, um, Mahi' is down, but my uncles aren't the friendly type," he explained. "I can see them taking offense at a human being allowed into Mahi's home. It could give them a reason to replace her with one of her brothers."

Michael frowned. "I admit I have very little knowledge

of your culture. Perhaps you and your parents would join us for dinner one night so we can rectify that."

Trey's face dropped. "Taka gave his life to save Mahi' and me. Mahi' rules in his name until I reach my majority."

Tabitha frowned in sympathy. "I didn't know that, Trey."

Trey screwed up his face. "I shouldn't be talking about it at all. Dammit, why can't I just keep my big mouth shut? You won't tell Mahi' I said anything, will you?"

Michael chuckled. "Of course not. We are very interested in building bridges between our two peoples. You will pass on mine and Baba Yaga's invitation to your mother. We can arrange transport for the two of you if being seen outside the Enclave would cause an issue."

Trey nodded enthusiastically. "You bet!"

Michael nodded, satisfied he'd made a good start. "Very well. Thank you for allowing me to keep you from your, um," he eyed the smiling Tabitha before returning his focus to the Baka, "learning, Trey."

3

Devon, The Hexagon, Underground Hangar, QBS _Izanami_

Bethany Anne awoke feeling surprisingly refreshed.

"It's amazing what freedom to act does for you," Michael murmured beside her.

Bethany Anne turned into Michael's arms and kissed him before she climbed over him to get out of bed. "It's amazing what the prospect of kicking some tentacled ass does for me, you mean."

"That too." Michael joined her in the closet. "I have to admit, I'm pleased that Baba Yaga will be coming out to play."

Bethany Anne made a face as she selected a pair of black leggings and a long-sleeved t-shirt from a drawer. "I'm not sure how to react to your crush on my alter ego. Am I supposed to be jealous of myself?"

"Um, no?" Michael replied. He grabbed a handful of similar, easy-to-wear under-armor clothing and headed back to the bedroom. "But if you keep on this track, 'we

37

overslept' will have to suffice as an excuse for why you were late to the war today."

Bethany Anne stood on her tiptoes to reach a shoebox on the top shelf. "It's a good thing you didn't organize a state dinner yesterday," she teased.

Michael looked at Bethany Anne. "I didn't?"

"You invited the leader of the Devon Bakas to dinner. If you think it's going to be an intimate affair, you are sadly mistaken." Bethany Anne stayed on the balls of her feet to grab another box, this one containing Baba Yaga's cloak. "After what you told me about your meeting with Mahi'-Takar's son, the only way I see to do this without endangering her position is to ensure that her rivals know we *fully* support her."

"How do you intend to do that?" Michael asked. "I read the child's mind. He and his mother are good people, but their position appears to be somewhat precarious. If we do not support them, we risk her brothers gaining control of forty percent of Devon's population."

Bethany Anne sighed. "Ugh, politics. It's like every time I think I've escaped them, there they are, fucking my plans in the ass. You know I'll support them, but it's a one-time deal, Michael. And it's going to have to wait until we've dealt with Location Three. As much as I feel for the plight of the woman, Moen isn't going to wait."

"This is the problem with picking up planets like new outfits," Michael joked. "You have to make the alterations yourself or deal with discomfort."

Bethany Anne raised an eyebrow. "Maybe it won't be so boring with you there." Her eyes sparkled with mischief. "You can wear something pretty to make it up to me."

Michael grinned back. "Sweetheart, you *always* look pretty."

Bethany Anne threw an energy ball at him. "Ass. Breakfast is almost ready. I can smell Alexis' and Gabriel's pre-mission pancakes from here."

"I smell burning batter," Michael shot back, catching the ball and absorbing the energy. A soft chime rang out from the bedroom, and Michael went to see who was calling so early in the day. "Your father. Want me to take it? I have time before I meet with Addix."

"Give him my love," Bethany Anne replied. She dressed quickly, then took a moment to slip her feet into heels, since she would be replacing them with her armored boots soon enough, and picked up the box.

Michael sat at the small table by the bed, his shirt forgotten as Lance spoke. He turned his head when Bethany Anne entered. "You might want to hang on for a moment."

Lance waved. "Hey, Pumpkin. I thought you should know that you're causing a few rumors with your spending habits."

Bethany Anne scooped her husband's shirt up on her way past, then leaned over Michael's shoulder to wave at Lance. "Oh, yeah? What kind of rumors?"

Lance flashed a grin. "The kind where people are beginning to wonder just who the new player is."

Bethany Anne's mouth quirked. "Let them wonder. It suits me fine." She dropped Michael's shirt in his lap. "Gotta run, Dad. Breakfast with the twins, and then a to-do list as long as my arm before I can leave for Moen. I'm done waiting for answers there."

Lance raised an eyebrow. "I'm glad to hear you're getting some resolution on the issue. Don't have too much fun, you hear me?"

Bethany Anne broke into a grin. "I don't know if I can keep that promise. This has been a frustrating few months, so the Ooken on Moen have it coming more than most."

Lance frowned at that. "Then give them hell, sweetheart."

Bethany Anne flashed a grin and reaffirmed her grip on the box under her arm. "You know I'll do my damnedest." Her nose wrinkled as she caught another whiff of burned batter. "I'd better move. First rescue of the day looks to be breakfast."

Her fears were unfounded. She arrived in the galley to perfect pancakes keeping warm under a cover on the breakfast bar and her angels scraping the source of the smell into a container.

"All of the syrup," Alexis told Gabriel. "She's been up all night studying, and..."

Bethany Anne smiled, waving a hand to clear the air. "I take it you two are burning down the kitchen for K'aia's benefit. What good friends you are to risk Mama's wrath so early in the morning."

Gabriel looked up from his drowning of K'aia's breakfast, a grin playing over his face. "Mama can always turn off her olfactory senses if the smell is offending her."

Alexis snorted. "Or we could all stop talking about ourselves in the third person and eat." She took the container from Gabriel and sealed it. "There, all gone. Where's Dad?"

Bethany Anne lifted the cover on breakfast. "He's on a call with Grandpa."

The twins bolted for the bedroom, leaving Bethany Anne to roll her eyes while getting the plates out for breakfast.

>>**Bethany Anne, there's a report from the G'laxix Sphaea you should see.**<<

Bethany Anne scanned the report, her eyes flickering with the speed she read. "Damn you, Bart. I could have been there already."

Bethany Anne looked regretfully at breakfast and opened her mental link to Alexis and Gabriel. *Say goodbye to Grandpa and come get your breakfast. We're leaving in twenty minutes, and you will need to pick K'aia up from the arena. I have decided that the Admiral has a great deal to teach you all.*

Devon, First City, The Hexagon, Network Command, Michael's Office

Michael was still impressed by the effort Sabine had put into blending something reminiscent of Louis *Quatorze* style with modern conveniences for him when he'd asked her for a space to work.

He was going to miss it when his wife came to the inevitable conclusion that settling on Devon was impractical.

He adjusted his furniture while taking the time to consider his approach to the issue at the front of his mind while he waited for his next meeting.

It was but a moment's work to exchange his usual guest

chair for the one he placed in front of his desk. Like all the rest of the furniture, it was sourced from local artisans, upholstered in plush fabric, carved and gilded to perfection —and also suitable for the four-legged visitor he heard making her way toward his office.

He nodded amiably when the spymistress entered. "Good to see you, Addix. Have a seat."

Addix's mandibles twitched as she settled on the guest chair and adjusted her light robe around her four legs. "You wished to see me?"

Michael pushed a holofile across the desk toward her. "I have an assignment for you that may require some travel. How do Ixtalis do in low temperatures?"

Addix chuckled. "Quite poorly, traditionally," she replied. "However, I am not much for tradition, and I find myself without distraction these days. What is the assignment?

Michael laced his fingers on the desk. "I want some concrete information on the Bakas. They make up just over forty percent of Devon's population, and we've got nothing except hearsay and supposition. They could be a useful ally in this war—if they are indeed allies."

"You don't trust them?" Addix inquired.

Michael raised an eyebrow. "I don't *know* them. Bethany Anne and I intend to change that once the Moen issues are resolved. In the meantime, we would like you to monitor the situation until we can get to it. "

Addix ran her fingers over the arm of her chair, tracing the carvings. "The Bakas are extremely secretive about their culture and sensitive to questions about it."

Michael nodded. "I am aware of that. However, the

nominal leader is a potential ally. Bethany Anne and I would like you to reprise your role as our children's guardian as a way to protect the heir."

Addix's mandibles dropped open in shock. "You are joking. I would, of course, be honored, but how does that fit with protecting the Bakan heir?"

"Our information so far is based on my mind reading of the heir and his cousins. Trey, the name he appears to prefer, is a member of Alexis' and Gabriel's training group. He and his mother may be holding onto power by a thread, but until we learn whether an alliance is possible, I believe Trey especially to be at risk."

"You suspect they intend to have him murdered?"

Michael rubbed his chin in thought. "His cousins harbor no thoughts of it. In fact, they are mostly apathetic about everything. However, they are currently acting as his guard, and their fathers all stand to gain from his death. I do not think it would hurt to be cautious, which is where you come in."

Addix tucked the holofile into her pocket. "Not a problem. It will be an opportunity to pass on my knowledge to the students."

Michael tilted his head. "I suspected you would enjoy the chance to teach again."

Addix chuckled, her mandibles tapping in amusement. "I will wrap up my other current assignments and make myself available to Tabitha at the earliest opportunity."

Michael shook his head fondly. "Good luck. We leave for Moen as soon as Bethany Anne is done building the city's morale."

Addix headed for the door. "Victory be with you all."

Michael's mouth quirked. "Victory cannot fail to be with us while Bethany Anne leads the charge. Oh, and Addix? You will be remaining onworld for a while, The *Lady Princess* will be reassigned. You may requisition a ship for personal use."

Addix's mandibles twitched in anticipation. "I believe the *Sayomi* has been docked at the *Guardian* recently."

"I wouldn't get your heart set," Michael told her. "John loves that ship almost as much as he loves his wife who built it for him, so he won't leave it here when we depart for Moen. One moment." He opened the message that had interrupted him. "I have to go. Bethany Anne is about to leave."

"Good...bye." Addix shook her head at the empty air Michael had been occupying as the word left her mouth and left the office, grumbling to herself about not making more time to train in the Vid-docs. "I really must learn how to do that one of these days."

Devon, First City, The Hexagon, Training Center

K'aia

K'aia ducked the downswing of Trey's staff but did not move fast enough to avoid being clipped on the upswing. She turned her body to protect her rear legs from further attack and whipped her braid at him, scoring a direct hit to his chest plate. "Point each," she panted, twisting as she stepped into her next technique.

The three Bakas at the side watched with indifference.

"Your cousins are kinda rude," K'aia complained. "Don't they want to support you?"

Trey dodged K'aia's staff, hurling himself three feet clear of the floor to land in a roll on K'aia's vulnerable side. "Those assholes are only here because my mother made them come. Like I need an honor guard who benefits if I die."

K'aia gaped at him, taking the end of Trey's staff in the gut for her lapse in concentration. "You're kidding?" She saw he wasn't. "That sucks. Wanna ditch them when the twins get here?"

Trey considered the offer. "Not worth it. Mahi' would end up childless, and I can't do that to her."

K'aia chuckled. "What makes you think you'll die?"

Trey met her eyes solemnly. "I don't think, I know. Mahi' will tear me limb from limb, and then what will she do without me? No, I'm a good son. I'll stay behind."

K'aia wasn't completely sure Trey was joking. "Your mother terrifies me and I haven't even met her. Did she give you permission to train here or are you sneaking around still?"

Trey nodded, panting as he worked to avoid K'aia's staff. "Yeah, she agreed. It took some persuading, especially after she found out I had lied upfront about having her permission to train here. She's going to meet with Baba Yaga to discuss a formal alliance against the Ooken."

K'aia scored three points in quick succession. "That's pretty huge. How did your family take it? From what you've told me, they don't sound very progressive."

Trey snorted. "I believe you call that an 'understatement.' My uncles weren't pleased, and my cousins couldn't believe it. I'm pretty sure they only came here with me last week so they could run to their fathers. Doesn't take a genius to work out they wanted to see me get punished for making contact with humans."

K'aia was about to comment on Trey's bravery in breaking tradition when she heard Gabriel and Alexis. She found that since her enhancement, she was aware of the twins before she saw them, one of the many benefits of her upgrade in the Vid-doc. She took a step back and feinted with her staff, then took Trey's feet out from under him with a sweep of her foot.

The Baka landed on his back in a puff of orange robes and sand, ignoring his cousins' laughter. "Dammit, K'aia! Every time! No fair."

K'aia extended a hand to help Trey to his feet. "You'll get used to hearing what humans think of fighting fair." She nodded at Gabriel and Alexis, who had just entered the arena. "I better get going."

Trey's cousins glared at the humans and turned their backs.

K'aia made an obscene gesture at them. "Seriously, they need therapy. I hope their faces get stuck looking like an explosion in a genitalia factory."

Trey cracked up at the mental image. "How is that even... You know what? Who cares, I'm making a break for it."

"Good man," Gabriel cut in.

Trey narrowed his eyes at Gabriel, scrutinizing his features. He sniffed the air, and realization dawned. "I know who you are! Well, I don't, but I think I met your father yesterday." His voice dropped to a whisper. "Are you Baba Yaga's young?"

K'aia cut Trey off before his curiosity got the better of him. Maybe the kid did need a guard—to save him from himself. "Hey, you're early...and you're in armor. Are we going somewhere?"

Gabriel nodded, offering a fist for Trey to bump. "Yeah. We were sent to get you and meet the ship out front. Your gear is onboard."

Alexis looked at Trey, who was in the process of

collapsing his staff. "Do you want to come with us?"

Trey flashed two rows of strong white teeth. "Does Baba Yaga have a short fuse?"

Alexis snorted at the Baka's enthusiasm. "You'll find out about Baba Yaga's fuse. We're headed to Moen with her."

Trey's shaggy face twitched with disappointment. "Off-world? For real? Oh. You're not kidding." He sighed. "You know, I will just wave to you all as you leave this time. I'll save it for when I've been training for more than a few weeks, huh?"

"You sure?" Gabriel asked skeptically.

Trey nodded. "Yeah. I thought you were sticking around Devon. Like I said, next time."

"You'll have to work on your mother," K'aia commiserated.

Trey grinned. "Sure." He walked off, his posture a little downcast until he saw Addix talking to Hirotoshi, then he veered in that direction to investigate with all of his usual enthusiasm.

K'aia rolled her eyes at her new friend's distractible nature, smiling as she turned to follow the twins out of the training area. "He's a nice kid. Bit of a space cadet, but whatever."

"I like him," Alexis stated.

Gabriel nodded in agreement. "Me too. He can come train with us if things go well with his mom and ours."

"Yeah, it's pretty awkward while we have to hold him at a distance. It felt kind of mean." K'aia sniffed the air, feeling hungry now that her workout was done. "You two smell like sugar." A loud growl came from her abdomen. "The good kind."

Alexis dipped into her bag and retrieved the container within. "Your stomachs are telling me you haven't eaten yet. Your nanocytes need fuel, you know. It's a good thing we brought you some breakfast. Here, eat up."

K'aia took the container and tucked into the pancakes as they made their way out through the main arena. "Nice and crispy, just the way I like them. Mmmm. And that's *almost* enough syrup."

Alexis wrinkled her nose. "You know sugar rots your insides, right?"

"Not now that I have nanocytes." K'aia licked the spoon clean. "Yum. Did you two see the leaked vids from Moen?"

"Yes, we did," Alexis told her. "It was me who leaked them. I hacked Network Command to find out what's really happening, and decided the people needed to know what's going on there."

K'aia covered her mouth with the back of her hand. "Which is what, exactly?"

"You out-logicked Phyrro," Gabriel interrupted before Alexis could answer. "You shouldn't think ADAM doesn't know about it. I don't want to be there when Mom and Dad find out you were responsible for the leak."

Alexis raised a finger. "I out-logicked—which is not a word, by the way—Phyrro, *and* I made a deal with ADAM," she corrected. "We're good. Besides, nothing in the vids we were allowed to access covered those poor aliens being used as living shields. It's *disgusting*!"

K'aia's appetite vanished. "It happens all over. This planet was a dangerous place to live before your mother put a leash on the mercenaries." She dropped the spoon into the container as they passed under an arch into the atrium and dumped the whole thing into the nearest recycling port. "That's the reason I went so far to find your parents again—to be there for people who need help and do what I can to make it right. Tell us what else you know."

Alexis shrugged. "I don't see us getting off the ship at all, but sure."

Alexis was stopped in her tracks by the crowd gathered in front in Hexagon Plaza. "That's pretty much everyone who trains or works here. What's going on?"

Gabriel pointed out a number of faces none of the three recognized. "Those look like they came from the bazaar side of the building."

Alexis touched her fingers to her collar, activating her armor's helmet. "Mom must be making a speech. Come on!"

Gabriel did the same before they all exited the great glass doors into the crowd, K'aia moving to guard Alexis' and Gabriel's backs without a second thought.

The crowd parted at the sight of the two fully-armored humans.

Alexis picked up K'aia's moment of discomfort. *K'aia, you're not disguised. You can't be seen with us—Mom's rule.*

For my protection, I know. I'll be watching. K'aia walked out of the door alone and slipped into the crowd independent of Alexis and Gabriel. She made her way toward a group of fellow trainees who were headed for the center of the plaza, where the *Izanami* floated overhead. *There aren't many four-legged Yollins on this planet. It's not difficult to work out who I am, even in full armor.*

Yes, Gabriel agreed. *But the point is to keep the mystery, or*

Mom will take us all off guard rotation and we'll be back in the classroom before you can say, "Pepsi, please."

Alexis raised her eyebrow. *Only until we bat our eyes at Dad. He'll help us get around Mom if she gets overprotective.*

I'll get by. I'm just sore about missing out on being part of the show. K'aia tuned the twins out as they left her behind, hearing Trey's chatter behind her.

Trey fell in beside K'aia. "I heard Baba Yaga's ship is here." He glanced shrewdly at K'aia. "You think she's going to speak?"

K'aia nodded at the ship casting its shadow over the plaza. "The twins told me she would be. I have the duty, or I would stay to keep you company." She made sure to keep any pity she felt for the lone Baka out of her voice.

Still, she empathized, and she liked the kid. Alexis and Gabriel wouldn't be the only ones to welcome him into their group with open arms if talks went well.

"When *don't* you have the duty, or have to study?" Trey bumped his hairy shoulder against hers before moving ahead. "Live a little. You only have to make it onto the ship before it leaves, right? It's *Baba Yaga*! Everyone on the planet will be watching, except for the people on the ships. Come on, she won't be mad you wanted to watch. It's a moment in history!"

"I think she will understand." K'aia relented, only half-listening to Trey. Her attention was more on the crowd around Gabriel and Alexis. "Keep watching, it's about to begin."

The twins dashed into the center of the plaza just before the innermost circle of the mosaic-tiled floor began to rise up. The crowd gasped or stood in awestruck silence when the brightness of the morning was replaced by what could only be described as an absence of light.

K'aia shrugged at Trey's questioning look. She figured the effect was being created by the five other Shinigami-class ships surrounding the *Izanami*. Michael's scary-ass android must have programmed their cloaking to create a false night.

Gabriel and Alexis moved to meet the ramp and positioned themselves on either side as it touched down with their weapons at ease, ready to react at the first sign of trouble.

K'aia wished her exosuit wasn't aboard the *Izanami* already so she could be there with them.

Trey continued to chatter in that sliding musical tone of his. "You know every vid-caster in the city has a drone as close to the ship as Baba Yaga will allow. I can't believe I'm *here*! We all saw the leaked reports from the battle zones. I bet she's beyond mad. I wonder…do you think she can really spit fire? That would be beyond impressive."

K'aia repressed a snicker and threw her arm around Trey's shoulders to move him along. "Who knows? Come on, or I'll probably be the one to find out when I'm late to my post."

They halted near the base of the newly created platform. K'aia was no shy maiden, and she had no problem using her bulk to make space for her and Trey at the front of the crowd.

The *Izanami's* hatch opened, emitting a red glow that framed the hatch against the darkness. The temperature dropped sharply as the glow spilled down the ramp in a spray of fine mist.

Trey craned his muscular neck, wanting a better view of the hatch. "That light—it's too bright. I can't see inside."

K'aia shushed him with a hand. "Give it a minute."

Blood-bright mist continued to pour down the ramp. It licked the edge of the platform and washed back on itself, the tidal swirl almost hypnotic in the darkness.

The crowd waited with their breath held to see which face Baba Yaga would greet them with. Whether she appeared as the Mistress or the Witch, everyone knew that surviving contact with Baba Yaga depended entirely on whether or not you broke her cardinal rule.

Baba Yaga appeared at the hatch and stepped into the night, pausing to take in the crowd below her. Her moon-white hair lashed the air, sending up tendrils of glowing mist that were eclipsed by the twin points of fire burning in the inky blackness of her face.

She was *clearly* pissed off.

This would be somebody's last day breathing. However, the people of Devon weren't the ones who had angered her.

The planet ground to a halt as Baba Yaga spoke. All across Devon, people gathered in their homes, their businesses, and at public screens as word spread. They were drawn in by Baba Yaga's rage, their empathy easy to come by since they felt the same anger at the disruption the Ooken had caused to their lives.

The Mistress of the planet lifted her chin and spoke into the unnatural darkness, her grim voice needling the minds of everyone listening. "This is *my* planet, but it is also your home. When I came here looking for a fight, I had no intention of remaining any longer than it took to relieve my frustration about your pirate problem."

She grinned without joy, descending slowly to the platform. "None of us planned on the Ooken. How could we? We had no clue they existed until they attacked."

The crowd beneath the *Izanami* muttered angrily.

Baba Yaga spread her hands wide. "The Ooken are a gigantic pain in my ass and yours, but their days are numbered. Devon is safe, thanks to the efforts of my people to make it so. However, the contributions you have made to the defense of your homeworld have not gone unnoticed." She turned a circle, making sure to include the cameras. "I come before the people of Devon today with a damn sight more respect than I had when I arrived— respect that you as a people have *earned*. Sure, you're ornery and rebellious, but I can appreciate that. The desire to steer your own course is not just a whim. It's the right of every sentient being."

Her face softened, lending her terrible features a sense of sadness. "The Moen have got an Ooken infestation they can't take care of." A symphony of alerts rang out across the plaza. "Bear witness with me."

K'aia felt the mood shift another notch toward anger. She checked her holo, finding unedited HUD-footage taken by Guardian Marines on Moen. The slender aliens were chained to buildings, as Alexis had discovered.

She continued to watch for a moment before shutting the playback off, sickened by the continued abuse of the diminutive aliens. She sincerely hoped that the twins hadn't watched the whole video. Alexis and Gabriel had an unjaded innocence about them despite the nature of their upbringing, and she would hate for the ugliness the Ooken were capable of to rob them of that.

"This is going out all over the planet." Baba Yaga's tone sent shivers through the crowd, her icy fury somehow worse than the searing anger they were used to from their ruler. "I want everyone to watch closely. See the treatment the Moen endure. Understand their pain. I will *not* stand for slavery in any form, and where I find it, I will stamp it out without mercy."

"I want to help!" a voice yelled from the crowd.

More joined the first, a clamor rising up across the plaza.

This was why Bethany Anne had settled on this planet to be the new Devon. These people resented any kind of management they didn't agree to. They fought and played by their own rules when they thought she wasn't paying attention, but they took care of their families and their friends. They would fight for their worst enemy if they believed it was the right thing to do.

They had *honor*.

Across Devon, many of the people responded much as Bethany Anne had intended. They left their homes, their jobs, or their purchases behind and banded together. In the towns and cities, Tim Kinley's ground teams moved out to meet the mobs. It was their job to funnel the people's energy to some purpose before it spilled into riots and looting.

Some were more taciturn in their reactions. Inside the Bakan enclave, Mahi'Takar sat in the main hall with her sisters, scrutinizing the human on the screen. Perhaps Tu'Reigd's dreams were not so impossible after all.

In Hexagon Plaza, K'aia allowed the movement of the crowd to carry her away from Trey and around the other side of the platform to wait for her chance to get aboard the *Izanami* without being seen. She peered through the churning mist, amazed by the way the people in the plaza hung on Baba Yaga's every word.

"If you can fight, you're already in the right place. Anyone who is generous enough to drop everything to help the Moen rebuild should get to a Library and start preparing for a change of scenery, because once I've cleared out the garbage, they're going to need every bit of help they can get. This shit will get messy fast, and the more we can do to make the transition smooth by returning their infrastructure to them undamaged, the better." Baba Yaga turned and placed a foot on the ramp. "If you fight for Devon, I welcome you."

She vanished as suddenly as she'd appeared and the mist expanded rapidly, running over the edge of the platform now that it was no longer held in place.

K'aia hopped onto the platform and darted up the ramp behind Gabriel and Alexis, grateful once again for the enhanced speed and agility her nanocytes gave her. The last thing she saw before the hatch closed was the rush for the doors of the Hexagon.

4

Devon, The Hexagon, Outdoor Arena

The arena echoed with the steady hum of a large gathering. Bethany Anne's appearance as Baba Yaga yesterday had gone viral in Devon's three cities within hours of her speech, and it seemed to Tabitha that she'd processed half of the planet's population in the last day—with the other half still to go.

Tabitha walked the lines of potential trainees, speaking for a moment with each candidate to assess their skill set before sending them on their way to meet their new teammates.

Hirotoshi, Ryu, Akio, Tim, and Sabine were carrying out similar assessments around the arena to determine how to make the most of this unexpected resource. They'd been doing this while still running scheduled classes in the indoor training center. Assigning a hundred thousand or more civilians to the track that most suited them took time to do right, yet the people of Devon waited their turn patiently.

Well, mostly patiently.

Hirotoshi touched Tabitha's mind. *Trouble is brewing between those two Bakas and Trey.*

Tabitha rolled her eyes. *Seriously? They can't just wait their turns like everybody else? I'll take care of it.* She stomped over to the two males at the center of the altercation, her tolerance for this kind of shit precisely zero. "What's going on here?"

The bullies ignored her, too wrapped up in their posturing to realize the foolishness of their choice. They were almost identical in size and had an equal amount of scarring showing under their matted fur. Both had their hands over their blades' hilts, ready to draw if their offense wasn't answered.

Tabitha snapped her fingers at them. "Hey! I asked you a question. Do you have a problem with my student?"

"I wouldn't anger her," Trey warned.

The two adults laughed at Trey. "Little worm, always letting the females fight his battles for him."

Trey bared his teeth. "It's called being smart, Ch'Irzt. She can take you, and that's double the dishonor for you. Then again, I could take you down myself...if I wanted to risk getting your ass-wodge stink on my fur."

Ch'Irzt and his buddy lunged at Trey, who didn't flinch a millimeter. "You little..."

Trey bared his teeth and cocked a fist. "What? I dare you. Just try it and see."

Tabitha grunted in consternation and shouldered her way between them before it got ugly. "Hey! Back up!" She planted her hands on the older Bakas' chests and pushed them farther apart. "No fighting. Keep your dick waving outside of this arena, or you're both out of here, you got me?"

Ch'Irzt bristled. "I do not answer to any human, much less one I could snap between my fingers."

Tabitha pressed her lips together and nodded. "Is that right? Your name is Chet? Well, *Chet*, let's get something straight right off the bat. You're here because *you* want to be trained by *me*, so you'd better hope you don't piss me off, or I might decide to make an example of you." She pointed at the stone arch leading to the changing area. "Exit's that way. If you don't like it, I'm happy to kick your furry ass out."

The Baka snorted and spat at Tabitha's feet. "Pah. I'd like to see you try."

Tabitha moved without warning, and the Baka landed hard on his ass before his brain was done processing that she'd hit him. "You were saying?"

Two females came forward and glared at the male on the ground.

"Get up, Ch'Irzt," the first grunted at him. "How dare you insult our host this way?" She held her hands out palms up to Tabitha. "I can only apologize. My son is resistant to change. He will obey you, or I will no longer have three sons." The last was said through the female's gritted teeth and aimed toward her eldest son.

"You behave like a youth still," the other scolded, wagging a long, painted claw in Ch'Irtz's face as he got to his feet. "Why do you always bring shame on our clan? Why can you not learn from my Tu'Reigd like the others?"

Tabitha glanced at the young Baka, who shrugged as if to agree he hadn't seen his cousins learning much except what curse words they could pick up from the training fighters. She grinned at the two females. "No offense taken. But your family's permission to take Chet here in hand would ensure he doesn't get himself or anyone else killed with his dumb-ass mouth."

The females returned Tabitha's devious smirk. "It would be our honor," his mother told her. "You may have his life to use as you see fit in the hope my boy returns to me a warrior."

Tabitha wasn't too sure about that. "Not necessary. Six months of living and training with the youth teams will beat some manners into him."

She raised her voice to make sure every being there could hear. "Anyone else who wants to spend time training with the kids should start acting up right now to save me the trouble of busting your asses later. This is not a summer camp, people. I *will* break you and turn you out stronger than before, but only if you *want* it. You don't like that? It sounds too hard? Like I just told Chet, the exit is that way."

Tabitha's voice echoed around the arena, her passion overpowering the murmurs of those present. "The Ooken aren't dicking around. They want our home, and they want us wiped out or enslaved. Sure as hell itself, I don't intend to let that happen. Do you?"

Tabitha stood with her hands on her hips as the lines began to reform. "That's what I thought," she finished softly, heading back to her line.

. . .

Location Three, Orbiting Moen, QBS *Izanami*, Queen's Armory

Bethany Anne arched her back as the last section of her armor locked into place. "Here's hoping Jean managed to work all the bugs out of the nanos."

"Any improvement to the energy drain taking armor into the Etheric causes you is to be applauded," Michael called from the armor case next to Bethany Anne's. "Perhaps in the near future Jean will find a way to eliminate it altogether."

"It's taken long enough to get to this point." Bethany Anne stepped down and walked over to collect her katanas from the wall mount. "Between Eve, William, and Jean, I'm hoping we'll see a hell of a lot of applicable tech coming from their findings on the nanocytes in the Ooken substance, however slowly the discovery phase is moving." She held her swords to her back and her armor moved to secure them.

"Especially once TOM and ADAM crack that Kurtherian code," Michael agreed. He detached his armor's gauntlets in favor of the ones Bethany Anne had given him, smiling when the nanocytes in his armor adapted to create a seal at his wrist. "Although the advances Jean has made despite the scant discoveries at the locations we've taken are not to be sniffed at. Who could have imagined splicing the two technologies could give us the ability to change the properties of a material at the atomic level? It will certainly make a change to sneaking around the darkest corners of the Ooken colonies in an attempt to avoid discovery."

"You're preaching to the choir." Bethany Anne waved her finger in a circle to indicate Michael do a turn. Her mouth twitched with satisfaction when he gave her that look of his and complied. She tapped the same finger on her lip. "The red looks good. Hmmm… Could be a *little* more fitted in the rear aspect."

Michael looked over his shoulder, then raised an eyebrow at Bethany Anne. "Looks fine to me."

Bethany Anne winked, chuckling as he turned back to her, "I'm teasing. Looks just fine to me, too."

Izanami's voice came over the speaker, ending the moment. "We are one Gate away from Location Three, my Queen," she announced. "Alexis and Gabriel are making their way to the bridge with K'aia."

Bethany Anne arched an eyebrow, a rueful smile spreading over her face. "Are you getting that date-night vibe? I'm not saying I'd change a thing, but finding time alone together is becoming somewhat difficult now that our children are getting older."

"Just hold onto the memory, my love." Michael took the hand Bethany Anne offered. "I expect the difficulty will ease once we are no longer living aboard the ship."

Bethany Anne half-shrugged and took them both into the Etheric. "I don't know if that's looking any closer. I'm not completely sold on the lake house. It's so close to the cities. Shit, this is still a drag."

Michael chuckled dryly. "There are at least a hundred kilometers of empty land around it on all sides. How much space do you *want?*" he asked as they stepped out into the transfer area on the bridge.

Bethany Anne pressed her lips together. "More than *that*. It's not the biggest buffer. It's not like we can Gate the whole planet out of here if the Ooken somehow find a way through the defenses around Devon." Her eyes flicked to the Ooken satellites around the planet that were displayed on the wraparound screens. It was quiet. *Too* quiet. "They must be wondering why I've pulled back."

Michael sat and activated the workstation at his couch. "That isn't a likely scenario. Let them wonder. Uncertainty breeds fear, which leads to errors we can take advantage of."

"True." Bethany Anne continued to scan the almost empty space beyond, settling down as the Gates bringing the rest of her Shinigami-class ships into the system came into being. "Izanami, what's the word on the Ooken reinforcements?"

Izanami's avatar appeared beside the console, her blocky red aura rippling with flashes of black. "ArchAngel tells me we should expect them to be inbound in just under twelve hours."

Bethany Anne eyed Izanami for a moment before turning her attention back to the center screen. "Then this is a perfect time to speak to my Admiral about miscommunication."

Izanami's mouth moved fractionally. "I will inform ArchAngel you expect his call, my Queen." Her avatar vanished in its usual spray of pixelated light.

Bethany Anne turned to Michael after the AI disappeared. "Does she look strange to you?"

Michael looked up from the console. "Izanami? No more than usual."

Bethany Anne pressed her lips together. "Her hair, I think. And her face moved."

Michael shrugged. "I didn't notice."

Bethany Anne wondered if she were imagining things. Admiral Thomas appeared onscreen, ending the discussion. "What do you have to say for yourself?"

Admiral Thomas winced. "I hope you rested well?" he tendered, looking somewhat sheepish.

Bethany Anne narrowed her eyes. "I did, and then I woke up to your report."

The Admiral held up his hands. "There was nothing to be gained by you getting here any sooner."

Bethany Anne glared at him for a moment longer. "Be grateful we're pressed for time. What's the status here?"

Admiral Thomas looked down for a moment and sent Bethany Anne a file. "We own everything around the planet, including the Ooken platforms at the stable Lagrange Points. Jean and Qui'nan's teams have fortified them with the big-ass battle station out at L3. Nothing is getting past the BYPS, and even if it could, we have two grudge-bearing superdreadnoughts stationed here at all times."

Bethany Anne chuckled. "Adrastea is still pissed about getting cut in two?"

Admiral Thomas raised an eyebrow. "You're kidding, right? She's got a hate on for the Ooken, and she doesn't care who knows about it."

Michael nodded in appreciation. "Understandable. What are we looking at planetside?"

Admiral Thomas grimaced. "The Ooken withdrew the moment we pulled the ground units back. Intel is coming up with all sorts of suppositions. The best they have is that the Ooken believe we withdrew to stop them from killing the Moen. It's uneasy but stable for the moment."

Bethany Anne's eyes flickered as she scanned the latest from every ship, satellite, and outpost she had around Moen. "There isn't much the Ooken can do, which is exactly the position I want them in. Let them hide for the moment. It makes accessing the Moen that much easier."

Admiral Thomas lifted his hands. "I wish I could tell you that's the case, but if anything, they've closed ranks even further. It's damned infuriating. They won't talk to us at all. You've read the reports. We go in and take the Ooken out, and the Moen just stare at us silently until we leave, then go right back to work."

Michael frowned. "I don't get their mentality. Are they brainwashed?"

Bethany Anne tilted her head to look at Michael. "What, like a planet-wide case of super-Stockholm syndrome? It's worth considering, but I can't see it. There's something deeper going on here."

Michael shrugged. "I'm not convinced. Interdependence of some kind is the only thing that makes sense." He sat back, lacing his hands behind his head. "The Ooken and the Moen need each other for something. Otherwise, the Moen would have fought back, and the Ooken would have killed them to the last and stripped the planet long before we got here."

Bethany Anne and Michael turned to see what the commotion was when the elevator opened, spilling Alexis, Gabriel, and K'aia onto the bridge.

K'aia had her braid wrapped around Alexis, pinning her arms to her side. Gabriel had K'aia in a chokehold, bracing himself to stay balanced as she bucked on all four feet to dislodge him from her back.

Bethany Anne snickered. "Play nice, children." She turned back to the screen and continued to grill the Admiral.

Michael pointed at the couches, his smile belying his stern tone. "The bridge is *not* the best place to roughhouse, children."

Gabriel loosened his hold on K'aia's neck fractionally. "Sorry, Dad. K'aia decided that the elevator would be a good place to test our reflexes."

K'aia dropped Alexis, then wrapped her braid around Gabriel's waist and pulled him from her back to deposit him gently on the floor. "I'll be more thoughtful in the future."

Michael chuckled. "It's done now. Make yourselves useful until it is time to leave."

K'aia leaned over to Gabriel and Alexis as they crossed to the couches. "What's going on out there?"

Alexis shook her head minutely at K'aia, flicking her eyes at the adults. "I have no idea, K'aia. Let's get to work."

Bethany Anne was well aware that her daughter had access and was elbows-deep in the Moen report. She kept her smile to herself, returning her focus to Admiral Thomas. "We've identified where the Moen leaders are hiding, right?"

Admiral Thomas nodded. "Elset, one of the larger western cities. It wasn't easy since they don't use any kind of electronic communication."

Bethany Anne tapped her fingers on her armrest while she pulled up the map in her HUD and found Elset. "I think it's about time I went and introduced myself. Stay alert. Oh, and Admiral? My children and K'aia will be shadowing you for the duration of this operation. Expect them shortly." She cut the connection and opened a new one to the bridge of the *Sayomi*. "Are you all in position?"

John grinned. "Primed and ready. The Ooken won't know what hit them when they get here. Literally, with this cloaking system. Did Jean tell you that the secondary weapons system—"

Bethany Anne waved a hand. "You can gush about your ship-mance later. We're going down to the planet just as soon as you're done dropping the children off at the *G'laxix Sphaea*."

John nodded and looked to his left. "I'm on my way."

Alexis made a sound of consternation. "No fair, Mom!"

Bethany Anne raised an eyebrow at her daughter. "It is perfectly fair. Did you expect me to allow you to come down to the planet with us?"

Alexis pouted. "Well, yeah. It's kind of redundant to bring us out here and then leave us behind. What are we learning?"

Bethany Anne raised a finger to silence her daughter's protests. "You three will stay where it's safe. This will be a good opportunity for you both to get some experience with fleet command."

Gabriel groaned. "Why do we have to study? I wanna see you slap the stupid out of the leaders, Mom."

John snorted. "Accurate description, BA."

"Goodbye, John." Bethany Anne waved a hand, and the screen went dark. She turned back to face Gabriel. "I can't see that I'll have to 'slap the stupid' out of anybody today."

Michael snickered. "Give it time. The day is still early."

Bethany Anne raised an eyebrow. "We're going down

there to have a *discussion*, with the aim of understanding the situation the Moen are in."

Alexis nodded along with her mother's every word. "They've had too much of tha—OW!"

Gabriel pulled his foot back quickly. "Got it, Mom. Can we watch the video when you get back?" He grinned disarmingly. "For educational purposes, of course."

5

Moen, Western Continent

The *Izanami* came in low over the ancient dunes, great sand mountains that stretched from one side of the continent to the other. Bethany Anne scanned the forests that grew in the wide valleys cut by shining yellow rivers.

It looks like fall, Bethany Anne commented as the city appeared on the horizon. *Any second the leaves will begin to drop.*

Michael nodded toward the retreating *Sayomi*. *Just like the penny when Alexis gets aboard the* ArchAngel II *and works out you and ADAM have been restricting her little hacking hobby by guiding her access.*

>>Just don't tell her I was the one who told you she'd hacked Phyrro,<< ADAM begged. >>She's spent enough time with Tabitha to pick up both her "snitches get stitches" attitude and the ability to put it into practice. <<

Don't tell me you're scared of a little girl, Bethany Anne teased.

>>**Damn right I am. She's your daughter, isn't she?**<<

He has a point, Michael admitted.

Bethany Anne chuckled as ADAM retreated to wherever he went when he wasn't talking to her. He'd explained it once or twice, but she hadn't really listened. Everyone needed their private space, and God knew she'd made enough of them for herself over the years.

She twined her fingers through Michael's, The action was made somewhat awkward by their armor, but they managed. They looked out together as the terraces on the seven dunes of Elset came into view. "Ooken everywhere."

Michael's lip curled at the blue splotches marking the Ooken among the Moen people below. "They do not blend well with the desert shades. It should make killing them that much easier."

Bethany Anne nodded, her mind turning over the possibilities of the situation they were about to walk into as Izanami brought the ship in over the city. "We'll leave the ship up here."

Moen, Elset, QBS *Izanami*, Cargo Bay

Izanami appeared by the drop doors while Bethany Anne and Michael were checking their equipment. "My Queen, I have located an extensive underground network stretching for kilometers under the surface of the dunes. There are indications of life in the deepest part of the northernmost dune."

Bethany Anne leaned out to look down on the dunes. "What about the Ooken inside?"

Izanami inclined her head. "The Ooken patrols we can

see above-ground are the only ones my scanners are picking up on this dune."

Bethany Anne turned to Michael for confirmation.

Michael finished his mental scan and nodded. "It's clear down there."

"Thank you, Izanami." Bethany Anne grabbed one of the support straps over the drop door and leaned out again. "We'll make a quiet rooftop incursion and avoid contact with the Ooken completely."

Michael gave Bethany Anne a wry smile. "An opportunity to begin the discussion without violence—how novel. Perhaps you were right after all."

Bethany Anne raised an eyebrow. "'Perhaps?' Perhaps you should think again. When am I *not* right?"

Michael's eyes crinkled with laughter. "You have set a precedent. It has to be considered."

Bethany Anne narrowed her eyes in return. "So does where you expect to be sleeping tonight." She walked over to the drop doors. "Are you ready?"

"When you are," Michael told her, grabbing the strap opposite hers.

Bethany Anne lifted a finger. "I'm going first. Once I'm sure it's not a trap, you can join me."

Michael grunted. "I don't like it."

Bethany Anne shrugged. "You don't have to like it. Unless you can take your armor through the Etheric without me to take the strain?"

Michael shook his head, his scowl deepening. "Well, no. But it doesn't mean I am okay with you going down there alone."

Bethany Anne knew she *should* be annoyed by Michael's

overprotective nature. She bumped her hip against his. "I'm a big girl. Izanami, the doors, please."

A rush of dry air filled the cargo bay as the doors opened to admit the desert heat.

Bethany Anne drew her katana, then stepped out onto empty air and into the Etheric. Half a breath later she came out on the top terrace of the dune over a hundred feet beneath the ship. *I'm on the roof.*

Any contact? Michael asked.

Empty so far, Bethany Anne reported, glancing around the hard-baked sand. She walked over to the edge and looked down at the dizzying drop from the rooftop to the terrace below.

Can you see a way in?

Bethany Anne caught sight of a dip in the otherwise unbroken wall. She pulled a spark from the Etheric and set off toward the anomaly. *It looks like there's a set of stairs in the wall up ahead. I'm going to check it out.* She walked across the flat expanse toward the blip, the spark of her energy ball cradled in one hand.

Bethany Anne reached out with her mind. There was a distant hum from the level below the terrace she was standing on. *We're good. Come on down.*

I'm making the jump, Michael replied. *Wait for me.*

Bethany Anne picked out Michael's slightly darker shadow against the pre-dawn sky as Michael made his spiraling descent.

Michael landed effortlessly beside her, barely disturbing the dust as his feet touched the hard-baked rooftop. The air was still and heavy, the rising sun hot at this elevation from the moment it began to crest the horizon.

The object of Bethany Anne's attention was blurred by the heat rising from the dune. She moved off at a brisk pace toward the blemish on the otherwise uniform wall.

What is it? Michael asked as the indent came into range of his eyesight.

Bethany Anne willed the spark in her hand to life. ***Our way in.***

Location Three, QBBS *L3*, Orbiting Moen

Aboard the QBBS *L3*, Second Lieutenant Soraya Petrovna double-checked the readings CEREBRO was giving her.

Then she triple-checked just to be sure.

"Shit… No, worse. *Shitshitshitshit!*"

She jumped up and clattered into her CO's office, forgetting about the comm altogether. "Sir, you need to get hold of the Admiral immediately."

Location Three, QBS *Sayomi*

John had just left the *G'laxix Sphaea* and was making his way to the bridge at a light jog when Sayomi's avatar appeared beside him.

"Dammit, Sayomi! Like the Baba Yaga face isn't enough without you making yourself look like a fucking zombie to boot. You have to stop sneaking up on me, or one of these days I'm not going to stop myself in time, and your hard light core is gonna get smashed."

Sayomi sniffed and reverted to her usual appearance. "Jean would kill you outright for destroying one of her hard light drives. Although…at least *something* would be getting destroyed." She lifted her chin. "How else can a war-born AI entertain herself when she hasn't a thing to do besides keep her human on his toes?"

John sighed as he rubbed a hand over his face. "You *wait.* It's not like you get much downtime." He paused for Sayomi to admit him to the elevator. "You wanna be careful," he told the AI. "That's the kind of thinking that gets your core wiped faster than you can say 'what homicidal thoughts?'"

Sayomi narrowed her eyes and flashed an x-ray version of herself at John, emitting a dark laugh when he flinched. "I have to hand it to Jean for giving up the thing that creeps out a big tough warrior like you."

John chuckled. "I think your appearance has much more to do with my wife's possessive streak than any attempt to keep you entertained."

"Whatever you say." Sayomi grinned, floating around John as he left the elevator. "I thought you would like to know that the commander of *L3* is in contact with the Admiral. CEREBRO has picked up seven large, fast-moving objects approaching Moen on separate attack vectors."

John frowned at the screen. "Clearly the Ooken didn't get the memo about us owning this neighborhood. Get them up, and let's see what kind of party crashers we have." He leaned in to scrutinize the outline of the closest. "Not ships. Asteroids? No, comets. They're firing *comets* at us?"

A flash of red lit Sayomi's eyes and the screen zoomed in. "Look again."

John growled, seeing the hint of a smooth curve in the tail of the hurtling comet. "The bastards are getting sneakier. Tell the Admiral we'll take care of it."

"I did that the moment I intercepted his message." Sayomi returned the screen to its previous perspective. "Perhaps *now* you will allow me to have some fun."

John placed a tiny comm bud in his ear. "Your idea of fun is somewhat different than most. What do you have in mind?"

"Ah, but our tastes in entertainment run along much the same track." Sayomi flashed her sharp smile at him. "The utter destruction of the Ooken isn't exactly your least favorite thing to contemplate. I simply thought a spot of competition would be the icing on the exploding cake."

John's jaw twitched. "I like it. Do the guys know about this incursion yet?"

Sayomi's avatar flickered as she contacted her sister AIs. "They do."

John grunted. "Then why are we still talking? Give me the Etheric comm to Weapons Control, and inform the Admiral that we'll all be cloaked out there."

"Message relayed," Sayomi informed him. "Etheric comm will be live in 3...2...1."

John grasped the holocontrollers that emerged from his chair arms as he reclined. The comm bud in his ear connected his chip to the HUD that manifested around his headrest and the faces of his brothers and sister in arms popped up one at a time.

John grinned. *Ladies. Ready to dance?*

Fuck you very much, Scott retorted. *Have you seen this?*

John toggled through his controller functions to calibrate his neural pathways with the *Sayomi's* weapons systems. *No, I missed the seven comets being steered our way by Ooken ships. I was just calling to ask how your day's going.*

Hoping it's about to brighten up when we explode those Ooken, Scott returned.

We're guarding Bethany Anne, Gabrielle pointed out. *We should let the BYPS take care of them.*

Or, Darryl countered, *we could make the wait for BA a little more interesting. Taking them out is technically still guarding her, right?*

John chuckled. *See, this is why we get along. I already told the Admiral we'll deal with them. ETA is twelve minutes. What are you thinking for the losers' forfeit?*

Peter told me Tabitha is looking for instructors, Eric supplied.

I already volunteered, Darryl cut in. *Soon as we get back, I'm down for duty.*

Us too, Gabrielle and Eric chimed.

All of you? Scott asked.

Yup, John confirmed.

Damn, I hadn't heard, Scott admitted. *I'll sign up as soon as we get back to Devon. Okay, how about losers get to train the Bakas?*

Gabrielle cracked up. *Tabitha isn't going to let you guys anywhere near her Bakas. She's put too much effort into gaining their trust. I spoke to one of the males, and they remind me a little of Michael.*

That's not so bad, Darryl argued. *I don't have any experi-*

ence with the Bakas, but Michael's calmed down some since he came back.

Gabrielle sighed. *Uh-uh. I'm talking about the Michael who ruled the UnknownWorld with a bloody fist for all the centuries before Bethany Anne came along. Don't kid yourself that he's mellowed any, either. That man is still the Patriarch at heart.*

John cracked up as a thought occurred to him. *Losers get to persuade Tabitha to let us train* with *her class. I'm not averse to learning a new fighting style.*

Sounds good to me, Scott agreed.

Gotta keep the cultural relations going, Darryl supplied.

Cultural relations, my ass, Eric managed through his laughter. *You just wanna play with a lightsaber. You* do *know they're not actual Wookiees?*

Who doesn't want to play with a lightsaber? John asked.

Boys? Gabrielle interrupted. *The comets?*

6

Moen, Elset, Underground

Bethany Anne raised her hand as they reached the indent, a switchback at the top of a twin staircase. *That explains the break in the wall. The easy entry to the building is a plus.*

Michael didn't relax his guard a millimeter. *Wait while I make sure it is safe.*

Bethany Anne extended a hand toward the head of the stairwell. *Be my guest. I quit bitching about safety checks right around the time you went backpacking in Colorado.*

I love the way you frame the ultimate sacrifice as a happy jaunt through nature, Michael retorted. He peered down the stairs cut into the outer wall leading to the lower terrace, then moved to the stairwell going down into the building.

Bethany Anne continued to keep watch for threats. *What are you looking for?*

Boobytraps, Michael answered, running a finger over the frame of the entrance. *We are not invulnerable, however hard to hurt we are. The things that* can *hurt beings as enhanced as we are should not be taken lightly.*

Bethany Anne turned her hand over, setting her energy ball dancing. ***But we're good now, right?***

Michael nodded and headed down the stairs. *We are.*

Bethany Anne's eyes darted over every surface as they descended into the cool, softly-lit interior. ***This place is so old. Look how the striations in the compressed sand get closer together the lower down we go. The Moen must have dug this out thousands of years ago.***

Michael ran his fingers over the pattern in the wall. *I guess we have one answer before we begin. The Moen have always been here.*

Bethany Anne was hoping for a little bit more than a geology report on the place. ***I'll add that to the knowledge that underground cities are a gigantic pain in the backside to navigate.***

Michael came to stand beside her. *Can't ADAM do something to map the way ahead?*

Bethany Anne narrowed her eyes at him. ***Short of me clicking like a fucking dolphin while we walk so he can learn to echolocate in the next minute? No. There isn't anything down here for ADAM to connect to.***

Michael frowned. *It would have been good to bring the children with us. Alexis has a second sense when it comes to direction.*

That's beside the question. Bethany Anne paused to process her thought. ***My concern is that they aren't ready emotionally. There's a hell of a difference between training scenarios or a guard rotation at the Hexagon and bringing them along on a live mission.***

Michael sent a wave of comfort through their mental link. *I think it is you who is not ready emotionally, my love. Consider it this way: since the dawn of time, parents have watched their children go off to fight in this war or that, power-less to protect them from the dangers of a warrior's life.*

Bethany Anne shook her head. **It's not like I haven't considered that. I haven't forgotten the relief in my father's eyes when I told him I wasn't joining the military.**

Michael played devil's advocate, as he often found himself doing on their children's behalf. *Our children also have the distinct advantage of us to guide and shape them until they are ready to spread their wings.* He hadn't thought himself to be any kind of libertarian, but the adage, "he came from a different time" truly applied to this situation. He had been blooded at the first sign of a hair on his chest, but it was another thing entirely for his son and daughter.

Bethany Anne narrowed her eyes. **I'd prefer less talk about spreading wings, but I see your point.** She paused as they came out where the stairs let out into a low chamber carved out of the compacted sand.

Bethany Anne caught a movement in the corner of her eye. **Michael. Behind you.**

Michael spun at Bethany Anne's warning with his Jean Dukes raised and ready.

He was confronted by an angry, weathered face the color of sunshine and the pointy end of a walking staff.

"What are you doing?" the elderly male Moen hissed, waving his staff at Michael. "You can't be in here!"

Bethany Anne moved to stand between the Moen and Michael. "We can be wherever we want." She deactivated her faceplate and flashed Baba Yaga's red eyes at the Moen. "I want to speak to whoever is in charge here."

"Baba Yaga!" The Moen held up trembling hands, concern for his life deepening the creases in his face. "Nobody is permitted to disturb the Alders. I apologize, but I have to ask you to leave immediately. Please don't kill me!"

Bethany Anne flexed her control on the energy ball in her hand, allowing it to surge momentarily. "Do I sound like I'm asking for permission? I'm here with peaceful intentions, but I didn't say *anything* about keeping my temper if I'm not met with cooperation."

"The easiest thing to do is exactly what Baba Yaga tells you," Michael told the quivering Moen in a soft tone.

Good cop? Really?

It's rare I get the chance, so why not?

Bethany Anne snickered in Michael's mind.

The Moen was glad of a reason to look away from the face of the Witch. He dropped his eyes to the floor and shuffled back the way he came. "This way, Mistress."

Bethany Anne looked back at Michael, then released the energy ball she was holding into the air and led the way after the retreating Moen.

He led them deeper into the dunes, muttering increasingly dire predictions of the consequences he faced for guiding them with every step. Twice, the Moen had to be persuaded to continue on through the labyrinth.

Bethany Anne rolled her eyes mentally as they neared the Alders' chambers and their guide was hit by a fresh wave of doubt.

"I'll lose my head for this, surely," he grumbled, taking

them into what looked to be an antechamber, filled with the scent of permanently damp sand.

I'd settle for his tongue, Michael decided. *Can't he think his thoughts like the rest of us?*

Bethany Anne lifted a shoulder. **He doesn't know this won't end in violence. Just tune him out.**

The Moen shuffled across the chamber, pausing by a stone door set into the wall between two columns. "I should go in first—"

"Yeah, hell, no." Bethany Anne pushed him aside, then threw open the door with much less care than she'd just shown their guide.

The six Moen seated around the stone table inside the chamber erupted toward the exit at the other end of the chamber when the door slammed open and Baba Yaga stalked in.

Bethany Anne redirected her energy ball, growing it as it shot across the chamber until the escape was blocked by a barrier of crackling Etheric energy. "Sit down. We have a few things to discuss."

The Moen hung back while Michael walked around Bethany Anne and pulled out the chair at the head of the table for her.

Baba Yaga took her seat, and Michael moved to stand silently behind her. "*Sit,*" she repeated, waving a finger at the empty chairs. "I won't ask a third time."

The Moen obeyed, returning to the table somewhat reluctantly.

One of the females spoke up angrily. "Why are you here, Baba Yaga? We did not ask you to come."

Bethany Anne crossed her legs and steepled her fingers

in her lap, scrutinizing the six as they shuffled nervously in their seats. "I'm done." She paused to allow her words to sink in around the table. "I have other people in need of my time. You will not continue to sit on the fence. I want the truth. Why haven't you taken the lifeline I'm offering?"

The female spoke up again, her tone somewhat sulky to Bethany Anne's ears. "We don't have to answer that."

Bethany Anne frowned at the Alder's attitude. "I don't get you as a people. Why don't you protect yourselves or fight for your freedom? You have the means to resist."

The Moen stared at Bethany Anne, her eyes wise, tired, and full of lies. "Why fight what the universe has sent our way? It is not for us to reason why, just to weather the storm."

Bethany Anne raised an eyebrow. "Well, *that's* the biggest load of bullshit I've heard since I got out of politics."

The Moen looked away. "Who are you to judge us?"

Bethany Anne growled through bared teeth, "You better hope to fuck I *don't* decide to judge you, because I give no quarter to anyone in league with the fucking Kurtherians. *Do you understand me?* Or are you really nothing more than a bunch of fucking mercy-killings waiting to happen?"

The Alders found their tongues at last. Their denial of the presence of Kurtherians was unanimous, their offense at the accusation strong enough to outweigh their fear of Baba Yaga for the moment.

Keep them nervous, Michael requested. *It's making it easier to read their minds.*

You're having trouble? Bethany Anne asked.

Not trouble, Michael clarified. *I'm getting a good read on them. I admit, maybe I should have complained less during the days when the only minds I had to read were human to some degree or another. These aliens we have met? Dipping into their minds is comparable to attending a buffet where every taste you are offered is an experience you have to come to terms with before you can process it.*

The Moen noticed nothing as Michael flicked through their memories.

Bethany Anne snapped, making the Moen jump in their seats, "*Enough!* If you don't stop answering my questions with more questions, my patience is going to run dry extremely quickly. That isn't likely to end well for you."

The Alder lifted her chin and looked Bethany Anne in the eye. "Answer me this, Baba Yaga. Without all you have endured, would you be the same person?"

Bethany Anne raised an eyebrow. "Essentially, yes." She uncrossed her legs and leaned forward to fix the Alders with a hard look. "You are prevaricating. What aren't you telling me?"

The Alders' eyes slid away.

Bethany Anne beckoned Michael forward with a finger. **Let's see what scaring the crap out of them turns up.** "Don't say I didn't try to play nice," she told the Alders as Michael made his eyes glow. "This shouldn't hurt...too much."

The Moen glanced nervously at Michael, then back at Bethany Anne.

You have scared them plenty already. Michael paused with a hand on the back of Bethany Anne's chair while he probed the Moen for information. *Oh, this is interesting. Ask them about the substance and see what that shakes loose.*

The Ooken substance? Bethany Anne was beginning to get an idea of the larger picture.

Yes, Michael confirmed. *It is the clearest image at the forefront of their minds, like someone told them not to think about an elephant.*

That is *interesting. Keep digging.* Bethany Anne tapped her fingers on the arm of the chair. "Tell me, what interests you about the nanocyte substance the Ooken use?" She noted the ripple of alarm that ran through the chamber.

Still, the Alders said nothing.

Bethany Anne lifted a foot and kicked the edge of the table, flashing her red eyes once again. The Alders jumped inside their skins at the resulting deep crack that echoed through the chamber.

Bethany Anne winced internally at the break she'd made along the center of the fairly ancient-looking stone. Outwardly, she was cold and calm. The light behind her turned from pale blue to violet to red. "Start. Talking. Either you work with me to rid this planet of the Ooken, or I have no choice but to think you're allied with the Seven."

The female who had spoken previously got to her feet, balancing with the walking staff all the Moen seemed to carry.

Meon

The male beside her made a half-attempt to grab her sleeve when Michael stepped forward. "Meon, no!"

Meon shook him off with a look that suggested he might feel the hard side of her hand if he touched her again. "Leave us. I will take the consequences of speaking with Baba Yaga."

The other Alders capitulated gratefully, looking at Baba Yaga for permission.

Bethany Anne dropped the barrier over the door, allowing the others to file nervously past her. "I will speak to *you*, Meon," she corrected. "You have this opportunity and this one only to convince me that your people aren't in bed with the Ooken."

Meon fixed Bethany Anne with a steely glare. "We are no allies of theirs, and neither are we yours. I remind you, we did not *ask* for your assistance."

Bethany Anne narrowed her eyes. "You are not in a

position to remind me of anything. Most would be at least a little grateful for my intervention, but you have something to hide, don't you?" She waved a hand at the bristling female. "Tell me what interest you have in the nanocyte substance the Ooken use. I won't ask again, and I won't lose any sleep over having your mind stripped. Your choice. "

Meon took her seat with an affected sigh. "I have nothing to say on that subject."

Michael placed a hand on Bethany Anne's shoulder. *I have something.*

Bethany Anne met Meon's gaze unblinkingly, tapping her fingers on the arm of her chair in the drawn-out silence. **What is it?**

I get the impression she believes they are making a sacrifice, Michael told her.

Bethany Anne frowned, the motion enough to cause the Moen to emit a hitched breath. **What do you mean, a sacrifice?** She put two and two together and came to the rock and the hard place the Moen were in. "So your people have some kind of genetic disease. Is it worth dying by the thousands to get your hands on the nanocytes?" She snorted in disgust. "Who am I kidding? You don't give two shits about your people, do you?"

Meon squirmed under Bethany Anne's unforgiving glare. "Of course, we do. Our people are already dying. With every generation that passes, the corruption that was planted in our genetic coding mutates further." The Moen brushed her fingers over the damage in the table. "We are bound to this planet until we can undo what was done to us by the Seven."

Bethany Anne held up a hand, feeling Michael stiffen behind her at the mention of Kurtherians.

Meon sighed—genuinely this time. "We cannot risk all that we have suffered for on the hope that you will leave us the cure we seek."

"Mother of…" Bethany Anne touched her fingers to her temples. "Why is it that every damn place I go, there's another planet full of self-serving, passive-aggressive *politicians* in my way? Do you even know what it is you're failing to steal?"

Meon nodded. "We have been working on learning where the nanocyte suspension is kept, but access is restricted, and our guards are vigilant."

Bethany Anne rolled her eyes. "Your guards don't scare me." She raised a finger at Meon before the alder could interrupt. "I told you, I'm *done*. This is how you're going to operate from here on out. I'm going to reverse my withdrawal and wipe out the Ooken, and you are going to work a fucking sight harder than you have been to get the location of that substance." She sent a comm bud skittering across the table. "Get everyone else out of the city unless you want to go out as Ooken shields."

"You cannot destroy our planet," Meon squawked, banging her staff on the floor. "That makes you no better than our masters."

Bethany Anne shrugged. "I've spent too much time chasing my tail to care about your feelings. In fact, I'm not just done with this conversation, I'm done with this planet. Consider yourselves sanctioned. You will get your cure, but no Moen will leave this planet until you grow the fuck up."

She got to her feet with a last look of disgust and swept out of the chamber.

Michael was close behind her. *Nicely done, although I thought you went a little easy on them.*

Bethany Anne opened the way into the Etheric, tempering her compulsion to collapse the dune around them as they left. *I don't want to be here a minute longer than I have to be. We will pick up the children the moment we get back to the ship, then we'll hightail it to Devon, where we can make some actual progress instead of playacting in this trumped-up fucking farce.*

Michael followed Bethany Anne into the swirling mist. *I would have killed one of them as an example to the others.*

Bethany Anne snarled as she swept a hand to open the way back to the ship. **Fuck them. Seriously, they can sit and rot. If I thought it would get those low-bellied ass pimples motivated, I'd have killed however many it took to make it happen. As it is, I have better uses for my energy, like getting everyone together and getting a handle on this fucking war.**

I can't argue with your logic, Michael conceded. *Leave gathering everyone to me. I'll take care of it once I've gotten the children aboard. I'm guessing you have some working out of your own to do.*

You guessed right, and thank you. Bethany Anne prodded Michael to show him where to exit to the transport bay, then strode out of the Etheric onto the bridge. She headed straight for her couch, collapsing onto it with a frustrated sigh. "Izanami, take us over to the *ArchAngel*, and inform the Admiral that I expect my children to be ready to leave when we get there."

7

Location Three, Leaving Moen, QBS *Izanami*

Bethany Anne dropped her Baba Yaga mask when Izanami appeared on the screen wearing an exact replica of her, well, *everything*.

The AI turned Baba Yaga's face to Bethany Anne, lifting a hand to indicate the shattered rock carpeting the empty space beyond Moen's BYPS. "It appears your honor guard found something to defend us against."

Bethany Anne took one look at the QBS *Cambridge*, which was finishing up with the final Ooken destroyer. "Leave them to their fun, but tell John we're leaving shortly. If I have to stay here, I might change my mind about collapsing that dune." Izanami raised an eyebrow, distracting Bethany Anne momentarily from the rage she was building to a head once again. She waved a finger to encompass the AI's sudden expansion to her wardrobe and emotive range. "What is this?"

"I have decided to imprint on you." Izanami's features

morphed to match Bethany Anne's. "I am currently making the decision as to which of your faces I shall wear."

Bethany Anne raised an eyebrow. "You can stick with Baba Yaga. I see enough of my face looking back at me from screens. I don't need to bump into myself when I'm walking the corridors as well." She wrinkled her nose and waved a finger at Izanami's armor. "You need to do something about that."

Izanami inclined her head. "Of course, my Queen." A halo of light passed over her avatar from head to toe, leaving behind Baba Yaga's black skin, white hair, and snow-white armor.

Bethany Anne put a hand on her hip. "How does white not make you look fat?"

Izanami winked. "I may have played with my avatar's dimensions a little."

Michael walked out of the elevator just as the transformation was complete. He looked from Bethany Anne to Izanami, who for some reason now resembled Baba Yaga. He saw immediately that Bethany Anne was in need of a distraction before she lost her temper. "You were right about Izanami. She looks…different."

Bethany Anne raised an eyebrow, a corner of her mouth turning up in amusement at Michael's momentary confusion. "You look like a man who has just seen a sandwich he'd like to be the main ingredient in."

Michael wondered for a split second if this was a trap. He had only meant to draw attention to Izanami's new look, not fall headlong into sudden danger.

Backing down, however, was not in his nature. He decided to bite and take the consequences—in the name of brightening his wife's mood, of course. "What an imagination you have. I was thinking no such thing."

Izanami moved to mirror Bethany Anne, her hand on her hip and a smirk playing over her lips. "His blood pressure just rose considerably. I'd say he's thinking about it now."

Bethany Anne snickered, her eyebrow arching mischievously at the way Michael's mouth worked to provide a comeback. "We're just playing with you, Michael. Don't have a stroke."

Michael narrowed his eyes at Bethany Anne. "Oh, well, if this is a *game…*" He sat back on one of the side couches with his hands laced behind his head and pinned her with his gaze while he let his mind run free.

Bethany Anne's mouth fell open. "You're such an *ass*, Michael."

Michael raised an eyebrow, his grin deepening. "Hard light technology is a marvel, is it not?"

Izanami looked from one human to the other, knowing there were layers of silent communication between them but understanding none of it. "Now *your* heart rate has spiked, my Queen."

Michael snorted. "I'll just bet it has."

Izanami rolled her eyes and scoffed. "Organics." She vanished in her usual spray of falling light.

Bethany Anne folded her arms, enjoying the joke somewhat less now that Michael had turned it back on her. She looked around, coming up empty for anything she could throw at Michael without ripping it from the ship. "Be grateful everything in here is bolted down," she grumbled.

Michael raised a finger. "Now, there can't *possibly* be any reason for you to be angry with *me* when you are the one who put the thought into my head in the first place." He paused to amend his defense when Bethany Anne called him on it with a twitch of her eyebrow. "Thoughts, for the sake of accuracy."

Bethany Anne was about to make sure *all* of his next thoughts were about her and her alone when she remembered that they weren't alone on the ship. "Shit, I didn't think. The children might be listening in."

Michael waved off her concern. "I permitted the three of them some game time as a reward for their good conduct while we make the trip to Devon," he informed her. "They were in the Vid-docs before I'd even finished telling them it was an option."

Bethany Anne nodded, satisfied they hadn't been overheard. "That's fine by me. They'll be rested for Tabitha's class when we get back." She ran through her mental to-do list for when they returned. "Speaking of which, I'm calling everyone in for a meeting now that we have Moen contained. After that, you're going to learn how to harness an Etheric storm. It's time to stop holding back because I'm afraid to lose you. We will do this together."

Michael's eyes flashed red. "It's about time you agreed with me on that. The weight has been on your shoulders for too long."

Bethany Anne dropped the snarky comeback forming on her tongue when she realized how much it had cost him to hold back while she risked her life every time she went up against the storms. *Michael.*

Michael lifted his hands, his expression dark and enticing all at once. *I can only be who I am. It may be your duty to protect this whole damned universe, but it is mine, and my honor, to protect you.*

Bethany Anne closed her eyes briefly, her focus stolen. She opened them again to meet his gaze. **Dammit, you romantic bastard! I'm wearing armor.**

Michael crooked a finger. *Let me help you with that.*

No need. Bethany Anne flickered between the bridge and the Etheric, shedding her armor with a single step toward him. "Izanami, seal the bridge and take us out. I don't want to be disturbed until we reach Devon."

Devon, The Hexagon, Training Center

Addix entered the weapons room in search of Tabitha, finding Hirotoshi instead.

The ancient human stood humming quietly to himself as he fed pieces of broken mechanical tentacles from his antigrav cart into the matter recycling unit. He straightened when Addix clicked her mandibles politely to get his attention. "Ah, Addix. How pleasant to see you here, if unusual. Is there something I can help you with?"

Addix skirted a laundry bin on her way over to Hirotoshi. "It's more, how can I help you help me. I need access to the Bakas, so I've come to offer my services with the youths."

Hirotoshi looked doubtfully at her and raised his hands. "You will have to speak to Tabitha about that. She's getting rather too much enjoyment by keeping the Bakas all to herself."

Addix's mandibles rippled in confusion. "I was under

the impression that the majority of the Bakas were against closer relations with us."

Hirotoshi lifted his hands. "Their leader has allowed her people to join forces with ours for the duration of the war. Whether we reach an actual treaty with them is a different matter."

"How so?" Addix found a spot to rest against. "Michael led me to believe that we are likely to ally in the face of Kurtherian involvement in this war."

Hirotoshi's brow furrowed as he tried to come up with a respectful way to express his opinion. "I don't know what to say. The Bakas are first-class assholes, although Tabitha is taking steps to amend that."

"She's making headway with cultural relations through her training program?" Addix asked.

"You could paint it in that light." Hirotoshi chuckled as he pressed a button on the recycling unit. He turned back to Addix with a soft grin. "She's taken a page from Bethany Anne's book and is beating respect into her new students at every opportunity."

Addix frowned at the matter recycling unit when it made a noise on starting much like two male Bistok clashing in breeding season. "That doesn't sound very much like Tabitha."

Hirotoshi looked over his shoulder at the machine, then back at Addix after seeing it was fine. "It is *exactly* like Tabitha," he stated. "Trust me, she's having a ball. Her group is comprised entirely of large males with egos to match their body weight."

Addix's mandibles rippled in understanding. "Ah. That must be a sight to behold."

Hirotoshi flicked a finger toward the exit. "See for yourself if you care to. She's training the male groups in the outdoor arena all day today. If you hurry, you might catch the end of the current session."

"I believe I will." Addix gathered her robe and turned to leave. "Thank you, Hirotoshi."

True to Hirotoshi's word, Addix arrived in the six-sided outdoor arena to a cacophony of Baka calls. She made her way to the front row of the bleachers and took a seat to wait for Tabitha's training session to end.

The opportunity to observe how the Bakas operated was more than useful to Addix's assignment. What information she had was mostly from hearsay and word of mouth. She had discovered so far that Bakas made little effort to work together outside their family groups, that they were natural fighters, and that their internal battles kept the species from turning their aggression outward.

Addix wasn't impressed by the Bakas as a whole. They had interstellar flight, but that was all she could see they had going for them in terms of technology. Back in days almost too distant to recall, she would have dismissed them entirely.

Maybe she was biased since her closest encounter with a Baka so far had been the time she'd torn that kidnapper's throat out on the mall world when the twins were younger.

However, she wasn't a person to hold the actions of one being against a whole species. She looked on this as an opportunity to educate herself, as well as completing Michael's assignment to protect Trey.

Addix wondered what Tabitha had done to unite the Bakas despite their allegedly fractious history. The unit of twenty on the sands seemed to have gotten over their rumored squabbles well enough—which was good for them, since Tabitha was taking no prisoners whatsoever among her students.

The Bakas had no chance of misinterpreting Tabitha's lesson.

Addix's mandibles twitched in thought as she continued to watch.

Tabitha yelled her own specific brand of encouragement from the top of a six-foot pedestal in the center of the training area. Her body was surrounded by a 360-degree holo display, which she was using to manipulate the mass of tentacled Ooken droids around the base while the Bakas attacked them in twos and threes. "Do you want to die out there? No? Then stop acting like it! Fight *together*!"

She shifted a quarter-step and set a droid to whip the closest Baka. "Li'Orin, you're down to one arm, you assmunch. Where was your backup?"

Tabitha left Li'Orin to work it out, concentrating on using her Ooken droids to push back the rest. "Where did all my warriors go? My infant son has bigger balls than all of you put together."

The largest Baka hefted his staff at Tabitha like a spear. "Eat *these* balls!" The spear sailed through the upward part of its arc without incident.

Tabitha twitched her finger on her display as it peaked, her wicked laugh ringing out across the arena as the corresponding tentacle snapped the staff in two. "The Ooken are going to laugh in your faces, right before they fucking eat them. *Now put some effort into it, damn you!*"

The warriors redoubled their efforts despite the fact they had no chance of taking Tabitha down.

Addix realized this was no training session. These warriors were here to learn a new way to *think*, and to discover what could be achieved when they worked together. They were already fearsome on the floor with their martial technique and prowess. It was about putting those strengths to their best use in battle for the survival of them all.

One by one the Ooken droids fell to the Bakas until only two were left standing—if the way the misshapen knots of metal gripped each other for support like the last two boards of a lean-to in a gale could be classed as standing.

Tabitha dropped her holodisplay and jumped down to the bloodstained sand to walk through the carnage toward Addix. Her head turned this way and that as she inspected the damage to her students. She winced as she passed the unmoving ones, her voice carrying over the pained grunts of the mobile contingent. "Great job, guys. C'mon, get yourselves to medical."

Tabitha clapped her hands as the Bakas filtered from the arena. "Aren't you forgetting something?" She pointed at the three unconscious warriors on the sand. "Or does this unit need another lesson in how not to be assholes to each other?"

She left her students to recover their teammates,

making her way to where Addix waited for her. "Hey! Long time no see. How's it going for you?"

Addix returned Tabitha's hug carefully. "It is good to see you too, Tabitha. I have been enjoying the freedom of movement I have now that Gabriel and Alexis have no need of a guardian when Bethany Anne and Michael are away."

Tabitha peered at Addix, curiosity evident in her scrutiny. "Oh, yeah? Who are you spying on now?"

Addix let her gaze drift to the Bakas leaving the arena.

Tabitha snorted. "Yeah, no. Not a chance."

Addix's mandibles twitched. "Perhaps I should explain. Michael has assigned me to guard the Baka known as Trey."

Tabitha raised her chin. "I swear, that man is going to be the death of me. Or himself, if I get to him first." She threw her hands up in exasperation. "Fine. I can use all the help I can get after Bethany Anne invited the whole damn city in to train."

Addix frowned. "You're oversubscribed?"

Tabitha placed a hand on her hip. "You did see her speech? I'm not the only one with more volunteers than I know what to do with. Tim's security teams, Joel's ground units, even the *Guardian* has a waiting list of ex-mercenaries looking to step up. Devon loves a fight. Just ask the Civilian Defense Force."

Addix tilted her head in question.

Tabitha shrugged. "I didn't pick the name. It's how we're organizing them all," she clarified. "Or at least we're making it look that way until the kinks are worked out. You know, Bethany Anne did all this and arranged an evacuation with a hell of a lot less. Did *not* look this difficult to my eyes back then."

Addix chuckled. "I imagine the motivation there was that Bethany Anne was the one everyone answered to. How is all of this affecting the Hexagon?"

Tabitha's eyes widened. "Oh, hell, the kids are moving just as fast as the changes are happening. Their latest idea is a behind-the-scenes candid-camera reality show. They want to show the people's stories—how their lives are changing as they adjust to life in the defense force." She waved a hand. "Never mind, you'll see it when it airs. What do you want with Trey? I can't see his family making it easy for you to cut them out."

Addix didn't disagree with Tabitha's assessment. "They will only see me in my role as Alexis' and Gabriel's guard. Besides, you are over-subscribed, yes?"

Tabitha nodded, still skeptical. "Yeah? And?"

Addix patted Tabitha's shoulder. "Don't look so worried. I am offering to train the youths on your behalf. While their development is vital to the future, your focus has to be on teaching their parents to stay alive."

Tabitha's nose wrinkled as she considered the offer. "I *could* use the help..."

Addix clicked her mandibles in delight. "Then it is settled."

Tabitha's mouth opened and closed. "Um..."

Addix was already at the exit. "Send me the schedule and current training regimens. I will begin first thing tomorrow."

8

Devon, QBBS *Guardian*, Commander's Deck

Bethany Anne left Tim's office, satisfied with their meeting on the progress with the shipyard. His section of the volunteer forces was training hard, and construction was moving fast enough to please her.

Tim was happy she hadn't demanded anything too impossible as his reward for efficient management of the station, although Bethany Anne couldn't come up with anything Tim hadn't covered—and she'd tried.

Some people just took a few decades to sort their shit out and realize their potential. Tim was one of those. The former bouncer was making the most of his third life, as Bethany Anne saw it. He'd come a long way from the aggressive young man who had come to her so long ago looking for a way to leave the path of destruction he was heading down.

How many people had she taken in with similar stories?

It was no hardship to have missed Rickie. Luckily for the verbally-challenged Were, Tim was smart enough to keep his right hand tucked out of sight when Bethany Anne was onboard, lest he run his mouth one time too many and she cut it off.

Bethany Anne snorted softly as the elevator doors closed on her, luxuriating in the sudden silence. She couldn't recall the last time she'd had a moment alone in her own mind, but there it was.

Meeting with Tim had left her feeling somewhat nostalgic for the *Guardian's* much larger sister station. For old times, when her face opened whatever door she needed —or her boot did.

Then her good sense kicked in. She realized she'd already made the decision not to move her base permanently to Devon. Why else would she be so hesitant to build there? Nor did she want to return to High Tortuga and undo all of her work to hide the planet. No, that place would remain hidden, a safe haven for her people who needed one until they could return to Earth.

Whenever that turned out to be.

It wasn't so much the *Meredith Reynolds* she missed as the ability to move as the need took her. Issues with the size and capability of their current home aside, there was much to be said for her ability to remain mobile.

Bethany Anne stepped into the Etheric before the elevator came to a full stop, exiting again on a stretch of the viewing platform that was separated into cubicles for privacy. Sometimes it seemed like the only place large enough to contain her thinking was the universe itself.

She slipped into the farthest cubicle and took a seat on the rectangular box in front of the window. The box shifted beneath her, flowing upward and out to cup her body as she reclined with her gaze on the stars and her thoughts on Moen.

If it wasn't for the fact that Michael was right about there being a deeper game in action, Bethany Anne wouldn't have been so easily distracted on the ride here, and the Moen would be a dune or two short of a city.

The single snaggly fucking weed among the well-tended patches of productivity she'd made from the more advanced Ooken locations they had taken, she was relieved to know the truth about them. If they liked it so much on the fence, they could look at the one she'd just put them behind. They'd have a long time to do it.

In the meantime, she had a war to win.

Bethany Anne watched the traffic between the station and the shipyard absentmindedly, the roamers inside the tubes appearing no larger than the miniature AT rover Gabriel and Alexis were building for Todd's birthday next month.

The luxury of time to contrast her immediate instinct with her considered reaction was an advantage she would not give up easily. Devon's three rings of protection kept the daily lives of the people intact, and the continuing expansion out at QT2 was large enough to put any attackers off.

The wider issue was the supply chain. While the salvage from the Ooken sites was more than plentiful, it was potluck what they found each time. Jean had been specific about the requirements they had for maintaining the fleet and how they could fill those requirements without stripping everything Bethany Anne was protecting.

She had a plan for that.

Nothing moved fast enough for her liking, not even her. Time was the one fucking thing beyond her control. That, and her wonky GPS when it came to locating the fuck-sucking bitch-gobbets otherwise known as the Ooken.

I have a theory about that.

Bethany Anne snapped out of her reverie. *Dammit, TOM. Can't you knock first or something? I'm going to install firewalls in my mind soon if I don't get five fucking minutes alone with my thoughts.*

I'll take my solution elsewhere if you like, TOM grumped. **It's not like we're verging on desperate for it.**

Bethany Anne sighed, giving up on the idea of solitude for the moment. *Sorry. Go on, I'm listening.*

TOM drew the explanation out carefully. **I've been doing some math,** he began.

>>You mean *we* did the math,<< ADAM cut in.

That too, TOM amended. **Whoever doesn't matter. The result was that I found a way to recreate the mind map in the real world. I think.**

Bethany Anne's fire cooled instantly. *Show me how.* Her eyes flickered briefly while TOM flashed the solution through her mind. *You want to attempt to touch every location simultaneously?*

TOM made a sound of agreement. **ADAM isn't restricted on how far he can spread himself if you can power the windows. What do you think?**

Bethany Anne couldn't see how she was meant to spread the energy it took to open one window to open...a hell of a lot of windows. *I think you sound pretty pleased with yourself, considering the practical application of your theory is theoretically not possible. Unless you have a super-massive Etheric storm up your ass you've been hiding all this time?*

ADAM snickered. >>**That would explain a couple of things.**<<

Actually, TOM told them archly, **we can find what we need in the Etheric. We just have to locate the place where the storms are created, which to my memory is... somewhere in the dimension. It shouldn't be too diffi-cult with the four of us working together.**

Are we basing this on a rumor you heard over a thousand years ago? Bethany Anne asked. *Because it sounds like bull-shit to me.*

TOM grunted in agreement. **It could very well be. It was a long time ago, Bethany Anne.**

Given that, we'd better make a start on finding it. Bethany Anne *should* have been surprised that TOM had information she didn't, but she was not. This wasn't the first time he'd neglected to tell her something until it was useful, and she didn't think it would be the last. *Wait, the four of us? You mean three, right?*

Four is correct, TOM confirmed. *You didn't think I'd suggest we do this without backup? Michael is coming with us.*

High Tortuga, Space Fleet Base, Barnabas' Office

Barnabas wondered if the information he held in his hand would be better kept to himself. However, it wasn't his to keep, and Tabitha had already arrived to take him over to Devon for Bethany Anne's impromptu conclave.

He put the tablet down and returned his attention to ensuring he wouldn't be missed on High Tortuga for a short time. Unfortunately for Stephen and Jennifer, that meant a disruption to their marital bliss.

That was how the cookie crumbled; some things could only be left to family. Especially since Shinigami was staying behind.

The door opened, and Tabitha came in. "Hey, stranger!"

Barnabas' eyes crinkled in pleasure. "Hello, yourself. Did you get here without any issues?"

Tabitha nodded. "Nobody suspected a thing. Achronyx isn't too happy about the makeover, though."

Barnabas shook his head. "That AI is as vain as the night is long. I can't imagine where he gets it from."

Tabitha winked. "I wouldn't know." She perched on the edge of the desk and glanced at the tablet. "Ooh, who's the cutie?"

Barnabas slid the tablet over to Tabitha, the decision made for him by his inaction. It was the right thing; Tabitha deserved to know. "Prepare yourself."

Tabitha frowned and took the tablet. "What is it?"

"Just watch," he told her gently.

Tabitha pressed Play and watched the short message in silence. Then she watched again, and yet again. She was about to play it a fourth time when Barnabas eased the tablet from her hands. She looked up with tears tracking down her cheeks. "Does this mean…"

Barnabas nodded. "Yes, Tabitha. She is beginning to heal."

Tabitha's tears continued to flow, unheeded. "Sending Grim was the right thing. I knew it."

"It appears so." Barnabas chose not to hear her whispered admission. He looked down to place the tablet in his desk drawer. "She's on the right path."

"Nickie was never a bad person. Just angry." Tabitha's face worked through a series of emotions, settling on none of them. "*Just.* As if anger like that is a small thing. I want her home, Barnabas. I don't want her out there without her family for a minute longer than she needs to be. I want to see her happy and whole. I want Todd to know her."

Barnabas didn't know what to do to ease Tabitha's heartache. "Her seven years are up. She can return whenever she's ready."

Tabitha scrubbed her eyes with the back of her hand. "I don't want to accept that she might choose not to come home."

Barnabas reached out and took Tabitha's hand. "Have you spoken to Bethany Anne about this?"

Tabitha nodded. "Mmhmm. You were there, remember? Bethany Anne was frowning at Kael-ven about something, I asked for permission to send something to give her a nudge." She pouted at Barnabas' blank expression. "You were the one who said it was a good idea."

Barnabas raised an eyebrow, searching his memory for the event and coming up with nothing. "I remember interceding on your behalf shortly before Grim'zee mysteriously lost a few decades and showed up in her life."

Tabitha nodded, grinning in a way she hoped wasn't too shifty. "Yeah, I sent her a friend, and maybe a few messages."

Barnabas resisted the temptation to sigh. "And Bethany

Anne has no idea that you've been in communication with Nickie this whole time?

Tabitha's eyes widened in horror. "*No!* She better not find out, either. Besides, I've been really careful to make sure Nickie thinks my messages are old."

She did her best not to think about how she'd hacked Meredith, Nickie's EI, before her niece was sent out into the unknown. She didn't want to implicate Barnabas if Bethany Anne ever found out what she'd done.

Barnabas chuckled dryly as he got up from his chair. "She won't find out from me. Unless she asks."

Tabitha laughed aloud. "You're the best."

9

Devon, The Hexagon, Network Command Center

Bethany Anne looked around the wide oval table, relaxed for the moment in the relative comfort of having almost everyone in the same place for a short time. There were some unavoidable absences, those who were on duty, or holding down the fort elsewhere.

Michael, her rock, was by her side, at ease for once. Along the table to her left, Admiral Thomas and Jean were there via holoprojection. To the right was her father, also holocalling from his office on the *Meredith Reynolds*, then Tabitha, who had arrived with Barnabas from High Tortuga moments earlier.

All of her Guards were present, John at the other end of the table with the rest of the Bitches around him. The other places were filled by Akio, Hirotoshi, Ryu, Tim, and Sabine.

"Thank you all for being here." Bethany Anne placed her hands flat on the table. "For those who haven't caught up yet, why the fuck haven't you caught up yet?" She paused a beat before continuing. "Moen was a massive time-suck. As of my departure, the planet is under a no-travel order for the foreseeable future. We'll take care of that later. Right now the focus has to be on the bigger picture. We need to be on the same page, because the Ooken—the Collective, or whatever the fuck they're called—have noticed we're kicking over their nests. Staying ahead of them would be preferable."

Barnabas lifted a finger. "I suggest we keep calling the enemy 'Ooken,' since they have been altered by the Kurtherians from the original Collective species."

Bethany Anne waved a hand. "Suits me, as long as history records us as the winner in this. I don't give two shits what name gets listed afterward as long as it doesn't take a century to remove them. I want this *over*, with minimal cost to my people and minimal impact on my planets."

Jean's not-so-measured breath cut the silence that followed. "It's just not possible this time, BA. We're pushing the limits, and it's going to show when I start shutting the shipyards down. You know there's no damn way I'm sending out anything that isn't up to standard, and that means ship maintenance comes first."

"We do still have the advantage at this time," Michael countered. "The salvaged materials from the sites we've taken so far has to be making some difference?"

"It's giving us months," Jean clarified. "Not anything to get excited about. I've made the projections available to the room."

"I'm with Michael on this," John argued, filling the silence left as everyone else checked. "I've been over all the numbers with Jean, and we've done more with less, comparatively. If we need to, we can hold them back for a few months while we strip the empty systems in the buffer zones."

Bethany Anne's fingers beat a rapid staccato on the wood. "Not practical without the infrastructure to process it in place." She turned to Lance. "What we need is a supplier large enough to meet our needs, but there is the small issue of my 'exile' in the way. I need your help, Dad."

Lance's hologram flickered, his face set in serious lines. "I'm here to do whatever I can, you know that. The last thing the Federation needs is a war on this scale."

Bethany Anne flashed a rueful grin. "That's why *I'm* here—to be the barrier that keeps the Federation safe, whether they want it or not."

Lance nodded abruptly, his pride too large to speak around for a second. "That's my girl. I'm sure you already have a plan that leaves everyone's behind covered."

Bethany Anne's grin grew a touch wider. "Funny you should say that, Dad. How would the Federation feel about trade relations with an independent planet?"

Lance raised an eyebrow. "What, Devon?"

Bethany Anne shook her head. "No. High Tortuga. I want it under another layer of protection until this war is over. Federation protection. There's no saying we can't use a trade agreement to make that happen without anyone getting suspicious, and nobody has to know exactly who is pulling the strings on this end."

Lance grinned. "Sounds like we're about to get into something of a gray area."

Bethany Anne shrugged. "I could play fair and do this

out in the open. How would the Federation leaders react to my sudden reappearance? It would be a hell of a lot easier than pandering to their fears."

Lance's eyes widened momentarily. "Poorly, as you know. A trade agreement with an independent power looks to me to be the best option here."

Barnabas cut in, "How is that going to work with the Interdiction? We spent all of this time hiding High Tortuga, and now you plan to hand it over to the Federation?"

Bethany Anne turned her attention to him. "That was always the plan. It will still be hidden, just in plain sight, with the strength of a thousand worlds in the background. Permitted ships will have right of passage, using specified routes that will be monitored by you and my father."

Jean slumped, dropping her head to the backrest of her chair. "Right, so how soon can we get these shipments started?"

Lance looked down for a moment, and his hologram shifted around as he worked out what was feasible. "I don't know. I can get the ball rolling pretty much right away, but we'll need all the backstops in place before High Tortuga applies for trade status. How many hidden stashes do you have left, Bethany Anne?"

"I haven't touched a single one yet," Bethany Anne confirmed. "And I don't intend to. Those are for rainy days, and there's barely a cloud on the horizon to justify tapping them as a resource. ADAM will take care of the backstops so everything will look above board in the application."

Lance nodded. "Then I will do what I can to expedite the process."

Bethany Anne raised an eyebrow. "I sincerely hope that means you're going to light a fire under whoever gets the application on their desk. We have no fucking time for bureaucracy. We need ships."

Admiral Thomas sighed. "How did I know *that* was coming? And what impossible feat would my Queen like me to pull out of my ass this time?"

Bethany Anne tilted her head at the Admiral. "I could always arrange for you to take extended leave if you're not happy with your work. How are those beautiful children of yours? Growing fast? Twins are such a joy, right?"

The Admiral's eyes widened. "Of course they're a joy—for the short bursts when they're asleep. Giselle and I have decided that parenthood is a war of wills against tiny little terrorists. Why didn't any of you tell me toddlers have an inherent death wish? They seem determined to stick their fingers into whatever is the most dangerous thing in the room. Or eat it."

Snickers erupted from the parents in the room.

"My fleet, Bart," Bethany Anne reminded him.

"Indeed," the Admiral replied, gathering himself. "Once the issues with materials are smoothed over, there should be no problem with continuing growth."

"Good." All amusement dropped from Bethany Anne's expression. "I expect you will have no problems replicating the success you've had with the *Helena's* shipyard over at Devon."

Admiral Thomas looked relieved. "I thought you had a challenge for me."

Bethany Anne lifted a shoulder. "I don't know about a

challenge, but I want an identical setup at High Tortuga, attached to the platform. And Bart? I want it done—"

"Yesterday?" he finished.

Bethany Anne narrowed her eyes at the Admiral's hologram. "I *was* going to give you six months, but if after all these years you finally worked out how to manipulate time and provide me with what I asked for *when* I wanted it, then where the fuck are my shipyards?"

Admiral Thomas huffed, knowing when he was out-snarked. "Barnabas and I will get with Lance to make arrangements."

"That's the kind of attitude that gets us places." Bethany Anne winked at him and moved on to the next item on her agenda. "The Ooken. Or more precisely, progress with the nanocyte substance."

"That's a whole new lot of sweet fuck-all," Jean grumbled. "I can tell you that we've gotten everything we're going to get from the nanocytes in the suspension you found out at the staging post. We will need fresh, uncontaminated samples to make any further headway on reverse-engineering the advances the Kurtherians who made them had over a thousand years to figure out."

Bethany Anne pressed her lips together. "It's a good thing you're up to the task. We have a possible lead on your samples since we found out the Moen have access to the suspension."

Jean's demeanor brightened. "Yeah? Where are my samples, then?"

Bethany Anne snickered. "You'll have them soon enough."

Tim shifted in his seat, feeling like a kid at the adults'

table. "Sooner. I got with Peter, and there are four teams with boots on Moen as we speak. They'll be back with those samples before the fleet has finished extracting the rest of our Guardian Marines post-cleanup."

Bethany Anne raised an eyebrow. "You keep impressing me, Tim."

Sabine flicked her ponytail over her shoulder. "He's an impressive guy. We have vid crews with the fleet, and the footage they're sending back could be used in wider circulation if you have no issues with it being shared to a wider audience."

Tim nodded. "I like that. There's always a small trickle from the Federation coming into our military, but we need to open the floodgates a crack."

Bethany Anne shook her head. "The only problem with opening the gates a crack is convincing the water not to drown you. I do not want the majority of the Federation turning up on the doorstep of the planet my children are living on."

Michael flourished a hand. "It would hardly be an issue if you settled on somewhere to *settle*. I would, however, suggest we find somewhere that has the room for a more suitable base of operations than the kids' place of business soon."

Sabine narrowed her eyes at Michael. "Who are you calling kids? Then again…" She flashed a crooked grin at him, and he returned a stern look. "Oh, lighten up." She chuckled as she turned to look at Bethany Anne. "Do you want our help finding somewhere to live? I can get Mark on it as soon as we're done here."

Bethany Anne lifted her hands. "Well, I don't want to

keep living on the *Izanami* forever. But..." She lifted a finger. "But I don't have time to build right now, and I don't want to be confined to any one planet. Barnabas, will High Tortuga fall apart without us?"

Barnabas gave that serene smile of his. "I already spoke with Stephen and Jennifer about taking on a more active role again, and I am well prepared to put the logistics network into place with Lance's assistance. You can rest assured that everything on High Tortuga will remain under control, Bethany Anne. Phase Five can begin whenever you are ready."

Bethany Anne nodded in satisfaction. "Good to know. Even better is knowing that when we do eventually get back to Earth, we will be able to fix whatever we find."

John shook his head. "Boss, you can't possibly still blame yourself for what happened on Earth?"

Bethany Anne raised an eyebrow. "You know I'm past all that, but I'm still holding myself responsible for repairing whatever mess we find when we get back there. Those are still my people, no matter how different we might be after all this time. As long as I have the power to protect them, I will."

A murmur of agreement went around the room.

"See?" Bethany Anne waved a finger at them all. "None of you feel any differently. Returning to Earth is still our end goal. We just have a mountain or two to climb before we get there and give them the advantage of what we've learned."

"MPPS, baby!" Scott and Darryl whooped, drumming their hands on the table.

Bethany Anne inclined her head and waited for silence.

"MPPS. What a fucking blessing. We institute the same provisions for healthcare, education, and employment that have changed High Tortuga into somewhere worth living. We aren't getting back to Earth any time soon, so we can figure out if and how the system needs adjusting to fit with humanity's needs along the way."

Michael nodded in appreciation. "That does solve the problem."

"As well as giving us the opportunity to look into how the MPPS translates from planet to planet and culture to culture without taking too much attention from the larger picture." Bethany Anne looked around the table once more. "Okay, if nobody else has anything they would like to bring up, I think we're done here. You all know where you need to be. Michael and I are leaving for an extended stay in the Etheric sometime in the next twelve hours. We will be gone for a couple of days, and I don't want to find out everything went to shit while I was gone. Tabitha, give me a moment, please."

Tabitha gave Bethany Anne a thumbs-up. "You got it." She took a moment to update Peter on the meeting while everyone except her, Bethany Anne, and Michael left the meeting room, her fingers twitching over invisible keys. "Let me guess—the Bakas."

Bethany Anne raised an eyebrow. "Good guess. It's almost like you're working with them on a daily basis. Have there been any incidents we should be aware of before we meet with Mahi'Takar?"

Tabitha smirked. "No, but I'm betting there's going to be one when you arrive at the enclave."

"That's where you're mistaken," Bethany Anne

corrected. "Prior to any official agreements, our relationship with her is to remain a secret, and I do not mean the usual kind of secret that everyone from here to High Tortuga knows within five minutes of it leaving my lips. I mean blanket secrecy to protect her and her son from assassination."

Tabitha pressed a hand to her forehead. "Yeah, their family politics isn't going to make that easy to achieve. What you need is a reason for Mahi'Takar and Trey to leave the enclave without her guards."

"We have Addix," Michael reminded them. "She's been working with the adolescents as I requested, yes?" He grinned at Tabitha's slightly bewildered nod. "Then have her call Mahi'Takar after hours to discuss her son's progress."

Tabitha snorted. "You want me to do what?"

Bethany Anne glanced at Michael. "I like where you're going, but it will look suspicious if Mahi' is the only parent called. We need to think bigger. Tabitha, how many minors do you have in your classes? How long would it take you to put together a review on each?"

Tabitha groaned. "Don't do this to me."

Michael spoke over Tabitha's protest. "We would be truthful in presenting this as a community event. A full Hexagon would make it much easier to cover Mahi'Takar's absence for a while. Long enough for us to learn what our commonalities are."

Bethany Anne winked. "Who doesn't love a get-together to celebrate their children? You can arrange student demonstrations, and encourage people to bring food and their younger children. Make a day of it if that's what you need. Open it up to Sabine's vid-crew and share it with the city. Whatever boost to morale we can give people."

Tabitha's groan increased in intensity for a second before she dropped her head onto her arms. "That would actually help in other ways." She sat up, her sulk replaced by a sunny smile. "I'm on it. It won't take more than a few hours. The event will take a little longer, since you can bet I'm going to have a bunch of parents who need the concept explained."

Bethany Anne tapped her nails on the table. "Use the Library to take care of that. Issue a brief explanation, along with a movie clip or two from the archives to give them a visual. "

Tabitha nodded slowly. "Okay… I can see this working. Give me three days to get everyone on board and arrange everything we need for the event. How do you plan on getting Mahi'Takar away from her guards?"

Bethany Anne's mouth twitched. "We aren't going to be there. Her son is in Alexis' and Gabriel's teaching group. Since that is the advanced class and her son has high status, it wouldn't be unreasonable for you to have your meeting away from the rest of the instructors."

"We need you at the meeting," Michael assured her.

Bethany Anne grinned. "Which we're going to have over dinner at yours and Peter's place. You just bring Mahi'Takar and Trey to us once they are safe with you."

Tabitha got to her feet and headed for the door. "Fine by me, but I'd better get started." She turned back and grinned at Bethany Anne and Michael. "This is just what this city needs…as long as you don't expect me to cook for everyone."

"Heaven forbid we get accused of poisoning the Bakan leader," Bethany Anne returned as Tabitha exited the meeting room in a swish of leather.

Devon, First City, The Bakan Quarter

Bethany Anne had not seen this part of the city in person yet.

Nevertheless, she made her way through the enclave without pausing for directions, a shadow under a cloak of indeterminate species, working her way through narrow streets and winding passageways until she came to the center of the low sprawling buildings and the residence of Mahi'Takar.

While Bethany Anne trusted her children's judgment when it came to accepting 'Trey' as a friend and teammate, she wanted to get the full measure of his regent mother before committing to supporting them both. Michael had begun by insisting he accompany her.

Bethany Anne's offer to take Alexis to guard her instead had been enough to give her husband a clue that this was a matter between two women and divert him to insisting their daughter remain behind.

The guards at the gate of Mahi'Takar's home stared at

Bethany Anne as she walked by. Bethany Anne wasn't planning to use the gate. She noted the security was mainly of the muscular type, although she detected a few nasty surprises hidden in the guard towers around the walls. "Good for you," she murmured, stepping into the Etheric. "But none of that can keep me out."

A mental scan as she emerged on the other side of the wall told Bethany Anne that her targets were on the floor below, alone. The Bakas built down rather than up, which to Bethany Anne's human mindset was all kinds of backward. She wasn't there to judge anyone on their preferences when it came to infrastructure, though.

She stepped back into the Etheric and came out again in the kitchen, where she found Mahi'Takar at the table with Trey. "Mahi'Takar."

Mahi'Takar was on her feet and in front of her son with a broadsword in her hands faster than Bethany Anne knew their species could move. "Leave or die."

Bethany Anne pushed her hood back, revealing her face to the two Bakas.

"Baba Yaga!" Trey tried unsuccessfully to get out from behind Mahi'Takar. "Mahi', I told you she would come."

Mahi'Takar remained in front of her child, her sword raised between them. "Baba Yaga. I have been expecting you. Do you come in peace?"

Bethany Anne nodded. "Yes. I was hoping we could talk before the circus gets going. Work out what we can offer each other, if anything."

Mahi'Takar lowered her sword to her side and gestured toward the free chair. "My son is headstrong. You will forgive him."

Trey emitted a high-pitched noise. "This is the best, Mahi'. I told you we could work with the humans. Baba Yaga has honor; you will see."

Mahi'Takar looked at her son with a mixture of fondness and bemusement. "Take yourself off to practice while I speak to Baba Yaga, Takar'Tu'Reigd."

Trey grumped a little but obeyed his mother.

Bethany Anne took the seat she was offered, an overstuffed chair built for someone more than twice her size—which Mahi'Takar was. "Thank you. Your home is beautiful, by the way."

Mahi'Takar glanced around distractedly at the polished wood and stone of her kitchen. "We have had a decade or more to make life comfortable here, although Devon isn't ideal. It has taken some adjustment to get used to living on the skin of the planet."

Bethany Anne's eyebrow twitched at the classification of forty feet underground as the surface. She crossed her feet at the ankle and settled into the oversized chair. "What is your homeworld like?"

Mahi'Takar's expression became wistful for a moment. "Above ground, it's frozen. Staying up there is certain death. Below ground, there's just as much chance of death, but you will at least be warm when you get torn to shreds by a pack of wild *kolak*."

"Sounds delightful," Bethany Anne offered. "I can see why you settled on Devon while it was still a dead spot."

Mahi'Takar lost the dreamy look, regarding Bethany Anne with skepticism. "What is your purpose in my home? Surely you did not risk my son's life simply to discuss frivolities."

Bethany Anne arched her eyebrow. "You know why I'm here. It's to save your son's life, and yours too. That's if you aren't too proud to accept you're not the one in control here."

The sound of air being sucked rapidly over clenched teeth came from beyond the wooden-beaded curtain.

Mahi'Takar's head whipped toward the door. "That had better have been the ghosts of your brothers I just heard, Tu'Reigd. Don't make me take the flat of my sword to your behind."

Bethany Anne couldn't help but snicker at the sound of his unceremonious retreat.

Mahi'Takar released a measured breath as she turned back to the conversation. "You would find that less amusing were you not also a mother, but I sense you understand."

"Oh, hell, yeah." Bethany Anne chuckled, the tension between them broken. "I believe we can trust each other. My children are your son's human friends. *That* was how I came to be aware of your situation," she clarified. "Not because Trey spoke out of turn."

Mahi'Takar nodded. "I have heard rumors of your ability to pull the thoughts from someone's head. They're true?" She shook her head in disbelief when Bethany Anne confirmed it with a nod. "You're reading my mind right now?"

Bethany Anne shook her head. "No. That shit gets tedious, and nobody gets into the Hexagon without their intentions being cleared by my security."

Mahi'Takar registered the information that Baba Yaga was not the only human who could read minds. "The

Hexagon must be the most secure building on the planet."

"It's damn near impregnable under normal circumstances," Bethany Anne told her softly. "Under siege, it's the second most secure building from here to the farthest reaches of the Federation."

"Only the second?" Mahi'Takar asked. "Which building outdoes the place Baba Yaga's children live?"

Bethany Anne inclined her head, a tiny smile appearing at the corner of her mouth. "The one where I gave birth to them. Our children are everything to us, and there is our common ground. What else do we need to agree on? Nothing else matters when our children are threatened."

Mahi'Takar's fur rippled and she turned her head to one side, then the other, searching Bethany Anne's eyes for the lie. Finding none, she grasped the human's forearm with a massive hand. "You have honor, Baba Yaga. I agree to lash my ship to yours, under the condition that you take Takar'Tu'Reigd under your personal protection."

Bethany Anne grinned. "Nothing would make me happier. There's a guard who you can trust, and her name is Addix." She pulled her cloak around her body, settling further into her chair. "As for the sharks circling you both, here's what we're going to do…"

Outside Federation Borders, Star System XG-3-560

Lance was a man of experience. Therefore, he knew the best way to draw the suspicions of the Federation leaders was to try to not look suspicious. Of course, he could have done all this out in the open since Bethany Anne had made sure nothing could be traced back to her, but where was the fun in that?

He hadn't tried to hide his departure from the *Meredith Reynolds*, or his destination. The ship he was in was even registered to him. After all, he was simply taking advantage of an unexpected break in session and the recommendation of a friend to kick back and catch something resembling a fish in the name of relaxation.

Nothing suspicious about that whatsoever.

Patricia knew better, as always. "Give Barnabas my love," she had told him when he'd said his goodbyes to her and Kevin two days previously.

Biorillium appeared in the far distance, a faint speck that grew larger and brighter with each passing second of Lance's approach. Soon it was a blue-green ball wrapped in wisps of white cloud.

Lance had no issues with planetary security since his stay had been booked in advance at a resort for those looking to get away from the rigors of life. He docked his ship and headed through the spaceport, taking only a single pack and a carryall with him.

An android waited in the foyer for him. "Greetings, General Reynolds. It is a pleasure to meet you. I am Ojon, and I'll be your attendant during your stay."

Lance made a face, holding his bags a little closer. "I don't know about having an attendant. Doesn't that defeat the purpose of coming here for some solitude? I've had enough of company for a while."

Ojon broke into a grin. "Haven't we all, General? You will, however, require sustenance and such, and that is where I come in. If you will follow me, please, I'll take you to your cabin."

Lance shouldered his bags and did as he was asked. Stepping outside into a world he'd only ever seen on the screen, he was momentarily jarred by the contrast to the high-gloss interior of the spaceport.

The spaceport opened onto a neat square at the top of a gentle slope. Animal or hand-drawn carts looked to be the transport choices for the planet. Lance was instantly enamored of the simplicity of it. He could almost feel the sleepiness of the place, and somehow he knew that nothing here happened any time before *mañana*.

"You like it, yes?"

Lance dragged his gaze from the hand-painted shingle hung above the wooden doors of the nearest store and chuckled. "Damn right, I do. It's beautiful here."

Ojon chuckled, indicating that Lance should follow him to a cart waiting in the street. "Don't mind Old Tassie. She's as docile as they come."

Lance dropped his pack into the cart and eyed "Tassie," all two hundred and fifty kilos of adult bistok harnessed to the front, before climbing into the back. "That thing isn't likely to try to separate me from my innards now, is she?"

Ojon hopped up and took the reins. "Not unless you're thinking of pissing her off," he replied airily. "She's a happy beast."

"Where I come from, bistok aren't thought of as working animals, and I've sure as hell never heard one described as 'happy.'" Lance glanced around at the scenery as the cart rolled out of the square and into open country. "Tell me about this place. I skimmed the brochure, but to be honest, you had me at 'well-stocked lakes.'" He nodded at Ojon. "Start with yourself. How does an android live on a world without connectivity?"

"Peacefully," his guide replied, geeing Tassie gently to gain momentum as they reached the bottom of the slope. "I am unable to filter signals, which not only leaves me vulnerable to attack, it's the equivalent of having a million voices in your head at once."

Lance patted the android's back. "That sucks."

Ojon lifted a shoulder. "Sometimes it does, but I have a home and a purpose."

They chatted amiably about nothing much for the next few kilometers, until the cart crested a low range of hills and the land dipped again toward a sparkling lake lined with trees.

"That's Lake Ponderance," Ojon informed him. "You are situated on the east shore, far from the activity. Your cabin is completely self-contained, but if you care for company at mealtime, there are a variety of eating establishments around the north shore."

The lane widened, then culminated in a pretty marina stuffed with pleasure craft filled with people determined to squeeze every drop of fun from the day. Ojon turned Tassie onto the boardwalk that divided the sandy shore and the soft loam at the tree line, then again to take a path through the forest around the lake.

Ojon made a chirping sound to slow Tassie to a jerky stop when they reached a gate on the forested east shore.

He turned around and handed Lance a bunch of keys. "This is you, General. The large key is for your cabin, and the smaller ones will give you access to the boat shed and the jetty. The cabin is fully stocked, as per the list your wife sent. Just use the tubes to order anything else you need. "

Lance took the keys with a smile and jumped down from the cart. "Thanks, Ojon."

"My pleasure, General. Enjoy your stay." Ojon waited for Lance to collect his bags, then shook the reins to get moving.

Lance lifted a hand in farewell as he headed through the gate. He made his way to his cabin, which looked to have been built from the trees felled to make the clearing it stood in, and let himself in.

The inside smelled of woodsmoke and winter. Lance took his bags to the kitchen and left them on the counter while he poked through what Patricia had deemed as suitable supplies.

Much to his surprise, the fridge was filled to bursting and not a leafy green in sight. Lance did a double-take when he found two rib-eye steaks as thick as his forearm tucked behind the Coke and beer with a note from Patricia.

He tucked the note into his pocket for later and went to explore the rest of his cabin. There was no point in having a vacation as cover if you didn't take the vacation, and besides, he had a day or so before Barnabas was due to arrive.

He jingled the keys, wondering what was in the boat shed.

The Etheric

The storm dissipated as Bethany Anne lowered her hands and released the energy. "Did you get that?" She glanced at Michael when he didn't reply immediately. "Michael?"

Michael lost his thoughtful look. "I think so. How soon can you do that again?"

"Right now." Bethany Anne waved a hand to move the golf ball-sized drone hovering around her head. "But it's your turn to try."

Michael eyed the storm in the near distance before facing Bethany Anne. "Very well, but I cannot see why we needed to record this. There doesn't appear to be much difference between controlling cloud systems and controlling these storms."

Bethany Anne raised an eyebrow. "Except the stakes if you fuck it up. Weather can't kill either of us if we make a mistake." She held out her hand, palm up. "I agreed to teach you on the condition you didn't get all manly and heroic, which is why we are starting with an extremely small storm."

A fast-moving cloud of Etheric energy detached from the storm and landed on Bethany Anne's outstretched hand. The storm fragment grew to the size of a football before she stabilized it. "This is about will, pure and simple. You have the self-control to ride the energy and shape it without losing yourself to it. You can do this."

Michael narrowed his eyes at the tiny vortex, his expression giving away what he thought about the training storm.

Bethany Anne nodded toward her hand. "Touch it."

Michael extended a hand.

"With your mind," Bethany Anne told him, pulling the

mini-storm back. "It would be a shame if our session was cut short because you had to regrow an arm."

Michael's hand fell to his side when he did as Bethany Anne directed and the energy *pulled* at him. "Is it sentient?"

Bethany Anne shook her head. "Not in any way we'd recognize. It's just energy, and energy wants to be used."

Michael nodded, his brow furrowing in concentration as he felt a connection to the energy he'd never noticed before. "It's nothing like controlling the weather," he admitted.

What he didn't admit to was his discomfort with the pull.

Bethany Anne smiled knowingly. "It's okay, you get used to it." She flicked her fingers to send the scrap of energy back into the storm. "You did well, but we need to save our energy. We have a long hike ahead of us, and there are no shortcuts."

Michael grinned, shucking his pack to rummage in one of the side compartments. "We're not exactly going to suffer from the effort of traveling a long distance." He handed her one of the two packages of tracker beacons Eve had provided. "We have food to last a couple of days."

Bethany Anne waved a finger in a circle. "Not forgetting the all-you-can-soak-up energy buffet." She took the trackers and set off at a brisk jog. "This way."

The mist around them lapped Bethany Anne and Michael's feet as they ate up the kilometers. Like a tide it moved, drawn toward their movement and then cast into their wake as they went against the current.

Michael controlled his breathing, matching Bethany Anne's slow heart rate beat for beat. "What are you searching for?" he asked as she dropped a beacon and made another turn with seemingly no guidance.

Bethany Anne pointed out a small but strong channel in the mists. "I'm backtracking the flow. TOM thinks there's a wall where all of the storms are generated, so that's what we're looking for."

Michael observed that the roiling mists were actually formed of a complex tapestry made from interwoven undercurrents. "This is how you locate the storms?"

Bethany Anne nodded, her attention on finding the point where the current she was backtracking split from the larger undertow. She found it a short way ahead. "Mmhmm. So far, I've found these undercurrents originate with a storm. I use the storm to follow the current to the next."

"So," Michael surmised, "your method of locating the storms by searching out these currents is sufficient, and what we're looking for is merely a larger current." He blinked to clear his vision of the patterns left behind when he looked away from the swirling mists. "Is there a connection between the storms we can use?"

Bethany Anne wrinkled her nose in consideration. "Sure. All energy is connected; that's probably the only constant no matter what universe you're in. Anne's research was actually a lot of help in figuring that out. Despite the apparent flatness of this place, the energy here runs outward from *somewhere*, like streams down a mountain. The physics here are screwy, but if there's an up, there's a down. I think TOM's 'wall' is going to look more like an ocean."

Michael picked up the pace, unable to unsee the paths

now that they had been revealed. "That would validate his theory that there is an originating point to be found."

Bethany Anne narrowed her eyes to focus on the far horizon, where a band gave the only hint of separation between ground and air. "We'll find out when we get there."

Devon, The Hexagon, Immersive Training Unit

Tabitha sat with her boots up on the teacher's desk she'd written into the classroom design based on her eighth-grade homeroom. She was waiting for her students to appear.

The teaching gig suited her, she had found.

Her time as Alexis' and Gabriel's guardian had prepared her for the demands and dramas of teen-equivalent students, as well as building her confidence as a mother before Todd was born.

She snorted softly, recalling the blind panic she'd been in when she'd found out she was pregnant with her son. It had all been for nothing, since loving Todd came as naturally as breathing. Besides, she had Pete to help her take care of the practical side of juggling parenthood with training the volunteer fighting force and teaching the Bakas some manners.

Peter wasn't the only one making her efforts look seamless. Addix was practical and pragmatic and was proving to be the perfect choice to assist her with the running of her classes. Tabitha had expected the Ixtali an hour earlier, but the spymistress had sent a message to say she was caught up in something with one of her assets.

It was her loss. Personally, Tabitha couldn't wait to see how her newest student dealt with her particular method of instruction, since her lessons were all structured around making the adolescent Bakas think about their preconceptions when it came to other species.

Her aim was simple: to teach them that not everything was a slight to their culture or their honor. That shit was cute as a plot device on a sci-fi show, but it wasn't going to cut it in the real world.

Neither was the superiority complex ingrained in the males from birth.

Rather than the Bakas getting exterminated when they faced Ooken, Tabitha needed them working *with* the rest of the civilian force. Those who didn't get it the first time had learned quickly enough when the consequences of their aggression played out the painful way.

Take Ch'Irzt, who was an extreme case. He had to learn that fucking up everyone's hard work because someone he deemed as socially inferior was ahead of him in line was not acceptable.

Most of the males had accepted her as the superior warrior, allowing them to submit to her demands without infringing their personal honor.

Of course, Tabitha had no problem playing dirty, and Mahi'Takar had made it clear she was to be obeyed, or they would face their leader's wrath.

Tabitha grinned. She hadn't had as much trouble with

the adolescents as with the older males. The youths had all been born on Devon, and while they tended to clump together with the siblings from their birth group, they were more amenable to new ideas when it came to mixing outside of their community.

Alexis and Gabriel appeared at the door first, their avatars dressed in dark shipsuits. Alexis flashed a huge grin when she saw Tabitha at the desk. "Aunt Tabbie! Where's Addix?"

Tabitha chuckled. "We've got a new student joining us today, and I'm here to make sure he integrates smoothly."

Gabriel's eyebrow went up. "Yeah? That should make it easier to form teams."

Tabitha shrugged. "Maybe. We'll just have to see how Ch'Irzt fits in."

K'aia came through the door just as Tabitha mentioned the Baka's name. "Not Trey's cousin Ch'Irzt?" she asked, going over to the seat shaped for her frame. "That ass rubs his own mother up the wrong way."

Tabitha winked at the disgruntled Yollin. "I met his mother. Nice lady. He won't be an issue. Take your seats," she told the twins. "The rest of the class is about to come in."

Gabriel and Alexis dropped dutiful kisses on Tabitha's cheek and took their seats as the other students filed through the door.

Trey was first in. He dropped into the seat next to Gabriel and gave Tabitha his brightest grin. *"Com és el meu professor favorit avui?"*

Tabitha frowned. "I'm good, if that's what you're asking."

Gabriel leaned in to whisper to Trey, "Try, '¿Cómo está mi profesora favorita hoy?'"

Tabitha nodded at Trey and pointed at Gabriel. "That I got."

Trey repeated the phrase slowly a few times. "Where did I go wrong?" he asked Alexis. "Don't tell me—dialect, again, right? Human has to be the most complex language I've ever come across. I don't know how you coped as a species before you developed translation software."

Alexis shrugged. "If my mother is to be believed, which she is, the translation software did nothing to help humanity understand one another. According to her, they just shouted all the louder until she…" She paused in thought for a moment. "You know, it just didn't help."

Em'Ain, Em'Eir, and Kn'Ille, otherwise known as Eamon, Emer, and Connal when they were in class, snickered at Trey as they walked past. "Stupid waste of time. We're here to learn how to fight with humans, not how to act like them."

Trey threw a sour glance at his cousins as they took seats on the other side of the classroom. "The desire to communicate has to be there to begin with—to listen as well as speak. How else do you find common ground to build on?"

"You're a special guy," Tabitha told him, throwing a sharp look at the other three Bakas. "Someday you're gonna make some pretty lady Baka—"

"Miserable and ashamed to be mated with him," a sour voice cut in from the door. Ch'Irzt leaned against the frame in full battle armor, somehow managing to convey the impression that his fur reeked even in the digital space.

"Who would have the runt? Talking about emotions like a female. He can't even grow a proper coat. He's a stain on his father's honor."

Trey shrank into himself, touching his dexterous fingers to his facial fur, which had yet to come in fully.

Tabitha's lip curled in distaste. "You're in my classroom now, asshole. I won't tolerate any of that puerile macho bullying crap in here, so sit down and shut your mouth before you earn another correction."

Ch'Irzt took a threatening step toward Tabitha and drew his blade. "How dare you insult me a second time?"

"Did you forget I already kicked your ass?" Tabitha reminded him. She snapped her fingers, and Ch'Irtz's avatar was transmuted into a naked, warty green blob with the Baka's eyes. "The penalties only get more embarrassing from here," she promised. "You don't want this to be your permanent avatar, do you?"

Trey snickered at the old film reference, along with the twins and K'aia. Eamon, Emer, and Connal missed the reference, having turned down Tabitha's extra credit class on moviegoing as a social activity.

Ch'Irzt glowered, his gelatinous body wobbling in a way Tabitha took as a no. She snapped her fingers again, returning the Baka to his own form, minus the armor and weapons. "I told you to sit, Chet."

Ch'Irzt took his seat without any more outbursts.

"Pity. He kind of deserves to be left that way," Alexis whispered to Trey.

Trey rolled his eyes in agreement. "Suits him, right?"

Tabitha removed her boots from the desk and sat up straight, smiling warmly at her students. "Okay, class. Let's continue with your homework assignments from last week. If you all recall, I asked you all to have a conversation with a Noel-ni and record the outcome in a report to share with the class. Who would like to go first?"

Emer raised her hand.

"Let's hear it, Emer," Tabitha encouraged.

Emer stood at her desk. "I spoke to Ricole. She did not understand the purpose of the encounter."

Tabitha nodded. "How so?"

Emer let out a small growl. "I inquired about her day, and she seemed to think I was looking for work because she took me to Network Command and gave me a series of increasingly dull tasks to complete."

Tabitha repressed her laughter. Mostly. "I'd say you got off lightly, Emer. Ricole was a bold choice. Well done. Who else would like to share?"

K'aia waved a hand in the air. "I had success," she called.

Tabitha gestured for her to continue.

K'aia leaned forward in her seat. "Well, after I left training the other night, I bumped into an old Yollin who said he knew you. We got to chatting and ended up in that bar over near the old Warehouse. You know the place?"

"Mmhmm," Tabitha hedged, wondering if this story was going to end in a place that was unsuitable for the younger ears in the room.

K'aia's mandibles chittered her laughter. "To cut a long story short, this Yollin caused an argument between two Noel-ni by sniffing one and declaring her to be a liar. Weirdest night, great brawl."

Tabitha raised an eyebrow. "I assume there was full-sugar Pepsi involved?"

K'aia winked. "I'm saying nothing."

Tabitha shook her head at K'aia. "Hmmm. Someone with a more appropriate report, please." She looked at Alexis and Trey, her good students—the two who never played around in class. She felt a sudden twinge of guilt for all the teachers she'd ever given a hard time.

Except for Barnabas, she thought to herself fondly. That fusty old ass deserved everything she could give him and ten percent more.

She called on Trey. "Wow me, kid."

Trey got to his overly large feet and cleared his throat nervously. "I volunteer at the hospital when I'm not here at the Hexagon or taking care of my mom. I share stories with the young on the children's ward in the evening." He tapped his wrist holo, showing them a holovid still of an infant Noel-ni in a hospital bed, his mother sitting beside him with her hands in her lap.

"This is Torraien. He has an ingrown claw that got infected, so he's segregated from the other young until the risk to him has passed. He was happy to tell me about his friends and how they play, and I recorded our talk for the class."

The class watched the small Noel-ni describe his life, helped along by gentle questions from Trey and explanations from his mother.

Tabitha got to her feet when Trey wrapped his report up. "Okay, I'm impressed. That was a thoughtful and sensitive interview." She smiled at the shy young male, then lifted her hands to get the rest of the class to stand. "We'll come back to the rest of you in the next lesson. It's time for today's practical."

The announcement caused excitement among the students, apart from Ch'Irzt, who remained sullen. Tabitha ignored him. He would get with the program soon enough —or he would learn to enjoy the loss of status that came with flunking a children's class. His choice.

She snapped her fingers again and the classroom dissolved around them, reforming a moment later into the scenario they were about to play. "Teams. Reds are Alexis, K'aia, Emer, and Connal. Blues are Gabriel, Trey, Eamon, and Chet."

"What are the requirements to pass the scenario?" Gabriel asked.

Tabitha counted them off on her fingers. "You must join a league, get to know three things about at least one member of your team, and play to win."

Ch'Irzt pounded a fist against his chest. "I always play to win. Out of my way, brats."

He pushed past Eamon and Trey, then vanished, only to reappear back where he'd been standing a moment before. "What is this?"

Tabitha smirked and continued to reel off the rules. "The scenario is timed, and you must complete each task before you can move on to the next. Failure to complete a task will result in a reset to the start of the task, as Chet so kindly demonstrated for us all."

Ch'Irzt continued to grumble.

Tabitha paid the big baby no attention. "Winning team gets a free afternoon to spend at the public venue of their choice with all the goodies."

Alexis perked up at that. "What goodies?"

Tabitha shrugged. "Play to win and find out."

. . .

Biorillium

Lance lit the grill as the night chorus got underway in the forest. A few insect repellant sticks took care of the worst of the bugs around the patio, and the smoke from the firepit took care of the rest.

He spread his afternoon catch out on the grill, then covered it with the lid before going back inside to find a cooler for the steaks and beers.

Having been so diligent in covering the food, Lance was perturbed to find the grill lid back in the upright position on his return to the patio.

"Damn animals." He reached back inside the door for the rifle he'd placed there after he'd heard a large *something* snuffling around the cabin last night.

Lance shouldered his weapon and locked the grill in his sights. If there was a fish in the lake that vaguely resembled a salmon, he was going to bet ten to one he'd drawn in the planet's version of a black bear.

He nosed the barrel of his rifle around the grill lid...and found Barnabas tending to their supper.

"I hope you didn't forget I was coming." Barnabas spoke softly as always, his teasing accompanied by a serene smile.

Lance lowered his rifle. "It's traditional to let your host know you've arrived so you don't get your funny ass shot off," he told him, retrieving the cooler. "Did you make it down here without being noticed?"

Barnabas nodded. "There was a sticky moment with a malfunctioning android, but Shinigami fixed the problem."

Lance winced, thinking of the pleasant exchange he'd

had with Ojon on the journey from the spaceport. "Did you have to terminate him?"

Barnabas frowned. "Of course not! I repaired his issue with some help from ADAM and wiped our meeting from his memory core."

Lance held up his hands. "Just asking." He opened the cooler and took out the steaks. "We have more important things to discuss. Medium or rare?"

Barnabas took a seat at the table. "Whichever you can manage with that primitive contraption," he replied.

Lance scoffed, brandishing the tongs over the top of the grill. "Don't sell the old girl short."

Barnabas peered into the cooler and rummaged around the bottles. "Who said I was talking about the grill?"

Lance offered Barnabas the traditional middle finger salute. "Extremely well done. Got you."

Barnabas raised an eyebrow. "Please don't ruin a good beef steak to prove a point."

Lance paled at the suggestion. "I wonder how difficult it would be to modify a herd of cows or two to populate the grasslands on High Tortuga?"

Barnabas chuckled. "Easy enough. However, the only ones eating beef would be the dinosaurs. We have bistok, and they are at least fast-breeding and aggressive enough to stand a chance."

"Did you see the android's animal?" Lance inquired, turning the meat. "Damn thing is as tame as a gelding. Never seen anything like it."

Barnabas smiled serenely. "A peaceable bistok is a sight to behold. It goes to show that we do not have to give in to our nature if we choose differently. Look at the Federation."

Lance groaned. "Not for another three days, and nobody can make it happen sooner."

"You still haven't resolved the issue with your dying king," Barnabas deduced.

Lance wiped a hand over his eyes. "No. There doesn't look to be a solution that leaves our hands clean," he admitted. "The king has days left. A couple of weeks at the most. It got heated enough for me to call a break to give everyone a chance to cool off." He piled the steak on a plate and handed it to Barnabas. "Maybe we *do* need a vigilante."

Barnabas accepted the plate from Lance. "Say no more."

The Etheric

Bethany Anne and Michael had been running through the mist for at least three eternities. At least it felt that way, time and the unchanging Etheric blurring together to become one and the same until the moment that the moody gray line on the horizon began to grow larger in their perception.

Bethany Anne grinned. "Am I seeing things?"

"It's real," Michael confirmed.

The break in the monotony was enough to spur them into a race for the last few dozen kilometers at the end of the hundreds they had crossed in the uncounted hours they had been running.

They pushed hard, wringing the strength out of their bodies and pausing only when the thin stripe had become a towering cliff that dwarfed them despite their relatively large distance from it.

Michael tipped his head back and shaded his eyes, squinting up to try to make out the top of the storm wall. "That is definitely not an ocean," he stated.

The corner of Bethany Anne's mouth twitched with amusement. "No, honey. It's…" Her voice trailed off as she sensed a huge mass of energy approaching the edge of the storm wall. "Fuck me."

Michael got a sense of the enormous power in the storm at almost the same moment as Bethany Anne. "It's headed this way."

Bethany Anne halted a few hundred feet from the storm wall with a distant expression on her face. "We just proved TOM's theory, which means we have an opportunity to test the practical application of it."

Michael's chuckle died quickly when Bethany Anne did not join in. "You're not joking? I do not think TOM meant for you to die attempting to control the largest single storm in the Etheric."

Bethany Anne shrugged and walked in the direction of the storm wall. "We need an increase in available energy to test the theory, and there's a shit-ton of energy headed right for us. The equation isn't difficult."

Michael stared at his wife's back for a moment before replying, "An increase in available energy is one thing. This storm stretches for," he felt for the edges of the approaching pressure with his mind, "a kilometer or so."

"I won't be chasing it alone. Do you think I would risk orphaning our children?" Bethany Anne's eyes unfocused for a moment. "TOM needs to pull up his panties and get with the program here. Besides, a storm of *that* size would prove his theory one way or the other, and if he's right, we have a way to get to the homeworld."

"I thought the goal was for me to learn how to handle these storms?" Michael reminded her.

Bethany Anne took out one of the beacons and activated it. "And you will. However, I won't pass up an opportunity this good."

Michael wasn't sure why Bethany Anne perceived this monumental challenge as a "good" thing, but he knew better than to argue when his wife got that look. "You're going to let ADAM and TOM do their part, right?"

Bethany Anne snorted softly. "They're already at work," she told him. "I need you to be my anchor until I have control of the storm, which should help you figure out exactly how I'm controlling the energy."

Her gaze shifted for a moment and Michael saw the minute changes to her expression that told him she was ripping either ADAM or TOM a new asshole. Possibly both. "Whatever you need," he agreed in the name of keeping his own ass intact for the time being. "What do you want me to do?"

Bethany Anne sat cross-legged on the ground, waved away a tendril of overly curious mist, and settled her hands into her meditation pose. "Hold my mind and don't let it go. Number two on the list of reasons not to fuck around with Etheric storms is that it's too easy to forget what keeps you from ascending."

Michael frowned. "That's a concern?"

Bethany Anne shrugged. "Not usually, but what's coming our way is a bit beyond what I've been working with so far. I'm doing this, but I'm not taking risks I don't have to."

Michael felt Bethany Anne's consciousness unfurl and stretch.

She looked up at him, raising a finger. "No laughing at my deepest, darkest fantasies," she warned.

Michael suppressed the urge to snicker. "If you are referring to the temple to footwear I can see in the deepest recesses of your mind, I wouldn't dream of it," he replied.

Bethany Anne pressed her lips together. "*Thinking* about laughing is still laughing," she responded archly.

Michael put a hand to his chest. "I swear, on the inside, I was crying tears of sorrow that your temple is not a reality."

Bethany Anne narrowed her eyes. "*Yet*. Now, if we're all done being amusing?" She returned her focus to the approaching storm. "This requires total concentration."

Michael sat directly behind Bethany Anne and wrapped his arms around her middle, his legs on either side of hers. "Then concentrate. I've got you."

"I know you do." Bethany Anne centered herself, holding onto the sensation of being cocooned by her husband's body. She reached her calm space and extended her mind toward the wall of roiling energy, where the gigantic storm was fighting to break free.

Just a little bit farther, she coaxed. **Come to me.** Her inner voice was soft. However, beneath the silky tone, she did not bend an inch. She called the energy to her, enticing it with the promise of purpose.

The storm obeyed, attracted to the bright spark of Bethany Anne's mind. It spilled from the wall in a spray of lightning, streaking the mist above her and Michael silver-blue.

Bethany Anne grasped the storm energy as the tumult parted to eject the leading edge.

Michael felt her grow distant. *Bethany Anne.*

I'm okay. Pay attention now, but don't listen to the storm.

Bethany Anne opened her mind to it.

The storm sang to her of power untamed, release from worldly concerns, and the peace of becoming one with its energy in exchange for simply giving in and becoming part of the song. It was a siren serenade she heard snatches of every time she called a storm, something she'd learned to ignore while she wielded the power of the Etheric to locate the Ooken.

Bethany Anne realized she'd had no idea of the true potential of the Etheric until now. She was barely aware of Michael, ADAM and TOM speaking to her, enraptured by the wild beauty she was there to tame.

The storm was an orchestra, playing her as its instrument.

She saw it all—the purpose of existence, the secrets of the cosmos, just one step away. She briefly understood how to create or destroy entire universes with nothing more than a thought. The knowledge slipped away before she could grasp it, but it didn't matter that the storm tempted her.

ADAM and TOM saw everything she did.

Michael was experiencing it along with her.

The smallest of satisfied smiles graced the corner of Bethany Anne's lips.

Come to me. Be mine.

The Etheric

Michael held Bethany Anne tightly as the storm grew closer.

Fully half of it had emerged by this point, and she was beginning to breathe harder under the strain. He entwined his mind around hers to lighten the load.

What are you doing? Bethany Anne's inner voice was tense.

Michael added his strength to hers. *You showed me enough that I've figured it out.*

Then we face this together. Bethany Anne slipped out of Michael's arms, taking his hand before she got to her feet to maintain the physical connection.

Michael took his place by Bethany Anne's side, his fingers tightening on hers. *As it should be.*

Michael deflected the lightning as they turned to face the storm, their combined will drawing it toward them with ever more speed.

Bethany Anne created a shield of hardened Etheric energy overhead to protect them from being scoured by the bombardment of particles and the wind decreased almost immediately, the lightning running harmlessly down the sides after being drawn to the spikes protruding from the top.

Michael indicated the cascading energy with a nod. *That certainly improves matters.*

No shit, Bethany Anne replied, pushing the shield up and out to give them space to work. The edge of the storm began to whip her hair despite the protection. **Okay, we got the energy here. Now we take control.** She tightened her grip on Michael's hand, raising the other to the maelstrom. **You should increase your weight. This is likely going to get bumpy.**

"Bumpy" was a somewhat underwhelming description of the cyclonic force that hit Bethany Anne and Michael when the raging mist swallowed them whole.

Michael had already increased his weight some earlier, when they got up from their meditative position. Now he dialed his body mass up until he was certain the wind would not steal his legs from under him or snap his spine. *I am beginning to understand why our children find your lessons so scintillating.* He felt Bethany Anne grin and the pressure build in her brain. *A margin for error of practically zero is every bit as effective as stimulating the nervous system for sharpening the mind.*

We all have to grow. Beating common sense into everyone personally takes up a lot of time I don't have. Bethany Anne didn't miss a beat despite the battle they were waging. She continued to exert herself, laying her will over the energy like she'd done so many times before. *It's much more efficient for me to provide a sink-or-swim experience.*

Michael grinned as he followed Bethany Anne's every move. *How enlightened of you.*

"Enlightened?" Bethany Anne chuckled darkly. *There are enough assholes in this universe for me to spend every second of my life kicking them into shape. It makes the times I do go to the effort of applying pain to expedite the learning process that bit more special, don't you think?*

Michael chuckled. *I don't disagree.*

They battled on in stoic silence as the lightning pounded the ground around the shield, which was holding —by what power Michael didn't know at this point. He could discern no end to himself and no beginning to Bethany Anne. He felt blood welling up, but it wasn't *his* nose that poured crimson.

Bethany Anne dismissed the concern she felt from Michael. She gritted her teeth, her jaw clenched with the effort it was taking to master the storm. *TOM is dealing with it. We're almost there, so don't get distracted now.*

She felt the pressure shift as the energy came under her control. *It's different.*

How so? Michael inquired.

Bethany Anne narrowed her eyes in consideration. *I'm not sure yet. I'm going to open a window.*

Michael nodded. *Be careful.*

Bethany Anne rolled her eyes internally.

Thinking about rolling your eyes is still rolling your eyes, Michael teased.

Bethany Anne turned her hard look on her husband. *Are you* **trying** *to piss me off?*

Of course, Michael replied. *I wouldn't want you to go into this at anything less than your best.*

You're an ass. Bethany Anne retorted, her mouth quirking as she began the process of opening the window. It took a gargantuan effort that started her nose bleeding again.

Bethany Anne?

Am I about to die?

Well, no, but—

Then it will wait. She heaved with all her mental power and everything she dared take from Michael.

It was enough...*just.*

The mist drew back and began to coalesce around them as Bethany Anne's knees gave way.

Michael caught Bethany Anne before she fell and held her steady under his arm until her face resumed its usual color. *Are you hurt?*

Bethany Anne pressed her temple to Michael's shoulder and rubbed her eyes in the hope whatever was causing the blurriness in her vision would hurry up and heal. *No, just drained. I'll be fine in a minute.*

They stood that way for a bit, watching the milky grayness leach out of the opaque mist as it hardened into a wall that surrounded them.

Bethany Anne drew long and hard on the Etheric as the window stabilized around them. *But that took everything I had and then some. If you ask me to do it again in the next five minutes, the answer will be screw that—and have some fuckdamn hell NO to go with it.*

Michael looked at the window. *Don't they usually open a distance from the inhabited planet?*

Bethany Anne nodded, her surroundings slowly coming back into focus as TOM repaired her brain and the dizziness receded.

Michael flicked a finger at the view beyond. *Then I believe you may have been correct in your assessment. This is certainly different than your previous outcomes.*

Bethany Anne rubbed her eyes again while the window crystallized. The landscape beyond was alien to her, but she had no trouble processing that the window had opened right onto the planet instead of hundreds of kilometers away. **What the...** She turned to Michael. **We did it. We opened a window to the Ooken homeworld!**

Michael released Bethany Anne and went over to touch the window. He looked back at her, his eyes wide with surprise. *You have done more than that. Come and see.*

Bethany Anne walked the few steps to him and reached out to investigate for herself. The membrane between the Etheric and the planet flexed under her fingertips before giving. She pulled her hand back and turned to Michael with an identical look of amazement. "I can't believe this. We've opened a fucking *door*."

QT2, QBBS *Helena*, Robinson Memorial Park

Admiral Thomas was enjoying a rare quiet lunch with his wife when CEREBRO interrupted.

"Apologies, Admiral, Mrs. Foxton-Thomas. We have a location on Bethany Anne and Michael. One of Eve's tracker beacons just came online. Tabitha is awaiting your call."

Admiral Thomas looked at Giselle regretfully. "Looks like that's the end of our date. I'm sorry, dear."

Giselle took his champagne flute with a smile. "Don't be silly. Our Queen needs you, so you must answer the call of duty."

The Admiral kissed his wife soundly. "Whatever did I do to deserve you?" he asked.

Giselle touched her finger to his nose. "You didn't pretend you didn't need me," she teased. "Now, Tabitha is a mite impatient when it comes to Bethany Anne, and much more likely to injure you if you keep her waiting. Go on, now."

"Yes, dear." Admiral Thomas kissed Giselle one more time just to be sure she was real and not a figment of his tired mind and left the park in a dignified dash.

Tabitha was already onscreen in his ready room when he got aboard the *ArchAngel II* ten minutes later. "No time to talk," she began, shifting in her seat as though she couldn't wait to be gone. "This is the one. Take the whole fleet and be ready to go in hot, because Bethany Anne isn't going to wait."

Admiral Thomas slid into his chair and pulled up his holoscreen to send out the orders. He paled when he saw the coordinates. "This is… Tabitha, only the superdreadnoughts can make this distance in time to be of any help to Bethany Anne, and even they will be cutting it fine. The smaller ships just flat don't have the Gate capacity."

Tabitha frowned. "Then load the smaller ships into the

superdreadnoughts like Russian dolls, or stick them to the hulls. I don't know. Just get them there."

Admiral Thomas sighed. "That's not in question."

Tabitha got to her feet. "Good, and stay in touch. I can't leave Devon."

She was gone before Admiral Thomas could reply.

He shook his head. "CEREBRO, you heard the lady. All hands to their stations."

The Etheric

Ooken

Bethany Anne turned slowly in the center of the circle, soaking up every detail of the gas planet revealed by the mists. ***It doesn't look very hospitable to humans out there.***

It doesn't appear to be hospitable to any species, Michael returned, indicating rust-colored rain falling around the craggy platform on the other side. *I'd say that's acidic.*

Bethany Anne shrugged. **There's shielding. It's definitely Ooken since that platform is made of their crystal.**

I wouldn't call it a platform. A sky base, maybe. Michael's gaze remained on the churning gases beyond the shield. *Do we know where it's located?*

ADAM is poking around. Bethany Anne frowned. **Dammit. It looks like it's seventeen Gates from Devon for the superdreadnoughts.**

More for the smaller ships—if they can make that many Gates consecutively. Michael looked hard at his wife. *You do plan to wait for the fleet?*

Bethany Anne flashed a grin at her husband. **It's like you know me. They will catch up soon enough. I want to see how much trouble we can cause before they get there.**

Michael's expression did not falter. *We have no idea what awaits us on the other side of this door. Prudence would suggest waiting for Bart and the fleet.*

Bethany Anne narrowed her eyes. **Yes, but if we do it my way, we'll be closer to done by the time the fleet arrives. Let them clean up, and we can all get back to Devon before Totto's closes for the evening. This kind of operation deserves a carbtastic ending.**

You are angling for an impromptu date night while our children are with Tabitha? Michael grinned at Bethany Anne's raised eyebrow. *I'm in. Can you get us back here if we need a sharp exit?*

Bethany Anne shook her head, drawing her right katana. **I can get us back into the Etheric, not to this place. I** *don't think we have much longer to decide. The door isn't going to stay open forever.*

Michael offered his hand to Bethany Anne as the circle of mist began to close in around them. *That's good enough for me. Shall we, my love?*

Such a gentleman. Bethany Anne took Michael's hand and stepped into the membrane. She activated her helmet, getting the sensation of moving through thick jelly. **That shit had better not have stuck to my hair.**

Michael activated his own helmet and brought up Bethany Anne's face-cam in his HUD. *Your hair is safe.*

She created the spark of an energy ball in her free hand as the membrane shrank to nothing around them. **Thank fuck for small mercies. Goop is always a nightmare to get out.**

That will be the only mercy this place sees today, Michael murmured as they emerged onto the rough crystal drop-off at the edge of the Ooken construction.

Bethany Anne peered over the perpendicular drop. **That's some shielding.**

You're telling me. Michael frowned up at the faint glow that was all that stood between them and the churning gases beyond. *I cannot see any structure that looks like a generator. What's the shield powered by?*

Bethany Anne pressed her lips together as she looked into the distance. **My guess would be Etheric energy. ADAM is telling me there are hundreds of thousands of small energy signatures coming from those towers.**

Michael turned to scrutinize the towering constructions that stretched in lines all the way to the horizon. *My guess is that the answers lie that way.*

Bethany Anne hadn't missed the unmistakable shapes covering every level of the towers. *The faster we move, the sooner we'll find out for sure.*

The rough crystal smoothed out as they walked, making the high technology sprouting from the ground appear all the more out of place against the backdrop of clinical desolation.

Bethany Anne sidestepped to get ahead of Michael as they approached the nearest of the eldritch constructions.

She paused for a moment in the shadows to scout ahead for other minds, spotting an entrance into the tower a short way around the curved wall. *I can tell there's a fuck-ton of Ooken, but all I'm hearing from the hive mind is static. What are you getting?*

Michael frowned, concentrating. *The hive mind is strong, but only in number.* He raised a finger, indicating the level above. *The majority are somewhere above us, present but not active. Perhaps the crystal obscures the hive mind in some way?*

Bethany Anne considered the thousands upon thousands of energy signatures ADAM had picked up. *That's not beyond the realm of possibility. I want to get a closer look before I act.* She ducked into the nearest passage. *There's not a chance in hell I'm allowing this many Ooken to be set loose.*

Michael finished examining the outside of the tower and headed after Bethany Anne, his sword held loosely in one hand.

Bethany Anne activated the spikes on the soles of her boots to improve her traction on the smooth floor and began to ascend the crystalline spiral. *All these decades and*

Jean still hasn't found a way to build the heels I want into my armor.

Michael rolled his eyes at Bethany Anne's back. *I can't imagine running across a battlefield in six-inch stilettos would be very practical.*

I didn't say they had to be stilettos, she retorted. **But there's no reason I can't kick ass and look good at the same time. I don't expect you to understand. Your job as a man is to appreciate my good taste.**

Michael chuckled. *Except that your good taste doesn't matter in this instance since Jean hasn't found a way to make a heel that can withstand the demands you would put on it.*

Bethany Anne glanced over her shoulder. **Except for that.** She held up a hand to halt Michael's progress as the passage opened onto a wide landing lined with Pod-docs. **Wait, there could be guards.**

Michael moved past her, sweeping the landing for any unwelcome arrivals. *I cannot sense any active Ooken in the immediate area, so we're good for the moment.*

Bethany Anne returned her katana to its place on her back but kept the spark in her palm alive. **Me either, but I'm not taking any chances. They might not be able to see us from a distance, but that won't mean a thing if a guard comes by.**

Michael made a noise of agreement, his focus on their surroundings. *These are Pod-docs. There's no mistaking them.*

Bethany Anne walked to the nearest Pod and stood on her tiptoes to look through the viewing window, getting confirmation of their suspicions. The Pod held a twitching nest of steel-blue tentacles wrapped around red fur contained within a glowing amniotic sac. **This explains why the Ooken aren't connected to the hive mind.**

Michael came over to see what she was seeing. *I wondered. These are much larger than any Pod-doc I've seen before, even the ones Eve built for Alexis' and Gabriel's toddler years.*

Bethany Anne pointed out the shimmering cocoon around the Ooken's body. ***More interesting, that's the nanocyte suspension, and now we know what it's used for—growing Ooken***

Michael peered into the window for a closer look. *Although this sample looks...active, somehow. The samples we have do not give off light.*

Bethany Anne's face hardened, and she waved a hand to encompass everything around them. ***All of this is comparable to our Pod-doc technology, it's just different.*** Her eyes became distant for a moment. ***TOM agrees with me. The Ooken didn't build this. The Kurtherians are directly responsible, and there's no way they would give this technology away.***

Michael's mouth tightened as he came to his own conclusions. *And these aren't Pod-docs. They're incubators.* He turned to stare at the towers of Pod-docs stretching off to the horizon. *But that's...*

An answer to another question, Bethany Anne finished, heading back toward the passage. ***We now know how the Ooken can afford to lose so many.***

Michael grumbled as he followed Bethany Anne into the passage, *It's an answer that just raised more questions. Are we saying that the homeworld doesn't exist? That this...factory, for want of a better word, is where the Ooken are created?*

Sometimes those hoofbeats you hear belong to zebras, Bethany Anne concluded as they descended the spiral. *It* *looks to me like this is a mass-production factory, and the Ooken are both the workers and the product. Based on the evidence so far, we have to acknowledge that the Ooken homeworld was a figment of our mindset. We didn't consider this as an option.*

She tightened her lips, her mind running with the concept and coming to a hundred and one conclusions, none of them pleasant. *If there's one factory, who's to say there aren't more of them churning out Ooken by the billions?*

Then we need to up our efforts to exterminate them at the source, Michael stated, his tone icy.

That isn't a solution, just a way to spend another lifetime running circles. We are facing an enemy who gives exactly zero fucks how many of their soldiers are killed. Bethany Anne's lip curled as she paused by the exit to scan for Ooken. *Creating life for the express purpose of sending it to its death? This whole setup disgusts me, and I want it wiped from this universe.*

You and me both. Michael put a hand on Bethany Anne's shoulder. *Small steps, and if there are any more factories, we will find them.*

Bethany Anne slipped out into the night. *Not fucking fast enough for my liking. I want a better resolution to this than another long, dragged-out war; one that doesn't require spending the lives of my people in order to win their safety.* She sighed. *Either way, we don't have time to wait for the fleet.*

Michael matched her step for step. *I can't see us making it for dinner. It will still be some time before they arrive.*

The spark in Bethany Anne's hand flared momentarily,

her eyes glowing to match the surge of anger she felt. *We need to work out where the weaknesses are so we can concentrate on grinding this place and all the Ooken here into a fine paste.*

Michael nodded his agreement, his eyes flaring to match hers. *Lead the way.*

They flitted beneath the towers without being spotted by any of the Ooken working above, until they came to a break in the monotonous grid layout.

Bethany Anne crouched in a hollow in the ridge where the crystal crumpled before taking a rough dip down to the valley below.

Michael dropped to his stomach beside her. *A map would be more than useful at this juncture.*

Bethany Anne considered the available routes. *We don't need a map. We've got ADAM.* She opened her connection to ADAM and TOM up to Michael. *He was about to fill me in on everything he and TOM have found so far.*

>>I can tell you what we haven't found,<< ADAM complained. >>*Any* connecting infrastructure. Every one of these towers is self-contained, with its own power source.<<

Michael frowned. **There goes Plan A.**

Bethany Anne waved him off. *Nothing is invulnerable. Did either of you come across anything that looked to be out of place?*

Well, there *is* all of the Kurtherian technology, TOM reminded them. **The curious thing is that I cannot say with certainty which clan created this place, only that it was none of the Five.**

Michael paused his careful inspection of the tower

opposite. *That is curious. What about outside the towers? There must be something generating the power for the shielding, or this whole place would be torn to pieces by the atmosphere.*

There was one strong energy signature. However, it is not emanating from any of the towers or the shielding. There is an undeveloped area just over two kilometers away, to the western end of the valley. It's coming from below the surface there.

Then that's where we're going. Bethany Anne set off down the slope. She winked at Michael's face-cam window. *One plan goes to shit, and the universe presents another opportunity. ADAM, TOM, keep up the good work. I want to know every way those Pod-docs differ from ours by the time you're done.*

Michael caught up with Bethany Anne at the bottom of the slope and they darted into the space between the crystal piles that acted as foundations, pausing to scout the way ahead.

Michael nodded upward. *There are more active Ooken above than there were in any of the previous towers.*

Bethany Anne followed his gaze, sensing the same. *They will wait. For now.*

Michael's mouth twitched. *I was thinking along the lines of remaining undetected.*

Bethany Anne waved off his concern. *Jean didn't spend so long tweaking our armor and not provide a few goodies. Check your HUD menu and select "Extras."*

Michael opened the menu and scrolled through the available options. *While it is genius, the oxygen extraction system might be overkill. Unless you are expecting to get caught underwater?*

Bethany Anne lifted a shoulder. *I expect everything. It saves time when I'm caught by surprise.* She braced herself for the pull her armor made on the Etheric through her body, then selected the kanji reading Shinigami from the icon menu. *I'll feel a lot better once this level of protection is available to all of us, not just me, you, and our children.*

Michael made a face of appreciation when Bethany Anne vanished. *I don't know how that woman managed to miniaturize the cloaking system enough to be used in armor,* he marveled, activating his own cloaking. *As for the armor, it will be available to all of our loved ones as their training with the Etheric advances and they are able to use it without danger to themselves.*

You're right. Both Tabitha and Gabrielle are getting close. The others will follow, or I'll just have to put everyone back in the Pod-doc to make sure they are all protected. Bethany Anne raised an eyebrow, a small smile appearing at the corner of her mouth. *As to Jean, that's easy: I tell her what I need, and she works out who to scare the shit out of to make it happen. Do you need a moment longer to recover?*

Michael shook his head. *I'm good. We should get going.*

Bethany Anne turned her thoughts over as they resumed their progress along the valley. *That substance could be a solution to the armor issue that doesn't require my level of Etheric control. What is Eve doing at the moment?*

Michael repressed a sigh. *She has mostly been complaining about being stationed on High Tortuga. What are you thinking?*

Bethany Anne's eyebrows met as she considered. *Too much to put into words right now. We've learned so much from the technology we've claimed during these battles, and I'm not the only one who has come to a détente with the Etheric. We're about to get our hands on up-to-date Kurtherian technology, Michael. Think about it: everything we've built has been based on technology over a thousand years behind theirs.*

TOM's discourse on the nature of the Etheric has been extremely useful in expanding my own understanding. Michael chuckled dryly. *If only we all had your innate ability to control it.*

Bethany Anne snickered. ***The universe would be completely fucked within a week. But I have an idea that will make it possible for those closest to me to use Etheric travel with refinements to our technology based on what we gain here.*** She waved a hand, already three thoughts ahead of Michael. ***If I decide to go that route, you'll be the first to know.***

Michael frowned. *Why does that sound less like considera-tion and exactly like I just became your guinea pig?*

Because you're the manliest man I know. Bethany Anne blew a kiss to her husband. ***And you're not the only guinea pig.***

Michael snorted. *You want to make it into a contest of masculinity?*

Bethany Anne's mouth twitched at Michael's protest. ***Competition—such a useful tool for getting the cooperation of a bunch of headstrong males. Besides, who doesn't enjoy a contest of masculinity?***

Michael shook his head at the wicked glint in Bethany Anne's eyes. *As long as you don't expect me to pose for a calen-dar,* he conceded.

They came to the location TOM had told them about, a

plain, rectangular crystal structure in the center of an open square surrounded by towers.

Bethany Anne's nose wrinkled. *Not exactly impressive, is it?*

What did you expect? Michael asked.

I told you: everything. This, however, she circled a finger as she regarded the building, *wasn't very high on my list of expectations.*

Michael stopped walking when an alien mind brushed against his. *We aren't alone.*

Bethany Anne didn't hesitate. *I can sense them too,* she told him, heading for the building. *Can you smell water?*

Yes, underground, Michael replied. *We need to be careful. There are plenty of Ooken around to make things difficult if we set off any alarms.*

Bethany Anne reached for Michael's hand. *I'll take us through the Etheric.*

TOM broke in, startling them both. **STOP!**

Bethany Anne froze just before she opened their way. *What the fuck, TOM?*

If I had a clue, I would have led with that. There's something...*wrong* inside that building.

Bethany Anne was thrown by the bewilderment in TOM's tone. *ADAM, can you shed any light on what's in that building?*

>>This is the source of the Etheric energy we picked up,<< ADAM ventured. >>Other than that, I'm still working on the Pod-docs, so I'm in the same position as TOM.<<

Which is?

>>We'll know more when you're looking at it.<<

ADAM's voice held a touch of regret. >>**Downside to all three of us sharing the same pair of eyes. If I had a body, I— <<**

Bethany Anne rolled her eyes. *The answer is still no. Are there any nasty surprises waiting for us outside the building?*

ADAM and TOM conferred for a moment.

>>**Not that we can detect,**<< ADAM told her.

Bethany Anne glanced at Michael in her HUD. *Then we're going in.*

Devon, The Hexagon

Trixa caught her reflection in the glass doors as they swung inward to admit Ricole. She immediately put her claws to use smoothing out her fur. There was *no* way she was appearing on the planet's main holonetwork with messy fur.

Not that she expected to get much screen time. However, Ricole was being shadowed by a vid-crew as today's feature story on *Devon's Defenders*, which her mother never missed. She fully expected to be wrung dry of every detail when she got home that night.

She dipped her head as the crew swept in behind Ricole, and her face burned when Ricole waved and the camera drone swiveled to the reception desk.

Ricole barely noticed the younger Noel-ni's sudden stage fright. She was too wrapped up in her concerns about taking the vid-crew around the classes without them seeing any of the Bakas training. She didn't have to understand why Tabitha was being a total hardass about it, she just had to figure a way to prevent it from happening.

She opened the team's comm. *We have nosey parkers. Are we good?*

Ricole, you worry too much, Demon drawled. *I should think my presence would be enough to ensure our pet journalists don't wander too far.*

Mark chuckled. *Yeah, and I've got a nasty bite waiting for any attempted hackers. Thank you, Eve.*

Thank you, Eve, Ricole repeated with a dry laugh of her own. *Okay, we're headed in. They're about to start the first segment.*

The tiny blond human who had introduced herself to Ricole as Fran Arthur stepped up to the camera and gave a dazzlingly warm smile. "Good evening, Defenders. I'm Fran Arthur, coming to you with a very special episode. We're joined by none other than Ricole, who has graciously invited me to spend the day here at the Hexagon. Ricole, thank you for having us."

Ricole was sure her attempt at a friendly smile came across more like an embarrassed half-snarl. "It's a pleasure to have you here, Fran. I'm a huge fan of the show, as are we all." She tried not to think about the camera as she gestured for Fran to join her. "Do you mind walking and talking? We'll never get through everything otherwise."

She pointed out areas of interest to Fran as they made their way into the original part of the building. "This is where we used to hold Fight Night when we started out. It's now the main indoor training area."

Fran nodded along with Ricole as they walked. "I hear

construction has begun again. Is the Hexagon going to keep expanding indefinitely?"

Ricole lifted her hands. "I don't know? As long as we're serving the community, I don't see why Baba Yaga would halt the progress. Since we opened for business, Hex has funded regeneration and infrastructure for the poorest parts of the city without displacing the hundreds of thousands of people who live there."

Fran grinned as she turned to the camera. "You can see the impact of Hex investment all over First City. We catch up now with Varia Schnell, whom viewers of *The Franarth Files* will recognize. She's no longer in despair about where her children will sleep at night or how she will feed them with no employment. We go to Gavin over at the Hope Docks to find out how Ricole and everyone else at Hex changed her life."

She held the grin a moment longer, then dropped it when the green light on the camera drone turned red.

"You done for now?" Ricole asked.

Fran shook her head and pointed at a second and third camera drone, then at her cyborg cameraman. "Stuart will use these to get all the stock footage we need. I have the passkey codes for your security department."

I've got them, Mark confirmed. *Okay, tell Fran she's been granted the access clearance she requested. That's thinking ahead. I like that in a woman.*

Demon padded into sight, pausing to touch her forehead to Ricole's hand in greeting before circling Fran and Stuart. *You do?* she purred. *Jacqueline will be interested to hear your assessment of the merits of human females.*

I will keep you in steak for a month if you don't, Mark

bargained. *The answer to "Do I want to die today?" is always no.*

That sounds fair, Demon agreed. *I will expect three kilos of prime cuts delivered to my loft every morning. You can speak to my butcher.*

You have a butcher? Mark asked.

Demon's tail flicked as she walked, startling Fran. *Did you think I would eat bushmeat given the choice? I sincerely hope for your sake your account is as large as your promise.*

Ricole ignored them, used to the mental chatter. She glanced instead at the cameraman, who was at the center of a number of strange whirring noises as his drones came in to land on his shoulders. "Is he okay?" she asked Fran.

The cameraman's eyes flickered, his awareness elsewhere for the moment.

Fran frowned prettily, a small line appearing between her eyebrows. "Stuart? Don't mind him," she told Ricole. "We'll do a short intro piece in a few locations and he'll take care of the rest. He had everything we need installed as firmware when we got the gig with the holonetwork. I'm guessing you have an EI? He gets like that whenever there's an EI."

Ricole nodded. As far as she knew, the holonetwork's explosion in popularity had a lot to do with this woman's persistence when it came to what was happening around Devon. "Fair enough. What about you? Where are you from originally?"

Fran flicked her hair over her shoulder. "Same as every other human out here. I grew up on the *Meredith Reynolds* and followed my Empress. Nobody has actually seen Bethany Anne since the Federation was founded, but the resurgence of her inner circle on Devon hasn't gone unnoticed. Baba Yaga hasn't been anywhere near so shy. I want to interview her—the Mistress. That's my dream."

Ricole smirked. "Careful what you wish for. Come on, let's get you some of that training footage. Commander Silvers is running drills in Arena Four, and he's expecting us any time now."

High Tortuga, Space Fleet Base, Barnabas' Office

Barnabas answered the voice call, somewhat surprised by Lance's relatively rapid response to his message regarding possible companies to fold into the logistics effort. "Is everything okay?"

"You sonofabitch sneaky bastard. You've known where my Merry has been all this time, and you didn't say a fucking *word*!"

"Hello, Lillian," Barnabas replied, wishing calls still came via a receiver you could hold at a distance to protect your hearing from women on the warpath. "Is Lance aware you are using his top-secret encrypted line to contact me?"

Lillian snorted. "What do you think? I just found out from Roh'dun that his cousin Grim'zee has been with Merry for who knows how long, and I came straight here. Now, you better spill before I find a way to get to High Tortuga and slap it out of you. Where is my daughter?"

While Barnabas appreciated the predicament John's and Jean's daughter was in, there wasn't too much he could tell her at this juncture. "I can't tell you."

There was silence on the other end of the line, punctuated by a few dull thuds. When Lillian spoke again, the fire was gone from her voice, replaced by icy anger. "Can't, or won't?"

"A little of both," Barnabas replied. "In all honesty, Tabitha is a much more suitable target for your ire. Grim was her doing. I was just the patsy for getting her plan past Bethany Anne, as much as I hate to admit she got one over on me."

"Oh." Lillian sighed. "Tabitha is covering her ass like there was a sudden temperature drop, and Dad won't hear her name mentioned. What can you tell me, Barnabas? Is she doing okay at least?"

Barnabas wanted to continue this conversation like he wanted the base to collapse on top of him. "Lillian, I suspect you know who to speak to for answers."

Lillian's retort didn't bear repeating.

Barnabas sighed. "My dear, I cannot help you. All I can do is promise I'm taking a more active role in Nickie's return to the fold. Will that suffice for us to say goodbye so I can continue making arrangements?"

The line went dead, leaving Barnabas to assume the ever-efficient juggernaut was satisfied with his offer. He poured himself a glass of water and messaged Lance directly using the Etheric comm.

Lance called back a few minutes later, his mental voice gruff. *What's up? Take your time. I'm in session, and it's moving slower than molasses in winter.*

Barnabas sniffed. *I do not envy your role, my friend. Government is a sword many a good person had fallen on. What is the topic of debate currently?*

Lance's internal groan said it all. *Vietania's entry into the Federation. It's a fuckbucket full of fairy feces, is what it is.*

Barnabas grimaced. *I expect that situation will resolve itself presently,* he consoled the General. *You will know the moment I do.*

Lance sighed. *That would be a load off my mind. Too many colonies, too many petty squabbles threatening the lives of the people living there.*

There's a fair amount of that going around, Barnabas conceded ruefully. *It amazes me how many colonies chose to institute monarchy as their governmental model when the expansion began in earnest.*

Lance made a semi-interested noise. *One moment.*

Barnabas listened in as Lance tore into some idiot in his General's voice.

"Are you fucking insane? You want to *assassinate* them? It's a damn good thing Bethany Anne isn't here to hear that shit come out of your mouth, Sorreg. Find another solution—one that doesn't involve the Federation getting blood on its hands."

Barnabas shrugged to himself, grateful again for the relative quiet of High Tortuga. *You need an assassin?*

Lance snorted. *Over financial corruption? I think not. I'm guessing you have a whole bunch of contract killers you can call,* he snarked. *All untraceable, right? Where do you even find these people?*

Barnabas *could* have told Lance he had something of a family affair in mind as a solution to both his and Lance's problem and his promise to Lillian. *If your fraudsters happen to have businesses that would fold into our network, it would save a great deal of time on your part to seize them.*

Lance snorted. *You're not kidding? That's not the way I'm running this. The Federation operates within regulations for a reason. If we start stripping people of their assets without a trial, we're no better than the preconceptions I've worked to debunk.*

Barnabas found Lance's particular brand of honor when it came to ensuring Federation actions were above board admirable. However, he had lived too long to expect everyone to play fair, and deep down, the General knew it too. *Do you have another idea how else you will arrange for millions of tons of cargo to be shipped out of the Federation without any suspicions being raised?*

Lance paused. *For now, I intend to keep this debate running. They'll argue whatever minute issue they're given for six weeks straight with little or no encouragement; it wouldn't be the first time. What are you going to do?*

Barnabas had barely formed the idea that had hit him before he called Lance. *I'm going to put Nickie in charge of the logistics network.*

Lance choked. *You're going to do* what? *The idea is to* prevent *word from getting out, not to drunk-crash a ship full of evidence in the Federation's lap.*

Barnabas sighed. *You don't know Nickie these days. She's fighting the good fight, her and her crew. She's ready to come home, although she requires freedom to roam. I'm going to try her suitability for logistics, and if she does herself justice, I'll make her the commander of the fleet. Once we have a logistics fleet to command, that is."*

Lance chuckled. *That's a mighty turnaround from the willful child Bethany Anne exiled. John and Jean will be relieved.*

He and Jean are in the dark, Barnabas told him. *It's early days, but something to build is something to stay for.*

Lance couldn't hide his shock. He'd had no idea Nickie —if that's what she was calling herself these days—was so close to redemption. *It could work. How does Lillian feel about that?*

Why don't you ask her? Barnabas returned. *She's probably about ready to break out of your office as we speak. Your secret line is not much of a secret, by the way. Lillian would appreciate you keeping her informed of Nickie's progress as much as I would appreciate avoiding awkward conversations with her in the future.*

Lance groaned. *You know, there is no point in having a secret anything if everyone in the family knows where all the secrets are hidden. I'll keep in touch with Lillian, and you will owe me a glass of something that burns all the way down to my stomach when I see you next.*

Barnabas lifted a shoulder. *I'll owe you a whole bottle, my friend. Thank you.*

In Transit, QBS *ArchAngel II*, Admiral Thomas' Office

The fleet had one more Gate to cross before they reached the coordinates ADAM had provided. Admiral Thomas wasn't *quite* at the point of spontaneously birthing felines, but he wasn't far from it.

The scale of the impending maneuver was evident in the slew of captains requesting permission from CEREBRO for their ships to debark the superdreadnoughts they'd been berthed on for the journey.

They'd been stalled for two hours while the superdreadnoughts slowly disgorged the contents of their hangars and cargo decks in a coordinated ballet, every ship of every class getting into position relative to their designated incursion point into the Ooken system.

The dance came to a close as the SSE fleet slid into place.

"You are exhibiting signs of agitation, Admiral," CEREBRO commented.

Admiral Thomas paused his continual comparison of the ships' coordinates against the carefully planned play on his datapad. "The sooner the new ships are ready, the better," he grumbled to the EI group. "At least I have you to keep everything running smoothly, CEREBRO."

"You are too kind," CEREBRO replied. "The scout ships are in position and awaiting your orders."

Admiral Thomas nodded. "Send them in. The sooner we get eyes on that system, the sooner we can get Bethany Anne and Michael out of there and lay waste to it."

"The report from ADAM has you concerned," CEREBRO surmised.

Admiral Thomas got up to pace. "Damn right it does!" He waved his datapad. "Once, just *once,* it would be nice if Bethany Anne waited for her backup before storming in."

"We would be happy to pass your concerns along to ADAM for the Queen's consideration," CEREBRO offered.

"That won't be necessary, thank you." Admiral Thomas rubbed his temple to ease the growing throb behind his eyes. "What are the scouts coming up with?"

"We are receiving preliminary reports," CEREBRO informed him. "The scouts have identified high-level defenses all around the sixth planet from the star, which is rather odd since the planet is not habitable by the Ooken."

Admiral Thomas frowned. "It's not? Show me."

"Not unless nitrogen-dependent life forms can suddenly develop the ability to exist in an atmosphere consisting mainly of sulfides." CEREBRO brought the viewscreen to life. "We are building a map of the system as the data comes in, but it will take a few minutes. Perhaps you would care to answer your correspondence while we wait for the scouts to complete their survey?"

The Admiral's head throbbed again. "I have plenty to do." He smiled to himself. "Besides, Giselle and her mother are not seeing eye-to-eye presently. If I don't *know* I have a message, I don't have to respond to it."

"Of course, Admiral." CEREBRO paused before continuing, "The challenges of an overenthusiastic mother-in-law are a staple of human comedy. Perhaps we could share some humor along those lines to pass the time?"

Admiral Thomas chuckled. "I don't think *that* will be necessary, either. Don't get me wrong," he clarified, "I love my wife, and as mothers-in-law go, Helena is not the worst. However, I would prefer to be served my own entrails for dinner on a nightly basis than get dragged back into Giselle's debate with her mother on the merits of traditional child-rearing over what Helena calls 'modern parenting.' Giselle will understand."

"The majority of us, being of military design, were under the impression that raising biological young required nothing more than attention to the child's physical and emotional needs on the parents' part," CEREBRO admitted. "Our insights on the various childrearing tactics of the different species we have come into contact with aboard the *Helena* have led us to conclude that is less than accurate."

Admiral Thomas shrugged, his focus on the developing picture of the Ooken system. "You know my opinion.

Parenting is more like an extended negotiation with tiny terrorists bent on self-destruction, as much as I've been told differently by my wife and everyone else. Children should mainly be seen at breakfast and bedtime."

"We would suggest it is fortunate that your wife is of a more nurturing mindset," CEREBRO teased.

The Admiral ignored the EIs. "What is your conclusion so far about the positioning of the defenses? There are three perfectly good rocky planets closer to the star. One of them even has an almost ideal oxygen/nitrogen atmosphere." He rubbed his chin in thought. "But they're hidden inside that gas giant. It isn't exactly screaming 'homeworld' to me."

"We have to agree, Admiral." CEREBRO highlighted a spot on the planet's swirling surface. "There is a great deal of Etheric energy being expended in this area."

Admiral Thomas nodded. "I don't have to guess; that's where we will find Bethany Anne." He tapped a few buttons on his wrist holo and the map on the screen appeared over his desk in all its three-dimensional hard-light glory. "Is the map complete?"

"It is," CEREBRO confirmed.

Admiral Thomas rolled his shoulders. "Then let's find out what we're up against."

14

Gas Planet, Ooken Sky Base

Bethany Anne and Michael entered the building cautiously. The inside was dim, lit only by a muted glow that pulsed gently within the smoky crystal walls.

Bethany Anne scanned the sparse atrium they walked into over the barrel of her Jean Dukes. *Creepy lair vibe much? Seeing what we have so far, I kind of keep expecting Cthulhu's uglier cousin to jump out from every shadow.*

Michael made a face as he passed Bethany Anne to explore the exits leading off the atrium. *It's the scent of soaked-in blood that does it.*

The room gave way to another, this one clearly a laboratory.

Bethany Anne blocked her olfactory senses before the stench of death crawled up her nostrils and took root in her brain. *This is where the Collective are turned into Ooken. You'd think they would do something about the smell.*

Michael shrugged, glancing at the equipment-covered

workstations. *It's not the worst thing I've ever smelled. Burning Were hair—now* that's *an odor that takes a while to depart.*

Bethany Anne pointed out a blue-smeared device that looked as though its primary function was to mince whatever was put into it. **What the fuck is that? And where are all the Ooken?**

Michael glanced at the arched passageways leading off from the back of the lab, then at Bethany Anne. *I don't sense any active Ooken, just the mind I felt when we were outside.*

Bethany Anne stepped lightly around a workbench, her Jean Dukes raised and ready. **There's more than one mind down there, and we've found the source of TOM's freakout.** She pointed to the darkened arch in the center of the wall. **Can you feel the barrier across that passage?**

Michael nodded, moving closer to investigate the invisible barrier. *I can, and my guess is that we will find the prisoners on the other side. What do TOM and ADAM have to say about it, now that we are here?*

>>**I say it's interesting. The arch has what I can only describe as a curtain of nanocytes suspended across it.** <<

Bethany Anne raised an eyebrow. **Can we pass through the nano-curtain?**

TOM spluttered incoherently for a moment.

>>**I wouldn't recommend it,**<< ADAM advised. >>**The nanocytes are programmed to consume everything except Ooken DNA.**<<

Bethany Anne shuddered at the thought of that grizzly end. **Okay, so we skip through the Etheric, no getting eaten alive by nanocytes.**

Not an option, TOM cut in. **The curtain is active in**

the Etheric as well. It looks like they weren't taking any chances.

Bethany Anne growled softly. *So how* **do** *we get through?*

Michael turned back from his inspection. *We could always force an Ooken to let us through.*

There aren't any around, Bethany Anne reminded him. She looked toward the exit. **We'll have to go back to the nearest tower.**

We will have to split up, Michael told her. *I only saw one guard on each level.*

Bethany Anne pressed her lips together. **Want to bet I can get back here with my Ooken before you get back with yours?**

Michael broke into a grin. *Why would I do that when it's a sure bet I'll win?* His armor sagged as he Mysted out of it and was gone before Bethany Anne could say a word.

Bethany Anne grumbled as she made her way to the nearest tower. **Cheat all you like. It's not going to help you.**

Are you sure about that? Michael inquired. *I have my prize in sight.*

Bethany Anne pressed herself into the shadows cast by the foundations and created a small ball of light over her palm. **Mmhmm.** She added a couple of touches to the energy construct while she listened for the *slap-slap* of slithering tentacles above that indicated a passing guard.

Hearing the sound she was waiting for, Bethany Anne released the energy ball to float up toward the first level. **You'd better do more than look, then. I have mine.**

The Ooken trilled curiously when the twinkling light appeared before it.

Bethany Anne made her bait hover just beyond the edge

of the walkway, paying attention to the Ooken's proximity through her connection to the energy ball while she created another ball of energy to stun it with.

She made the energy ball twinkle invitingly. *Here, Ooken Ooken Ooken. Come and get the shiny...*

The Ooken's chin jutted over the edge, the tentacles around its mouth writhing to taste the air around the mysterious light source. It turned its head from side to side, its pupils dilating and expanding as the ball danced for it.

Bethany Anne flicked her fingers and the energy ball exploded into a sonic wave, preventing the Ooken from calling the hive mind for help. She released the other energy ball at the same time with the intention of landing it on the Ooken's jaw.

However, the Ooken jerked its head back when the bait exploded, and the second energy ball shattered the crystal above its head instead.

Fuckdammit!

A failure is still an attempt, Michael told her lightly.

The Ooken screeched, clawing at its head in a vain attempt to dislodge the ringing in its skull.

Don't say another fucking word, Bethany Anne retorted as the Ooken screeched in distress.

I hadn't intended to, Michael assured her. *However, my Ooken is about to pass out from lack of oxygen so you might want to get a move on.*

Bethany Anne laughed. *Nice trick, Mysting into its lungs. You do know that they can breathe through their suckers?*

I do, and I'm having the damndest time keeping them all covered.

Bethany Anne's right hand found the hilt of her katana as she formed another energy ball in her left. **Okayyy, so being fancy wasn't the way to go. I can admit when I'm wrong.**

Michael feigned surprise. *You can?*

Bethany Anne's mouth twitched as she left the cover of the foundation. **A lesser woman would be annoyed by that and make you sleep on the couch tonight.**

My love, you could never be a lesser anything, Michael assured her.

Bethany Anne chuckled in Michael's mind. **Being smooth isn't likely to get you out of the doghouse, but I can understand why you might be confused since I'm so rarely wrong. Consider yourself forgiven.**

Michael's laughter cut off suddenly, replaced by a soft curse. *Consider yourself a distraction. I just killed my Ooken.*

Bethany Anne wound up for the jump. **That's priceless! Exactly what you get for being so big-headed. Got to go.** What she *didn't* tell Michael was that the Ooken had spotted her. **Good luck finding another one and getting back to the curtain before I do.**

The Ooken screeched and lunged from the walkway above, wrapping its tail tentacle around a protrusion in the crystal. It came at Bethany Anne tentacles-first, all three rows of razor-sharp teeth in its mouth dripping toxin-laden saliva and alien bacteria.

Bethany Anne had no intention whatsoever of getting bitten, either by those teeth *or* the ones lining its suckers. She dropped into a roll, turning as she came to her feet to fend off the attack with an upswing and a practiced flick of her left wrist to release the energy ball.

The Ooken screeched and retracted its tentacles when her katana sheared the tip from the largest. The crystal creaked under the pressure but did not give as the Ooken put its full weight on its tail, turning its body from side to side to ascertain the damage the energy ball had done.

It screeched again and swung around for another attack.

Bethany Anne pulled six sparks of energy, forming arrowheads from them as they hurtled toward the Ooken flying toward her. She was rewarded with a pained screech and a shower of dust when one of the energy darts passed right through the Ooken's tail, shattering the opalescent crystal it was gripping with the thick tentacle.

The Ooken plummeted toward her, spraying the ground with thick, dark blood from the stump where its tail had been a few seconds previously. It struggled to get to its feet, its claws scrabbling uselessly against the slick crystal.

Bethany Anne avoided the blood as she walked the three steps to the crumpled heap of Ooken. It stirred as she bent to pick it up, stilling again when she punched it in the head.

She gripped the Ooken by the nest of small, tender tentacles around its mouth and the two large ones protruding from its back, then hoisted it over her shoulders before leaving the tower.

Michael was nowhere to be seen when Bethany Anne arrived at the nano-curtain with her get-out-of-instant-death-free card over her shoulder.

His armor sat empty ten feet from the archway.

Bethany Anne dropped the unconscious Ooken to the floor. *Looks like victory is mine.*

Michael strode into the lab dragging a fifteen-foot Ooken, its tentacles trailing behind him like a grotesque wedding train. His shirt was torn, revealing drying blood from freshly healed injuries. *You made the better choice. Adapting to the situation turned out to be somewhat challenging.*

Bethany Anne looked at Michael's barely-breathing Ooken. *How many did you kill before you managed to knock this one out?*

Three, Michael admitted. He nodded at the smaller Ooken by Bethany Anne's feet. *Nice catch.*

Bethany Anne raised an eyebrow. *What's that guys are always saying about size not mattering?*

Michael shrugged his Ooken onto the floor. *I wouldn't care to comment on matters that don't concern me.* He knelt by his Ooken and placed a hand on its forehead ridges.

Bethany Anne stood guard, watching for the slightest twitch from the two Ooken. *Do you need them awake for this?*

Michael shook his head. *No, since they can't fight us if they don't know we're in there.* He was quiet for a moment while he and TOM rummaged through the Ooken's mind.

Well? Bethany Anne asked when Michael looked up again.

It's simpler than I expected. If our Ooken go through first, the curtain will read us as prisoners and refrain from attacking our DNA.

Prisoners? Bethany Anne narrowed her eyes, wishing the Ooken before her weren't vital to the rescue. *The*

191

fuckers are keeping more than the Collective down there? I know we can't kill them, but do they have to be conscious, or will carrying them ahead of us work?

Michael closed his eyes, concentrating on finding the information in the Ooken' heads. *I can't be certain.*

An alarm began to shriek, followed by another.

The alarm may not be for us, Michael speculated. *It could be that the fleet has arrived.*

Bethany Anne and Michael shared a glance as the first two alarms were joined by a whole chorus of blaring klaxons. *There's only one way to find out. I don't want to be here if the Ooken have worked out where we are. There are prisoners to be freed before we can destroy this fucking abomination.*

The ground beneath their feet shook.

I'm going to say that's the fleet knocking to come in. Bethany Anne bent to pick up her Ooken from the floor but paused when the platform shuddered from the force of another impact on the shields. *Wait, I want to talk to Alexis and Gabriel before we go.*

Michael nodded. *Can you reach them from this far away?*

Bethany Anne raised an eyebrow as she searched for her children's minds. *I grew them cell by cell inside my body. I can reach them from wherever I am.*

Alexis was the first to answer. *Hi, Mom! Did you and Dad win already?*

Bethany Anne chuckled. *Not yet, sweetheart. The fleet has just arrived, we think.*

Gabriel spoke over Bethany Anne. *Are you and Dad in trouble?*

Your father and I are fine, Bethany Anne assured them.

We found some prisoners who need to be rescued. I just wanted to hear your voices before we help them.

Tell the children I love them, Michael cut in. *I can barely hear them.*

Your father sends his love too.

I can hear him just fine, Alexis replied.

Bethany Anne narrowed her eyes at the distant note in her daughter's voice. **I hope you're not trying to read my mind right now, Alexis.**

Gabriel chipped in, distracting her for the moment. *Hurry up and kick the Ooken' asses, Mom! Aunt Tabbie's going to kill us all with her boot camp.*

Bethany Anne raised an eyebrow. **We will. You can think about your forfeit for that poor language when your father and I get home.**

Mooooom!

Bethany Anne smirked at Gabriel's groan. **You've had this coming for a long time, son. Get creative or suffer the consequences, and don't say I never warned you about payback all the times you took joy in my slip-ups.**

Alexis snickered as Gabriel continued to grumble.

The ground shook under Bethany Anne's feet again. **We have to go. I love you both, and we'll be home soon.**

She dropped the link and looked at Michael with concern. **That link was between the children and me. How could Alexis hear you?**

I heard her too. Michael pressed his lips together. *It's not surprising that she would be a natural amplifier since her mental abilities have always been a challenge for us to restrain. The question is, what did she* see? He picked up his Ooken. *The sooner we're home, the sooner I can relax.*

Bethany Anne shook her head at the idea of Michael relaxing as she adjusted her hold on her Ooken so it was in an upright position. *Don't worry, Gabriel and Alexis are safe on Devon. Tabitha won't let them out of her sight.*

Devon, First City, The Hexagon

Gabriel spoke first when Bethany Anne dropped the link. *That was weird. Why would Mom call us out of the blue like that?*

Alexis didn't reply.

Gabriel touched her arm. *Alexis? What's wrong, are you okay?*

Alexis glanced at Tabitha, who was waving them back to class. *I saw where they are in Mom's mind. The Ooken... There's so many of them. I don't want to go back to class, Gabriel.*

Gabriel's brow furrowed. *One minute.* He ran over to Tabitha, returning a moment later. *I told her you were upset by Mom's call. She said to get some rest and feel better.*

Trey had paused in his kata when Alexis broke away. Gabriel gave him a thumbs-up and wrapped his arm around Alexis' shoulders. "Come on, I'll take you back to the ship."

Alexis nodded glumly, allowing Gabriel to steer her out of the training area. *That's a good idea, but I can take myself, thanks.*

Gabriel waited until they were out of sight before speaking again. *We're not going back to the ship so you can rest. We're going to go help Mom and Dad.*

Alexis shrugged off Gabriel's arm. *Are you crazy?* She

looked at her brother as though he were a Coke short of a six-pack. *We can't go tearing off to who-knows-where! I'm worried, but I know Mom and Dad have it handled.*

Gabriel raised an eyebrow. *Why else did Mom call us? Trust me, when we get to Mom and Dad, they'll be glad to see us. All we have to do is persuade Izanami to take the ship out.*

You have a point. Alexis sighed, seeing endless crystal towers again when she closed her eyes. *Okay, I'm in.*

That's the spirit, Gabriel replied, making the turn for the elevator down to the underground hangar.

Are you sure we're ready for this? Alexis fretted as they stood under the camera to be identified by Winstanley. *It's not training or the game. It's a real war.*

Sure I'm sure, Gabriel told her. The elevator arrived at their floor and he stepped in, looking back at Alexis. *All we do is train, so we're ready. We've got our armor, and it's virtually Ooken-proof.*

Okay... Alexis led them out into the hangar when the elevator doors opened again. *Mom and Dad will be mad we snuck out, but if there are as many Ooken as you say, they really might need us as backup.*

Gabriel leaned over Alexis' shoulder to look in on her holo as they walked into the brightly-lit underground space. *Look, I don't like sneaking around any more than you do. If it helps, pretend we're doing it as a covert ops assignment. Call Izanami, and follow my lead.*

They paused for a moment while Alexis tapped her wrist holo to open a video link to the ship. Gabriel flashed a subdued grin when the AI's avatar appeared above the screen in miniature. "Hey, it's the prettiest, most deadly AI in the fleet."

Izanami arched an eyebrow. "What mischief are you two up to this time?"

Gabriel smiled disarmingly. "No mischief. We're on our way to the ship to pick up our armor."

Alexis nodded. "Can you get the crates out of storage, please?"

Izanami tilted her head. "Your battle armor?"

"Yes, please," Gabriel answered.

Alexis smiled. "Thank you, Izanami." She grabbed Gabriel by the sleeve the instant the tiny hologram vanished. *What's your play here?* she demanded. *I'm not taking another step until you tell me how you intend to get Izanami to take us to the Ooken planet.*

Gabriel grinned. *Relax, all we have to do is talk about how many Ooken there are and how concerned we are for Mom's safety. Izanami is imprinted on Mom now, and she will get so angry that she'll forget we're onboard and tear off to her rescue.*

Alexis rolled her eyes at how pleased with himself Gabriel sounded. *It's not the worst plan. Izanami is very protective of Mom.* She began tapping on her wrist holo again.

Gabriel shuffled on the spot. *What are you doing? We need to get going.*

Just a second...aaand...done. You'll thank me, I promise. Alexis set off across the hangar. *Come on, then. We haven't got all day.*

Gabriel narrowed his eyes at his sister. *What did you do?*

Alexis grinned. *I got something from network command to help us. I have a better idea than trying to lie to Izanami.*

I didn't say we should lie to her, Gabriel protested. *What do you think we should go with?*

Um, how about the truth? Alexis dropped the grin when they neared the ship and she spotted the ramp descending in preparation for their arrival. *There's no need for deception. Well, not a* lot *of deception. Maybe an exaggeration to smooth the way, but nothing that will get us in trouble. It's for a good reason, and besides, what you're planning is much, much worse.*

Gabriel shrugged. *Fine, but if you think either of us is getting out of this without being punished, you're kidding yourself.*

Alexis snorted. *Want to bet? We're* both *going to be in a world of hurt when it's over. I'm relying on Mom and Dad being so mad at you for stealing the ship that when they decide to cut their losses and kill one of us as an object lesson, I get to live.*

That's never going to happen, Gabriel shot back. *You know I'm the favorite. I just want you to know that when Mom finally settles on somewhere to live, I'll really enjoy having all that space to myself.*

Alexis snickered and punched her brother in the arm. *Yeah, right. You'd be so lost without me it would be tragic to watch.*

They mounted the ramp and headed straight to the armory, where Izanami's avatar waited for them at the door. "I did not realize you had full-contact combat on your schedule today," she remarked.

Alexis looked up at Izanami with wide eyes. "We don't. Can you keep a secret?"

Izanami's aura flickered. "That would depend on whether the secret being kept would result in someone being harmed."

Alexis shook her head. "No, nothing like that. I broke the rules about spying, and I wish I hadn't."

Izanami tilted her head. "I am not surprised, child. I will hear your secret."

Alexis' bottom lip trembled slightly. "Mom called us, and I peeked and saw where she and Dad are. She said that they're fine, but I know they're in trouble. Then I hacked network command to find out what's really happening out there. It's bad, Izanami."

Gabriel nodded. "Alexis was upset and Tabitha told her to rest, but I thought it would be better to train."

Izanami froze. "The Queen is not in the Etheric?"

Alexis shook her head. "She's on a planet filled with so many Ooken I couldn't count them."

Izanami's avatar rippled, the flash of light she emitted turning her armor blood-red for a split second.

Gabriel glanced at the armory door. "Can we get our armor?"

"Yes, children." The armory door began to cycle open and Izanami winked out of existence, leaving Alexis and Gabriel by themselves.

They entered the armory and found their armor crates waiting on one of the long benches.

Gabriel looked at his sister uncertainly as they opened their crates. *Do you think it worked?*

If it didn't, this will. Alexis removed her wrist holo. She set it down on the bench to display the video and turned to her crate. "It's the scout ship footage from the Ooken planet. Look how the defenses are positioned; there's no easy way through for the fleet. Even the *Ballista* will struggle to hurl a rock large enough to get to the inner atmosphere intact."

Gabriel frowned at the projected scene. "I bet Izanami could get through. This is the best ship in the fleet."

Alexis gave her brother a mental nudge. *Subtle.*

I'm just putting the idea out there, Gabriel assured her.

Izanami reappeared in a burst of red pixels. "Phyrro informed me of your plan to take part in the battle. Did you really think I would lose my temper and forget you were here?"

Alexis sighed and hung her head. "No, Izanami."

"Sorry we tried to trick you, Izanami." Gabriel dropped his chest plate back into the crate. "But you have to understand that we're worried about Mom and Dad being on that planet without us there to back them up."

"Your parents were very clear about the two of you remaining here while they are off-world," Izanami reminded them. "It's important to them to know you are both safe while they fight."

Gabriel grunted. "Yeah, and if it was up to Mom, we would stay nice and safe for*ever.*"

"I hate to admit it, but he's got a point." Alexis shrugged when Izanami's stern gaze landed on her. "We've been training practically since we could walk. Fighting is what we are *made* for. How else can we prove we're ready if Mom and Dad are too afraid we'll get hurt to give us a chance? None of what we said was a lie. They're in danger."

Gabriel banged his crate with a hand. "We had to do *something.* Mom and Dad are going to be facing hundreds of thousands of Ooken alone if the fleet can't get through, and *you* could get to them."

"There's something I didn't tell Gabriel earlier," Alexis admitted. "Mom was thinking about Kurtherians."

Izanami remained silent as Alexis and Gabriel continued to argue their case. She *could* get Alexis and Gabriel to their mother and father. A quick check of Alexis' holo had given her the coordinates of the Ooken planet, and it was within range of her ship's Gate drive.

Further inquiries had given her the details of the impending battle and her Queen's situation. It did not look at all promising from a mathematical perspective, but then Bethany Anne was forever one to defy the odds.

Her decision came down to one factor: would the twins benefit from being prevented from making this choice for themselves? The answer to that was beyond her ability to fathom, but her decision was already made.

Izanami held up a hand to halt the twins' persuasion. "Enough. I will take you to your parents."

15

Ooken Sky Base, Laboratory

Bethany Anne hesitated a fraction from the nano-curtain.

Second thoughts? Michael asked.

She frowned. ***No. Just...we might not get out of this. It's been a long fucking time since I had to face the prospect that I might not survive. The thought of orphaning our children is frankly the most frightening vision in my life.***

Michael didn't conceal his own concerns, but like Bethany Anne, he preferred to reach for dark humor in these moments. *I would have thought that would have been awarded to the revelation of the UnknownWorld.*

Bethany Anne snickered. ***What, that bunch of overgrown superpowered toddlers? Don't imagine they rattled me for a second. There was a reason you chose me to replace you, you sneaky bastard. You'd been parenting them so long you wanted the world's longest nap.***

Some of those overgrown toddlers are your closest friends, Michael reminded her.

Bethany Anne held the Ooken in front of her like a shield. *I stand by my statement. They needed a nanny. Nathan still needs one; just ask Ecaterina.* She lifted the Ooken's hand and pressed it to the nano-curtain. *ADAM, is it working?*

>>You're not screaming, so I'll say yes.<<

Bethany Anne raised an eyebrow. *I hope you're not still sulking over the body thing.*

>>No,<< ADAM replied tersely. >>I'm having a hard time convincing the Pods to stay closed.<<

Do what you can. Bethany Anne restored Michael's connection to their link and turned her attention to her other ridealong. *TOM, why are the Pod-docs opening?*

The Pod-docs are opening? Michael asked.

Mmhmm, unless ADAM can prevent it. TOM is about to tell me how it came about.

Not because of anything we did. TOM huffed. **ADAM is causing delays across every tower, as well as tracing the location of whoever sent the order to rouse every Ooken on the platform.**

Michael frowned in consideration. *Are the Ooken aware of our presence?*

Not yet, TOM confirmed. **However, remaining here might leave you in a tight spot. The Pod-docs *will* open. It's only a matter of time.**

Bethany Anne tightened her grip on the Ooken and stepped into the passage. *Then I suggest we hurry the fuck up before I'm forced to make so much of a mess it puts me off calamari forever.*

Her body tingled as she passed through the nanocytes. *Are you feeling that?* she asked Michael.

All the way to the marrow of my bones, he replied. *I have to agree, this is not the most comfortable situation to be in.*

We should be grateful the Ooken don't know how to use half of the tech they have. Bethany Anne almost slipped on a slick patch as they descended the twisting tube. **Why are these lairs always underground? Is there some realtor to the evil who finds these places? It almost makes me think fondly of trashing mansions and palaces like we did in the good old days.**

Her Ooken twitched when a long, desperate cry echoed through the mental space. It opened its eyes a crack when more pained wails joined the first.

Bethany Anne slammed her fist into its nose ridges, sending it back to sleep instantly.

Don't you have night-night cartridges for your JD Special? Michael asked.

Bethany Anne shrugged. **Yes. I just didn't feel the need to waste one on this sorry mothersucker.**

Michael chuckled dryly. *Fair enough.* He stepped over the wet spot as he passed it. *Did you look to see what you stepped in?*

No, Bethany Anne answered without looking back. **Why?**

It appears to be a puddle of the substance.

I don't think stopping to investigate inside the nano-curtain would be the best idea.

Michael nodded, continuing to press through resistance that wasn't there. *I agree wholeheartedly. Nevertheless, we should not leave without obtaining a workable amount of the substance if we get the opportunity.*

It would alleviate the need to return to Moen, Bethany

Anne agreed. She cautiously felt ahead with her mind. *The first thing on the list is getting the prisoners out of here. I have a feeling we'll have another opportunity to collect samples once we reach the end of this passage.*

Two turns later, the passage ended in a chamber lit by the same glow inside the walls as the rooms above. The only ways out were back the way they'd just come or through another darkened archway.

Bethany Anne formed a trio of energy balls over her left hand to light the chamber. *The smell of water is stronger down here,* she murmured. *We're getting close to where the prisoners are being kept.*

Michael flexed the hand not holding his Ooken to activate his gauntlet. *Looks like there's only one way to go.*

Looks like it. Bethany Anne released two of the energy balls to float a short way in front of them and readied her katana in her free hand.

They walked side by side through the archway into an expansive cavern.

Which was empty.

Michael winced at the echo their boots made on the polished crystal. *Where are the Ooken?*

Bethany Anne had different concerns. *Fuck the Ooken. Where are the prisoners?*

Michael glanced around, looking for another exit. *You said we were getting close. Maybe the prisoners are in the next chamber?*

Bethany Anne shook her head and dropped her Ooken. *I can feel them. They're in this one.*

Michael frowned in confusion. *Then where are they?*

She waved him off and walked toward the center of the huge, empty space. *Shhh. I'm listening.*

You do that, Michael told her, dropping his Ooken next to Bethany Anne's. *I'm going to search for another way out of here.* His armor slumped as he Mysted out of it.

Bethany Anne's eyes drifted over the pattern of light in the walls as she walked, her focus on reaching out to the Collective mind.

It took a few moments to breathe away her frustration. She knew the prisoners were here somewhere. Finding them was simply a matter of attaining a clear state of mind.

She opened her mind a fraction as the storm inside her was quelled by her determination to calm her emotions. *Can you hear me?*

The Collective ceased their dirge and shied away from Bethany Anne's mind.

I'm your ally, Bethany Anne continued, *Do you understand what an ally is? A friend?*

Apparently not, since there was no response from the Collective.

Bethany Anne's heart ached for them and her chin dropped to her chest, her eyes closed against the wave of sadness that washed through her. Any other time, she would have forced the situation. However, all she could do was shed tears for beings too broken to see the good in anything.

"*Please.*" Her voice cracked, her hold on her emotions slipping as she spoke. "I want to help, but I can't find you."

She waited as the silence stretched, hoping that just one of the prisoners would see that she was there to save them from the horrors they had suffered. *TOM, can they hear me?*

I assume so, he replied.

A voice came from beneath Bethany Anne's feet.

What do you want from us?

Bethany Anne opened her eyes and found herself meeting the blind eyes of a Collective through the floor. As always, she was jarred by how they could look so different from the Ooken despite wearing the same face. She dropped to her knees and placed a hand to the floor. *I don't want anything from you. I want to get you out of there.*

The tentacles around the Collective's mouth wavered in the water. *Leave us. We will not be tricked by the lies of a god again.*

Bethany Anne almost laughed aloud. *I'm a bitch to cross, but I'm no god. My name is Bethany Anne, and I'm human...mostly.*

Much stronger gods than you have taken ownership of our destiny.

Bethany Anne counted seven more voices as dark chuckles rippled through the Collective mind. *I told you, I'm no god. And neither are the Seven, no matter how thoroughly they believe their own bullshit. I should know. I've spent two hundred years exterminating them.*

A baby god, then, the being corrected, *since you have barely seen two centuries. You cannot save us, Baby God.* There was silence for a moment. The being below attached itself to the underside of the floor, the tiny serrated teeth in its suckers gripping the crystal for purchase. *We have agreed to speak with you. I will be the conduit.*

Bethany Anne's eyebrow shot up. *In my experience,*

those claiming to be gods are usually nothing more than pain-in-the-ass Kurtherians in need of my attention. Are you saying you know of one?

We know of many, the Collective replied as one. *The gods of old came to our world and tricked us with promises of Ascension. By the time we discovered the danger and fought back, it was too late.*

You would be surprised how many times I've heard a similar story. Bethany Anne sat down beside the conduit and crossed her legs. *Eradicating the Seven has already taken up too fucking much of my life.*

There are many who have suffered at the hands of the gods, the conduit told her resignedly. *We can only bend to their will or die faster.*

There are also many Kurtherians who aren't breathing well enough to continue fucking around with innocent civilizations, Bethany Anne retorted. *Let me show you what I do to your "gods."*

She gave them what they needed to see.

The eight Collective gathered around like children at story time while she showed them her memories of the death of every Kurtherian who had met their end at her hand so far.

The conduit spoke from the mass of undulating tentacles. *Gods do not die. Kurtherians bleed and die like any other being.*

That's right, Bethany Anne affirmed. *Where do you come from? What did they do to you? I've come across one of your kind before, isolated and dying. I honored their last request, and they shared their memory with me. I'm happy to share that with you once we get you out of that tank.*

We thank you for that. The conduit's tone became melancholy. *We lived in peace in the giant kelp forests of our world. The water was sweet and clear, and we spent our lives contemplating the key to Ascension.*

Sounds perfect, Bethany Anne murmured.

It was, the conduit agreed. *Until the Kurtherians came. They took us far from home, imprisoned us in their ships, and cut us off from our kin and the Mind. We are scattered and alone now. The gods only wanted us for our genetic material. They tear us apart, corrupt us with the DNA of other species they have here, and remake us into the abominations that enslave us.*

Bethany Anne covered the crystal over the conduit's tentacle with a hand. **The Ooken.**

We see the Corrupt in your mind. You name them differently?

Bethany Anne pursed her lips. **Human trait, I'm afraid. Nicknames are kind of our thing. You'll have to get used to the concept of being named.**

We will accept these nicknames from you, Baby God, the conduit replied. A ripple of alarm went through its body. *The Corrupt are beginning to wake.*

Don't worry about it. Bethany Anne got to her feet. **Will you allow me to help? I have a ship here that can take you home, just as soon as I work out where that is and make it safe for your people.**

The conduit's tentacles rippled. *It is too late for that. The seas were polluted in the war, the kelp killed.*

Bethany Anne nodded as she considered where she could possibly house nine beings the general size and shape of krakens. **Then we will find a new world for you to settle, somewhere I can protect you easily. You are welcome to** *stay aboard one of my stations that is fitted to accommodate water or vacuum dwellers until we find a suitable planet.*

The harmony of voices murmured among themselves for a moment before the conduit spoke again. *Maybe you are not a baby god after all. We thank you, Bethany Anne.*

Don't mention it. Bethany Anne turned at the sound of Michael's footsteps behind her. ***Did you find a way out?***

Michael indicated the western side of the cavern. *There's an upper level. It's sealed, but there's definitely someone in there.*

Bethany Anne narrowed her eyes. *"Someone?" Not an Ooken?*

Not an Ooken. Michael confirmed. He lifted his hands. *Whoever it is, they were capable of blocking me. What about you? Did you find the prisoners?*

Bethany Anne swept a hand at the mass of tentacles beneath his feet. ***All eight of them, and they're not just being held prisoner. They're trapped.***

We have a similar issue, TOM added, cutting in. **One of the captured Ooken has just expired.**

Bethany Anne spun to look at the two Ooken they'd left by the entrance. Michael's was twitching in its sleep. Hers lay still, its head in a slow-spreading puddle of yellowish fluid.

She turned to Michael. ***Maybe the night-night round wouldn't have been such a waste after all.***

Michael grimaced. *I'm going to guess the second punch to its head did it.*

Of-fucking-course it did. Bethany Anne sighed at the problem she'd made for herself. ***Fuckdammit, how do we both get out of here now?***

There is still another possible exit, Michael reminded her.

Bethany Anne waved over her shoulder as she turned away from the dead Ooken. ***Okay, here's what we're going to do. You get hold of Bart and have him send down the* Polaris *to pick up our friends here.***

Michael nodded. *It would be nice if they brought us a fresh Ooken to replace the dead one so we can get out of here in one piece*

Bethany Anne held out her hand, and an energy ball appeared briefly over her palm. ***That shouldn't be a problem. I believe the solution is behind that door.***

Michael glanced at a hair-fine crack in the floor. *What's your plan to get the Collective out of there and onto the ship?*

Bethany Anne snorted. ***Give me a second. I haven't gotten that far yet.*** She increased the intensity of the energy ball as the whole cavern shook, showering dust all around them. ***This minute my plan is to introduce my size seven to that door and make whoever is behind it shut down the nano-curtain.***

Michael pointed out the crack, which was spreading alongside them as they walked. *We should hurry up, whatever we're doing. This crystal is reacting poorly to the impact vibrations resonating from the shield. If it disintegrates, we're going for an unexpected swim.*

Bethany Anne picked up her pace. ***I have no intention of allowing that to happen.***

Michael showed Bethany Anne to the door, an iron rectangle cut into the crystal that came up to Bethany Anne's chest. *No Ooken would fit through there.*

Bethany Anne tossed the energy ball from one hand to

the other. *There's only one way to find out who does,* she replied, throwing the energy ball.

The door melted on impact, the resulting spray of molten iron turning the resulting hole cherry red for a brief second.

It was enough to save their lives.

GET BACK! TOM screamed as another nano-curtain came down on the other side of the hole.

Bethany Anne screamed in frustration and blasted the curtain with Etheric energy. "You fucking coward! Stop hiding behind your tech and *FACE ME!*"

Kurtherian, TOM growled.

A silhouette passed across the hole.

Bethany Anne stamped her foot. *FUCK! Michael, there's a Kurtherian in there.*

Michael's hands clenched into fists. *There isn't a lot we can do with that curtain in place.*

Bethany Anne put a hand to his arm. *There's plenty we can do. Watch my back, and get the* Polaris *here. I'm going to find a way around that curtain. There are still more prisoners somewhere in this building, and I mean to find them.*

Just as soon as I rip that fucker's still-beating heart from its chest.

Ooken System, QBS *ArchAngel II*

The fleet arrived with a bang.

Heavy weapons fire from the ancillary fleet preceded the superdreadnoughts through the Gates they opened simultaneously at strategic points around the sixth planet.

The Ooken were quick to react. Their ships spilled

from the larger platforms, while the smaller satellite stations released thick clouds of drones into the vacuum.

Admiral Thomas was prepared. He paced the bridge, waving his datapad like a baton as he conducted the attack. "ArchAngel, keep that Gate covered. CEREBRO, send out the order to fry those damned drones, and get ready for the dreadnoughts. They won't be far behind. Get the *Ballista* in place and defended."

True to his expectations, a Gate opened between the fleet and the planet. A nest of metallic tentacles burst from the center, crackling with energy.

Admiral Thomas spotted one of his ships between the SD *Ballista* and the Gate. "CEREBRO, get Kael-ven onscreen," he called.

The captain of the *G'laxix Sphaea* was less than pleased to be disturbed. "I'm in the middle of something here."

"Yes," Admiral Thomas replied. "The firing line."

Kael-ven shrugged, unconcerned about his ship's proximity to the Ooken Gate. "Meh, all the Ooken have is those plasma weapons. Damn amateurs. I'd shoot *myself* with plasma." He leaned out of the shot for a few moments. "Watch that Gate."

Admiral Thomas shifted his gaze to the Gate and the emerging dreadnought. "What now?"

Kael-ven lifted a finger. "Kiel?"

A moment later, the Gate vanished in a flash of light, nothing left of it or the Ooken ship but a cloud of dust that was stolen by the solar wind.

Admiral Thomas picked his jaw up. "What in Heaven's name was *that?*"

"You're looking at the prototype for our latest weapons

system." Kael-ven chuckled. "We took shore leave at the *Helena* after we were done at Moen, and Jean gave us a bunch of stuff she has in mind for the new ships to test."

The Admiral threw his hands up. "Why is it that nobody ever thinks to tell me about these developments? I'm only the damn admiral, for crying out loud. It's not like I need to know what I've got to fight with or anything."

Kael-ven chuckled. "Jean told us you'd say that, and to tell you that you'll get yours soon enough."

"Did she now?" Admiral Thomas wasn't sure if that was a threat or a promise. Had he offended her? He hoped not. That shit could get painful.

"She also said a few things that don't bear repeating, sir," Kiel piped up offscreen, clarifying everything by exactly zero percent.

"I'll just bet she did." Admiral Thomas leaned over his console as CEREBRO spoke in his ear. "You have drones inbound. Stay safe, now." He returned Kael-ven's nod and cut the call. "CEREBRO, sitrep."

The holomap lit up to illustrate CEREBRO's rundown of the fleet's progress. "The *Defiant*, the *Wright*, and the *Queen's Fury* were all headed for attack point seven when the Ooken opened a Gate close to point six."

Admiral Thomas could see no markers indicating the Shinigami-class ships on the map. "Let me guess: they all dropped off."

"Within seconds of the Gate's activation," CEREBRO confirmed. "Wait, I have them...and they're gone again. Along with the Gate and the four destroyers that made it through."

Admiral Thomas frowned. "Damn, they're good. Never

mind the Bitches, CEREBRO. They can operate just fine without us. Tell me about something we *can* track. Where are the other ships?"

"The *Ballista* and the *G'laxix Sphaea* are holding by the planet," CEREBRO replied. "The *Astraea* and the *Adrastea* are taking care of a cluster of Gates between points three and four."

A flash of light washed over the viewscreen, and the floor beneath the Admiral's feet hitched. "ArchAngel, report."

ArchAngel replaced the outside view on the screen. "The Ooken have worked out our shield phase frequencies," the AI replied. "They got a fragmentary explosive through. We have hull breaches on decks Three to Five. I have dispatched repair bots ahead of the maintenance crews to assess the damage."

Admiral Thomas had no time for commiseration. He scrolled through the preliminary damage reports as they started coming in from the bots. "Were the weapons affected?"

ArchAngel looked off to the side. "Weapons are online and still fully functional, Admiral."

"Then keep pounding the crap out of them." He dropped into his chair, watching the *Ballista* fling another chunk of asteroid into the planet's gaseous atmosphere while ArchAngel loosed a steady blanket of kinetics, explosives, and energy discharges at the enemy around the scuppered ship.

The impact from the asteroid displaced high loops of gas as large as the superdreadnought itself, lighting the battlefield a ghostly orange as the gas refracted light from the local star.

Admiral Thomas knuckled his eyes to rub away the bright coronas that remained in his vision. "CEREBRO, how many times have they missed the shield?"

"None," CEREBRO replied. "However, due to the acidity of the atmosphere, our asteroids are more the size of baseballs by the time they impact. Still effective, but hardly the same power."

Admiral Thomas kept his gaze on the screen. "What's your recommendation?"

CEREBRO's answer held a note of amusement. "There's nothing else to do, Admiral. We're gonna need a bigger asteroid."

Admiral Thomas groaned. "Did someone spill coffee in one of your cradles, CEREBRO? Your understanding of humor appears to be malfunctioning horribly."

CEREBRO made a raspberry sound. "Killjoy. You have an incoming transmission from the platform."

"Put it through," he told the EI group. "Bethany Anne?"

Michael's voice came crackling from the speaker. "Sorry to disappoint you, Bart. We're in a tight spot. Technology we haven't encountered before. Bethany Anne is requesting the *Polaris*, plus pickup for us two plus eight of the Collective and all the other prisoners we expect to find before we're done."

Admiral Thomas grimaced at the viewscreen. "The moment we get through the shield, I'll have it there waiting."

Michael sighed. "What's the delay with the shield? If

those towers remain operational much longer, things are going to get hairy down here." He paused. "And tentacle-y."

"Too late," Bethany Anne cut in. "ADAM can't keep them all locked in anymore. I've pulled him back to work with us on the nano-curtain since we're already trapped in here."

Admiral Thomas sucked in a breath. "Trapped? How deep in the shit are you?"

"Pretty fucking deep," Bethany Anne replied. "But not so deep we can't pull it back. We'll keep working on getting out of here. Just make sure you're ready with our ride when we do."

Admiral Thomas got up to resume his pacing. "CERE-BRO, you heard the Queen's orders. Get the *Polaris* into position, and have the fleet focus on getting access to that platform. We need to get to Bethany Anne and Michael."

16

Ooken Sky Base, Cavern

Bethany Anne, TOM interrupted, **I don't think we have much time.**

Bethany Anne narrowed her eyes at the hole in the wall, leaving Michael to figure it out. *ADAM, the nano-curtain?*

>>**This is...there's no way into the programming.**<<

The Kurtherian passed the hole again, leaving Bethany Anne no clearer on what species the diminutive figure was wearing beneath its robe.

Michael cut in, *Can't you create a backdoor or something?*

>>**I don't think so,**<< ADAM admitted. >>**There's nothing to work with. Whoever wrote this didn't make any mistakes.**<<

TOM's concern was clear in his tone. **I was afraid of this.**

Everybody makes mistakes. Bethany Anne frowned. *Get ready, TOM. If ADAM can't make a backdoor into the curtain, we're going to make one for him.*

TOM sighed. **If I had an eyebrow. Just one...**

Bethany Anne raised her own. *You'd look like an ass, that's what. Who the fuck wants a monobrow? Concentrate on your cousin in there.*

Do you know how offensive that is? TOM asked.

I assume very. Bethany Anne snickered. *If you can't laugh in the face of death, what can you do?* She probed at the Kurtherian's consciousness with her own. *Hey, asshole! Whose body are you treating like fucking couture right now?*

The Kurtherian ignored her, although Bethany Anne felt a ripple of amusement at the edges of its mind.

You're so brave, hiding behind your little curtain. When I get through it, I'm going to tear your wormy ass out of your host and grind you to paste under my heel. Bethany Anne adjusted her position to take the pressure of her left knee from her right ankle. *I have to learn to meditate standing up. TOM, do we know who we're working with yet?*

Hmmm. TOM considered the options. **Not aggressive or very talkative. Not arrogant enough to brag.** He made a sound that could only be described as a gasp when the Kurtherian came over to the curtain to stare at Bethany Anne, who was sitting cross-legged in front of the nano-curtain. **Holy** *fuckballs*!

Bethany Anne got to her feet in an instant. *Shit, TOM. What brought that on?*

TOM's voice wavered as he spoke. **The clan just became the least of our concerns. That's no host body.**

Bethany Anne raised her chin, meeting the Kurtherian's glowing red eyes with a dazzling flash from her own. *It's a real Kurtherian? I've always wondered what you guys looked like when you weren't wearing other people like meat puppets. You guys don't wear clothes?*

We wear clothes. He stopped chuckling when a flash of light from behind the curtain raked her vision.

TOM cursed softly. **Bethany Anne, it's gone.**

Bethany Anne glared into the returning gloom as the afterimage faded, confirming her certainty that the room beyond had been vacated. *Fuck it! Inches! It was fucking inches away from me!* She stamped her foot in frustration. *I want that curtain tech, and I want a way around it so this doesn't happen again.*

Michael glanced down, detecting an almost indiscernible reverberation in the crystal under their feet. *Do that again.*

Do what again? Bethany Anne asked.

Michael stamped his foot. *Did you feel that? The space beneath us is hollow.*

Bethany Anne raised an eyebrow and confirmed it by stamping again.

NO! Michael's eyes widened, his hand coming up a fraction too late.

A deep crack reverberated from the walls, and the ground beneath their feet parted.

Bethany Anne dropped almost all of her weight immediately when they plummeted to the level below, halting her plunge and floating down at a more survivable pace.

She dropped the last step to the ground as Michael landed beside her in a crouch, sending up a cloud of pulverized crystal. **We aren't the only living beings down here. We must be close to where the other prisoners are being kept.**

Michael got up from his crouch and brushed off the dust as he glanced around. *This looks like it leads toward the cavern on the upper level. Perhaps we will find a way to free the trapped Collective without endangering them.*

Only one way to find out. Bethany Anne walked in the direction of the faint heartbeats, energy ball and katana at the ready.

The conduit spoke up in her mind as they neared the end of the passage. *Bethany Anne, there are Corrupt in the over-chamber.*

Bethany Anne exhaled. **Well, isn't that just fan-fucking-tastic?**

What is? Michael asked.

Our friends have just informed me there are Ooken above

us. I'm going to guess the dead one's absence in the hive mind alerted them.

Michael grimaced, anticipation putting a gleam in his eyes. *We expected that. The only surprise is that it took this long. What do you want to do?*

Bethany Anne paused to consider the options. ***Prisoners first, then we'll figure a way out of here.***

Michael glanced back at the hole they'd fallen through. *And when the Ooken realize we are down here?*

Bethany Anne turned her katana in one fluid movement, scribing a circle in the air with her blade before setting off again. ***We'll make sushi out of them.***

The passage they were in began to widen out a short distance ahead, opening up as the wall tapered gradually to the left.

Michael tapped the crystal lightly with a finger. *There's water behind this.*

Mmhmm. The tank. Bethany Anne was distracted by the nearness of the Collective consciousness. ***We're getting to the end of this passage.***

Michael sensed the change in the air currents ahead. *The Collective are directing you?*

No, but they're sticking close by. Bethany Anne's lip curled as the conduit continued to report on the Ooken. ***They want to protect us.***

Michael indicated the culmination of the passage. *Can they tell us what we're going to find behind that door?*

Bethany Anne shook her head. ***We're on our own.***

Not for long, Michael told her. *Bart says they've broken through the outer shield.*

Bethany Anne deactivated her armor's cloaking,

keeping tight control of her energy ball to prevent it from surging when the drain on her energy ceased. *Keep in touch with him. I need my mind clear to maintain the mental link with the Collective.*

Not a problem. Michael tried the door. *It's locked. We might activate another nano-curtain if we blow it open.*

Bethany Anne raised the hand holding her energy ball. *Stand back. I'm going to try something different.* She flicked her hand at the metal slab blocking their way when he moved aside.

The energy vaporized the door without any disturbance to the surrounding crystal, leaving the way ahead clear.

Michael made a face of appreciation at the sudden absence of door. *What did you do there?*

Bethany Anne peered through the hole in the wall at the six-foot-wide crystal walkway. *I was thinking about the nano-curtain and how those nanocytes are programmed to consume matter. I instructed the energy to feed on the metal at the atomic level.* She reactivated her cloaking and stepped cautiously through the door onto the crystal floor beyond with her weapons raised.

Michael turned a spark of energy over above his gauntlet as he followed Bethany Anne through the hole. *You're saying that you coded the energy to consume inorganic matter? How is that possible?*

Bethany Anne raised an eyebrow. *It's more complicated than that, but yes. As to how I did it, fuck if I know. I wanted it, it happened.*

Michael accepted her answer—for now. How Bethany Anne had done something confusing yet appropriate once more would have to wait for a time where they weren't in the bowels of the enemy lair. *Coded it, instructed it. Same thing.*

Bethany Anne scanned the area around them, indicating hollow-eyed beings of different species huddled in cramped cells cut out of the crystal. ***More proof that the Seven are sicker than the drip at the end of a gangrenous dick. Just look at it; this place is laid out like a fucking concentration camp. I don't recognize any of these species, but I'll wipe every fucking Ooken off the face of this platform by hand for what's been done to them.***

Michael glanced around at the forcefields containing the prisoners, noting that a few of them seemed to feel his gaze upon them. *No argument from me. Some of these beings have psionic abilities.*

Either that or heightened ability to sense danger. Bethany Anne halted where the crystal was intersected by a metal walkway with a circular Ooken-sized gap in the cross-section. She leaned over to look at the floor below, then turned her head to look over her shoulder at Michael. ***See? Same equipment as the lab above, but scaled right up. This must be where they cook up the special sauce, with the prisoners as the ingredients.***

Michael looked over the rail. *There's no shortage of Ooken down there.*

Bethany Anne hopped onto the railing and scanned for a suitable landing place, ignoring the easy way down. ***They won't even know we're here. Come on, we need to find a way to free the prisoners.***

Michael perched on the rail beside her. *You're thinking there's some equivalent of a generator room down there?*

You bet that peachy ass of yours I do. Bethany Anne pushed off, landing on top of the machine she'd picked out. *I've got ADAM tracing the route now, and you'll get it in your HUD as soon as I have it.*

Michael's HUD display was overlaid with a filter a moment later that showed ghostly arrows pointing toward Bethany Anne. He made the leap, landing cat-like beside her. *This could be another opportunity to gain some new technical knowledge. Imagine if we combine the nano-curtain technology with the advanced forcefields they've got. That would be game-changing in terms of defense.*

Bethany Anne grinned at Michael's shared passion. *Game-changing isn't the word for it. You're talking about upgrading the BYPS systems, right? That was my first consideration.* She made her way along the machine, careful not to make a sound that would alert the Ooken just meters away from them. *My second was to wonder how I can use the tech offensively once we have it.*

Michael chuckled dryly. *Of course, it was.* He paused for an Ooken to pass between two machines before crossing the gap between them.

Bethany Anne took the lead again when they reached the other side of the factory floor, waiting for Michael to reach her before she lowered herself to the ground. *We're right by the Collective.*

Michael narrowed his eyes in the direction of Bethany Anne's gaze. *Look behind there. Isn't that the tank the Collective are imprisoned in?*

Bethany Anne nodded. *Looks like it.*

Michael lifted a finger to indicate a hair-fine crack

creeping at a snail's pace down the crystal toward them. *Whatever we're doing, we'd better do it fast.*

In Transit, QBS *Izanami*, Pod Bay

Alexis stamped her foot in frustration. "I don't see why we can't get there faster, Gabriel. If we can make lots of small folds in the fabric of space-time to travel, why can't we make a much larger fold and sidestep the Gate system altogether?"

Izanami chuckled. "Give me the drive capacity and your wish is my command, Alexis. Until then, we must be patient. Four Gates to go."

"Four Gates too many," Gabriel grumbled.

Izanami arched an eyebrow at Alexis and Gabriel. "Would the two of you care to get out and walk the rest of the way?"

The twins looked at her in confusion.

Izanami lifted a shoulder. "It seemed like something your parents might say. Be patient, children. If I could push the ship any harder without damaging my Gate drive, I would have done so already."

Alexis abandoned her position over the console with a sigh and put her face in her hands. "I've got a feeling Mom's in trouble, or that she's going to be if we don't get there soon."

Izanami gestured toward the open transport Pod with a tilt of her chin. "We will reach her in time. We are only one Gate away now."

Gabriel rolled his eyes at the precaution but followed the AI's instruction.

Alexis turned to Izanami before climbing in after her brother, her hazel eyes ringed with dark circles. "Don't hesitate, Izanami. Mom is going to need you."

Izanami considered the warning in the seconds it took for the Pod ramp to shut, a hesitation—for her, at least—as her logic processes came to terms with the utter veracity in Alexis' words despite there being no way the child could have seen the future.

As her Gate drive engaged, Izanami sent a probe ahead to contact CEREBRO.

The EI group responded to her hail as the probes crossed the event horizon, transferring the event logs of the siege so far. *Izanami. We were not expecting you.*

Izanami materialized her avatar on the bridge. *My Queen has need of me, and I have the Prince and Princess aboard my ship. Connect me with the Admiral. Their safety must be secured first.*

Alexis cut in, revealing her presence in the mindspace. *Izanami! You agreed to let us help!*

Izanami's eyes flared red. *Do not argue, Alexis.*

Admiral Thomas flinched at the sight of Izanami when he appeared on the viewscreen. "Izanami?"

Izanami inclined her head a fraction, a sharp-fanged grimace on her lips. "Admiral. Send John to my coordinates to collect Alexis and Gabriel. I am here to rescue my Queen."

Admiral Thomas grimaced. "I'll pass your request along."

Izanami's eyes flashed red. "See that you do. I will be waiting, Admiral."

17

Ooken Sky Base, Prison Level

Bethany Anne reached out to the conduit. *How are you guys doing in there?*

The conduit's voice sounded distant to Bethany Anne, as though they were communicating long-distance over a shitty landline. Nevertheless, the victorious note in its voice could not be hidden by mental static. *The Corrupt will not hold us for much longer. The bombardment from above is causing conflicting resonance waves. The integrity of these walls is failing.*

Can you survive out of the water? Bethany Anne asked.

For a short period of time, the conduit replied. *We will provide a distraction for the Corrupt, and you must free the prisoners soon or they will all drown.*

Bethany Anne glanced at the ring of cells above, considering the options. *Michael, that isn't the only crack in the tank. This floor is going to be flooded at any time. We need to switch focus to getting the prisoners out. I have to stay behind.*

What are you thinking? Michael asked. *I can work to get them into the Etheric while you find the substance and assist the Collective with the transfer.*

Bethany Anne didn't register that Michael was agreeing with her. **It's got to be me because there's no way in a month of frozen Sundays I'm allowing you to leave your armor behind.** She frowned as his words sank in. **You don't disagree?**

Not at all. You are harder to kill than me, and I can always get new armor. Michael considered the logistics. *How long have we got?*

Bethany Anne narrowed her eyes. **I'm half-tempted to shoot you just to make sure you're not an Ooken changeling.**

Michael shrugged. *Lives only come in multiples for Buddhists and felines.*

They looked up as a prickle of awareness tingled up the backs of their necks at the same instant. There was an Ooken leaning over the rail.

Then, there was no Ooken—just a bloody rain of flesh over the factory floor.

Bethany Anne threw up her hands as their cover was lost. **Did you forget they can't see us? Or at least they couldn't until you decided to paint the damned place black.**

Michael shrugged. *We need to move it along, right? Job done.* He deactivated his cloaking and braced himself, hesitating when no attack came. *Huh. They're just carrying on with their work.*

Bethany Anne narrowed her eyes, suspicious of the lack of response to the sudden appearance of two blood-coated humans in their midst. **It's like they can't see us.**

Michael walked the six steps to the nearest Ooken and

waved a hand in front of its face. *No reaction whatsoever. Do you think they're programmed in a different way?*

Bethany Anne frowned. **Maybe...** She detected no communication between the workers when she reached out, just a single, solitary purpose. **They're not connected to the hive mind.** She crossed to Michael and poked the Ooken with a finger.

It still did not react, simply continued going about its various tasks as though nothing but the next step existed.

Michael's reply was cut off by two tons of slavering, snarling Ooken landing on him from above.

MICHAEL! Bethany Anne was by his side before she realized she'd moved.

Stay clear. Michael shocked the Ooken with a jolt of electricity, apparently encouraging it to tighten the eight-armed hug it was giving him. *I'm okay, but short of Mysting out of my armor, I can't get free.*

Bethany Anne fought the urge to tear the Ooken off her husband using her teeth and nails. His voice calmed her as always, but only slightly. She reached for the Etheric instead, her unanswered question still hanging in the air. Not into the realm, but the energy around her.

The call was muted here, easy to decline despite its strength. Bethany Anne took control of it all, the symphony hers to conduct. She searched for the notes she wanted to hear.

They were there. Quiet, almost inaudible, but the song was there, contorted into rage inside the Ooken.

Fucking GOT you. Michael, get ready.

Bethany Anne's eyes *blazed*, the flood of light deepening the walls to the color of fresh blood. A wave of her hand

and the Ooken rose into the air, its tentacles shooting out to the sides at impossible angles as it released Michael.

Michael turned as he dropped and landed on his feet. *I'm good.*

I didn't doubt it. Bethany Anne waited until he was clear before lowering the Ooken to the floor. She didn't miss the progress of the cracks in the tank, now running through the wall like veins.

Neither did Michael. *You ready to go?*

Bethany Anne hesitated to begin the countdown to the shitstorm. **The sooner I master stopping time, the better. We never fucking have any.** She sighed and gave in to the inevitable. **Okay. You focus on getting the cells open, and I'll do what I can to find the substance before the walls give.**

Michael went to return to the upper level. *We can't be too far from the controls for the cells now.*

Bethany Anne's mouth curled in a cold smile. **Good. Have fun smashing that shit up. I'm about to get us some answers.** She opened her internal connection to her secret weapons. **ADAM, get inside that fucking abomination and wipe its nanocytes back to factory settings.**

What's your thinking here? TOM asked.

Bethany Anne wrinkled her nose. **Since we're short on time, I'm going to limit this to finding out if the Ooken are sentient beings.**

>>You want to see what it does without its nanocytes running it,<< ADAM surmised. >>They're powering down now.<<

Bethany Anne felt her hold on the Ooken weaken as the dark light leached from its eyes. It dropped to the floor, the impact sending a shockwave through its flaccid muscles.

Bethany Anne felt the complete absence of anything that could be construed as a thought from the quivering mass of directionlessness. *Question answered. Michael, how much time do I have?*

A few more minutes, Michael replied. *The control room was not unguarded.*

She looked out over the procession of moving parts, a thousand arms gripping, cutting, stirring, and grinding away along the line. *I'm going for the secret sauce,* she told her husband, turning away from the Ooken.

>>**Follow the assembly line back to the start,**<< ADAM advised. >> **I spotted what looked to be a vat on the other side of this...um...whatever it makes.**<<

Bethany Anne broke into a run. Three steps in she leapt, using the skull of one of the larger worker Ooken as a steppingstone up onto the machinery. *I see it.*

>>**You could hardly miss it. It's thirty feet tall.**<<

Bethany Anne raised an eyebrow. *You're pretty snarky for someone who's meant to be convincing me they're mature enough to be allowed out to play by themselves again.*

ADAM chose to cut his losses before Bethany Anne decided against ever allowing him to pilot a body. >>**Thirty feet isn't so high.**<<

Bethany Anne snickered as she activated her armor's climbing mode and the palms of her gauntlets extruded an almost invisible adhesive. She scaled the side and hauled herself onto the meter-wide rim. *Jackpot. We've got our blank nanocytes.*

>>**There are enough nanocytes in that vat to upgrade everyone on High Tortuga,**<< ADAM estimated, only half-joking.

Bethany Anne considered the ramifications of upgrading the entire civilian population as she balanced in a crouch on the rim of the vat. *Not High Tortuga, but Tabitha is getting a pretty decent fighting force together. I'll give those who fight for me whatever advantage I can without compromising our position.* She peered down into the open tank, which was filled almost to the brim with a glowing light blue substance, shot through with miniscule flecks of dancing, sparkling energy.

TOM snickered. **You call those ragtag rebels a fighting force? The Bakas fight among themselves as much as they listen to Tabitha.**

Bethany Anne rolled her eyes. *Careful there, your Kurtherian is showing. Mahi Takar's sideshow aside, I happen to appreciate the Bakas' loyalty to their family groups. It's one of the reasons I gave Tabitha permission to indulge her Eliza Doolittle fantasies with them.* She hesitated before dipping a hand into the vat. *What happens when I ingest these?*

Nothing should happen, TOM assured her. **The nanocytes are not programmed, so as far as I can see, they should be absorbed into your bloodstream within seconds and remain inactive. I'll isolate the suspension in your stomach until we're in a position to do something with it.**

"As far as you can see" is not the most rousing endorsement.

Do you want me to lie?

Bethany Anne rolled her eyes and immersed her cupped hand. *No. Okay, here goes.* She lifted her hand to her lips with some trepidation and drank the suspension.

She didn't drop dead, which she appreciated greatly. *How much of this shit do I need to drink?*

As much as you can take in as quickly as you can take it, TOM told her. **We don't have our sample yet. I have to alter your stomach to neutralize the PH of the suspension without damaging the nanocytes.**

Bethany Anne dropped to her knees on the edge of the vat and used both her hands to scoop the suspension into her mouth. *It tastes fucking vile. Did they make this to taste like Pepsi mixed with battery acid just to piss me off? I'm telling you, it's working.*

No, that's the acid, Tom informed her. **Okay, you can store the suspension safely. Drink up. We need to move.**

Bethany Anne was well aware that the disintegration of the factory walls was progressing. She took one more mouthful and got to her feet. *That's plenty. Michael?*

Good to go when you're ready, he confirmed. *I'll be on the upper level in less than a minute.*

Bethany Anne tilted her chin to glance at the access to the upper level. *Meet you there.*

An explosion sounded from somewhere nearby and a fresh round of alarms went off, bringing the discord she had tuned out earlier to the front and center again.

Bethany Anne felt the hive mind approaching, a boiling rage of biting tentacles headed right for the cells. She stepped off the edge of the vat, adjusting her weight as she dropped to glide easily to the floor. Landing at a run, she darted through the worker Ooken in a blur. Her only thought was to get to the prisoners before they fell prey to the mass of certain death headed their way.

Plenty of the prisoners had decided not to wait for assistance to arrive.

The Ooken poured through the hole Bethany Anne and Michael had made to get down to the prison, heedless of where they landed, driven to kill by their nanocytes.

Bethany Anne vaulted the rail and landed in the middle of the melee. She fired her gauntlet blades with Etheric energy and threw herself at the nearest Ooken. Sidestepping the Ooken's tentacles, she parted it from its face with a downward slash that prevented it from stuffing the bite-sized aliens it had in its clawed hands into its mouth.

The aliens screeched and swarmed the fallen Ooken, biting and tearing into its fur with teeth and claws.

"I'm going to get you out of here," Bethany Anne told the tiny aliens, hoping like hell her translation software wasn't fucking it up too badly.

The aliens flashed sharp teeth much like the Ooken's at her and scattered, their shocking blue skin lost among the crush in an instant.

Bethany Anne moved on. As she obliterated the Ooken, she pushed every prisoner she came across into the Etheric, not giving any of them a choice in case they vanished like the tiny blue aliens.

Tentacles flew, heads rolled, and Ooken fell wherever she stepped. Her blades burned, her speed the deciding factor in one life-or-death confrontation after another. The death part fell to the Ooken each time, but she wasn't counting.

Not out loud, anyway.

Michael arrived in a blast of lightning, scattering Ooken like bowling pins. He flew up and over the railing, hurtling feet-first into an Ooken that had managed to get the drop on a pair of horned aliens who were fighting back-to-back against two more Ooken.

Asking permission didn't so much as occur to him. He shoved the large aliens into the Etheric and moved on to the next prisoner, who he spotted through the burning hole he created in the tentacle wall with another precision application of lightning.

Bethany Anne felt Michael's presence before she saw him. She ducked and pivoted, clearing the immediate area of Ooken with a concussive wave.

Another tumult of tentacles spilled in from the hole above the prison floor, which was at least fifty feet wide now by Bethany Anne's estimate. The press from above caused great chunks of crystal to fall and smash the combatants below, killing Ooken and prisoners alike.

Bethany Anne drew hard on the Etheric, calling the energy and directing it to create a seal over the hole before the entire level came down on their heads. *Time's up*, she told Michael. *You need to shield yourself. This is about to get real.*

She gave Michael a moment to protect himself, then pulled again on the Etheric and sent out another wave of energy over the prison level. This wave she made heavy. Prisoners and Ooken alike dropped to the floor, pinned by Bethany Anne's makeshift suppression blanket.

Only Bethany Anne and Michael remained standing, the beating of tentacles on the crystal above the only sound in the manufactured silence.

Michael scanned the remaining prisoners. *It would be faster to Myst, but I'll lose my armor.*

There's nothing I can do once the crystal degrades past a certain point, Bethany Anne told him, pouring her strength into holding the ever-growing network of cracks in the crystal together. *Get them into the Etheric.*

Michael mopped up the last of the prisoners and turned to find Bethany Anne. He saw her strain under the massive amount of power it was taking to hold the walls together. *Bethany Anne, that's all of them.*

GO! she ground out, her mental voice giving Michael all the motivation he needed. *Get out of here before you can't.*

I will be waiting for you. Michael left his armor behind and stepped into the Etheric after the rescued aliens.

QBS *Izanami*, Pod Bay, Transport Pod

John's eyes were on the battle ahead of him, giving Alexis, Gabriel, and Izanami a side view of his jaw on the screen. "I'll be there just as soon as I get a break in the action. Hang tight, kids."

Alexis cut the call and turned to Izanami. "We don't need a babysitter, Izanami. Let us stay with you. We're safe on the ship."

"You are safe on the ship as long as I remain cloaked and tucked out of the way," Izanami corrected. Her avatar paced in front of the viewscreen.

"You look just like Mom when she's impatient," Alexis teased. Her smile faded instantly.

Izanami turned red eyes on the twins. "I am not impatient," she denied, her outward appearance wavering between Bethany Anne in her usual armor and Baba Yaga in her white armor. "I am frustrated with waiting for John to arrive."

Alexis raised a finger. "You know, we could help you get in close to the planet. I came up with something while Uncle Admiral Thomas was telling you all the reasons we have to wait back here. He just has a grudge against Shinigami, and you are inhabiting a Mark II *Shinigami*-class ship, after all."

Izanami sniffed. "Perhaps I should just threaten the Admiral into letting me pass. I should drop this Pod off with him as payback for putting me out."

Gabriel frowned. "Why would that be revenge?"

Izanami raised an eyebrow. "I'm an ultra-advanced super-quantum AI, and you two are too much for me at times. The Admiral could use your help for the next few hours, don't you think?"

Alexis raised an eyebrow. "Or we could do this since Mom is in danger." She sent Izanami a modified blueprint. "See, with just a few tweaks to your hard light drive, we can get in closer than the *Ballista* or any of the other Shinigami-class ships. Wouldn't you like to be the best in the fleet?"

Izanami laughed. "Child, I am already the best in the fleet. However, I do like your thinking here. Did you compensate for the stress boundaries in this math?"

Alexis nodded, her eyes widening at the suggestion she would skip a step. "Of course. If you check, you'll see I calculated for multiple tolerances. The construct will hold long enough."

Izanami's avatar rippled. "Long enough is all I need."

Gabriel nodded toward the Pod door. "So, can we get

out of here before Alexis starts explaining and I glaze over completely? I have to get started on the modification to the Gate drive if we're doing this."

Izanami hesitated. These were only children, and ones she was honor bound to protect. "What makes you so certain your mother is in danger?" she asked Alexis.

Alexis shrugged, the confusion on her face making her appear much younger for a moment. "I don't know, Izanami, I swear. But it's true. I feel it in my bones, no matter how uncomfortable the lack of physical evidence makes me."

Izanami looked for holes in Alexis' plans and found none. She fixed the two of them with Baba Yaga's sternest stare. "At no point will the two of you engage in any activity other than what is agreed upon beforehand. Do I have your word?"

She scrutinized the twins' wholehearted agreement for any sign of deception, intentional or not, and found none. "Very well. Your plan is good, but I have a few adjustments to make to improve its efficacy."

18

Ooken System, QBS *Izanami*, Bridge

Izanami flitted from screen to screen, her confinement to the ship's systems while the twins worked on her hard light drive grating to her very being.

Every part of her ached to be between Bethany Anne and whatever danger Alexis had foreseen. Logically, prescience made little sense. However, her examination of Alexis' brain activity through Phyrro's monitoring showed her there was something to the child's claims.

Izanami called to the children's EI. *Phyrro, I need you to take a message for me.*

Gabriel came out of the elevator with his arms full and dropped his bounty on the floor by Alexis. "Okay, I stripped the Vid-docs. Where next?"

Alexis pointed at the floor opposite her. "That was the last of it. Strip out the neural nets, then we need to mount these to the central processors I'm almost done building." She indicated a tray with two small chips immersed in a clear fluid and passed Gabriel the device she was working on to inspect. "There are thirteen more ready to go, twelve reserves and the two regulators for the system."

"I see now. Spread out the energy intake to give *Izanami* more power without burning out her hard light drive." Gabriel passed the processor back to Alexis and cut the mat open along the seam to remove the mess of wiring inside. He bent his head to his task, working quickly to finish and move on

Alexis growled when the final hair-fine connection she had to solder slipped. "Stupid, stupid... Get *in* there!" Her tongue appeared at the corner of her mouth as she rectified the mistake. "Done."

Gabriel replaced the cover on his micro-soldering kit. "Me too."

Alexis shook her head. "We're not moving fast enough. Come on, we need to go EVA to place these. Izanami, get ready for your hard light drive coming back online." She touched a finger to the cube in her palm, and it pulsed with white light as it rose from her hand.

Izanami reappeared in her customary spray of light, the corona casting a blood-red glow over the pearlescent white of her armor and hair. "I have withdrawn from the ship's systems. Phyrro is now in control, and has been adjusted so you cannot meddle in his code a second time."

Alexis blushed. "I wouldn't. I owe him an apology for the first time I did it."

Izanami nodded. "Then I believe there is nothing else to discuss."

The twins gathered their equipment.

Alexis turned to Izanami as they headed for the access corridor. "Izanami, thank you for believing me."

Izanami wasn't sure what the appropriate response was. These children affected her as much as they did their parents. They had also given her the justification for what she was about to do.

Gabriel and Alexis would not end this day as orphans. Not if she had anything to do with it.

Ooken Sky Base, Prison Level

Bethany Anne felt the crystal above her give way completely, now held by her will alone. All prisoners except the eight Collective were gone, and so was Michael, safe in the Etheric. She was free to work.

She reached out to the conduit. *I hope you're prepared to make a splash.*

Release us and see what we make of the abominations, the conduit hissed in her mind.

Bethany Anne directed the energy holding the tank together to tear the cracks wide open. The air pressure shifted as the water slammed into the factory floor, rushing in on all sides to send up a wave that washed the prison level clean of dead Ooken.

The Collective cried out as the wall of the tank gave way at last.

Let the Corrupt come, they sang. *Let them die at our teeth.*

Bethany Anne released her barrier above, freeing the Ooken to fall through the hole. She was sickened to see they had resorted to eating one another in their uncontrollable pursuit of destruction. She raised her arms and seized the Etheric energy in the Ooken's nanocytes.

They resisted, and her efforts were hampered by the need

to keep herself tentacle-free. Bethany Anne saw it all and none of it, her only focus on burning the Ooken from existence. She threw out lightning, energy balls, and wave after wave of blistering Etheric energy, hammering at the hive mind.

The Ooken closed as she searched for a way in. Bethany Anne made precise steps as she fought, conserving her energy for killing. The water rose steadily, lapping at her legs as she moved. The dead landed with flochy thuds in the knee-high wash.

Bethany Anne spotted a flash of movement beneath the surface. The Collective had made it out of the tank. *Can you guys clear the space around me? I can take them out in one fell swoop once I get into their nanocytes.*

A mass of dull gray tentacles broke the surface of the water all around and scooped the seven Ooken nearest Bethany Anne into the water.

To her left, the conduit hauled itself over the railing with its two lesser tentacles and propelled itself like a slingshot to Bethany Anne's side. It opened its beak and ripped the air with a screech before lunging at the Ooken.

The Ooken moved like a pack of raptors, right into the conduit's waiting mouth. It swiped a tentacle and they were gone, crushed and devoured before they could lift a claw to defend themselves.

Bethany Anne ran up the conduit's dorsal tentacle. She kicked the first Ooken like she was opening the Superbowl and drove her gauntlets blades-first into the one still latched onto the Collective's shoulder, having no intention of allowing them to take another bite. She leapt after the one she'd kicked and snatched a handful of the tentacles around its mouth. *Open fucking sesame. I want in, and I'm not playing.*

The Ooken fought her, thrashing her with tentacle and claw in an attempt to latch onto her armor.

Bethany Anne electrified her gauntlet in response, grinning as the Ooken stiffened with the fifty thousand volts she sent into its body through the extremely sensitive ganglia. *Not today, or any day.* She took full advantage of the temporary fritz to the Ooken's central nervous system to slide into the hive mind, reaching for the nanocytes in their brains. *Wipe them as soon I take control,* she told ADAM and TOM.

Like wildfire she spread through the hive, leaving a void in place of every mind she touched. All around her, the Ooken dropped where they stood as the programming in their nanocytes was erased by ADAM.

The Collective fell back, satisfied with Bethany Anne's revenge against their captors. They clung to the railing as the water rose farther, their bodies floating in place, surrounded by remnants of Ooken corpses.

The exterior wall is still holding, the conduit told her. *We cannot break it without exposing ourselves to the void.*

Bethany Anne shook her boot free and waded over to the railing. *We need to get you out of here before you get turned into blobsicles.*

It turned its owlish eyes on Bethany Anne, each sightless pool the size of her head. *Where is our escape? We will die long before we reach your ship.*

Bethany Anne raised an eyebrow, a slow smile appearing on her lips as she opened herself to the Etheric.

Leave that to me. I have an idea. She jumped onto the railing and looked down into the water.

The Collective murmured among themselves, and the conduit surfaced. *We sense you have a difficulty.*

Bethany Anne lifted her hands. *I'm considering how to get a single escape bubble into the Polaris, she told them. Just one of you is large enough to fill the doors, although the hold is large enough for maybe ten of you. Spread out a bit. It'll be easier to get you into the ship one at a time.*

The Collective separated and Bethany Anne enclosed each of them in Etheric energy, which she hardened and insulated to prevent the water inside from freezing once the bubbles hit the vacuum. *How are you doing in there?* she asked when she was done.

We can tolerate this for a short time, the conduit replied.

Bethany Anne stepped over the railing into the water. *Then let's get the fuck out of here.*

Ooken System, Open Space

Izanami crouched on the bow of her ship, both feet on the mat Gabriel and Alexis had affixed to the hull. Her connection to the rear mat was inside her drive, waiting for her to activate it. The battle still raged on, keeping her from reaching her Queen easily.

Her hard light drive hummed as it worked to transform Etheric energy into hard light at a rate Jean hadn't designed it to tolerate. She removed the regulators one by one, testing as she went despite the fact she had already calculated the odds of the modified drive being in any way salvageable afterward to be less than 0.00001 percent.

The restriction on how much power the drive could pull from the Etheric no longer prevented her from doing what was necessary.

Still, there was nothing to say that the moment had to pass without a display of elegant magnificence for her to be remembered by.

Izanami opened her arms and loosed her hair to fly free behind her. She shifted her stance as her avatar grew to the size of the *Ballista* off in the distance, lifting a foot and placing it on the mat on the stern to set her center of gravity low over the body of the ship.

How are you feeling, Izanami? Alexis asked. *The construct looks to be holding from here.*

I believe we should make haste, Izanami replied, seeing the *Ballista* surrounded by small Gates.

Connecting the Gate drive to the neural mats, Gabriel told her. *Remember to maintain contact with the mats, or you'll lose control and drop out too soon.*

Izanami narrowed her eyes, focusing on the gas giant in the distance. She checked to make sure Alexis and Gabriel were harnessed in their couches while she quadruple-checked that what she was about to attempt was indeed possible.

Then she reached out. *Bethany Anne.*

Bethany Anne almost lost control of the escape bubbles, then reaffirmed her hold on the Etheric energy tethering the Collective to her and resumed her descent. ***Izanami?***

Yes, my Queen, the AI replied.

Bethany Anne didn't understand how in hell she was hearing her ship's AI when she'd left her ship on Devon. *ADAM, where is Izanami?*

There's no need to ask, Izanami replied. *I am above the planet. You are trapped, and I'm going to break you out.*

Izanami closed the connection, moved her back heel a fraction, and dropped the ship into the open Gate below. She set it to head for the inner atmosphere of the planet, her bandwidth constantly splitting to deal with the multiple warnings going off in her peripheral vision.

She opened a new Gate onto the churning orange acid surrounding the Ooken platform and slid into the maelstrom with her scanners hot, detecting the huge expenditure of Etheric energy that marked Bethany Anne's location as she erupted through the Gate, her ship propelling her at high speed toward the platform.

Bethany Anne was near the base of the platform, behind almost a kilometer of crystal. Izanami considered destroying the entire structure to get to her Queen, but the loss of life to the Guardians would be unacceptable.

This was old thinking, covered in the space between nanoseconds.

Izanami had already shifted her feet again to bring the ship around underneath the platform to the place her scanners told her was the weakest.

Alexis and Gabriel were speaking to her, but she didn't hear them.

Bethany Anne was running out of time.

John's voice replaced the children's. She vaguely made out that he wanted access to the children. She let him into the ship, which left her free to concentrate on examining the crystal to select her point of impact.

Izanami found a fissure created by a single air bubble deep inside the crystal. She crouched, coiled her body tightly, and *leapt*.

The crystal gave out even as her avatar crumbled. As Izanami pushed on, driving herself into the cracks, she felt what it was like to be the unstoppable force meeting the immovable object. She deactivated the regulators in her hard light drive and *pulled* to draw every drop of power from it before it burned out.

She had no sensation of being torn to pieces by the collision, and no awareness of the moment her hard light drive imploded from her demands on it.

Her last thought process was the image of water rushing toward her.

Alexis and Gabriel watched Izanami leave the mats, shock turning them cold.

John came onto the bridge at a run. "Kids, thank God you're all right."

Alexis pointed wordlessly at the screen, tears pouring down her ashen face.

"Izanami," Gabriel choked out. "She lied to us."

John looked at the screen just as Izanami's behemoth avatar hit the bottom of the platform, shattering the hard light drive and the crystal into a million and one fragments.

Water flooded out, turning to ice on contact with the vacuum of space. It captured the shattered crystal and the shards of dying light, creating an icy prism that lit the battlefield as it poured out of the platform. The tumult halted as suddenly as it had begun when the water hit zero gravity and began to accumulate, forming an inverted mountain that grew larger with every passing second.

"Hell if she didn't make a damned rainbow," John muttered, thinking his own AI would be more likely to exit this life as a flock of ravens.

He scrutinized the ejecta for any signs of life and any signs of Bethany Anne. *Boss, Michael. You out there?*

I am on my way in the Polaris, Michael answered. *Bethany Anne should be somewhere on that ice with eight of the Collective.*

Gotcha, John told him. *We'll start the search without you.*

The icefield grew before their eyes until the surface was fully a third as wide as the platform. Somewhere in all of that was Bethany Anne.

"Who's going to find Mom?" Alexis asked.

John clapped a hand on each of the twins' shoulders. "That would be us and everyone else not currently fighting. C'mon, we're closest. We're her ride."

Bethany Anne ceased blasting the crystal when she felt an impact shake her bones. Although she didn't know what

Izanami had done to break through the wall in time, she was grateful.

She braced herself and the escape bubbles as they were sucked downward by the sudden evacuation of water, keeping a tight mental grip on the eight bubbles as they plummeted out the bottom of the platform and were ejected into space.

Her fall was halted by an impact before she had a chance to float away. She landed on her back on an ice ridge and scrambled to her feet to check the escape bubbles.

All eight were still intact. ***You all okay in there?*** she asked.

There was a pause before the conduit answered. *We are uninjured.*

That's about all any of us can ask for right now. A thud behind Bethany Anne made her turn around. A dead Ooken lay in the spot she'd landed a moment before.

She opened a link to the *ArchAngel*. ***Admiral, where is the* Polaris?**

Admiral Thomas' mental voice was full of relief. *On standby while I waited to find out where you would need it. Michael is aboard with the aliens you rescued, who are a laugh a second, let me tell you.*

Bethany Anne let out a long sigh. ***Just get me off this ice cube. Withdraw our troops and pulverize it. Burn it, knock it out of the damn sky—I don't care, just get it gone. I'm so done with this place that I haven't got two fucks to rub together, tech or not.***

Bethany Anne cut the connection and gathered her

strength to pick up the bubbles. *Hang on, this might get a little bumpy.*

Despite her fatigue, she felt good about their victory. She scanned the fleet reports as she walked, her mood further lifted by the lack of lives lost on her side.

The *Izanami* appeared on the horizon, followed by the QTS *Polaris*. Bethany Anne lowered the escape bubbles and waited for the ships to land.

She opened her link to Izanami, intending to thank her for getting them out of a tight spot.

Izanami wasn't anywhere to be found.

Izanami? ADAM, why isn't she answering?

ADAM came back almost immediately. >>**I can't find her either.**<<

Mom. Alexis spoke softly in Bethany Anne's mind. *Izanami is dead. She sacrificed herself to get you out of the trap.*

Bethany Anne refused to believe it. *IZANAMI! Answer me, damn you!*

Nothing.

ADAM, where is she? Find her!

>>**I have the last location of her hard light drive,**<< ADAM told her regretfully. >>**But I can't connect to it. She's gone. You still have time to find the drive, and it's giving out enough residual power to hold the ghost of the Izanami construct.**<<

Show me where to go. Bethany Anne followed the directions in her HUD across the newly formed ice field without a thought.

She came across a crag in the ice that was too wide to jump, and jumped anyway, throwing herself into the Etheric. Her boots scattered fragments of ice and crystal as she crunched over the jagged edges on her return, and on she ran.

The light trapped inside the ice had almost faded when Bethany Anne reached the place ADAM had marked in her HUD. Her traitor eyes burned with tears when the light vanished, making enhanced vision pointless since she couldn't see through the blur. *Where is it?*

>>**Somewhere here, in the ice.**<<

Bethany Anne began searching for Izanami's hard light drive, tearing at the ice in a frantic attempt to locate the drive before her chest did as it was threatening and stopped breathing.

Izanami had been a part of her life for only a short time, but the AI's simple grace and quiet caring nature when it came to the children had earned her a place in Bethany Anne's heart. She dug deeper, throwing up huge chunks of ice as she burrowed into it.

She left no one behind, and she refused to lose another loved one.

No more sacrifices; not *one* more in her name. If she had to lock everyone down again and fight this war alone to prevent the pain she felt right now, *she would do it.*

Someone was sobbing nearby. It wasn't until she felt Michael's hand on her shoulder that Bethany Anne realized it was coming from her.

"She is gone," he told her softly.

Bethany Anne blinked at Michael, not processing his words. She shrugged him off and dropped to her knees to keep on digging.

Michael spoke into her mind. *Bethany Anne, you need to come to the ship.*

Bethany Anne looked up at him, the hollows under her eyes painting her face in lines of grief. "I'm not leaving without her drive. She has no backup." She pounded the ice with her fists. "Why didn't I force her to back herself up?"

"Because you treated her with the respect of an individual. Izanami made her choice." Michael held out a hand and waited for her to take it. "The living need you, my love. Alexis and Gabriel are waiting for us."

Bethany Anne felt her chest loosen at the mention of her children. She looked around one last time as she got to her feet. "Give me a moment to say goodbye."

Michael nodded and walked off a short way, his eyes on the ground in respect.

Bethany Anne returned to his side a few minutes later, still looking paler than usual behind the visor of her helmet. "Let's go."

Michael called for the Pod he had waiting to take them to the *Polaris*. "You will bear this, as you have so many times before."

Bethany Anne's eyes flashed red. "I'll bear it, but I *won't* allow it to happen again."

19

QTS *Polaris*, Queen's Suite

Bethany Anne curled up on the bed, hugging her knees to her chest. She looked up when Michael entered the cabin. *Just let me be. I want to cry.*

Michael crossed the room wordlessly, pausing only to grab a blanket before he got onto the bed beside her.

Bethany Anne allowed him to wrap the comforter around her without argument. They sat as the silence between them built, thickening with the words she didn't know how to say. The tears came eventually, the first to escape followed quickly by a deluge as she poured out her broken heart to her husband.

Her emotion ebbed after a while, drained away with her tears. "*Why?* Why would she do that? She knew she wouldn't survive."

Michael held her while she vented. "Izanami loved you, Bethany Anne. Our children can tell you the lengths she went to in order to reach you."

Bethany Anne sniffed, pulling herself into an upright

position. "They might if I ever unground them. Or when I pull my shit together and go see how they're coping with their grief."

"She was part of their daily lives for a while, so I expect Alexis and Gabriel are feeling what death truly means for the first time in their lives." Michael let his hands fall into his lap. "Time will tell if the deaths they have experienced in-game have provided them with any immunity."

Bethany Anne closed her eyes. "There is no immunity, Michael. Loss fucking *hurts*."

Michael got up from the bed and bent to pick up Bethany Anne's shoes from the floor. "Our AIs are loyal to a fault, and Izanami was especially focused on protecting you."

"We have to protect *them* better," Bethany Anne's words hitched in her throat, unable to make it past the emotion wedged there.

Michael felt her grief harden into something altogether more productive. He held out Bethany Anne's shoes. "So, what are you going to do about it?"

Bethany Anne scrubbed a hand across her eyes, the puffiness beneath them vanishing as resolve returned to the line of her jaw. She took her pumps and slipped them on, her eyebrow returning to its usual imperial angle. "We take care of the meeting with Mahi'Takar. Then I'm going to QT2 to light a rocket under Jean's ass."

Outskirts of Yollin Space, Voidrux Logistics Head-quarters

Luther Voidrux came from a long line of assholes. His

father was an asshole, and his before him, all the way back to Earth. Being educated men whose sense of honor outweighed their tendencies to poor social intelligence, the Voidrux name had nevertheless been one that spoke to dependability and quality service for as long as humanity had been in space.

Luther had inherited all of his family's wealth when he inherited the company. Unfortunately for him, the family name, and the couple hundred thousand employees who had suffered since Luther's takeover, he had somehow missed out on even a drop of their sense of duty.

Voidrux Logistics was no longer the proud company it had once been. His habit of screwing his business partners out of their money, and most often their lives in the process, had forced him farther and farther from the welcoming bosom of the nascent Federation.

He was currently based on this shitty asteroid, but not for long.

Rumor had it someone was throwing credits around like they were going out of fashion, and Luther knew exactly what to do with a potentially huge score like that. He expected to be sunning himself on one of those luxury resort worlds he couldn't afford in his present financial circumstance within weeks.

Luther walked the warehouse floor, humming to himself.

Things were looking up for him at long last.

Devon, The Hexagon, Penthouse Apartment, Living Area

Alexis finished setting Todd's offerings to the world of finger-painting out to dry and went to wash her hands in the kitchen. "I wish Mom would just get mad at us."

Tabitha made room at the sink for Alexis, grabbing a towel to dry her hands. "I told you, you can't scare the crap out of your mom and get away with it." She passed Alexis the towel. "I thought you liked training with her?"

Alexis laughed, "Yeah, she's the most skilled fighter I've ever seen. It's just, I don't know. She was holding back before."

Peter returned from the bathroom with a paint-free Todd. He set the child down to play and came over to lean on the counter by Tabitha while their son ran over to the miniature fort that was his play area. "Say what you mean. Playing with the grown-ups is painful."

Alexis flicked her hair back. "Got it in one. She's merciless."

Tabitha's eyes lit up. "Welcome to the big leagues, where you learn, or you die."

Alexis rolled her eyes. "No kidding."

Tabitha snorted. "You'll appreciate it when you're too hard to kill for anyone to bother trying."

Alexis giggled. "Don't tell Mom, but I'm kind of enjoying it. It might be fun to zap my brother every once in a while when I have better control of the Etheric. Or that ass…inine…"

Her voice trailed off when no other word to describe Ch'Irzt presented itself, then accepted her fate and dropped to the floor and started doing push-ups before finishing her sentence. "That monumental ass Chet. I hate how he treats Trey. I wish I had laser vision. Corneas don't take *that* long to grow back, do they?" She counted off and got to her feet. "It would *so* be worth it."

Peter patted Alexis on the shoulder. "Kid in class giving you trouble?"

Tabitha threw up her hands. "Yeah, the fully-grown type I had to bump down from the adult classes before he even began. This dumbtastic wonder is the only one of his sibling group still alive, so I can't even use his brothers to knock him into line."

Peter grimaced as his protective instincts kicked in. "Want me to show him some brotherly love?" He pounded his fist into his hand. "Wouldn't take a minute."

Tabitha stood on tiptoe to kiss Peter. "I know, my hunk of sexy wolfman. But I can handle one moody male, and if I get bored with smacking him down, Mahi'Takar is always happy to reinforce my lessons."

Bethany Anne materialized in the center of the sitting area while Tabitha was speaking. "I can't say I disagree with her methods." She dropped onto the couch with a relieved sigh and bent to remove her boots.

Alexis came over and tucked herself under Bethany Anne's arm. "Hey, Mom. I'm glad you're home. Tough day?"

Bethany Anne held her daughter tightly. "Good day." She raised an eyebrow at Alexis' hair. "I see you had some pampering from Tabitha."

Alexis released Bethany Anne and looked at her uncertainly as she touched her fingers to the frosted tips. "Mmhmm. Do you like it?"

Bethany Anne narrowed her eyes at Tabitha as she brushed her lips against her daughter's head. "Of course I do."

Alexis let go of the breath she'd been holding and flashed a grin at Tabitha. "Told you."

Todd poked his head over the wall of his fort, his face creasing with joy when his eyes confirmed what his nose and ears had already told him. "Auntie Bethany Anne! Come and play!"

Bethany Anne chuckled and got to her feet. "What are we playing?" she asked, stepping over the fort's wall.

Todd handed her a small box with a solemn expression. "Keep the treasure safe from the pirates. I gotta fight them."

Tabitha sighed loudly. "Did those pesky pirates come back, Todd?"

"Yeah, Mama," her son agreed. "Me and Auntie Bethany Anne will show them."

"We will," Bethany Anne agreed. "I bet we'll defeat them just in time for dinner, huh?"

Todd forgot about the pirates at the mention of food. "Is dinner soon?" he asked Tabitha.

Tabitha looked at Peter.

Peter held out his hands. "You already had dinner, Todd. It's almost bedtime."

Todd pouted, folding his arms. "Don't wanna go bed. I wanna play with Auntie Bethany Anne."

Bethany Anne made a sad face. "I have to go to a boring meeting soon, sweetheart. It wouldn't be any fun for you to sit quietly while the adults talk about the rules, would it?"

Todd's brow furrowed as he worked through the logic. "Nooo…"

Bethany Anne lifted her hands. "That's what you would have to do if you stay up late. How about you get ready for bed, and I'll tell you a story before you go to sleep?"

Todd narrowed his eyes. "A story about pirates?"

Bethany Anne lifted her hands. "What else?" She grinned at the resulting joy on his little face.

Tabitha grinned as her son dived into Peter's arms. "I'd better get my fine behind out the door. Mahi'Takar is due at the open day in a few minutes." She tossed Alexis her jacket. "You ready?"

Alexis caught her jacket midair. "You bet I am. It's killing us to keep things from Trey. The sooner we can get him away from his so-called family, the better." She flounced out with a hair-swish worthy of Tabitha.

Tabitha looked at Bethany Anne over her shoulder as she followed Alexis out the door. "Do you remember being that righteous at her age?"

Bethany Anne waved them off, snickering. "Weren't *you* a little ball of sunshine at that age? I know I was."

"Bet your dad would tell us differently," Tabitha called back.

Devon, The Hexagon, Main Arena

The hum of many languages met Tabitha and Alexis when they got to the back corridor leading to the arena.

"Maybe the open day wasn't just a good cover," Alexis commented as they got to the doors. "Sounds like half the city turned up to take a look round."

Tabitha nodded at John as they passed his position by the door. "It won't be a bad thing if we get more support." She scanned the arena, looking for Trey's slightly golden fur among the pinks, yellows, greens, and blues of the crowd. "I don't see any new Bakas."

Alexis shrugged. "They'll come around. They won't have much choice if Trey's mom signs a treaty with us."

Tabitha spotted Trey at the entrance. "There he is. No sign of his mom, though."

"How's my best student?" Tabitha asked when they reached him.

"I thought *I* was your best student," Alexis teased.

Trey grinned. "Nervous, honestly. Mahi' is almost here, and she sent me ahead to tell you she has her two youngest brothers guarding her. They'll do as she tells them."

Tabitha tilted her head, greeting Mahi'Takar with a warm smile when she arrived with two large guards in tow. "Hey. Glad you could make it. This is Alexis, another of my students."

Mahi'Takar inclined her head a fraction, her regal nod offset by the warmth in her eyes. "We are not so different when it comes to wanting to know our children are on the right path. I look forward to hearing about my son's accomplishments."

Tabitha noted the dissatisfaction the two guards flanking Mahi'Takar failed to conceal at their leader's friendly tone. "He has a lot of accomplishments to talk about. Trey has shown intelligence and perseverance in his training."

Mahi'Takar looked over the assembled Devonians. "I assume you have somewhere quieter in mind for our discussion?"

Tabitha played along, the attitudes of the two male guards at Mahi'Takar's back not impressing her. "Actually, I wanted to invite you to a small gathering I've arranged for my star students and their parents."

Mahi'Takar raised a hand to still Trey's reaction. "Very well." She turned to her guards. "You will remain here to ensure we are not interrupted at this gathering."

"Not happening, Mahi'," the tallest told her roughly. "We don't know that these humans will obey the laws of hospitality."

Tabitha sighed. "You're talking to your sister about hospitality, and you haven't even bothered to introduce yourselves? What rights do nameless guests have? None."

The shorter male peered out from under his shaggy fringe of hair. "You have learned our ways."

"I told you," Trey cut in. "We can be allies and exchange culture. Humans are not so different from us. They fight for family and honor, and they despise the Seven." He waved his arms as he spoke, somehow managing to tangle up his gangly limbs for a second. He blinked, then continued as though nothing happened. "You could learn a lot from them if your head wasn't made of wood."

The taller brother snorted. "You have to be joking. These small, hairless creatures?" He leaned over to Mahi'-Takar. "Sister, why are you allowing our future Takar to be influenced by lesser warriors?"

Mahi'Takar wheeled around and backhanded her brother across the face. "I warned you, Da'Mahin. Do not force me to make a point."

Da'Mahin bared his teeth at Mahi'Takar, and Trey jumped in front of his mother. "Do you want to live out your days in exile?"

The rise in the level of tension drew John's attention. He swerved to intervene, but Tabitha waved him off behind her back, wanting to avoid a confrontation.

John ignored Tabitha, approaching Mahi'Takar with a winsome smile. "These guys bothering you, ma'am?" he asked.

Mahi'Takar fanned herself with a hand. "Since the day they were born. Unfortunately, it is the role of male siblings to make life difficult for a female."

John chuckled. "You sure? I can throw their behinds out of here, no problem."

Da'Mahin scoffed. "You barely reach my chest. How do you expect to make us do anything?"

John met Da'Mahin's eyes calmly. "Keep being an asshole and you'll find out."

Trey snorted. "This is John Grimes. He's one of the humans' most celebrated warriors."

Mahi'Takar dipped her head fractionally. "Then it is our honor to meet you, John Grimes. Perhaps you would care to share stories of battle with us?"

John lifted a shoulder. "I dunno about celebrated. I live my life and kick what ass is necessary, is all. Same as the rest of us. No need to make a big deal out of it."

Tabitha raised an eyebrow, wondering why John was slinging humble pie like he was moonlighting as a short-order cook. "You could give these guys a tour while Mahi'-Takar and I talk about Trey."

John folded his arms across his chest. "The guys and I are sparring in the outdoor arena with the CDF. If you guys aren't bothered by a little pain, you're welcome to join us."

Tabitha pressed her lips together. "You want to fight the Bakas?"

John shrugged. "Group consensus."

"Challenge accepted." The smaller of Mahi'Takar's brothers grunted, inflating his chest to loom over John. "How many are in your group? It should be a fair fight, or there is no honor in winning."

John grinned. "You're no cowards, I'll give you that. We six against you two. We'll tag-team."

"If you insist on putting yourselves at a disadvantage, we will not argue," the Baka replied. He bowed slightly. "I am Li'Kein, and I will be your better today."

John walked off. "This way, guys. This is gonna be interesting."

Tabitha turned to Trey and Mahi'Takar and chuckled. "These guys haven't been training here, so they have no clue what's about to hit them."

John turned back and lifted his hands. "Well, I've only got a left and a right. It's not rocket science."

Mahi'Takar scrutinized John for a moment, then turned to her brothers. "Da'Mahin, I will allow your challenge to stand. Go with this John Grimes, both of you. Learn what he has to teach you. This is my will."

Da'Mahin and Li'Kein glanced at John, then set off after him.

"Do not leave this building, Mahi'," Da'Mahin ordered.

"Go piss in the wind," Mahi'Takar retorted. "I will go where I please, and you will remain on the premises until I have conducted my business." She growled low in her chest as she turned away from her brothers. "Bistok-headed males."

Tabitha gestured for Mahi'Takar to walk with her. "How long do you think we have before they come looking for you?"

Mahi'Takar shrugged. "That will depend upon your males' endurance when it comes to pissing contests." She shrugged at Tabitha's sideways glance. "What, did you expect me to dress it up?"

Tabitha snickered. "We should be fine for hours. Let me show you two up to the penthouse. Dinner should be about ready by now." She led them through the crowded arena to the restricted access corridor she'd had put in to separate the private elevator from the general-use ones.

Trey darted back and forth as they walked, chattering nonstop the whole time.

Tabitha had already decided she liked Mahi'Takar. "Trey's right, you know. We have a lot in common when it comes to family. I know this whole thing was about getting you here, but I want you to know you've got a good kid there." She moved ahead to call the private elevator.

Mahi'Takar took the compliment with practiced grace, ruffling her son's fur as she ducked to enter the elevator. "He brings joy to my life, and one day he will make a fine leader."

Tabitha finished the start Trey's mother had made on messing his fur up. "'Course he will. He's got a good mom to back him up, and now he has us, too."

20

Devon, The Hexagon, Penthouse Apartment

There was an awkward silence as Tabitha walked into her apartment and everyone turned to look at Mahi'Takar and Trey.

Bethany Anne, wearing Baba Yaga's face, came over to greet the Bakan leader. "Good to see you again, Mahi'Takar."

"Your invitation to eat was a welcome one," she replied. "If only we did not have to go to such lengths to meet."

Michael gestured to the living area. "We should begin since time is short."

Alexis snickered. "Not likely. Uncle John took Mahi'-Takar's brothers to spar with Gabrielle and the guys."

Tabitha nodded in confirmation. "We have a couple of hours at the least."

Peter came out of the kitchen, red-faced and flustered. "Dinner is ready."

Tabitha led them all into the dining room. It took a few

minutes for everyone to decide where to sit while Peter brought the food in. The discussion during dinner centered around the effects the war was having on the population, and soon enough they were all seated around the table with almost empty plates.

Bethany Anne sipped her Coke, watching the interaction between the children for a moment before turning her attention to Mahi'Takar. "They seem to get on just fine without any treaties to tell them how to behave toward one another."

Mahi'Takar raised her cup to that. "Here's to an existence run by children. May we all perish with minimal suffering."

Gabriel and Trey cracked up at that. Alexis rolled her eyes at them but couldn't resist their laughter.

Bethany Anne leaned back in her chair. "My daughter already believes she holds the solutions to all existence," she told Mahi'Takar, a smirk touching her lips.

Michael waved his fork. "Who's to say she doesn't?"

The children cracked up completely.

Bethany Anne raised a hand. "You wake Todd, and you'll be reading him pirate stories until he goes back to sleep," she told them.

"May we be excused?" Gabriel asked.

"To the living area, yes," Michael replied.

Trey followed the twins out of the dining room, not needing to be asked twice.

Mahi'Takar shook her head as her son bounced out of the door. She turned to Bethany Anne. "What guarantee do I have that my son will be safe if I agree to this?"

Bethany Anne placed her glass on the table and met Mahi'Takar's questioning gaze. "What guarantee do I have that you're not just using me to secure your own leadership?" She held up a finger before Mahi'Takar could interject. "I'm not here to force anyone to fight for me, but those who do will obey me. We have two choices: we either trust one another, or we part ways after this evening without resolving anything. I need to grow my military, and you need to keep your family at bay until Trey can fight for himself. What's holding you back?"

Mahi'Takar sat stiffly in the chair. "You have to understand that being made to submit was what forced our people to split. Many would choose to move on before kneeling."

Bethany Anne waved a hand. "I'm not asking for kneelers. That shit bores the life out of me. I want fighters—people who will give their last drop of blood to protect their families' lives. Do you understand? This will not be an equal partnership, but it will be a partnership nonetheless."

Mahi'Takar glanced at the door. "That sounds—"

"'Fair' is the word you are searching for," Tabitha supplied. "We will protect Trey, I promise."

"Don't kid yourself," Bethany Anne told her. "The children are listening to every word we say. What we decide now will shape them as future leaders, so make the right choice for your son and the future of your people."

Mahi'Takar closed her eyes for a long moment. When she opened them, her face was set in resolved lines. "The right choice is not always clear, which the Empress could have told you if you had asked before she was exiled. She was a female who understood the nature of personal sacrifice for the good of her people."

Bethany Anne narrowed her eyes. "Hmm. So if you were speaking to Bethany Anne, it would be different?"

Mahi'Takar snorted. "Of course it would. Don't be dense." She dipped her head. "Apologies. That was out of line. I mean to say that although you are powerful, you are not the Empress. She alone has the power to rid my people of the Seven's influence. All you can do is kill."

Michael cut in. "The Seven? Again? Explain what you are referring to."

Mahi'Takar shook her head. "This is neither the time nor the place. I will speak on that once our peoples are bound by law and I am assured that Tu'Reigd is no longer at risk from my brothers' machinations."

Bethany Anne glanced at Michael. *You think telling her will seal the deal? Six hundred thousand fighters aren't anything to sniff at. More, when I kick whatever Kurtherians are messing with her homeworld into the next life.*

Michael's face gave away nothing. *Your choice. I can restrict her from being able to talk about it if it makes any difference.*

Bethany Anne made her decision. *It's time I stopped hiding, out here at least. The Federation doesn't need to know anything, but I can't expect loyalty from my allies if I don't give them the same.* She dropped her mask, revealing her true face to the Bakan regent. "Mahi'Takar, I will do whatever is in my power to save your people. Will you fight for me?"

Mahi'Takar watched the change with wide eyes, then lifted a clenched fist to her chest and looked at Bethany Anne with the tears of a mother in her eyes. "Yes, my Empress. We will fight for you."

High Tortuga, Space Fleet Base, Barnabas' Office

Barnabas chuckled as little Kevin zoomed away with his toy spaceship, leaving Lance alone on the screen. "So, what can I do for you? I'm guessing this isn't a social call."

Lance grinned, watching his son go. "You guessed right. I've had an unexpected contact from the Six. They've resolved their issues, and are ready to sign the agreements. However, the monarch of Vietania is not the person I was expecting."

Barnabas was pleasantly surprised. He hadn't heard from Nickie to confirm the result of her assignment, although the news of Cynthia's abdication had spread quickly through the grapevine. "That was fast. I believe Queen Jolie's confirmation was a resounding success."

Lance narrowed his eyes. "Yes. I can't help but wonder what you had to do with that, although after suffering through a meeting with the other queen, I have to say I'm grateful for the change."

Barnabas touched the side of his nose. "A vigilante never tells, Lance. You should know that by now."

Lance regarded him skeptically. "I know for a fact that you haven't left High Tortuga, yet you look like the cat that got the cream. Come on, spill. How did you resolve it? You *did* resolve it, right?"

Barnabas lifted a shoulder. "In a manner of speaking. I outsourced it." He closed the video link, the smirk still hovering on his mouth as he contemplated how far Nickie had come.

Tabitha would be expecting to hear from him soon. Hopefully not too soon, since CEREBRO had just informed him the *Penitent Granddaughter* was about to touch down in Hangar Three.

Why his niece insisted on keeping that heap of Skaine trash when she could have it scrapped in favor of a new ship was beyond him. He left his office in a hurry before she decided to visit him there. The repair bills for his furniture after her visits were becoming off-putting.

He intercepted Nickie at the elevators. "Did you leave anything for anyone else to buy?"

She lifted a heavily-laden arm to give him the finger, then thought better of it when her bags slid jerkily toward her elbow. "Hey, Uncle B. I got your message. I need to put all this in my office for now, and we can talk in there."

Barnabas nodded at her reference to the office Tabitha had set up across the corridor from his as hers. "Very well. I will be interested to see how you treat your own belongings."

Nickie pushed the door open with her shoulder. "You're gonna have to keep waiting, I haven't had the renovators in yet."

Barnabas followed Nickie into her office, which was exactly as Tabitha had left it, save for the Ranger badge nailed to the wall. "Nice to see you didn't hesitate to put your stamp on the space."

Nickie snorted. "You wound me. Wherever I lay my ass

is fine by me. I'm not fancy." She dumped her bags in the corner and dropped into her chair with a sigh, putting her feet up on her desk. "So what's my assignment? I assume you have one for me."

Barnabas inclined his head. "Something like that." He ignored Nickie's impatient glare, taking the guest chair opposite her desk. "It's time for you to decide."

Nickie raised an eyebrow. "Time for me to decide what, exactly?"

Barnabas folded his hands in his lap. "Your sabbatical is over, and you've seen the kind of work I'm offering. Are you ready to come home?"

Nickie flushed and sat upright. "I don't have to answer that."

Barnabas nodded. If Nickie wasn't ready, his waiting game would continue. That didn't mean he was going to make it easy on her. "You don't *want* to answer. There is a difference, you know."

Nickie's lip curled. "When I start giving a fuck about that, you'll be the first to know. Do you have an assignment for me or not? I've got a crew to pay and a ship to run. Sitting around talking about feelings like a bunch of old women doesn't pay well enough to waste time on."

Barnabas sighed. "There *is* an assignment if you want to take it. Your cover from the Vietania operation is still viable, which suits my needs right now."

"You want me to run cargo?" Nickie affected a yawn. "Boring. If you think trapping me in a nice little routine is going to make me settle down, you've got another think coming. I don't care what the pay is. I'd rather die fighting on some nameless world than waste away doing *nothing*."

"I am aware of your proclivity for chasing adrenaline," Barnabas assured her. "However, as I said, it is time to acknowledge your decision to return to your family. We are at war, Meredith Nicole. It's time to step up or go your own way."

Nickie sat back again and returned her feet to their spot on the desk. "When is Aunt Bethany Anne *not* at war? She'll wipe out whatever alien menace there is this time and go back to micromanaging everyone's lives, and I'll be chained down again. You honestly think I'm going to agree to that?"

Barnabas frowned. "Grow up, child. Do you believe Bethany Anne fights because she wants to?"

Nickie shrugged. "Dunno. Hadn't thought about it much beyond her always being pissed about something when I was a kid."

Barnabas sat back. "There has to come a point in your life where you stop seeing your family as infallible beings who failed you and accept responsibility for your choices." He smiled gently, diffusing the argument on Nickie's lips. "Bethany Anne fights because she sees no other way to protect those she loves."

"She must love the whole fucking universe then," Nickie retorted.

Barnabas let it pass since the seed had taken root in her mind. "The Ooken invasion is no joke, Nickie. It puts the Kurtherians two steps away from the Federation. The fleet is the only thing holding them back, and without a supply line to support it, well…"

Nickie rolled her eyes. "Yeah, yeah, I get it. I guess now you're going to tell me how playing delivery girl is vital to

Bethany Anne succeeding. Just skip the pep talk and get to what you want."

Barnabas smiled, satisfied by her capitulation. "As you wish. The Silver Line Company has been transferred to your name and is now registered here on High Tortuga. The company has been granted permits to transport cargo between the Federation and High Tortuga, and as far as the Federation is aware, this is a simple trade agreement."

Nickie narrowed her eyes at the mention of subterfuge. "What's the real deal?"

"You are aware that the Federation treaty exists on the condition Bethany Anne remains in exile. Our brief is to obtain the materials for building without endangering the stability of everything we have all worked toward for almost two centuries."

Nickie dropped the attitude for a second, but just one. "Wait…" She jumped to her feet and leaned over the desk. "You've been steering me toward this the whole fucking time, haven't you?" she demanded.

Barnabas got to his feet as well, looking as though butter wouldn't melt in his mouth. "I have no idea where you get these ideas, Nickie."

Nickie glared daggers at him. "Get out of my office, you manipulative sonofabitch," she seethed. "I'll take the fucking assignment, but you can send my orders to Meredith. I don't want to see your face for a long fucking time."

Barnabas nodded. "If that's what you need. I'm proud of you for doing your duty, Merry."

He closed the door behind him to avoid being hit by the paperweight she threw at him, which smashed through the glass and thudded into the wall opposite the door. He couldn't, however, miss the loud "Fuck you" that accompanied his departure.

Nickie would calm down. She always did. He just had to avoid the projectiles until she was ready to play nice again.

The problem with young children was they always threw the biggest tantrums right before they folded.

Considering the severity of her tantrums of late, she was just a few moments from accepting true adulthood.

QT2, QBBS Helena, Shipyard

Jean heard Bethany Anne's heels echoing in the access corridor long before she saw her.

She wiped her hands on a clean rag as her closest friend glided purposefully toward her with a gleam in her eyes and a devilish grin on her lips.

"What have you got for me?" Bethany Anne asked, looking over Jean's shoulder into the workshop beyond.

Jean folded her arms and imitated Bethany Anne's voice. "Oh, *hi*, Jean. How's it going? Have you spent a minute with your husband that wasn't work-related since I saw you last? Did you know your estranged granddaughter has reappeared?"

Bethany Anne paused in her tracks. "I'm sorry, did you say Nickie came back? I haven't seen her to permit her return."

Jean shrugged. "You should speak to Barnabas about that. He's had her working for him a while now, and she's grown up a hell of a lot."

Bethany Anne narrowed her eyes. "*Tabitha*. Just wait

until I get my hands on her." She waved the subject off. "You know, if Nickie is all done being an asshole, then she isn't my concern. And I would love nothing more than to send John out here, but he's needed elsewhere in the fight right now."

Jean sighed. "I know, I was just bitching. We agreed to this, but it doesn't make it any easier to be apart from my man, you know? I've been staying here instead of going home. It's better than working in silence without him there to make it comfortable."

Bethany Anne smirked. "So I should expect a hell of a lot of new ships to come out of this place as soon as you start getting regular shipments from Barnabas?"

Jean snorted. "Now who's thinking too small? I don't know how the Kurtherians come up with these advances and then fail to get every single use out of them. You can expect new ships, more advanced weapons, upgraded armor, and more efficient Gate drives. The list of possible applications goes on."

Bethany Anne pressed her lips together. "I'll be interested to see how Eve's project comes out."

Jean guided Bethany Anne through the workshop, swerving around the technicians working under the bellies of ships in various stages of completion. "Qui'nan hasn't come out of her office since she found out exactly what we're working with. The suspension you brought back from the factory was more than enough to reverse-engineer the nanocytes and make a start."

Bethany Anne grimaced. "I should fucking hope so since I won't be drinking it again any time soon. That shit was vile."

Jean chuckled. "Always taking one for the team. You should get a plaque or something."

Bethany Anne bumped Jean with her hip. "How about you find a way to finally put some damn heels in my armor so I can walk right?"

Jean grunted. "This again?"

Bethany Anne shrugged. "I could point out that I'm not known for letting go once my mind is set. I spend so much time in armor these days that I haven't even looked at a pair of pumps since the war began." Her hard expression softened a micro-second, just long enough for Jean to see the woman behind the façade. "It feels...*wrong*."

Jean looked at Bethany Anne with despair. "Seriously, how about I work on completely eliminating the drag when you walk the Etheric? Or on improving the nano-fabric to make it strong enough to make plate armor obsolete?"

Bethany Anne considered which she'd prefer. "Dammit. Okay, but I'm not going to be happy until I get what I want. You know that, right?"

Jean chuckled, moving ahead of Bethany Anne as they reached her operations hut in the center of the workshop. "I do know you."

Bethany Anne walked in and made a beeline for the chair in the corner she liked. She settled back while Jean rummaged in the fridge behind her horseshoe desk. "Has Qui'nan finished designing my home?"

"You're in luck, I have one Coke left." Jean handed the bottle to Bethany Anne and opened her water. "I told you she locked herself in her office? She's redesigning the whole fleet."

Bethany Anne paused with the bottle at her lips. "Don't fuck around, Jean. Show me the ship already."

Jean waved a hand over the console sensor in the center of her desk, the only surface in the room that wasn't piled with forgotten projects. Her grin turned into a frown when nothing happened. "CEREBRO, you're making me look bad. Where's my workstation, you bunch of fuckwits?"

An empty framework for a superdreadnought appeared over her desk. "Apologies," a single voice offered somewhat bashfully from the speaker. "We are with the Collective."

Jean tapped her console. "I keep hearing that from you. Do I need to restrict your access to them?"

"It is unavoidable," the solitary EI replied. "We are taken up with translating for them."

Bethany Anne frowned. "That can't keep happening. What percentage of you does it actually take to translate?"

"Close to sixty percent of the available remaining processing power, after accounting for the running of the station," CEREBRO replied. "It is stretching us to the point where we sent a request back to High Tortuga for more EIs to be assigned to our group. We expect the cradle containing them to arrive tomorrow."

Bethany Anne wrinkled her nose. "ADAM, see what you can do to help lighten the load around here until then."

Jean looked up from her console. "It's ready."

Bethany Anne scanned the image of the city-sized battleship, noting the separation between residential areas and the inner workings of the ship. "Can it take me long-range and flatten whatever I find when I get there?"

Jean grinned. "And then some. It has—"

Bethany Anne waved a hand to cut her off. "It will suffice. Build it."

Jean nodded, seeing the walls come down. There would be time to heal. "Yes, ma'am, my Queen, your Empr…"

"Don't you say it," Bethany Anne cut her off. "I can't replace you."

She winked at Jean.

21

QT2, QBBS *Helena*, No-Ox Habitat

Bethany Anne ran through her list of everyone who could possibly break the barrier that was hampering communication efforts with the Collective as her roamer descended into the deep.

The problem was, telepathy was the eight survivors' only form of speaking to anyone. The obstacle was that short of reassigning one of the very few people she had with mental abilities from the battle line where they were needed, there were no options she could figure out just yet.

She halted the roamer's plunge into the depths of the crystal-clear water and got to her feet to wait for the conduit to emerge from the kelp at the bottom of the habitat. The kelp was fast-growing, which was a good thing since the Collective ate twice their body weight in it every day.

Bethany Anne had been surprised to learn the Collective were vegetarians by choice. She would never have guessed that after witnessing them gorge on Ooken flesh during the fight in the factory.

A flash of gray indicated the conduit's arrival. It surged out of the kelp at speed, slowing its ascent by extending its tentacles to use the water as a brake. *Baby god, you have returned.*

Bethany Anne folded her arms. *I thought we agreed to stop the god talk?* she reminded it. *How is your temporary home? Any problems apart from communicating with my people?*

The conduit's body rippled. *We are comfortable here, if lonely still. We long to be reunited with our kin.*

Bethany Anne smiled sadly. *I'm going to do my best to recover as many as I can. I came here to ask if you would care to access the final memories of your...I want to say cousin. Does that relationship make any sense to you?*

It does not, the conduit replied. *We are one. However, we understand what you offer, and we accept with thanks.*

"Maybe one day soon we can speak about the concept of individuality." Bethany Anne muttered. She opened her mind to the conduit and showed the eight Collective the prisoner's last moments in detail.

She left them shortly thereafter with the promise to return with a solution to the Collective's isolation as soon as she had one.

Bethany Anne turned the problem over on her journey back to Devon. Practically, there was no way she could afford to lose anyone who could protect their team from the mental manipulation of the Ooken.

It occurred to her as Devon came into sight that Jean

was just about annoyed enough by the disruption to her schedule to find a way around it using technology.

It wasn't a problem. All she had to do was find a messenger with no fear of a painful death, and she was golden.

Devon, First City, Bazaar

Morning broke over First City, streaking the sky with purple and gold.

The traders milled around their stalls, huddled over hot drinks and gossip about the neighbors in the pre-business lull.

The bell in the clock tower rang for the start of business hours, and the gates groaned open to admit shoppers as the aromas of fresh baked goods from the food vendors floated out to greet them.

The morning passed as mornings do. The bazaar hummed with conversation from the knots of shoppers who filtered in and filled the streets between the stalls. The subject turned more often than not to the activity in the Enclave. The Bakas had lately become a presence in the city, something they had avoided prior to Baba Yaga's speech.

The general public was gripped by their emergence, although the network's coverage of the war just about beat them as the hot topic. The vendors were of a different opinion, even those making a killing on Baka-related merchandise.

While the open doors of the Hexagon were good for

business, the Bakas being at war with each other would fuck things up for everyone in the bazaar. Nobody thought for a second that Baba Yaga would stand for it, and then their customer base would get slashed into thirds.

Quite literally.

The general consensus was that the sooner the rumblings died down, the better. As the early rush ebbed and the lunch crowd began to arrive, the odds of that hope being realized plummeted.

Gabriel and Trey compared their purchases as they cut through the side street that would bring them out in the Hexagon section of the bazaar.

"Function over beauty every time," Gabriel argued. "If a blade is perfectly balanced, it will look good anyway." He replaced the dagger he'd bought in its sheath and slipped it into his bag with the other items they'd picked up.

Trey held up his choice so Gabriel could read the intricate etching on the blade. "Somebody did this by hand, and they put hours of work into it. The blade is just as strong as that plain thing you bought."

Gabriel shrugged. "I'm not judging. We'll see which is better when we get back to the Hexagon. Just don't tell Alexis or K'aia we went out. They won't get that this was important."

Trey snickered. "I hadn't planned on it. They have taken it upon themselves to be the substitute for Mahi' while I'm staying with you."

Gabriel grimaced. "Ooh. Sucks to be you."

Trey chuckled. "They care, is all. It's not like I'm dodging blades in my sleep. I can avoid them until they let me breathe." He raised his eyebrows. "You know, if this is what it is to be bonded to a female, I can see my people getting impatient with me to take a mate."

Gabriel snorted laughter. "Right? Girls think they know everything."

"That's because they do," Trey admitted. "We would be much unhappier without them. Doesn't mean I want to choose one to bond with."

"Well, yeah." Gabriel patted Trey on the back. "My dad says women are always right, even when they aren't, and a wise man knows to never admit any of that, or he'll never hear the end of it. I can't see why it's worth the effort."

Trey snorted. "You will soon enough."

They crossed at an intersection with a busy food stand on the far side.

"You wanna grab a bite?" Gabriel asked, indicating the food stand. "Smells like hotdogs to me."

Trey looked like he was about to vomit. "Yeah, no. I'll give hotdogs a miss, thanks. I can't believe humans eat their companions. It's just wrong."

Gabriel had no clue what his friend meant for a moment, then it clicked. "Trey, what do you think a hotdog is made from?"

"Well, dog meat, I assume," he replied. "But I met a dog recently, and they are delightful beings. I would never eat one."

Gabriel clapped Trey on the back. "Hotdogs are mostly chicken, which you love. C'mon, I'll treat you."

They waited in line for a few minutes and emerged with two fully loaded hotdogs.

Trey sniffed his skeptically. "Human food is confusing. Is all this plant matter on the meat necessary?" he asked, poking at the onions with a claw.

Gabriel wiped ketchup from the corner of his mouth. "Mmff, totally."

Trey closed his eyes, wrinkled his nose, and screwed up his courage to take a bite. He almost had the hotdog to his mouth when it was slapped out of his hand.

"You're a disgrace, Tu Keigd," Ch'Irzt sneered. "Dating with a human? It's bad enough we have to associate with them. My father says—"

"I don't care what that poisonous old shit has to say," Trey retorted, shoving his cousin. "That was my lunch!"

The street around them had cleared by this point, the vendors nearby pulling their shutters down in preparation for a fight breaking out.

Gabriel saw Ch'Irzt wasn't alone. Em'Eir and three other Bakas around Ch'Irzt's age egged him on from the background, and a few adults had recognized Trey and stopped shopping to gawk. He opened a mental link to Alexis. *We might be in a tight spot. You busy?*

Give me a minute, she replied. *Where are you?*

Fifty yards from the plaza, Gabriel told her. *Just follow the sound of Chet's dumb ass getting beaten. He's with Em'Eir and a couple of others, and Trey's not taking the interruption to his day all that well.*

Not taking it well was something of an understatement.

Trey looked for a moment like he was going to turn the other cheek as he'd done so many times when Ch'Irzt was making a point of proving what an absolute dick he was. Then he surprised everyone who knew him: he punched his cousin in the jaw and dived on top to hit him some more as he fell.

Trey pounded on Ch'Irzt with all the frustration of a childhood of sucking up his cousin's bullying in the name of keeping the peace.

Gabriel saw that intervening would resolve nothing. Em'Eir appeared to understand that too, since he did not assert himself on his older brother's behalf. This was a fight that had been brewing for a long time, and for the first time, Trey wasn't holding back for the sake of his mother. Gabriel cursed the family politics that prevented them from taking care of what really mattered—the Kurtherians.

Even in his rage Trey kept his composure, whereas Ch'Irzt fell back on his instinct to use his size and weight against his shorter, lankier cousin. Every time Ch'Irzt regained his feet, Trey knocked him down again without appearing to put much effort into it.

Ch'Irzt saw red and charged Trey, managing to catch him around the waist and drive him to the ground.

Gabriel whooped when Trey avoided a loss by twisting to land on Ch'Irtz's back with his cousin's arm in a high lock.

Alexis arrived to find her brother cheering Trey on instead of trying to diffuse the fight. "Why aren't you doing something?" she hissed at Gabriel.

Gabriel frowned. "I *am* doing something. I'm enjoying the hell out of seeing Chet get his ass handed to him. Look at Trey; he loves it, and it's giving him some positive attention for a change."

Alexis couldn't disagree. She glanced around the people

placing bets on the outcome of the fight, noting that the other Bakan youths were looking at their future leader with respect for the first time she'd seen since meeting him. Then she spotted a group of older Bakas with disapproving stares approaching.

Alexis worked out that the male was another of Trey's uncles—Da'Mahin she recalled. She readied an energy ball as he strode toward the fight with clenched fists. "We should call Mom."

"What is this about?" Da'Mahin demanded of Em'Eir. His face clouded further at the mumbled answer, and his companions were no happier to hear whatever Trey's cousin had told them.

Gabriel tensed, ready to act if Trey's uncle moved to lay a hand on his friend. "I think we can take care of it. Didn't Mom leave for Moen this morning?"

Alexis shook her head when one of Da'Mahin's companions dropped his hand to his belt. *This is going to get ugly if we don't get her or Aunt Tabitha here,* she reasoned. *Mom, are you still on Devon?*

I'm about to leave, Bethany Anne replied. *What's up?*

Alexis pared the story to its essentials. *Gabriel called me for help. Trey got into a fight with Chet in the bazaar, and some of the adults are getting invo—*

Bethany Anne stepped out of the Etheric with an energy ball in each hand and Baba Yaga's angry face. "What the hell is going on here?" she demanded, striding over to stand between the youths and Trey's family.

Trey and Ch'Irzt broke apart, panting. They looked around at the crowd, dazed by the apparent materialization of their uncle and his band.

Bethany Anne raised an eyebrow at Da'Mahin. "Well? I asked a question."

The large male dropped his eyes. "Family business does not concern you, Baba Yaga. My sister's son is out of line, and it is my duty to correct him in his father's absence."

"Children, get yourselves inside the Hexagon." Bethany Anne crooked a finger at Trey. "I will call your mother, and she can deal with your uncle. We will discuss why you three were in the bazaar later. You'd better have a damn good reason as to why you were outside without a guard."

Gabriel winced. "Don't blame Alexis. She only came because I called her."

Bethany Anne raised an eyebrow and pointed at the Hexagon. *"Later."* She opened her connection to Michael as the children headed inside. ***Our son decided that being grounded wasn't for him. He and Trey snuck out.***

They didn't take K'aia with them? Michael asked. *That boy is toast.*

Apparently not, Bethany Anne snarked. ***Alexis called me to break up a fight between Trey and that punch-drunk cousin of his in the bazaar. Gabriel called her in the first place, so I'm not mad at her. One of Mahi'Takar's brothers was about to take advantage of the situation until I stepped in.***

I will have words with our son, Michael replied. *Where are the children now?*

I sent them up to the apartment. I think we're going to have to make Trey's stay official.

So three become four. Michael's tone told her he was fine with that. *It's not an issue.*

Clearing out Moen can't wait any longer. I need you to take care of this while I'm gone.

Tabitha and I have things under control, he assured her.

That's all I needed to hear. Bethany Anne turned her finger on Trey's uncle. "You people make me *sick.* Takar'-Tu'Reigd and Mahi'Takar are under my personal protection from this moment on. Anyone who so much as hurts their *feelings* will learn what it is to live for an eternity without hope. Am I making myself clear to you, Da'Mahin?"

Da'Mahin glared at his feet. "Perfectly, Baba Yaga," he replied sullenly, wondering how the Witch knew his name when they had never met before.

Bethany Anne didn't need to read Da'Mahin's mind to know his thoughts, but since she was inside it, she would leave a little gift should he decide to betray his sister again. "You have it tattooed on your forearm," she told him, causing the Baka even more confusion since he was wearing greaves that covered the tattoo. "Your time of plotting against Mahi'Takar and her son is over. She has my support, which means you'd all better fall in line or take the next ship off my fucking planet before I put you in a box." Her lip curled as she looked at Mahi'Takar's brothers. "Tu'Reigd is no longer accessible to any member of his family who poses a risk to his life. That boy has spent most of his life in a constant battle to keep your fucking knives out of his mother's back. God help you *all* by the time I'm done training him. You sure as shit don't deserve the leader he's growing into."

Bethany Anne didn't care to hear any reply Da'Mahin

made; she had more important things on her mind than some ignorant asshole's butthurt. She stepped into the Etheric and took a shortcut to her private hangar.

The lights came on automatically when Bethany Anne's foot touched the floor of the transfer area. However, the illumination did nothing in her eyes to lend life to the uninhabited ship in the center of the hangar.

Bethany Anne walked over to the *Izanami* and lifted a hand to brush the strut. "You overly sentimental ass," she murmured, not caring that Izanami could no longer hear her. "I should have you reconstructed just so I can beat some sense into you."

The cold metal felt dead to her touch, compounding her sense of loss. She let her hand fall to her side and turned away from the empty husk, thinking about the events leading up to Izanami's suicide. "They keep giving me more reasons to lose my shit."

TOM spoke up as she walked out of hangar one and made the turn for Hangar Three. **You are stronger than that.**

Fucking right I am, she retorted. *Throwing a galaxy-sized tantrum isn't going to do anything except hand the Seven exactly what they want on a plate. I'm on to them, TOM. Whichever clan it is, wherever they're fuckin hiding, I'll track them down and exterminate them just like I did the Phraim-'Eh. They can't take anyone else from me if I kill them first.*

I don't doubt you will, TOM told her gently. **One step at a time, yes?**

Bethany Anne nodded as she entered the hangar. *Step*

one: wipe my hands of Moen permanently. She walked with purpose, missing the delicate click of the heels she loved so much, and reached out to touch the minds of her Guards as she passed their ships on the way to the QBS *Sayomi*.

Saddle up, Bitches. Saint Payback is ready to ride.

Devon, QBS *Sayomi*, Bridge

John began his pre-flight checklist, grinning at Bethany Anne's proclamation. *We're happy to preach that shit all day long, BA. Get your righteous ass on the damn ship so we can get started.*

Bethany Anne materialized behind John's chair and leaned over to stick her face into his HUD display, distorting the hologram. "You haven't even started the ship yet."

John flinched. "Jesus, Bethany Anne, you scared the shit out of me." He held up a finger when she burst out laughing. "It's bad enough Sayomi spends most of her time using your face to cut years off my life."

Bethany Anne snickered. "Jean told me all about her plan to make sure you miss her. I couldn't resist."

John frowned as he disengaged from the HUD. "Is that what this is about? Jean wants me thinking about her?" He sighed. "She should know I do already. Most wives would send a gift. Why does mine feel the need to terrify me into coming home?"

Bethany Anne took the co-pilot's seat. "You tell me? You're the one who's been married to her for so long. Did you do something to piss her off before we left?"

John shrugged. "Fuck if I know. I'll find out when I get back to her, that's a certainty." He raised his chair to its upright position. "We good to go?"

Bethany Anne laced her hands behind her head. "We're still in the hangar?"

2 2

Moen, Elset, QBS *Sayomi*

Silent, deadly, and invisible, five Shinigami-class ships cut through the atmosphere, their passing causing the clouds to swirl around silently as they passed. They came in to hover high above the underground complex where Bethany Anne had found the Alders on her previous trip.

Bethany Anne deactivated her chair's HUD and got to her feet. *Is everyone clear on their objectives?*

Simple, Scott replied. *Protect the civilians. Kill as many of those slippery motherfuckers as we can see. Don't die before you get done with the rest. That about cover it?*

Bethany Anne looked at John and shrugged. **Pretty much.**

What do we do if the Moen decide to take a hostile attitude toward us? Darryl asked.

Bethany Anne had already considered that. **The Moen have been made aware this is happening, so any you find fighting are there of their own free will.**

Gabrielle sniffed. *I still cannot believe they lied about being captives for so long.*

I can, John disagreed. *They'll do whatever they're told to do.*

That has more to do with their leadership, Bethany Anne told them, glancing at the cooler between her chair and John's. **Shouldn't be a problem after the next thirty minutes or so. You all have your targets, and the last one to reach theirs has to give Jean some bad news.**

John's eyes widened as the others dropped off the link and peeled off on trajectories that would take them to the other major population areas around the planet. "You can't be serious? I'm already living in the outer space equivalent of a house of horrors. Do you want her to murder me for real?"

Bethany Anne winked at him. "We're above our target. I'm not waking up on the first day aboard my new ship to have it turn on me because I pissed Jean off."

John shrugged. "Fair enough. What's your plan?"

"We have a delivery to make and five cities to clear." Bethany Anne picked up the cooler. "I'll tell you one thing. The Alders had better be damned fucking grateful I'm not sticking their cure where the sun doesn't shine."

John snorted as he held her wrist for a moment. "I mean, you *could*."

Bethany Anne sighed. "I really could." She took them into the Etheric and pulled John to the exit point that brought them out in the underground complex.

Bethany Anne hadn't been in this part of the complex on her last visit. She felt around in the mental space, finding the tacky-feeling minds she was looking for a short distance along the passage from where she and John stood. *Over here.*

They made their way along the corridor, pausing when they heard voices arguing nearby.

That them? John asked, bringing up his JD Special when the anger in the Moen voices spiked.

Unfortunately, yes, Bethany Anne confirmed, one ear on the Alders' heated debate over her sanctions. She picked out Meon as the most vocal proponent for screwing her over and held up a hand to stall John. *Wait a minute. This looks to have been going on for a while. I want to listen in.*

John grimaced. *Do they remind you of seagulls? They have that squawky tone to their speech.*

Like nails on a chalkboard, Bethany Anne agreed. *Fucking dumbasses. They couldn't get around me even if they had more than three brain cells to share between them.* Her lip curled as Meon's faction continued their attempt to persuade the others into an early demise at Bethany Anne's hands. *Let me tell you, none of this is making me feel any less inclined to apply the cure rectally.*

John tensed, suppressing his urge to shut the Alders' mouths permanently. *Why are you helping this bunch of snakes?*

Because I'm not an asshole Kurtherian, Bethany Anne replied. *Who would leave an entire species to go extinct slowly over generations?*

John didn't find the excuse to be valid. *I can understand the fucking reasoning behind the way they've chosen to be, but it's still wrong.*

Bethany Anne shrugged. *I'm past caring. I have an obligation to myself, which I'm about to fulfill, but I don't give a shit about these people. In fact...* She passed John the cooler as Mahi'Takar's words came back to her. *This is the perfect opportunity to remind everyone why it's a bad idea to piss off Baba Yaga.* She deactivated her helmet and stepped into the Etheric.

John chose the more conventional route into the room, opening the door with his size-fourteen skeleton key. He evaluated the situation as he strode over the remains of the door, counting twelve Moen around the long table in the center of the room.

Well, eleven.

Bethany Anne stood on the table with her back to him, bathed in a red glow, one hand raised. Across from her, a female Moen hung suspended in the air, looking like she was finding it difficult to draw sufficient breath to make her excuses.

"The cooler." Bethany Anne pointed at the table without turning around. She tightened her hold on Meon's throat when John placed it beside her. "A little faith would have gotten you a lot farther with me," she stated. "I was clear about what would happen if you crossed me." She clenched her hand, cutting off Meon's air supply for good.

She turned on the remaining Alders with a snarl as the body fell to the floor. "My sanctions will remain in place until such time as I decide they are no longer necessary to contain your fucking idiocy. Then I will turn over the task of babysitting you to the Federation. Does anyone else have a problem with that?"

The Alders cowered, heads bowed.

"Speak up," Bethany Anne demanded. "Give me a

reason not to end you all now and replace you, because I'm not getting that you understand."

The Alder who had argued with Meon at their last meeting somehow managed to find his balls and stood up. "You make us prisoners on our own planet, Baba Yaga."

Bethany Anne laughed. "Prisoners? You're fucking kidding, right? I offered you a way off this planet, and you fucksucking morons threw it back in my face. You can fucking rot here for all I care. I've got people in really bad situations to help."

The Alders burst into argument.

She turned her back on them and hopped down from the table. "Shut your whining mouths and accept it. You made yourselves slaves, and I'd say it's an upturn. Take your cure and grow the fuck up. If I have to come back here, I'll be leaving this planet in ashes."

Bethany Anne placed a hand on John's shoulder and took them back into the Etheric. *I have not missed dealing with petty politics one minute since I stepped down.*

John grunted, bracing himself for the drain being in the Etheric in his armor put on his energy. *I dunno. You have that ability to really connect with people. It was kind of like you never left.*

Bethany Anne's jaw twitched. *You think? I haven't got time to be distracted. They can sort their own shit out. Doesn't mean it frustrates me any less.*

John bumped her with his shoulder. *If only we could find a horde of mindless killing machines for you to take that frustration out on.*

Bethany Anne chuckled, waving her free hand to open a path back to the city. *Ask and you will receive.* She pulled

John out onto one of the lower terraces. *Welcome to Ooken Central.*

John grinned, his free hand dipping to his other Jean Dukes Special. *Are we starting the party or crashing it?*

Bethany Anne raised an eyebrow. *We're the law, coming in to bust this shit up.* She centered her connection to the Etheric and reached for the hive mind. *I have the majority. You take care of the ones that slip away.*

John frowned. *What are you planning?*

Bethany Anne walked onto the terrace. *This.*

John's jaw dropped when every Ooken on the terrace suddenly ceased whatever they were doing and stiffened briefly before collapsing on the spot. *What the fuck?*

Keep watching, and tell the others to be ready. I'm not done. Bethany Anne rose into the air as she worked her way out from the terrace, tearing into the hive mind to connect with every Ooken in Elset.

The Ooken fought Bethany Anne's control as awareness of her attack rippled outward through the hive mind. She was aware of the comm chatter between John and the others, but she didn't need to hear it when she trusted them to take care of their parts while she did hers. *ADAM, how long is this going to take?*

>>**No longer than a few minutes for each city,**<< he informed her. >>**The Ooken are concentrated around them, but I get the feeling that cleanup afterward isn't your concern here.**<<

The Moen can clean it up themselves. Do I look like a fucking maid service? Bethany Anne gritted her teeth and pushed harder.

. . .

Orbiting Moen, QBS *G'laxix Sphaea*, Bridge

Kiel turned in his chair without tearing his eyes from the screen, almost falling in his haste to get Kael-ven's attention. "Are you seeing this?"

Kael-ven waved him off, engrossed in what was happening on the terraces of Elset. "It's Bethany Anne; she's finally lost it with the situation. About damn time, too."

Kiel panned out as the circle of death around Bethany Anne seeped out of the city and across the dunes toward the nearest city. "But there are half a billion Ooken down there."

Kael-ven chuckled. "And that makes a difference why?"

Kiel shook his head. "I don't think she's been this angry since the end of the Leath war," he murmured, mostly to himself.

Kael-ven said what they were both thinking. "At least she found an appropriate outlet for it this time. Chasing her across galaxies was nobody's idea of a fun time."

Elset

Bethany Anne heard another voice in the mindspace. It was weak and faint, but it was definitely not Ooken. She focused, isolating the single sweet note in the grinding cacophony. *There's a Collective here. TOM, can you and ADAM hold the connection to the hive mind while I free it?*

No, was TOM's simple answer. **However, I can sense its proximity.**

Fuckdammit, Bethany Anne cursed. The voice was too

far gone for her to speak to them. *It might not be too late if someone could get there.*

Maybe? TOM hedged.

Good enough. Bethany Anne cut in on the Bitches' bitching. *There's a Collective somewhere under the city. It's near death, and I'm stuck here.*

On it, John told her. *Any idea where, exactly?*

Bethany Anne searched to refine the location of the Collective's voice. *It was coming from below the dune to the southeast of the city. I don't see a way in for you. Let me fix that.*

She flicked a spark of Etheric energy toward the rolling expanse, feeding it more energy as it hurtled toward its target. The sand imploded in a spray of molten glass on impact, leaving behind a glowing tunnel into the side of the dune. *There you go.*

Eric chuckled. *Should be cool by the time we get there. You know we'll do what we can to save them.*

I just called for the Polaris, Gabrielle informed the team. *They'll be here as soon as they can make it from QT2.*

Wrap up what you're doing and get your asses over to Elset, John told them. *BA has her own battle to fight.*

Bethany Anne returned her focus to resuming her attack on the Ooken. The mindspace was empty for kilometers around her. She reached out, cutting through the paltry resistance they had thrown up while she was distracted.

The challenge was the sheer numbers. Even together, they were no match for her will. The weight of their consciousness, however, was crushing in its volume.

Bethany Anne blocked it out, insulating herself with the

sound of the Etheric. Its heartsong strengthened her, just as Michael had earlier when she had spilled her grief. She became pure rage, sharpened to a keen edge by the loss of Izanami, immune to the grating screech of the Ooken attempting to shred her mind. She increased the pressure on the hive mind, forcing her way into hundreds and then thousands of minds at a time.

The song shifted as the energy cascading from Bethany Anne's body consumed more and more of the hive mind. She felt it strain to do her will, restricted only by her refusal to give up control. *This is getting to be too much to handle,* she told TOM. *What happens when I run out of Ooken on this planet? Will it try to find more?*

Bethany Anne, I can't say.

Bethany Anne pressed her lips together. *Why not? I want to know what will happen if I release this energy. Will it stop at the Ooken?*

TOM considered the question for a moment before replying. **Really, I can't say. What you are accomplishing with the Etheric is so far beyond even the most tenable theories I have studied that all I have been able to do recently is try to figure out what you did after you do it.**

Hmmm... Bethany Anne hadn't realized she'd finally surpassed the sum of TOM's knowledge on his own religion. *Then you'd better get started on "The Book of Thales of Miletus." We'll figure it out together—you, me, and ADAM. I'm going to let some of the energy go and see what it does.*

She isolated a section of the hive mind and allowed a small amount of the energy she was holding to run free. It was difficult not to pull it back immediately as she let go, her muscle memory demanded she hold tight to it. The song became exultant as the energy pulsed and burned through the nanocytes in the Ooken's brains, frying them simultaneously as it exploded outward from her.

The energy dissipated at the boundary Bethany Anne had created, rejoining the whole to be given fresh purpose.

You have your answer, TOM murmured, staggered by what he was witnessing.

Then let's blow this popsicle stand.

Bethany Anne released the energy and the Etheric erupted from her in a torrential rush that shook her to the core. The force flung her head and arms back, bowing her spine as her hair flew wildly around her body.

Lightning flashed overhead in the cloudless sky, pounding the terrace around her.

Bethany Anne felt no pain, just the knowledge that wherever the song was heard, Ooken died.

It was only now as she became one with the energy that she understood the siren song was no more than a plea for connection, for her to be part of the whole.

She had always operated on the assumption that the Etheric was something to be manipulated and controlled, and resisted at all costs. TOM's teachings had failed over and over to disabuse her of the notion, but her eyes were open now.

The glimpses she'd had of universal knowledge were a candle to the sun of her epiphany. There was something *beyond* Ascension.

Something more.

The Kurtherians had it all wrong. Ascension was weakness, an inability to hold onto individuality. It was not the goal, but the final tempting barrier between the initiate and true knowledge.

She did not have to ascend unless she chose to.

Not now…

Not ever.

23

Moen, Elset, Southeast Side

John looked over the barrel of his Jean Dukes Special, treading carefully on the still-malleable glass as he walked down the tunnel.

He'd debated decreasing his armor's weight, but the loss of advantage compared to the ruin of his boots was no choice at all. The decision was only partially clouded by Jean's gentle reminder of how long it had been since they'd last seen each other.

There were no Ooken here, save the dead he'd passed on his way to the tunnel. Bethany Anne hadn't had a blowup like this in...well, *ever*. Scott kept up a running commentary in his ear, checking off the kilometers as he sped to Elset.

Almost there. Don't go in without me.

Too late, John told him. *You should move faster.* He turned at a scuffle near the tunnel entrance.

Scott shucked his G-rig as he came to a stop, drawing

his Jean Dukes Specials as it hit the floor. "*Who* isn't fucking fast enough? Quit beating your chest and let's go already."

Gabrielle joined them a moment later, her face flushed from running. "You assholes could have waited." She looked around. "Darryl and Eric haven't made it yet?"

John waved them on. "They're on their way. They'll find us when they get here."

The three of them advanced, weapons ready for the first whisper of trouble. Bethany Anne's tunnel cut deep into the dune, the blast having fired the sand into murky crystalline glass that looked all too familiar to those who had been inside an Ooken structure.

"Guess we know what the Ooken want with this planet," John murmured, knocking on the brittle structure with his knuckles.

"Sand-mining." Scott sneered. "What a life."

John felt the same disgust for the generations of innocents who had been tricked into devoting their lives to no cause whatsoever. "We need to find a place where the tunnel intersects with the existing structure. Split up and start looking for anyplace lighter or darker than the rest."

They started examining the walls of the tunnel as they traveled deeper.

Scott was first to find something. "Check this out," he called back. "It could be our way in." He tapped the wall. "If you don't mind making a mess."

John and Gabrielle came over.

"What the… Well, we reached the complex." Gabrielle made a face at the cooked Ooken trapped in the glass, tapping in front of the dead creature with her pistol. "That had better not smell when we break it open."

John shrugged. "Why? Will it put you off barbeque?"

Gabrielle's eyes widened. "Not even. Michael's idea of eating a freaking dinosaur was enough to do that." She pinched her nose and fired at the dead Ooken.

The glass shattered, releasing the Ooken and a stench Gabrielle was glad she'd opted not to experience based on the tears the guys were trying not to release. "Boys, stop being dramatic." She fired again to widen the hole to a size she could get through without soiling herself on Ooken-splatter and stepped through, still holding her nose.

"Can you hear the Collective?" John asked as he came through the hole.

Gabrielle tested her tentative connection to the mind-space. "I think so." She looked left, then right, and pointed. "This way."

Scott was last in. He looked around the pillared chamber. "How do you know?"

Gabrielle tapped her head. "The smarter ones of us have been working on improving our ability with the Etheric. I can almost hear thoughts, like a stone skimming the surface of water."

She led them toward the place she'd felt an occupied emptiness.

They came to a huge block of stone set into the sand and John moved ahead of Scott and Gabrielle. "The sweet spot is higher on these." He lifted a boot and shattered the stone with a single kick.

Scott leapfrogged John with his JD Special raised. "I

hope the doors aren't load-bearing. The tomb vibe in here is gonna be totally ruined if you keep fucking them up."

Gabrielle put a hand on Scott's arm. "We're too late. I think it just died."

John and Scott entered the chamber beyond to confirm Gabrielle's sense.

"Shit, you're right," Scott called back to her.

Gabrielle rushed in, taking in the loose bag of flesh floating aimlessly in the tank. "We were so close!" she cried, punching the stone lintel into dust.

The doorframe shifted, and sand dusted their heads.

John looked up. "There's nothing we can do here, and we need to leave before it comes down on our heads. Bethany Anne should be about done up there, and I want to see my wife."

Scott nodded in agreement. "I wasn't planning on a desert burial."

Gabrielle wiped her eyes. "Okay, let's get out of here."

They made their way back to the glass tunnel at a sprint.

The hole Gabrielle had blown in the tunnel was half-filled with sand when they got there. It spilled out on both sides, partially blocking their escape.

"Gabrielle first," John demanded.

Gabrielle didn't waste time arguing the finer points of chivalry. She dived through head-first, knowing John wouldn't budge until she did.

Scott was next, his passage widening the way for John to get the bulk of his shoulders through sideways.

The glass creaked ominously as John forced his way

through the slowly diminishing hole into the tunnel. "Get moving!"

They drove for the surface as the glass began cracking under the pressure of the sand above. No one looked back or wasted breath to speak.

The interior grew steadily lighter as they neared the mouth the tunnel, the damp air becoming easier for their heaving lungs to bear.

Eric and Darryl came padding toward them with their weapons up as they reached the exit.

"Turn around," John barked. "It's gonna collapse."

A reverberation shook the ground, and as if to prove John's point a chunk of glass fell way back in the tunnel. The sand only needed the invitation of gravity to surge into the tunnel, spilling rapidly toward them.

Bethany Anne appeared and disappeared again.

John felt himself being dragged backward. His heart sank when the weight of the Etheric slammed down on him without warning.

"I'm beginning to think you pull shit like this just to test me," Bethany Anne bitched, bending at the waist to yell into his face. "Get your ass up. We're going back to Devon, and then we're going to have a discussion on your abilities."

John rubbed his face as he sat up, still dazed from the unexpected transfer. The others were in a similar state. He pulled his aching body up off the ground, Bethany Anne's words resolving into a coherent sentence. "What do you mean, 'our abilities?'"

Bethany Anne didn't stop to look back. "You'll find out when we get back. I'm holding a briefing."

. . .

High Tortuga, Space Fleet Base, Barnabas' Office

Barnabas had been waiting too long for Nickie's report. He'd fully expected her to be difficult for a while, which was why he had talked Tabitha out of her access to Nickie's iteration of Meredith.

Why he hadn't thought to do so the moment his recalcitrant niece had shown up on his doorstep out of the blue, he didn't know. Meredith was much more pleasant to deal with, even if being bonded with Nickie had made her one of the snarkier EIs he'd come across.

He read the text report that had accompanied the salient moments of Nickie's assignment, which Meredith had been thoughtful enough to provide video of.

Those had been eye-opening in the extreme. He had suspected Nickie had a softer side when it came to her crew but witnessing it was a different matter altogether.

Barnabas wasn't of a mind to intrude.

He closed the report and considered the snag her crew had come across. A certain company Barnabas had his eye on as a massive timesaver in the setup phase of the operation was being less than amicable when it came to honoring their side of the offer they had submitted to him.

Nickie had gone in to discover whether the distasteful Voidrux man actually had a company in liquidation or whether he was all hot air with no balloon to fill.

The answer turned out to be more complicated, as they were often turning out to be when Nickie was the one who went digging. The Grimes in her wouldn't allow that woman to rest until she had the truth.

If only she weren't so easily offended.

The company existed. It was not, however, in liquidation. Barnabas needed a closer look at what was going on there than Nickie had been able to get on her short expedition. Did he have anyone on his shit list at the moment? He could only think of Nickie, and he had to admit he was at fault despite the good intentions of his gradual manipulation of her path.

Bethany Anne had seemingly been fond of meetings recently. Perhaps he would find his solution with her. He checked with CEREBRO, finding Bethany Anne had a briefing scheduled for tomorrow morning Devon time.

Barnabas got up from his desk and grabbed his traveling robe from the hat stand by the fireplace. "CEREBRO, inform the Queen I will be attending the briefing. Ask if she would wait before leaving Devon to speak to me if I don't make it in time." He couldn't help but notice the temporary piece of wood nailed over the broken window of Nickie's office on his way to Hangar One. "And arrange an appointment with a decorator after my return."

Devon, First City, The Hexagon, Penthouse Apartment

Bethany Anne had postponed the briefing to give Jean and Barnabas time to travel quietly to Devon. There were getting to be far too many journalists around the Hexagon for her liking.

She left the penthouse apartment, thinking to spend the unexpected free time with the children. There was no way they would be traveling with her or Michael for the foreseeable future.

It wasn't the disobedience or even the breach of trust. It was the mind-altering terror of realizing they were not safe, as she had thought, but there in the middle of the battlefield where literally fucking *anything* could have happened to them in the time between Izanami leaving the ship and John arriving to pick them up.

She gave exactly no fucks that her children teetered on the cusp of adulthood.

They could live a thousand years, and she would still feel her heart drop out of her ass at the thought of existing for even a moment in this life without them.

However, locking them down would only serve to make them hate her. Bethany Anne recognized the fine line between being a parent and a jailer, a guardian and a dictator.

She couldn't hold them to her forever, but she could surround them with a network of protection starting with her and Michael and moving out from K'aia and Trey to others she deemed worthy.

It was still control, but Bethany Anne was who she was, and she wouldn't change even if she had the ability to love with anything less than the burning intensity of an entire universe going supernova.

Bethany Anne found the children training with Michael, Tabitha, Addix, and Mahi'Takar in the smaller APA by the outdoor arena. She blew a kiss to Michael when he paused briefly to acknowledge her presence as she made her way to the seating area.

They sparred in two teams, age against experience, split by ability. Alexis and Gabriel battled Tabitha and Michael with the Etheric while Addix and Mahi'Takar defended against physical attacks by K'aia and Trey.

Bethany Anne wrinkled her nose, thinking they had to

get popcorn makers installed in the APA viewing areas. She settled in to watch, more than impressed to see that the light show from the other team did not distract Trey.

Having spent time being interrogated by the adolescent leader-in-waiting, she knew for a fact he was fascinated by Etheric energy. The focus he had on his opponents and teammates showed Bethany Anne a glimpse of the warrior he would grow into, and at that moment, she didn't doubt her prophecy in the bazaar would become a reality.

Likewise, she saw the same easy confidence in the way Gabriel and Alexis fought. Bethany Anne had learned early in motherhood that her iron fist was as useful as nipples on a chest plate when it came to teaching the twins. They only needed to be shown the basics of something to work it out, which was the kind of independence she would usually find pleasing.

However, when it came to her children, independence was a double-edged sword.

Bethany Anne's challenge had always been giving them the space they needed to thrive, which had surprised her since she'd had Michael pegged as Captain No when they were born.

She supposed they would be in the same situation had she and Michael not raised them to be warriors and leaders. Would watching them go off to college without looking back be any different emotionally?

Somehow, Bethany Anne thought it might be worse.

Addix made a jerky movement, which caught her eye and pulled her from her wandering thoughts.

The rest of the Ixtali's team stood around watching her curiously.

The Spymistress' mandibles were clenched in concentration, and then all of a sudden she was holding the wisp of a faint energy ball above her hands. She looked up as the other team stopped fighting to stare. "I...I *did* it!" She thrust her hands out to show them all, accidentally flicking the energy ball straight at Mahi'Takar.

Trey screamed and dived toward his mother, completely unnecessarily since Bethany Anne had already reached out with her mind to snatch the energy out of the air. He landed at his mother's feet in a puff of sand and gave a pained groan as the air was knocked out of his body.

Mahi'Takar waved her hands at her son. "Get up, Tu'Reigd. These people are going to a lot of effort to keep you alive. Nobody here wants either of us killed in a training accident. Why do you try so hard to put me in an early grave?"

Bethany Anne walked over and slipped between Michael and Tabitha to get to Addix. "You kept this quiet."

Addix chittered with delight. "Well, I didn't want the pressure. It's taken months in the Vid-docs to retrain my nanocytes to reach this stage." She shimmied on the spot, the movement strangely graceful for someone of her shape. "I made an energy ball. How about that?"

Bethany Anne pressed her lips together in thought, the slightest hint of a smile on her face. "Hmm. The Etheric and our own technology have been holding out on us."

Mahi'Takar spoke up. "I want this technology for Tu'Reigd. It will make him invulnerable."

Bethany Anne shook her head. "It doesn't, and I don't

hand out high-level technology like party favors. If he earns it, he'll get it, same as anyone else."

K'aia jabbed Trey with an elbow. "Good luck with that."

Trey was not in a joking mood for once. He nodded solemnly. "Not my focus. Mahi' is right; I need to become invulnerable. Not by taking shortcuts to greatness like those we left behind, but by becoming the best warrior I can be through blood and sweat and the lessons learned in both victory and defeat."

Damn, get that kid in a Pod-doc, Michael murmured into Bethany Anne's mind. *That much idealism isn't generally survivable at the best of times, and he's going to keep throwing himself in at the deep end until he ends up in an ocean with no float.*

Bethany Anne didn't disagree.

She waved a hand. "Fine. I'll meet in the middle. Trey gets partial enhancement so he doesn't get his overenthusiastic ass killed. Level two only, and over a few weeks," she modified to block Trey's protest. "You have to be able to withstand training with Alexis, Gabriel, and K'aia. No arguments.

Mahi'Takar nodded. "That will be satisfactory."

Bethany Anne held up a hand. "Don't thank me yet. I want Trey to move into the Hexagon until things are settled."

Mahi'Takar opened her mouth to argue but thought better of it. "I will agree on the condition Tu'Reigd remains on Devon."

Bethany Anne lifted her hands. "Suits me just fine. My children's actions have just earned them the grounding of a lifetime, which coincidentally means they are also confined to Devon. To the Hexagon, in fact, unless they are out with permission and guards. Does that sound agreeable to you?"

Mahi'Takar snorted. "From one mother to another, that's music to my ears."

24

Devon, The Hexagon, Network Command

Bethany Anne walked into the meeting room ahead of Michael and Addix.

Tabitha had opted to wait in the anteroom with Mahi'-Takar until it was the regent's turn to speak. Everyone else was inside, waiting for Bethany Anne to arrive.

John, Jean, and Gabrielle sat together, Barnabas was deep in communication with someone over his wrist-holo. Eve had her head bent over a datapad on the table.

The chatter died as Bethany Anne took her seat. "Thank you all for being here, not that 'mandatory' means 'show up if you feel like it.' Pass that along, before I have to." She ordered her mental checklist of the items for discussion. "We'll start with the wins since it's the longer list. Want to go first, Eve?"

Eve blinked. "Good to see you too, Bethany Anne." She flicked her fingers at the holosensor in the center of the table to bring up her report. "As you can see, research into the possible applications of the nanocyte suspension have already begun to yield results. Jean will talk about the improvements in our defensive technology, I have been working on implementing the discoveries into our Pod-doc technology."

She waved, and the image switched to show the results of multiple sets of test results. "My prototypes are showing promise. Addix has agreed to work with me to fine-tune the integration between body and mind, and I expect to have results to share by the next meeting."

Bethany Anne nodded and turned to Jean. "The shipyard?"

Jean smirked. "Is back in full production, thank all the non-existent gods of war and destruction. Construction on the other shipyards is underway again also. Like Eve said, what we're doing with the suspension is mind-blowing. Put it this way: seventeen Gates is going to look like a hop across a puddle for our ships when I've finished refitting them. Anyone coming up against us can and should kiss their ass goodbye."

Bethany Anne tapped her nails on the table. "What about our hard light tech? Do we have improvements there?"

Everyone in the room turned to Jean, who was not fooled for a second by Bethany Anne's apparently calm exterior.

Jean nodded. "Working on it. It's going to take time."

Bethany Anne shook her head. "No, it isn't. Where is William at the moment?" She looked around, getting no answer. "Never mind. I'll have him come over to the *Helena* to give you a hand as soon as he's done with whatever has dragged him in. Marcus and Bobcat, too, if they're amenable."

Jean nodded. "That would be good. I've missed having those three knuckleheads around to interrupt my day. Tina would be more than useful too if you can persuade her to come all the way out there since she's got a knack for thinking around those tricky problems."

She sat up straight, recalling something else. "That reminds me. Armor is coming along faster since I found a file of old designs one of the kids in Tina's Academy class did a lifetime ago. They were way beyond our capability to produce back then without mortgaging every asset you had, but I saw something in them, so I had them archived."

"But it's not too expensive anymore?" Bethany Anne inquired, her interest piqued.

Jean grinned. "Not anymore, and that's not all. The designs inspired a way for me to grant your most impractical wish."

Bethany Anne raised an eyebrow, leaning a scant inch closer to the table. "You're shitting me. For real?"

Jean winked. "All I need is an idea of what style you want. The fashion world is your oyster, not that you deserve it after inflicting that ass Rickie on me."

Bethany Anne fixed Gabrielle with a hard look.

Gabrielle lifted her hands. "You think I'm stupid enough to annoy Jean? Not likely. I owed Sabine a favor, and it all worked out in the end."

Bethany Anne tilted her head. "Hmm. Maybe you don't want to come with me after the briefing to research designs for Jean. It's fine if you want to stay behind."

Gabrielle perked up at that. "I heard shopping. Did I hear shopping?"

"I think you did," Jean agreed. "I'll sit this trip out since I have too much to do at the shipyard."

"Nice try, Jean." Bethany Anne grinned. "I need you there to take notes. And this time, we choose our disguises *before* we leave for the Federation. Nobody gets lithly paint on my upholstery afterward.

Gabrielle blushed, her mouth opening and closing like a fish's a couple of times. "That was an *accident*."

The Queen shrugged. "I don't care, I still had to get it cleaned. Okay, who's next?"

Barnabas cleared his throat, straightening in his seat to stick his hands into the sleeves of his robe. "I have a matter that needs your attention. The owner of one of the prospective companies for the logistics network is behaving like a man with something to hide. I had one of my assets—"

Bethany Anne cut in, narrowing her eyes at Barnabas. "That wouldn't by any chance be Nickie, would it?"

Jean jumped up when Barnabas nodded. "What?" she blurted, leaning over the table to yell directly into Barnabas' face. "You didn't think to tell us *she was back?*"

Barnabas took her tirade calmly, looking her right in the eyes. "Jean, if you had spoken to Lillian, you would have known weeks ago."

Jean clenched her teeth and sat down again in a huff. "Butt out of my relationship with my daughter," she growled.

Barnabas held up his hands. "By all means. Your granddaughter is more than enough of a handful."

John caught Jean as she lunged across the table. "Babe, leave it. Barnabas knows what he's doing." He fixed Barnabas with the patented Grimes stare, no happier with the revelation than Jean. "You'd *better* know what you're doing."

"Enough." Bethany Anne clapped to bring them to order. "Don't make me kick your asses out of here. Next item, enhancements."

"Is that why Mahi'Takar is here?" Addix asked, looking at the Baka. "To discuss her son's enhancement?"

Bethany Anne made a see-saw motion with her hand. "Partly. For those who haven't already heard, Addix has managed to unlock basic Etheric ability with training in the Vid-docs."

Congratulations went around the table, making Addix's mandibles chitter as she waved it off.

Bethany Anne waited for everyone to settle before continuing. "Addix isn't the only one reaching the next level. Michael, Tabitha, Gabrielle, Gabriel, and Alexis, in particular, have all been working to discover the extent of their nanocytes' capability. We know now that we've barely scratched the surface, and what I learned about the Etheric on Moen changes everything for us. Forget what you think you believe, because I sure as shit got an education recently."

"What does that mean for us, though?" Gabrielle asked, frowning slightly.

"It means…" Bethany Anne waited for a beat to make sure everyone was paying attention. "That the minute Eve has the upgrades on the Pod-docs completed and tested, you and the others are getting upgrades of your own."

The news went down exactly as she expected, meaning everyone started talking over each other to get their opinions in, while John sat back in stoic acceptance with his arms folded across his chest and kept his thoughts to himself.

Bethany Anne turned her head to raise an eyebrow at Michael. *I told you.*

Michael shook his head. "I'll go first."

Gabrielle cut out halfway through her rant about the *last* time she'd gotten into a Pod-doc and lost years of her life. She waved a finger at Michael. "You can go in if you like. *I* will continue the natural way."

Bethany Anne frowned. "This isn't an option, and I *don't* have time to argue. You get the upgrades, or I send your asses back to High Tortuga and you can wait the war out in the base where I don't have to worry about anyone *dying*."

She heard herself getting louder, but she didn't give a damn. "The Ooken aren't just some random species one of the clans picked up. The Kurtherians are growing them from genetic material obtained from the murder of any species with an ability they like the look of, like the *fucking cowards they are*."

She glanced around the table. "You can all be hurt by the Ooken, and I won't abide it for one minute longer than necessary." She stabbed a finger on the table. "We have them on the run, and I refuse to sit by and let you go out there without doing everything I can to keep you alive." She eyed each of them in turn. "Besides, we're going after them soon, and dragging your asses through the Etheric is not on the list of things I want to do before I get there. I need my strength to take down as many Ooken as the Seven can throw at us."

John snorted. "Well, yeah." He scratched under his chin. "That was some crazy shit you pulled on Moen. I would appreciate having that ability."

Gabrielle tapped a finger on her lips in thought. "I can't argue that. Are you saying you can teach us to do...whatever it was you did to wipe out all those Ooken if we go into the Pod-doc?"

Bethany Anne shrugged. "I don't see why not. Michael understood handling the storms fast enough."

Michael raised an eyebrow, a glint of amusement in his eyes. "Sure. If the old man can learn a new trick, why not everyone else?"

Bethany Anne rolled her eyes at his dramatics. "Moving on. Same item, different track."

Tabitha, bring Mahi'Takar in, please.

Tabitha came in ahead of Mahi'Takar, her chin set at an angle that meant business. "I want in the Pod-doc first," she told Michael. "Beauty before age is long overdue as a concept, and I'm not waiting." She flounced over to Addix and Eve and dropped into the free chair. "Well?"

Bethany Anne waved a hand and turned to Mahi'Takar. "Take a seat. I want to hear more about how the royal family of a planet so far away we never heard of it ended up hiding among criminals and murderers on the edge of the Federation."

Mahi'Takar smiled. "There are not as many criminals on Devon these days."

"There are still plenty of murderous fucksacks, though,"

Bethany Anne returned. "Most of them in this city are related to you. Why are you so reasonable?"

Mahi'Takar sighed. "Unfortunately, that is our way, and has been since the dawn of our civilization. I was lucky to travel to the Empire with my father when I was around my son's age, and I spent some time at the Etheric Academy while he was in diplomatic meetings."

Bethany Anne frowned. "He did? Who was your father? I don't remember him."

John winced. "You were, um, away at the time," he told her. "Lance took care of it."

Bethany Anne shrugged it off. "So you got a look at the wider world and liked what you saw?"

"I did," Mahi'Takar replied. "As did Fi'Eireie, my betrothed. We decided we would build a republic when our time to rule came, but my brother Lu'Trein was jealous and set out to destroy our dreams. We were a small family, just us two. I was born first, and he never forgave me for it. From my coronation, he plotted to have me killed so he could claim the throne for himself."

Tabitha made a gagging noise. "I'm guessing Trey's arrival put a stop to that."

Michael snorted. "Unlikely. I'm guessing that was when your brother's focus switched to taking him out of the line of succession."

Mahi'Takar nodded. "Worse, he brought the Ascension cult to our homeworld and destroyed our honor, twisting it into something ugly in order to earn his new friends' favor. He had my Fi' killed, then he came after Tu'Reigd and me. I had no choice but to flee. Lu'Trein cut ties with the Federation as soon as he took control, so this seemed the safest place to go."

Bethany Anne nodded. "That's how the Seven work, but they don't usually give people a choice."

Mahi'Takar sighed and put her head in her hands. "It is so good to finally speak."

Bethany Anne's heart broke for her since she of all people understood the twin burden of womanhood and leadership. She placed a hand on the regent's forearm. "Let it out, Mahi'Takar. We're all friends here."

Mahi'Takar got hold of her emotions. "Mahi' will suffice. We are more than friends, regardless of the outcome between our two peoples. You have taken my son into your home and treat him as one of your own."

Bethany Anne shrugged. "It's the right thing to do. Decency costs nothing."

Mahi'Takar held up a hand. "I will not hear otherwise. Tu'Reigd is flourishing out of the shadow of my brothers, and I am forever in your debt." She paused. "And yet, I am about to ask more of you, my Empress."

The corner of Bethany Anne's mouth rose. "Let me ask something of you first. How widespread was this cult when you left?"

Mahi'Takar frowned. "It has been over a decade. Lu'Trein's rhetoric is powerful, and he was completely indoctrinated by the cult long before we fled. Nevertheless, many do not truly believe, and wait for Tu'Reigd to return once he is grown." She studied Bethany Anne with curiosity. "Are you asking because you have a mind to help my people?"

Bethany Anne tapped her nails on the table as she

considered how in the hell she could defend her territory and take back Mahi'Takar's for her. "I can't be everywhere, and my resources here are not infinite. The question is, how do we get your family on our side?"

Mahi'Takar smiled. "If you are agreeing to fight for our home, you just did."

Bethany Anne nodded. "Then we have reached an agreement we are both satisfied with. Take it to your family, and we will meet again when I return."

Federation Outskirts, Plunging Fallow Station

Jean glanced at the racks with barely concealed disinterest while they waited for Gabrielle to emerge from the changing room. "I hate high-end retail places like this. Damn overpriced flimsy crap is gonna tear the first fight you get into, and the sales assistants think they don't breathe the same air as the rest of us."

"If they knew who we were, they'd be all over us," Tabitha agreed.

"They *are* all over us," Bethany Anne told them, meeting the broody stare of the store guard with a bright smile. "Just not in the way you're used to."

Jean flipped the guard the finger. "This place sucks. Gabrielle. Hurry up so we can get out of here."

Bethany Anne didn't like a thing in the store anyway. "I saw a shoe boutique not far from here I want to check out."

"Curse your eagle eyes," Jean grumbled. "I want to shop where they don't look at you like you're about to trash the place because you have a spot of grease on your clothing,

Gabrielle snorted as she came out of the changing room

with her items. "You're just mad there's not a single gun shop on this level."

"Damn straight," Jean agreed. "Pay for your things and let's get out of here." She walked out of the store ahead of the other three, spotting someplace much more her style on the information broadcast screens directly across from the doors.

Bethany Anne, Tabitha, and Gabrielle joined her a few minutes later.

"I'm going to peel off for a while," Jean told them.

Bethany Anne checked the time. "I have to take care of Barnabas' thing after I'm done shopping. I'll meet you back at the ship in a few hours."

Tabitha wrinkled her nose at the window displays around them. "Yeah, I'm gonna go with Jean. I can't be seen in this kind of thing. I've got a reputation as a badass I'd like to keep." She sauntered after Jean, leaving Bethany Anne and Gabrielle alone with all the shoes.

"Boutique?" Gabrielle asked, mouth pursed.

"This way," Bethany Anne replied with a grin.

25

Outskirts of Yollin Space, Voidrux Residence, Bedroom

Luther had ended the day on a sour note.

For some unknown reason, every legitimate bank account he had was now frozen. He didn't dare check the ones nobody knew about in case he inadvertently led the responsible party right to his rainy day pots.

He was certain the culprit was not the Federation. Otherwise, his arrival at his twenty-six-room family home would have been more of a handcuffs and nightsticks affair than a sullen lope into the drawing room to drown his sorrows in his great-grandfather's priceless scotch.

Consequently, he was heading to bed three sheets to the wind, and although he knew he *had* legs, he wondered if perhaps he had left them by the fireplace in the drawing room with his slippers.

Do I care?

He stumbled into his bedroom, shedding his clothing as he crossed the twelve steps to the four-poster bed his great-great-great-whoever had smuggled from who knew where and fell face down onto the mattress.

"Well, aren't we just Sorry Central?" a voice that spoke of the possibility of endless pain asked.

Luther scrambled to a sitting position, dead sober. "Wha... Who's there?" He looked around frantically, hoping he'd hallucinated the voice

"I'm afraid," the voice purred dangerously, "that you've been a very bad man, Luther Voidrux. It's time you saw the *light*."

Luther shuffled back on the bed, feeling for the blaster he kept under his pillow for occasions such as this. "Who are you? Show yourself!" he demanded, regaining some of his confidence when no one appeared to go with the voice.

"You really are a dumbass, aren't you?" Baba Yaga grated in his ear from beside him on the bed.

Luther screamed at the sight of her. He threw himself sideways off the bed, firing his blaster indiscriminately.

Baba Yaga was not there.

He sat up, looking at the smoking ruins of his family heirlooms. "You're not the Witch," he whispered to himself, failing to buy his own lie. "*You can't be her.*"

The temperature dropped, chilling Luther to the bone. He backed out of his bedroom slowly, his head swiveling in every direction as his panicked brain told him that the Witch was hiding in every corner and shadow.

The mansion was dark since Luther hadn't bothered to turn on the lights for his journey to bed. He crept along the passage, blaster at the ready in his shaking hands should any more figments of his disordered imagination come to life.

Luther had calmed slightly by the time he reached the double staircase leading down to the foyer. He told himself he must have been hallucinating from drinking bad scotch. "You ass, you almost frightened yourself to death."

He wasn't too happy about the damage to his bedroom, either.

Deciding to sleep on the couch in the drawing room like he should have done in the first place, Luther headed downstairs to fix some warm milk and a sandwich before he sacked out.

Luther switched on the kitchen light and made his way to the cooling unit to get the fixings out.

Sharp pain in the back of his head made Luther's arms drop to his sides. Panic gripped him when the milk splashed his bare feet. He couldn't feel a thing.

Nor could he move from the spot.

"Don't worry," Baba Yaga's raspy voice ground out behind him. "You'll feel *everything* in a minute…"

The Witch waved a hand, and control returned to Luther's body. He looked down at the milk turning yellow on the floor, and his mind checked out as he realized that his bladder had given up.

Baba Yaga flashed a cold, sharp smile. "All this drama," she told Luther as she took a step toward him. "All I wanted was to have a conversation."

Luther pitched forward, Baba Yaga's soul-destroying laugh the last thing he heard before splashing in the puddle on the floor.

High Tortuga, Space Fleet Base

Barnabas received a message from Bethany Anne as he was walking to the hangar. Puzzled, he opened it, wondering why she had sent a text instead of calling him directly.

It all became clear once he skimmed over the documentation signing over Voidrux Industries to the CEO of Silver Line Company, who just happened to be Nickie.

There was a note attached.

Your man was nothing more than a greedy-ass individual with delusions of retiring on what he got out of us.

Strangely, he found religion last night.

The business includes over two hundred thousand workers of every description, and its headquarters is on an asteroid close to the border with Yoll.

I'm sure Voidrux will make a fine penitent.

Oh, and Barnabas? Speaking of penitents, I will enjoy picturing Nickie's reaction when you tell her most of her work will involve being pleasant to the Federation. Payback isn't the only bitch you're stuck with.

Until the next briefing,

Bethany Anne

Barnabas chuckled as he filed the documentation with CEREBRO. He couldn't wait to see Nickie's reaction either.

Uncharted Galaxy, Hidden Location

The Bitch. The Queen. The Empress.

Whatever she answered to, however primitive her beginnings, every remaining Kurtherian of the Seven clans knew her true name.

Death.

For two centuries now, Death had hunted them. Harried them. With no rest or remorse, she had searched out the Seven and cut away at their power, their resources, and their precious numbers. She had scattered them, driving them ever outward, and then pursued them some more.

The absence of the Phraim-'Eh at this assembly was an affront.

There were no living Phraim-'Eh left to attend.

No longer a Prime, a Secondary, or a single Pilot among them, the remainder of the Seven clans gathered in the shadows of a cavern that did not belong to them. Hooded to a person in order to conceal their identities, every Kurtherian present seethed in silence at being reduced to this deception by Death's ability to read minds.

Further, Gödel had culled those whose obsession with the moral high ground overrode their good sense to keep them all out of Death's crosshairs.

Here were the survivors, the ones whose former quests for glory had been satisfied by smaller progressions along the path to Ascension. The ones who had been adaptable enough to recognize Gödel's greater wisdom and knew that all of their lives depended upon her leadership.

The silence grew in volume as many more joined the summit by mental link from their hiding places across the galaxies, another precaution against total destruction should *she* find them. There were no snatches of conversation that might give away a connection. Even their exact number was hidden.

Gödel's law was simple to obey.

Give the humans *nothing.*

A low, reverberating chime sounded, signaling the arrival of the highest-ranking Kurtherian left alive to lead them. A solitary ball of Etheric energy came into being near the roof of the cavern. Its pallid light cast the ancient carvings on the dais into relief, a reminder to the Azzhur in the cavern of the species they'd wiped out when their clan took this planet centuries ago.

Gödel's entourage entered first. Two carried her throne onto the dais, and the other four fanned out at the base of the steps and raised their glowing hands to the roof. "Rejoice in supplication," they proclaimed. "Gödel has come."

Every Kurtherian of the clans found the human cryptonym distasteful in the extreme. No one present knew their leader's true designation.

None dared ask.

Gödel exercised her skills with the Etheric with clinical abandon and pinpoint accuracy, as did her faithful, meaning, she could call herself whatever she liked and there wasn't a Kurtherian who had the power to question her.

Everyone was aware of how badly the summit would go if everything was not exactly as Gödel expected it. The neutral silence took on an air of uncertainty as her armored guards mounted the dais and positioned themselves around the throne with their scepters charged and glowing.

Gödel appeared upon the throne in a flash of light and a swirl of semi-diaphanous robes. The relief in the cavern was palpable when she settled back without passing comment—or killing them all in a fit of displeasure.

The absolute ruler of the Seven adjusted the folds of her ornate hood against her veil before laying her gloved hands in her lap. "Explain," she ordered in a dispassionate tone, "Explain to Us how Death, that irrational, emotional *human*, has managed to gain even greater control over the Etheric."

A susurrus of denials rebounded off the roof of the cavern.

Gödel lifted a finger, and a Kurtherian in the front row stepped forward. "Speak, T'sehmion. Tell Us and your brethren what you witnessed."

The T'sehmion bowed his head and turned to the assembly. "Your Glory. My facility was attacked by Death and her consort. They gave me no choice but to initiate self-destruct measures. All was lost, including the Bl'kheth."

Gödel's veil rippled as her mandibles jabbed at it. "How did she get past Our defenses?"

The red glow beneath the Kurtherian's hood dimmed as he turned back to Gödel. "I do not believe what I saw, your Glory."

Gödel leaned forward on her throne. "I see it in your mind, and it is the truth. Tell them." Her voice hardened, making her request a demand the Kurtherian dared not disobey.

The T'selinion bowed lower. "She walked out of an Etheric storm, but..." he paused for barely a moment, "That is not possible."

Gödel straightened, and the room flinched.

Her chin protruded beneath her veil, every word icy. "Nothing to say? Not *one* of you can hypothesize how she lived through it? How she went into that storm and walked out at Our facility?"

No one spoke.

Gödel leaned toward the delegates. "Then what purpose does any of you *serve*?" she demanded. "We were not ready for her to discover Our factories. If none of you can protect Our interests, you are of no use to Us or to the future of the clans. We will replace you."

The room erupted in whispers as Gödel got to her feet.

"We d-d-dare not m-move against her, your Glory," one of the hooded figures stuttered. "She is too p-powerful, and the revelation of her ability to ride the st-storm wall p-proves it without a doubt."

Gödel pointed a gloved finger around the room, smiling as she landed on the speaker and took control of his nanocytes. "We are *Kurtherians*," she calmly told the assembly as the speaker gasped his final breath. "Superior to all, submissive to none. *We...You* and I... are the guardians of the path to Ascension, and we are at war."

She released the unfortunate to fall to the floor before she raised her voice. "No longer can your duty be disrupted by the will of a single...primitive...female. You will *all* purge this blasphemous line of thought and find a way to rein in the humans, or it will be Our duty to cleanse our genetic pool of your weakness. There must be something we can use to remove Death from the equation."

Gödel glowed with absorbed energy. "Death desecrates our ancestors with her every breath, and it is all we can do to keep her distracted by continuous war. The years she vanished, we could find no trace of her. Now she is returned, stronger, more powerful, and more of a denigration to our Ascension, and *We want her destroyed*!"

A curt voice broke the stillness of the cavern, taking the plunge for them all. "We are well aware of her weakness, Your Glory. However, unless we all have access to the knowledge you have gained..."

Gödel's laugh rang out across the cavern. "And have you begin to believe you can match Our Magnificence? We think not, Reben. It has become clear to Us, and to you, that the path to victory lies with Us, and Us alone. You are but weapons, and at the moment, ineffective ones at that."

The speaker's continued status as a living being encouraged another to speak up. "Your Glory, any move against the humans will result in disaster for us all. The charts—"

Everyone present found their ability to draw breath was no longer a given when Gödel lifted a hand and squeezed it into a fist. "We care not for the charts." She sneered. "We are *Gödel*. The prophecies are naught but amusements to such as Us. We care only that Death, and all of her allies, is removed as an obstacle to the Kurtherian shepherding all. This universe has a choice: obey Us and accept the Wisdom of Ascension, or *die* to bring that Age in."

Everyone in the cavern hitched a grateful gasp when Gödel dropped her grip on their airways and vanished.

Her voice echoed through the cavern—and their minds.

Our ways to threatened, and We will not tolerate failure. You will find a way to neutralize Death...

Or die trying.

EPILOGUE

QT2, QBBS *Helena*, Three months later

Bethany Anne left the No-Ox habitat, almost soothed by the time spent meditating with the Collective on their shared grief.

Today was the day Jean would reveal her new home, and Bethany Anne was alone in being underwhelmed by the whole occasion.

While Izanami's absence was no longer a knife in her heart every time she got aboard a ship, the loss was never far from her mind. Her meditation had guided her to the conclusion that time would heal her wound, as it had so many times before.

The difference this time was that she didn't try to close her emotions down. If she could not find her own joy in the day, she would share her family's, and that would be enough.

Nevertheless, it would carry a bittersweet note in her memory, and while she wasn't exactly fine with that, she accepted it was the way it would be.

She exchanged her roamer vehicle for a fresh one from the charging point outside the airlock and set off for the shipyard.

She could only stare in wonder at the size of the ship. It reminded her of that moment in one of the *Star Wars* movies when you saw Darth Vader's Executive...*no, that was an Executor-class star destroyer, right?* Either way, the other star destroyers had looked like toys next to that ship.

Hundreds of years later, that scene was still firmly implanted in her memories.

Alexis and Gabriel were waiting for Bethany Anne when she arrived.

Alexis elbowed her brother in the ribs as their mother climbed out of the roamer. "I told you she was still sad. She's been with the Collective again."

Gabriel scrutinized Bethany Anne's face. "She looks fine to me."

Alexis rolled her eyes and walked over to Bethany Anne. "You are *such* a guy sometimes."

Bethany Anne held out her arms to her children. "This is getting to be embarrassing since you two are taller than me now."

Alexis released Bethany Anne and clapped excitedly. "Not for long. Jean told me your armor is ready."

Now, *that* was a reason for Bethany Anne to embrace the celebratory mood. She shooed her children ahead as the first hint of a smile graced her lips. "What are we waiting for? Let's go so I can see how she did."

Gabriel looked over his shoulder. "You haven't seen it already?"

Bethany Anne shook her head. "Jean's kept this sewn up

tighter than... You know, you're not the right audience for that kind of snark. She's tested my patience, that's for sure."

"That's not saying much, Mom." Alexis giggled. "I mean, you don't exactly have an abundance of it when you want something."

Bethany Anne raised an eyebrow. "Whose side are you on?"

Alexis batted her eyelashes. "The side that says Gabriel and I should be ungrounded?"

Bethany Anne snorted. "Yeah, right. Not in a thousand years is that look going to work on me, Alexis Nacht. This is my payback for bitching about my Guards, I know, but it's not going to make any difference. You go out, you have guards. End of discussion."

Alexis pouted all the way to meeting Michael at the hangar entrance.

Michael noted immediately that Bethany Anne and Alexis were at odds. "Why don't we look like a family about to see their new home for the first time?" he asked, wishing it wasn't his job to mediate between his wife and daughter.

That was no different than most dads in history with daughters. He was not the first to deal with this problem, nor would he be the last. However, he would absolutely be the one in the middle of two of the most powerful. It was his burden to bear.

Gabriel sauntered past, waving a finger at Bethany Anne and Alexis. "Mom was already in a bad mood, Alexis made it worse and then decided to sulk about it, and now Mom is one rolled eyeball from being done."

Michael looked at his son for a moment before mulling

the reasons he sometimes checked for gray hairs in the mirror despite having nanocytes. "Is that accurate?"

Bethany Anne shrugged. "It's accurate enough. Jean will be waiting." She headed into the hangar to look for Jean, passing antigrav pallets piled high with supplies and equipment on her way to the open hangar doors leading out to the construction frame holding her super-dreadnought.

"You can't board until you name her," Jean teased, coming down the ramp from the frame. "Otherwise, she's ready for you to move in. I had all your belongings sent from High Tortuga, so you're good to go."

Bethany Anne turned to see Michael approaching the foot of the ramp. "You can name this one."

"Easy," Michael replied. "The *Baba Yaga*, in Izanami's memory."

Jean chuckled. "Funny you should choose that. I named this class of superdreadnoughts for her." She turned to the assistant hovering behind her. "You heard the man. Get it finished so they can go home."

Bethany Anne managed to pull a smile from somewhere. "I like that. Where are the children? We should take a tour while the painters finish up. We have an extended trip to plan for."

Gabriel and Alexis showed up a moment later with K'aia and Trey in tow.

Bethany Anne chuckled at Michael's instinctive movement to herd them toward the ramp. She headed over to Michael and linked her arm through his as the children ran onto the ship ahead of them.

Michael bent to kiss Bethany Anne's hair. "It is not such

a bad home, this ship. It is certainly the largest I've ever lived on."

Bethany Anne steered Michael up the ramp. "It's not a home." She frowned. "But we will make it one. Come on, Jean looks like she's going to have a fit if we don't hurry up."

Jean waved them aboard. "You've got as long as you like to suck face once I've shown you around. Don't pretend I haven't still got a full day's work to do after this." Her face told a different tale than her tone, her eyes crinkling at the corners as they walked onto the ship.

QSD *Baba Yaga*

Bethany Anne wandered away from the tour, wanting to get her first visit to the bridge and the meeting with the ship's AI out of the way before she built it into something impossible.

>>**What's the deal?**<< ADAM demanded. >>**You didn't lose me. We can talk, you know. I miss Izanami too. She was a part of me I'll never get back.**<<

Bethany Anne stopped in her tracks. *I never thought of Izanami as an extension of you,* she admitted. *She was so individual, so...her. I feel like I lost a friend.*

>>**You did,**<< ADAM reasoned. >>**You lived aboard her ship and spoke to her every day. She bonded with you, and she wasn't designed to do that. You bonded with her too, Bethany Anne. Be sad. Be angry. Miss her. You wouldn't be human if you didn't.**<< He paused. >>**But then get off your pity party and talk to the people who are here for you.**<<

Bethany Anne placed a hand on the bridge door as she remembered the time she had gone through as the dark one, the Witch of the Empire. *I'm not going to break. Not this time. I'll talk when I'm ready.*

The bridge door cycled open, and Bethany Anne strode in to find a space defined by clean lines in cream, silver, and blue.

It was a complete contrast to what she had been expecting, since what she had seen of the ship so far was more utilitarian in military gray and white.

Bethany Anne walked around the hard light projector in the center of the bridge on her way to the main console. She took her chair and engaged the ship systems, ignoring the tightness in her chest as the HLP whirred to life.

The children clattered onto the bridge, followed by Michael and Jean.

Bethany Anne turned from the console. "You made it just in time."

Gabriel dropped onto the arm of Bethany Anne's chair and draped his arm over her shoulders. "Mom, just wait until you see your armory. Ours is awesome, but yours is the coolest I've ever seen."

"Never mind the armory!" Alexis squealed, taking the other arm. "The closet, Mom! It's bigger than Aunt Tabitha's and Uncle Pete's apartment!"

Bethany Anne turned her eyebrow on Jean.

Jean lifted her hands. "What can I say? You had the space."

The console lit up, distracting Bethany Anne for the moment, and she checked the displays. "Looks like our new AI is coming online. Don't crowd her, children. Remember, this is her first experience as a sentient being."

Everyone moved back as the HLP's whirring kicked up a notch. The spindles moved into position and began to glow.

"This is always slow at first," Jean warned. "Give it a minute to warm up."

Bethany Anne was unable to look away despite herself. The AI was the heart of any ship, and the freedom to choose their own personality was a gamble at the best of times. Would she get another Meredith? An ArchAngel?

Hopefully not a Shinigami.

She didn't think she could take it.

The children gasped when light burst from the spindles at the top of the tubular encasement, pooling in the deep tray at the bottom. The spindles cut out when the tray was filled to the brim, and another arm emerged from the upper part of the apparatus and held a marble-sized sphere above the tray.

Bethany Anne held her breath as the light began to rise and coalesce around the hard light drive. This iteration was supposed to be virtually indestructible, needing the force of two colliding planets to crush it.

Or so Bobcat had told her.

Time would tell, and she had learned her lesson about getting attached to inorganic beings who resided outside her body. She would not get attached to this AI, even if she lived aboard the ship for a hundred years.

Bethany Anne held Gabriel close as the physical appearance of the AI came into focus.

The light around the drive now vaguely resembled a human form.

Bethany Anne's heart dropped when she made out the shape of a breastplate and greaves. Her hair hung loose. It was white.

No!

The AI remained stationary until the fine detail of her expressionless face resolved.

Alexis took Bethany Anne's hand as she squeezed her eyes shut to stop the tears threatening to fall. "It's okay, Mom," she whispered. "Look."

Bethany Anne opened her eyes to prove to her children that she could.

The first thing she saw was Michael staring open-mouthed at the projection.

The avatar inside the tube was glowing red. Not just red, she realized. Red and *gold?*

The AI stepped down from the tray and looked down at herself, her voice brought back from the grave. "How very...generic. This won't do at all."

Bethany Anne narrowed her eyes as the girls broke into squeals. "You're looking pretty good for a dead person."

Izanami grinned and dissolved into golden sparkles, coming back a split second later wearing her own white armor, her hair back at its usual hip length. "I am now. That's much more me." She turned a circle and lifted her hands. "Don't you think?"

"Perfect," Bethany Anne agreed. She leaned around Gabriel to look at Jean. "*You?*"

Jean chuckled. "Me. Happy Birthdays for a few decades my Queen. Now, I've got to get back to work."

Alexis and Gabriel had Izanami turning this way and that while they complimented the improvements to her avatar's range of movement.

Bethany Anne caught Michael gazing at her with a mixture of satisfaction and relief. ***Did you know about this?***

I did not, he replied. *Although I am relieved your burden has been lifted. Perhaps now you will think of this as home.*

Michael moved away to explore the bridge as Izanami extracted herself from the children.

Bethany Anne couldn't hold back her grin. "Jean really pulled a miracle out of her ass. You were *gone,* dammit. There was no bringing you back."

Izanami flashed her sharp smile. "Nobody told Jean that. ADAM tells me you took millions of Ooken lives in revenge for my death. I will have to make sure I repay that by killing twice as many in your name when we return to war."

Bethany Anne let the tears go. "Izanami, you can kill as many damn Ooken as you want. Have you seen your ship yet?"

"Of course." Izanami winked. "But have you seen my *guns?*"

Finis

Until we meet again
in ENTER INTO VALHALLA...

THANK YOU for not only reading this story but these *Author Notes* as well.

(I think I've been good with always opening with "thank you." If not, I need to edit the other *Author Notes*!)

RANDOM (*sometimes*) THOUGHTS?

I'm sitting in my (near) Los Angeles hotel room, the beginning of the 2019 SFWA Nebulas conference going on down below. (The Nebula is an award for Sci-Fi and Fantasy stories, and is given out this Saturday night.) I am finishing up these *Author Notes* before this book goes up on Amazon tonight, hoping we publish by the early morning.

It is three years and six months since I released the very first Kurtherian book, and now we are releasing the twenty-sixth book with Bethany Anne in the main Kurtherian timeline.

The stories are a bit different now.

As I edited this book, it struck me how all these characters have grown through the years, sometimes entering into the stories in odd ways (Sabine made me think of this) and wondering where everyone might be that we didn't shoehorn into this story.

(If you have missed Nickie Grimes in _Deuces Wild_, take a moment to read that storyline. It's a little harder because we attack a problem with families and misunderstandings. Then, you add the Grimes gene into the mix, and a whole backbone of "I don't give a shit," and you get Nickie.)

The universe and character list are too large to not give other characters a little bit of book time. Fans want to know what happened to XYZ characters, but then we have a couple of concerns from not giving Bethany Anne enough time because we spoke about others.

It is challenging, to say the least.

We are trying to figure out how to split the characters into their own storylines and perhaps do something else, maybe another book, with their stories. I don't know if we will be able to figure out a solution, but know that we ARE looking into it.

Well, that and we have finally been able to set up everything to move the plot forward. To get out of the children phase and get a space-sized ass-kicking moving forward with all these characters and one in particular.

THANK YOU for supporting Bethany Anne. She will forever be the special one in my heart out of all of the characters I've created.

She is the Queen Bitch, and I love her for that.

AROUND THE WORLD IN 80 DAYS

One of the most interesting (at least to me) aspects of my life is the ability to work from anywhere and at any time. In the future, I hope to re-read my own *Author Notes* and remember my life as a diary entry.

Woodland Hills Marriott, Woodland Hills, California, USA

It's a party!

Well, not really yet.

I understand that the Nebulas was just a one-night "thing" started a bit over fifty years ago as an excuse to get together and have a party with other authors.

Flash forward to today, and it is a conference that starts on Thursday and goes through Saturday, and the Nebula dinner (do dress nicely) will be held Saturday night. I was up past midnight out drinking (I really had a real honest-to-god alcoholic drink where I usually just have a Coke). For those curious, I like Drambuie neat. Usually, just one to sip.

I was with Ronnie Virdie (Author), Yudhanjaya Wijeratne (Author) and Dan Wood (Draft2Digital). Craig Martelle (Author) and Judith Anderle (CMO LMBPN Publishing and my wife) had already gone back to the hotel after dinner. We talked about books, the art of story, arguing about shit I doubt I remember much about (no, I wasn't drunk, but late night discussions don't stick around in my long-term memory very well.)

(Editor's Note: I will remember that for when you agree to something in one of our midnight convos, Anderle)

We will be here through Sunday for any meetings with those still hanging close and leave on Monday morning for the five-hour car trip back to the Cave in the Sky™ in Las Vegas.

One week in Vegas, then we hit the skies towards New York and Book Expo America and APAC (Audio).

Where I'm sure I will be lousy in the mornings as well, Mr. Campbell (he reviews these notes before publishing so Zen Master Walking™ will know I'm talking about him).

But at least this time YOU will have probably been out late with us and your mornings will suck as well.

(Zen Master Walking™ Note: My mornings never suck. It's a gift.)

Damn, I need a nap...

FAN PRICING

$0.99 Saturdays (new LMBPN stuff) and $0.99 Wednesday (both LMBPN books and friends of LMBPN books.) Get great stuff from us and others at tantalizing prices.

Go ahead. I bet you can't read just one.

Sign up here: http://lmbpn.com/email/.

HOW TO MARKET FOR BOOKS YOU LOVE

Review them so others have your thoughts, and tell friends and the dogs of your enemies (because who wants to talk to enemies?)... *Enough said ;-)*

Ad Aeternitatem,

Michael Anderle

CONNECT WITH MICHAEL ANDERLE

Michael Anderle Social
Website:
http://www.lmbpn.com

Email List:
http://lmbpn.com/email/

Facebook Here:
www.facebook.com/TheKurtherianGambitBooks/

Made in the USA
Las Vegas, NV
14 August 2024

93839574R00225